Fall of Snow

Frost Industries - Book Three

Montana Fyre

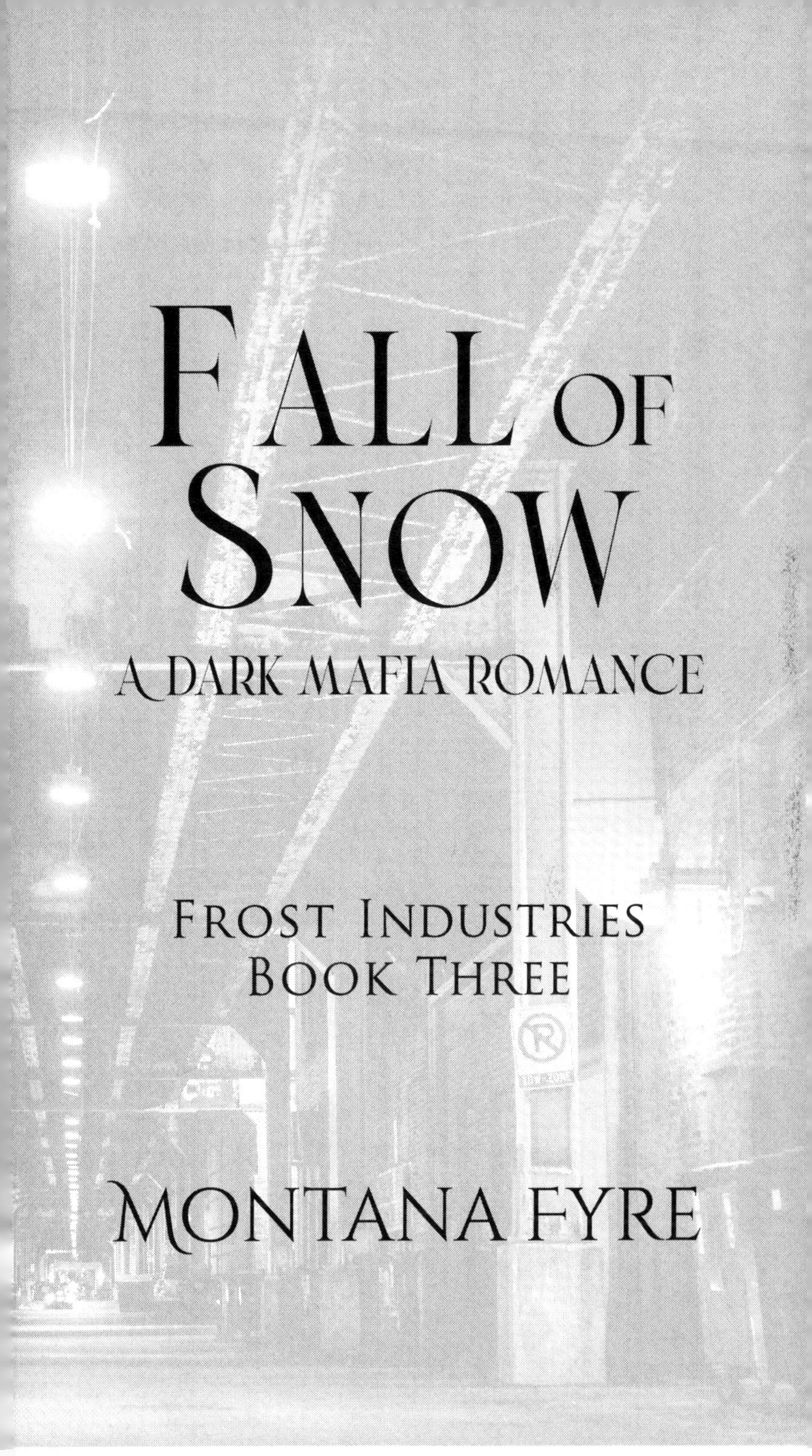

Fall of Snow

A Dark Mafia Romance

Frost Industries
Book Three

Montana Fyre

ISBN (Paperback) : 978-0-6454851-5-8

First edition, 2022.

Front cover and book design by Montana Fyre.

Edited by My Brother's Editor.

www.montanafyre.com

Acknowledgments

Frost Industries came to me years ago. It was four stories that seemed to work together, and a few names that I loved, but would never be able to pepper into any other series.

Over the last few years, I've plotted here and there. I've made notes in a thousand different note books (most of which I've lost), I've written quotes that found their way into the book, and I've fallen in love with the characters you'll meet in this book.

I've loved every second of writing this series so far, and I truly feel like I've found my author groove writing dark romance.

As always, I would first and foremost like to thank my wonderful husband. He supports me with every decision I make, he talks me down when I'm ready to throw in the towel, and he loves me even when I don't love myself. I wouldn't be where I am if he hadn't continually believed in me and pushed me to be the best version of myself.

My friends and family who support me endlessly and have been my cheerleaders since the beginning of this journey. For giving their opinions on covers and formatting, for listening to be talking out plot points just to work it out myself, and for loving me even though I'm almost always distracted.

Ellie, my wonderful editor, who picks up all my Australianisms and fixes the same mistakes in every book I write (will I ever learn? Clearly not).

And to all the readers who have been on this journey with me. It's an incredible adventure and I couldn't do it without you. Thank you for taking a chance on me. Thank you for reading the words I write. And thank you for taking the time to review my books. It honestly means the world to me.

Elijah and Snow tested me, but I think they may just be my favorite couple in the Frost world, and I hope you love them as much as I do.

Trigger Warning

This book contains dark themes that some readers may find distressing, including, but not limited to:

Violence

Elements of BDSM

Sexual Assault

Coercion

Play with an item used for hunting

Kidnapping

Stalking

Giving medication without knowledge

Dub Con / Non Con

To the villains who got a bad rap in fairytales, there's a redemption story for you yet

Love is not blind.
It sees you in the dark and chooses to be your light.

- SNEHA PAL

PROLOGUE

ELIJAH

My little Snowflake.

I've watched you for so many years, I feel as if I've always been a part of your life.

I've watched you cry when you're sad and smile when you're happy. I've watched you celebrate the good times and drown your sorrows in the bad. And each moment that I've followed you, is a little better I get to know you.

And soon, you'll be mine.

Your room is set up at my house, ready to cage the wildcat that hides under the surface. Most people wouldn't try to clip your wings, but I will. You need someone to take care of you, someone who knows you better than you know yourself to protect you from the world, even if that means protecting you from yourself.

The last few months have been hard on you, I understand that, but it doesn't give you the right to harm the body that belongs to me, even if you don't know it yet.

The moment you started down the road of self-destruction, I began moving things into place to ensure you wouldn't be your own demise.

I understand your heart is hurting, despite not having one myself, but I can no longer allow you the freedom you crave.

It is my hope that one day you'll understand why I did this, and you'll accept the life we are to have together.

You see, my little Snowflake, this plan has been in motion since the day we met when you were fifteen. Even then, you were the wild child of your family, as most youngest born are. There was something about you, something so completely entrancing that I found myself following you to see more. Like with most of my toys, I expected to grow bored, but if anything, the longer I spent following you, the more obsessed I became.

The feud between our families has certainly complicated things over the years, but now I'm running the show, I need a queen to stand by my side, and there is no one more fit for the job than you.

ONE

SNOW

The concept of freedom isn't nearly as grand as freedom itself. It's difficult to describe what exactly it feels like, but the moment I'm out of the confines my family place on me, it's like I'm another person. I'm someone other than the baby of the Saint James family.

Over the years, I've perfected the art of losing my security detail. Everyone my brothers hire underestimates me because, in their eyes, I'm the weak little Mafia princess. There's a balance of power they expect, but it's never the way they think it will be.

They, just like most people, make their minds up about me long before I say my first word to them. Ditzy. Dramatic. Spoiled. Socialite. They think because all I manage at Frost Industries is public relations, that I'm the most useless member of the family. And hey, that may be true, but when your brother is CEO, your sister is CFO, and your other brother is the enforcer of the largest criminal organization in the country, you have to expect you're probably going to be the disappointment of the family.

My phone buzzes in my pocket, telling me my idiot security team has finally realized I'm missing. I've already been out of the house for an hour. How it's taken them this long is beyond me. I am, however, looking forward to watching Storm fire them. There's this vein in his neck that pops out and pulses when he has to deal with the chaos I've caused him, and I get this sick satisfaction watching his barely contained rage.

I ignore my phone and take another sip of my cosmo. If they really want to find me, there's a tracker on my phone and in my bag, both of which do a better job at protecting me than any security my brothers have ever hired. One call to Everett, and they know my exact location to send the cavalry to save me like some kind of damsel in distress.

"Another?" the bartender asks, his long brown hair falling around his face and his green eyes dancing with mischief.

I've played this game before. Pretty girl walks into bar. Pretty girl orders a drink. Bartender likes the look of pretty girl and thinks he may be able to rail her if he plays his cards right. It's a tale as old as time and a game I like to play from time to time.

I nod, the corners of my lips quirking up in a coy smile. With my fire engine red lips and mess of blonde locks, I look anything but innocent sitting in a bar at three in the afternoon, but playing a part is half the fun. The man watches me for another moment, assessing me as I take another sip of my cocktail before tilting my head to the side. Men don't like when I hold their gaze. Men like submissive women and that's never been me, even in the bedroom. I'm not going to let a man walk all over me just because he has an extra appendage the world views as making him better than a weak little woman.

He turns and starts pouring alcohol into shakers, his hands shaking slightly as he does. I've been in here a few times and seen this same bartender, but he's never seemed anything but cocky.

I brush off the thought and glance around the mostly well-lit bar. It's early, so there are only a few people sitting at tables and one other man sitting at the other end of the bar. His face is shadowed by the dim lights in the corner, but it's the art on his arms that draws me in. The intricate lines, the gray wash coloring that stretches across his impressive forearms. There's something deep inside me begging to move closer, like a moth to the flame that will inevitably end them. I don't have the best track record with men, always running headfirst into toxic relationships whenever I feel this pull.

Even though I can only see the black shirt stretched across his hard chest and the ink on his arms, there's something familiar about the man. I've definitely never seen the tattoos before because I would remember them, but there's something eerily familiar I can't quite put my finger on.

A fresh martini glass appears on the bar in front of me, drawing my attention away from the mysterious stranger and back to the flirty bartender. His eyes linger on my mouth as I bring the fresh glass to my lips and take a healthy sip. The best part about hitting on the bartender is the more you flirt, the stronger your drinks get, and the drunker you become.

"Thanks." I smile up at him, my eyes dragging down his neck and across his wide chest. He may not be the inked mystery man, but he'll do.

Two
Elijah

She's like a little lamb on her way to the slaughter. She's trying so hard to be interested in the asshole behind the bar, but she can't keep her eyes off me. Although she's looked at me like this every time I've allowed myself to get this close, this is the first time she's seeing me. See, over the years, I've become a master of disguise. You don't know it's me unless I want you to know, and up until now, I haven't wanted Snow to see the real me. I've been careful to keep my face hidden though, because that's something she would recognize.

Not that it matters. Today is the day she becomes mine. My pretty little Snowflake. I've been planning for today for what feels like a lifetime, but I had to wait until my idiot father and useless uncles were out of the picture. The Saint James family doesn't know what a favor they did for me because I couldn't have my family's vile tendencies near my woman. The things I've seen at their hands turned even my stomach, and my soul is as black as hell itself. I get satisfaction out of tearing people apart limb by limb, but the shit they liked was too sick for me, and I would never put my precious Snowflake in that kind of danger.

The bartender pours her fourth cocktail. His gaze locked on her chest rather than what he's doing. I don't blame him. I've caught myself staring at them a time or two on these little missions to get to know her. These moments I allow myself have never been enough, but it's how I know her favorite cocktail, her favorite food, the brand of tequila she likes when she's had a particularly rough day. All the things a computer and a private investigator could never tell me, I know everything there is to know about my little pet to ease the transition into her new life.

I'm not so blind to think it won't be difficult for her, because it will. I'm clipping her wings and caging her in, just like she thinks her family has always done. But there will be no escaping me or my home. She won't be able to pull the same escape routines that have allowed me to follow her the way I have. At first, she'll think she's a prisoner, but she'll come to see it's for her own good and that everything I do, I do with her best interest in mind.

"I finish in ten. Do you want to get out of here?"

Snow nods, her lashes fluttering against her cheeks. The image she portrays in public dropping into place. The mask is firmly fitted most of the time, but there are moments when the real Snow slips out, and I'm mesmerized by the woman no one else knows.

The bartender sends her a sly smile and turns to cross to the people who have just sat at the opposite end of the bar.

Snow lets out a breath and picks her glass up, swishing the

pink liquid around a few times before bringing the rim to her lips.

I'll never get sick of watching her mouth. It's one of the first things that ever drew me in. The perfect little pout her lips form, the beauty that lights up her face when they tip into a smile, the image I've concocted in my mind of what they'll look like wrapped around my cock. That's the picture that has me wrapping my fist around my dick late at night.

My little Snowflake doesn't realize she's being led into a trap, one I carefully set for her. She doesn't know that leaving with that bartender will be the last free decision she makes.

I check my watch and fidget in my seat. The longer we sit here, the higher chance her brothers are going to realize she's gone and send someone to retrieve her. We've done this same routine so many times I'm surprised they haven't been able to keep her under control, but she won't be free for much longer.

The moment the bartender starts moving toward the opening at the other end of the bar, I'm out of my seat and heading for the door. Everything that's about to happen needs to do so seamlessly, starting with me being in position. I give her one last glance over my shoulder as I push the door open and find a smile tugging at the corners of my lips.

Time to come home, little Snowflake.

Three

Snow

As I step out of the bar with the bartender who I haven't bothered to ask his name, a shiver of question runs through my bones. I've done this a thousand times, gone home with random men, and then had my brothers knocking on their front door looking for me, but this time feels different.

His arm wraps around my waist and pulls me tight against him. His body towers over mine, and for the first time in all the years I've been running away from my security team, I think I've made a mistake. I can't quite put my finger on what exactly feels off, but there's something in the air that makes it hard to suck in a breath.

I look up at him and, for the first time, really see him. His cheekbones are high and pronounced, his jaw sharp and covered in the shadow of the day, but it's his eyes that have my heart skipping a beat, and not in a good way. It's the nervousness I don't expect to see, the way his gaze shoots from side to side as he walks us through the parking lot toward his car.

It's a trap.

My step falters, fear pushing through my carefully crafted exterior, but I can't allow him to realize I'm onto him, not if I want to get out of here safely. The phone in my pocket has been constantly vibrating for the last half hour. Surely someone will be coming for me soon. But they've never taken this long before. Usually, the calls start and fifteen minutes later, someone is collecting me. The only exception is when I'm in someone's apartment, and the team sends my brothers in to do their dirty work.

"Are you okay?" his deep voice rumbles.

I nod, steeling myself to reply. "Yeah, I just tripped." The lie rolls off my tongue so easily it should concern me, but if lying is the only way to get out of the mess I suspect I've made for myself, I'm going to lie through my fucking teeth.

He watches me for another second and then looks up toward the cars parked a few feet away. If I had to put money on which of the cars I'm about to get in, it would be the old beat-up white Honda. Beside it is a high-end Mercedes, too nice for this side of town. The matte black stands out in the dim parking lot, the surrounding buildings blocking any sunlight.

I take a deep breath and stop. "Oh shoot. I left my favorite lipstick in the bathroom." The pitch of my voice irritates me, but I learned a long time ago that the more stupid you can make yourself sound, the more the people around you will underestimate you, and that's exactly what I need right now.

"Leave it. I'll pick it up next time I'm in for you," he says dismissively as he tugs me forward roughly.

"You don't understand," I whine. "They discontinued this color, and it's my absolute favorite. If I lost it, I just don't know what I would do." I'm laying it on thick, hoping he'll think I'm the dumb blonde of the Saint James family, just like the rest of Chicago.

When his eyes turn down on me, there's nothing but annoyance behind the green I found so endearing earlier. This isn't a man interested in getting his dick wet, he's a man who has other plans, *darker* plans. "Listen here, you little—"

Before he can finish his insult, my hand wraps around the pepper spray in my bag, and I pull it out, spraying it straight into his eyes. As soon as he drops his grip on me and his hands fly to his face, I take off at a run. I'm not in the best outfit to be running away from an attacker, jeans, five-inch heels, and a knit sweater, but I'll have to make do with what I have.

The bartender's grunts of pain get farther and farther away the more I run, which gives me hope he's not following me. I just have to find a cab and get back to the estate, or at the very least, to Frost Industries. At least there I could find some security and maybe one of my siblings or Everett to take me home.

I chance a glance behind me and let out a breath when the bartender is still doubled over by his car, but before I can turn back around to watch where I'm going, I slam straight into a hard body.

"Hello, my little Snowflake," they rumble, their deep voice sending a shiver through my body.

My eyes drag up the man's body, the intricate tattoos I was admiring in the bar meeting my gaze. *Wait, did he say my name?* Usually, I wouldn't find it that worrying when a stranger knew my name, considering my family lives our lives in the public eye, but there's something about the way it rolls off his tongue that disarms me.

"What the fu—" Before I can finish my sentence, a sharp prick in my neck cuts the words off, and a moment later, my legs give way underneath me. No. This can't be happening. I can't let them take me.

Seconds pass that feel like hours. Every passing second, I have less control over my body, to the point I worry I may stop breathing. The body in front of me carefully lowers me to the ground, not letting me fall to the hard asphalt. His hands are gentle as they stroke over my body, and his words are the last thing I hear as whatever he's injected me with takes me under.

"It's okay, Snow. You're safe now."

Four
Elijah

I hold Snow in my arms the whole way back to my home. The driver didn't ask questions as I climbed into the back of my Mercedes with an unconscious woman in my arms. He's paid well not to stick his nose where it doesn't belong.

When I took over the business, I culled every last person that ever worked under my uncle. They were all liabilities I couldn't afford to have, especially when I wanted to align myself with the Saint James family. They wouldn't stand for any of the things those sick motherfuckers used to do under the previous boss, so they all had to go. Everything I've done from the moment my family died is put plans in place I've been plotting for years, but this part of the plan right here, my beautiful Snowflake coming home, that's the part I've obsessed over the most. Every single part of this plan centers around her standing by my side.

I brush her blonde hair from her cheeks and stare down at her. She looks so tiny in my lap, and I wonder how small she'll seem in my bed when she eventually moves to it. She'll have her own room for the first little while. It goes against my baser needs for her to be away from me, but my Snow has a fire inside I need to dim enough that she won't try to stab me in my sleep.

The car slows, and I finally draw my eyes away from my woman. I don't know how I'm going to get any work done now she's home, but I'll have to cross that bridge when I come to it. Maybe it's time I get a number two so I can spend more time with my Snowflake.

The driver comes around and opens the door, his eyes never dropping to the woman in my arms. He likes living, I suppose. Maybe it's time I remember his name if he's going to be a permanent employee.

I give him a short nod and close the distance between the curb and the unsuspecting brownstone. I bought the house years ago when I first got my trust fund. And then every time one of the other houses on this side of the street went up for sale, I bought those too. I knew I would eventually need a base of operations, and who would ever suspect a row of family homes to be converted into an impenetrable bulletproof fortress?

The work I did on the homes was done over years so as not to raise suspicion, but behind these doors is a mansion no one knows about but me and my staff and now Snow. At least she will know. For the first few days, she'll see very little of the home I've created for us. The little touches I insisted on to suit her tastes. I want her to be comfortable here and proving how much I know about her and what she needs should help me to prove that to her.

I unlock the door and step across the threshold with her in my arms. The scent of cinnamon, her favorite fragrance, hits me head-on. I'm all too aware that the move is usually reserved for husbands carrying their new brides into their shared home, and it gets me thinking. Maybe I could marry her while she's unconscious…

The thought is interrupted when Snow stirs in my arms, a soft whine filling the air around us. I'm running out of time to get her in her room before she wakes up. The drug I gave her was non-harmful, and I only gave her enough to get her here without a scene. Soon she'll come to know I won't ever do anything that would harm her. Well, maybe I should rephrase that. I won't ever do anything that could permanently harm her. I am tearing her away from her life and family without so much as a word, and I suppose that will have a negative impact on her in the short term, but nothing permanent.

I carry Snow into her room, the one right beside mine, and gently lay her out on the bed. For a moment, I can't tear my eyes away from her beauty, the space in my chest where a heart should beat constricts in a rare moment of feeling. She's the only person who's ever made me *feel* anything, and maybe that's how she found her way here. The little lamb in the lion's den. My pretty princess in her ivory tower.

Her mess of blonde hair splays across the pillow, framing her perfect face. I've spent so many hours staring at her that I've memorized every single angle of her face, the small dusting of freckles on her nose, the way her lashes whisper across her cheeks when she closes her eyes. Snow is ingrained in my mind, and some days I don't know where she ends and I begin. That's what obsession is though, the unhealthy need for another person, the person who occupies your mind during every waking minute and your dreams too. Just the way Snow has since the moment our eyes locked from across a crowded room ten years ago.

God, she was pretty that night. The white dress pooling around her legs, giving her the image of floating. Her hair pulled into an intricate braid on the top of her head, and I swear I thought she was an angel. She's too pure for this world, too pure for me. But there's the sick side of me that craves making her dirty. Dragging her down into the abyss I live my life in to tarnish her purity. It's all I've been able to think about for a decade, and now she's all mine to stain.

My poor little Snowflake won't know what hit her when I finally get my hands on her. The good little angel from all those years ago will kneel for me, and I can't fucking wait.

FIVE

SNOW

For as long as I can remember, I've dreamed in vivid color. Every morning I wake up, and I remember every last second of the dream I had the night before. There have only been two exceptions to that rule.

The first was when I had my tonsils taken out as a child. The sedative they gave me knocked me out, and not even my wild dreams could break through the drugs. And the other was right now.

It takes long moments for me to open my eyes, the haze behind them causing my stomach to flip uncomfortably. The sheets beneath me are foreign, just as soft as the ones I have at home, but they're new. They don't have the same lived-in smell mine do when they come out of the dryer at the estate.

I blink slowly, waiting for my eyes to come into focus, but when they finally do, I almost wish they never did.

This isn't my room, and this sure as hell isn't my house, but everything looks… familiar. The mattress I'm lying on is the same one I have at the estate. The bedside tables are the same too. Even the painting on the wall to my left is the same, but I know in my soul that I'm not in my house. My hands rub down my body, dread settling over me and making it hard to suck in a breath until I'm sure I'm still wearing the same clothes I was when I got dressed this morning. The button of my jeans digs painfully into my stomach, and the only piece of clothing I'm missing is my coat. Okay, at least that's a good sign.

I sit up, causing the world to spin around me, but I can't remember anything from before I woke up. This morning I was thinking about slipping my security detail to go for a drink. Did I do it? Where did I go? How did I find myself here?

Once the dizziness subsides, I shuffle to the edge of the bed and carefully stand, making sure to hold on to the bed in case my legs give out beneath me. They shake as I take careful steps toward the door. Every time I turn my head, it spins, and I have to grab a hold of the closest steady object, but everything about this room grabs my attention. The closer I get to the door, I realize the wallpaper is the same as my room at the estate, and so is the door, right down to the fucking handle.

Did I wake up in another goddamn dimension?

I reach for the handle and twist, but it doesn't budge. I turn it the other way. Nothing. What the hell?

A laugh claws up my throat. I'm so stupid, of course I know what's going on. My brothers are teaching me a lesson for sneaking out all the time, they're trying to show me the dangers of slipping my security team by scaring me. My racing heart starts to slow as I swallow the giggle lodged in my throat. I can't let them know I know what they're up to. It's more fun if I let whatever fucked-up plan they have run its course.

I cross to the window next, I'm interested to know where exactly they've brought me for this little lesson, but when I look out into the street, I don't expect what I see. We're in the old part of the city, the part where the rich singles live in fancy brownstones. Why on earth would they bring me here? We've never even been to this part of the city, and I've helped Wynter enough to know we don't own any property around here.

A flicker of doubt ignites in my belly. What if it wasn't Rayne and Storm playing a prank? What if someone actually took me? And not just any someone. A someone who knows exactly what my bedroom looks like from the inside, right down to the brand of sheets and the decorative pillows I bought in Paris last year on a girl's trip with Mom and Wynter.

The thing is, and the thing that has a cold sweat breaking out on my brow is that my brothers wouldn't get all these details right. Even an interior designer would have a hard time getting every single one of these aspects right.

I turn toward the door again, my eyes running over everything in the room once again. The dizziness I felt when I stood up returns, and a moment later, I crumple to the floor, the plush rug softening the blow when I hit the ground. The softness envelops my body, the familiar texture almost allowing me to pretend I'm at home in my room. When I was in high school, my friends and I used to lie on the rug while we flicked through magazines and talked about boys, and it's that memory that I allow to drag me back into unconsciousness.

Sometime later, I wake, my body surrounded by plush bedding. Someone moved me. Someone was in here, and they moved me back to the bed.

I sit straight up, fear beating through every fiber of my being as my eyes dart around the dark room. The moon shines brightly out the window, and the street below is quiet. What time is it?

Slowly, I slip out of bed, the rug I fell asleep on soft beneath my feet. Instead of feeling groggy like I did when I woke up the first time, energy courses through my blood. I need to figure out where I am, who has me, and how the hell I can get out of here.

My eyes fall on what I think may be the bathroom on the far side of the room, and I quickly cross to it. Once I've done my business, I look around the space and sigh with annoyance. The tiles are the same as the estate, the clawfoot tub almost identical, and even the products I use every day in the shower are lined up on a shelf just like the one at home.

This has to be a fucking parallel universe.

I pick up my favorite shampoo, the bottle full and unopened. My brothers wouldn't have thought of this much detail. They may be the best at organizing large shipments of weapons and wide-scale hacking into government databases, but there's no way they would think to stock wherever the fuck I am with my favorite beauty products.

I need a weapon. Something to protect myself when whoever has taken me comes in here to get whatever they want. There has to be a reason they've taken me, but I don't have a clue what it could be. I'm not involved in any of the shady shit my family does. I never have been, and I'm almost certain I never will be. They've always tried to protect me from the extent of what we're involved in, and I've never felt the need to stick my nose where it doesn't belong, but maybe I should have asked a few more questions.

It never occurred to me that I could still be in danger after the Russos were killed. I thought they were the end of the danger. Not that them being on the loose ever stopped me from slipping out from under my securities' nose occasionally.

But maybe I should have listened to my brothers when they told me how dangerous the city can be, especially for someone like me. I'm the weakness of my family, not because I'm not strong, but because I'm the youngest. There's nothing my brothers and sister won't do to protect me, and every bad guy in the city knows it.

I drop to my knees, the cool tiles making me wince on impact, but I ignore the pain and start rummaging through the cupboard below the vanity for anything I can use as a weapon. I know self-defense. My brothers insisted I know how to protect myself, considering how little I liked having a security detail, but something tells me this is different. This isn't a matter of fending off some two-bit thug on the street. This is someone who has planned to take me. Someone who has plotted over a long period of time, someone who has watched me, who has been in my house enough to know every single thing I have in my bedroom and bathroom. Whoever has me probably hasn't taken me just to extort my family out of money.

No. The man who took me wants something much more sinister. I just don't know what yet.

Six
Elijah

I'm not normally someone who smiles. Emotions are a liability in the life I was born into and certainly within my family. If you want to survive life as a Russo, you have to be cold and dead inside. There's no room for feelings, or love, or happiness. Those things are myths you hear about from other people, but you can never feel them yourself.

Except, I haven't stopped smiling since I left Snow asleep in her bed. The corners of my mouth and cheeks ache from the foreign gesture, but I can't help it. A part of me has clicked into place, and I've never felt so settled in myself. My whole life I've looked over my shoulder, waiting for something to go wrong. But now Snow's here. Everything in my world feels right.

In my family, happiness was always a weakness. One time when I was seven, a friend at school gave me a toy car. I'd never had one before because my father and uncles didn't believe Everett and I should have a childhood. Our sole purpose was to be the heirs to the Russo name, and we started training for that role almost from when we took our first steps. He was luckier than I was. His mother was alive for some of his life, so he felt love and compassion, even if he did experience such loss at a young age. My mother died when I was a baby, meaning the only parent I ever had was a cold, heartless father.

When my father found the car in my backpack, he threw it in the fire and forced me to watch it melt, and once it was nothing more than the metal frame, he made me reach into the open flame and retrieve the burning hot remnants of the toy I loved so much. I still have the scars from where he forced me to hold it until it was cool enough for him to throw in the trash.

That was the day I turned my emotions off, and I didn't turn them back on again until the day I laid eyes on my beautiful Snowflake. She's the only one to ever make me feel anything and having her in my home feels right.

I watch as she rummages through the bathroom looking for something to protect herself, just as I expected her to do. Every move she's made since she woke up has been exactly as I thought it would be. Confusion. Panic. Reasoning with herself. Survival. Each reaction is so uniquely Snow it only makes my smile grow wider.

She's incredible. The perfect mix of fire and uncertainty she's always lived her life with. I'm addicted to her rebellion and obsessed with the shyness she hides behind the mask she shows the world. I've been hooked on Snow Saint James since the first time our eyes met, and there isn't a drug on this earth I'd rather be addicted to.

I've planned everything from when I first laid her down on

her new bed. I should be walking in there any minute now, taunting her with who I am, but something inside me makes me stop. Dare I say my conscience? I didn't believe I had one up until now. Hell, when you've done the shit I have, the word itself is foreign, but there's something about my Snowflake that makes me second guess everything I've ever known.

She's scared. Whether she's willing to admit it or not, she's a frightened little lamb, and me going in there to taunt her is only going to make it harder to make her trust me. We have a long way to go to get her where I want her, and while my baser instincts call to me to hunt my prey, make sure she knows the danger lurking in the shadows and then pounce when she's least expecting it, the part of me that Snow softens wants to ease her into her new reality.

A knock at the door startles me. Already Snow has become a distraction, but I can't bring myself to care. One of the main reasons I partnered with the Saint James family was so I would have more time to spend with her when she arrived, and soon I'll start hiring some more staff to help me. A second in charge, maybe even an enforcer to do the dirty work. As much as I crave the blood of my enemies, the screams they let out as they get closer and closer to death, Snow won't like it if I come home covered in blood, so I may have to take a step back from that side of the business.

"Come in," I say just loud enough for whoever is outside the door to hear.

Mrs. Chambers sticks her head through the door, a warm smile on her lips. I was the most concerned about her going along with this plan and not running back to the Saint James family to tell them Snow is here against her will, but when I told her we would be having a houseguest who would eventually become my wife, she seemed almost excited. She's been a housekeeper in our family for my whole life, and the source of the only warmth I've ever felt. She's the one who raised me, and deep down, she knows I would never hurt a woman the way my father and uncles did.

"I have Miss Saint James's dinner here. Would you like me to take it in?"

"Please." I nod. "As we discussed, you can speak to her. She'll need someone to lean on, but for the moment, omit where she is and who has her." We've been over this a few times in the last couple of weeks. All the staff were made aware of our guest and what it would mean if they were to tell anyone she was here before the time was right, and each of them knew there was more than just their jobs on the line. I'll fucking slaughter their entire families while they watch and then torture them for as long as I can before their body finally gives up if they breathe a word of this to anyone.

"Of course, Mr. Russo." She gives me a kind smile before backing out of the room.

"Mrs. Chambers," I call out before she can close the door, and her head peeks back in. "Thank you for helping me make this easier on her."

"She's been here a few hours, and I can already see what she means to you, and you know all I've ever wanted for you is happiness. If this makes you happy, and you can make her feel safe and cherished, then I'm going to be on board. But mark my words, Elijah, if you ever lay a hand on that woman, I will do whatever it takes to get her away from you, regardless of the consequences."

I almost laugh. She's the only one who has ever gone toe to toe with a Russo and walked away with her life, and she's not looking to break that streak now. "You have my word. I will never raise my hand to Snow, never hurt her the way my father and uncles hurt the women in their lives."

"Then we won't have a problem." The door closes behind her, and I allow the chuckle to trickle from my chest. Maybe I have a soft spot for my fiery little Snowflake, because the woman who raised me is just the same way.

SEVEN

SNOW

There's nothing in this goddamn room I can use as a weapon. The only things that are in my room at the estate that are missing from this room is anything that could be used as one. There's nothing I can use in place of pepper spray. The nail scissors I keep by my bed aren't there. And the heaviest item I can lift is a goddamn bottle of moisturizer.

Once I've processed the fact I have nothing to protect myself with, I wander back into the bedroom and take a seat in the chair beneath the window. It's obvious this one is much newer than the one my mother used to cradle me in when I was young and we first moved into the estate. She loved that chair. She used to read to Wynter and me in it every night before bed. The boys were a little older, so by that time, they were more interested in playing with their new toys than listening to the fairy tales Mom would read to us. This one is firmer. It doesn't have her scent lingering in the fabric, or the memory of her woven into the stuffing. It smells brand new, and that only makes tears spring to my eyes.

The sound of a key in the door has me sitting upright and looking around the room again. What if they're coming to harm me? As much self-defense as I know, it's only going to do me so much good if I have to find my way out of an unfamiliar house. Best case scenario, the only person here is the one coming through the door, but the worst, and most likely, scenario is that there's a houseful of security holding me here, and there's no way I'm getting out unscathed.

The last thing I expect to see when the door swings open is a five-foot older lady with short gray hair and glasses balancing on the bridge of her nose. She wears a wide smile, and both hands are holding a tray.

"It's nice to see you up, dear. I came in to check on you earlier, but you were out for the count." She chuckles, placing the tray of what I can only assume is food on the table a few feet from where I'm sitting.

As much as I want to ask every question that rushes to the tip of my tongue, I can't tear my focus from the door she's left wide open. I'm almost certain it's a trap, but what if it's not?

"Sadly dear, I assure you it would be a fruitless endeavor. This place could give Guantanamo a run for its money," she muses. "I'm Mrs. Chambers, but you can call me Mary. No one else does, but I figure if I ask enough people, one of them eventually will."

"Where am I?" I ask quietly, pulling my knees to my chest and wrapping my arms around them.

She turns to me, her eyes glinting with sympathy. "All of your questions will be answered soon, dear. I know you must be frightened, but I promise no harm will come to you here." Her words are soft and kind, but she's avoiding the question.

"I was drugged and kidnapped. I think we're a little past harming me," I snap.

Mary sighs, her eyes casting down to the carpet. "You're right. But you're safe here. I brought you some soup. It should be kind on your belly considering the day you've had."

"I'm not eating that."

Confusion pulls her eyebrows together a moment before understanding crosses her features. She takes a few careful steps toward me so as not to startle me. "I know your arrival here was under precarious circumstances, however, I can assure you I would not drug your food. I'm here to make sure you're happy and healthy, and that includes making sure you're fed."

I consider her for a moment, wondering how I'm best to play this. She seems like a reasonable woman, but if that were the case, she wouldn't be a party to kidnapping an innocent woman. "I don't understand why I'm here. Please let me go. Please don't let them hurt me." The tears I intend to cry are crocodile tears. I've always been able to cry on demand, and believe me when I say, I've done it a time or two. But when the tears well in my eyes, I realize there's nothing fake about them and the telltale signs of a sob catches in my throat. I didn't intend to cry real tears. I don't want anyone to see my weakness, but hopelessness is eating away at me. What if I never see my family again? Our parents only died a few months ago, they can't lose someone else. Our family has been through so much. I don't want them to hurt anymore.

"Oh, sweetheart." Her eyes dart to the corner of the room,

where I spotted a camera the moment I curled up in the chair. She closes the distance between us, and I don't flinch when her arms wrap around me.

I find comfort in her warmth. I shouldn't allow myself to feel anything other than anger and fear, but there's something about the older woman that brings me calm.

"I know you're scared now, but I think if you allow yourself some grace and you let go of your preconceived notions, you could be very happy here."

"Please," I cry. "I just want to go home."

"I know, sweetheart. But this is your home now," Mary says quietly, but her words only make me cry harder. All hope that she might help me escape diminishes. I don't know where I am or who has me, but I allow myself to fall apart in the arms of a woman I've only just met, who works for whoever took me.

Eight
Elijah

Her tears are all I see. I've been watching her cry for the last half an hour. Mrs. Chambers left after ten minutes of trying to comfort my inconsolable little Snowflake. She's so pretty with tears streaming down her cheeks, and it's all I can do to stop myself from storming in there and fucking her so hard she sobs for me.

My cock hardens in my jeans, and my hand twitches with the need to relieve myself, but I don't. The next time I come, I'll be coating my Snowflake, marking her as mine. No other man will ever touch my woman, not if they want to keep their hands attached to their body.

My phone vibrates across my desk, drawing my attention away from the beautiful woman on the screen. My lips tip up into a smile. I've been expecting this call for hours, but it's taken him longer than I thought it would.

"Storm," I say evenly.

"My sister is missing. Can you let your guys know to keep

an eye out for her?" He hates asking me for anything. Hell, he hates this whole arrangement, but that's nothing compared to how much he's going to hate what's going to happen next.

"I don't need to."

Storm sighs, and an image of him sitting behind his desk, massaging his temples with frustration, pops into my mind. "Look, Elijah. We agreed to this truce because it was mutually beneficial, but if you're not going to be helpful, you can shove—"

"I don't need to tell my guys shit because I know exactly where Snow is."

Silence greets me on the other end of the phone and my eyes find their way back to Snow as she crosses the room to the soup Mrs. Chambers left for her. Maybe she's realized I would have no reason to drug her again, not when I've already got her at my mercy. She has to be hungry, and I'm relieved I'm not going to have to pin her down and force-feed her.

"Where is she, Elijah?" he growls.

"She's safe," I assure him. "I'll have her call you in the morning."

"You'll put her on the phone right this fucking minute, or I'll come down there and slit your fucking throat." The menace in his words only makes me smile more. He'll be seeing this as an attack on all of them, but really, it's just me claiming something that belongs to me.

"She's safe, Storm. I'm not going to hurt her. She's warm, and fed, and comfortable. I will have her call you tomorrow, but I won't wake her just to calm your rage. I suggest that when you speak to her in the morning, that you're calm and rational, because if you upset her, it will be the last call you have." I end the call and turn the phone to *Do Not Disturb*. He can call as much as he likes, but he won't be speaking to Snow tonight.

The bowl is empty by the time I look up at the screen again and she's crawled back into the bed beneath the sheets. She looks tiny in such a large bed, and I can't help but smile at the fact she's decided to stay in her jeans. I thought it would go a long way to build trust if I didn't change her while she was unconscious, but surely she's not comfortable.

I stare at the screen until her breathing evens out and a soft snore comes through the speaker. As if the cameras weren't enough, I wanted the closest thing I could get to being inside her pretty mind. I push the chair away from the desk and stalk out of the room I use as an office, making my way toward the wing of the house with the bedrooms. Mine is right next to the one Snow is asleep in, but it won't be long before she's moving in with me. Once I've eased her into her new life, she'll spend every night wrapped up in my arms.

I hesitate by her door for a moment, my hand twitching to reach for the key hanging on the wall. I should let her sleep. It's been a big day for her, but my body is drawn to her. Finally having Snow within my reach after so many years of planning makes me greedy. I've waited for what feels like a lifetime. So many times I considered throwing in the whole plan and running away with her, far away from our families and their influence, but now I have her here, I'm glad I waited. The moment I took her, all restraint should have diminished, but I find myself caring about something I've never given a fuck about before. Someone else's feelings. It's foreign to me, like waking up in another country where I don't speak the language, but I welcome the unfamiliar feeling.

I reach for the key and quietly unlock the door. I don't want to wake her, but the pull to be close to her is more than I can fight. And I shouldn't have to fight my baser needs anymore, not when I can be as close to Snow as I like now. No more living in the shadows. No more staring at her from the other end of the bar or bumping into her on the street just so I can get a whiff of her perfume. No, those days are over. She's mine now. All fucking mine.

Snow is curled up in the middle of the bed, the blankets tucked around her as if they'll do anything to protect her. I suppose the illusion of safety is enough to allow her tired body to rest.

The steady rise and fall of her shoulder brings me comfort as I cross to the chair she sat in and cried about the loss of her freedom. She doesn't understand yet, but she will. If she can just be patient and give herself to me, she will be freer than she has ever been in her life. There won't be any ivory tower for my woman because she'll be standing right by my side, ruling our kingdom.

She'll fight at first, defying the loss of her independence, but soon she'll see how good it can be.

I stare at her for hours, even staying put through a nightmare despite my need to comfort her. Being so close to her without being able to touch her is so familiar it's like breathing, but it's harder to restrain myself now. But I won't have to for much longer. Soon she'll know all about the future I've planned for us, and once she comes to terms with it, there will never be another moment I hesitate to touch her.

It's not until the sun starts to pool through the open window that I slip out of the room, heading to my own to shower and change. Today's the day I finally claim my woman.

Nine

Snow

I groan as I tug the pillow over my head. Why is the sun so bright this morning? Normally it doesn't hit my side of the house until late morning, and surely I didn't sleep that long.

My eyes snap open as memories filter back through my mind. The bar. Being drugged. The tattooed man. Waking up in a room that's too similar to my childhood bedroom. Each memory is a kick to my stomach, making it impossible to suck in a breath.

I'm not at home. Someone kidnapped me. I have no idea where I am, or if I'll see my family again. All I know is that somewhere in this house there's a woman named Mary who held me while I cried but denied me my freedom. I don't know what I've done to deserve this. I've never had anything to do with the darker sides of the family business, only participating when absolutely necessary. But what I do know is that all our threats have been neutralized. We have no enemies right now, and maybe that's why I'm so anxious. At least if Angelo Russo was still alive, I could surmise it was him who had orchestrated my kidnapping. But being in the dark, having no idea where I am or whose hands my fate lies in, it has a sense of dread washing over me and nausea bubbling in my belly.

Slowly I sit up and look at my surroundings again. Maybe I missed something last night. The light of day is meant to bring new opportunities, new hope, but as my eyes cast across the familiar setting, all I feel is dejected by my new reality. All I can do is hope my brothers come and save me, because they're my only chance of getting out of here.

The door swings open just like it did last night, and again Mary strolls in with a wide smile on her face. I wonder idly if this is how I'll wake up every morning or if this ruse is to lead me into a false sense of security, and soon, I'll find myself locked in some kind of dirty basement. Although, in most cases, that would be the option I would suspect, I don't think that's the case here. Why would someone go to all this effort to make the room look exactly the same as my bedroom at home? Why would they source all the same products, buy all the same toiletries, right down to my favorite perfume Mom had bought for me when I turned eighteen, if they only intended for me to stay here for a night or two?

"Good morning, dear," she chimes.

"Hi Mary," I murmur, my eyes casting down to the carpet beside the bed.

"Oh, finally someone calls me Mary! Maybe you can convince everyone else to as well."

She moves to the other side of the room, and I track her movements out of the corner of my eye. She's left the door wide open again, and my body twitches to make a run for it.

What's the worst that can happen? They catch me and bring me back here? *Or they kill you.* She moves into the closet and returns with a short cotton dress as well as a matching set of bra and panties.

"You're going to have breakfast in the main dining room this morning. When you're ready, pop out the door and turn left, follow the hallway all the way along and the dining room is at the end."

Before I can ask any other questions, she disappears out the door, leaving it open as she leaves. I stare after her for long moments. If I'm a prisoner, why are they letting me out of this room? A prisoner is confined to a small space, a cell of some sort, but they've just given me freedom to roam the house, and I don't know what to make of that.

When I finally regain the use of my limbs, I cross to the bathroom and turn the water on in the shower as hot as it will go. I've always enjoyed a hot shower, but I've never needed one like I do right now. Every part of me feels filthy, even if I haven't been anywhere the least bit unclean.

I take my time in the shower, only the slightest bit nervous about being naked in a foreign place when I hadn't had a chance to find all the hidden cameras. But at this point, I have bigger problems than someone seeing my tits.

Once I've scrubbed every inch of my body until my skin stings, I shut the water off and wrap a soft, fluffy towel around myself. I go through my normal motions, using the skincare someone has taken the time to collect and place in the exact same order I have mine, right down to the position of the headband I sometimes use to hold my hair back while I do my makeup.

I dry my hair but don't bother to style it before heading back into the bedroom and pulling the clothes Mary left for me on. The only room I didn't visit last night was the closet, and something pulls me toward it, like an invisible magnet dragging me along until I'm standing in the doorway. At first, the materialistic part of me is in awe of the rows of designer clothing in front of me, but then reality hits me so hard that the wind is knocked right out of my lungs. If all these clothes are my size, which on first inspection they are, whoever took me intends to keep me for a while… a long while.

Backing out of the closet slowly before I can fall down a rabbit hole I'm not sure I'll drag myself back out of, I turn and stare at the open door. Maybe I should just hang out in here and skip breakfast. It's probably the safer option. But if someone has gone to all this trouble to get me here, are they really just going to let me sit in my room and sulk?

I take tentative steps toward the open door, my heart pounding in my chest when my head sticks out into the hallway, and I look side to side. There isn't a sound in the house, and maybe that's just as disconcerting as the room that's eerily similar to my bedroom at the estate. My bare feet carry me across the deep pile carpet, my toes sinking into the softness and grounding me. Fear bleeds into my veins, I've never been that great at the unexpected, but this feels much more ominous than anything else I've ever faced.

The closer I get to what I assume is the dining room, the more the pit of my stomach aches with anxiety. The unknown has never felt more terrifying than it does right now. Each step is slow and calculated, barely trusting my body to remain upright as I near what could be my own demise.

My steps falter just outside the door, my eyes darting down the hallways on either side of me. Should I make a run for it? I'm already out of my room. I've got to be closer to the exit than I was before. Maybe I can make it. Maybe I can escape.

But the rational part of my mind reminds me I have no shoes on. I don't have my purse or my phone. Even if I make it out the door, which is unlikely, the chance of me actually getting home is so slim my heart aches for the life I've taken for granted all these years. All the times I ran away from the protection my family insisted I have played back in my mind. Every lecture about staying with my security team for my own safety is like a sitcom rerun. I did this to myself. I have no one else to blame but my own stupid self for putting myself in this position, and now I have to live with the consequences.

I step forward into the dining room. A long oak table stretches from one side of the room to the other, and a man stands at the window across from me. His back is muscular and wide, and familiar tattoos wind around his bare arms up to the black T-shirt obstructing my view of the rest. The man from the bar. The one in the shadows.

Slowly, so fucking slowly, he turns around and I get my first glance at the man who has torn me from my life, and my mouth drops open in surprise when my eyes lock with his familiar green ones.

"Welcome home, my little Snowflake."

Ten

Elijah

Each emotion that passes through her eyes has the corners of my lips quirking up into a smile. It's sick to get such pleasure from her pain, but I can't help it when it comes to Snow. Recognition comes first, then confusion, and then the anger burns to life in the pools of blue. The look of thunder that crosses her face makes me choke on a groan. I have a feeling a fired-up Snow is a fun Snow.

"Elijah? What the fuck do you think you're doing? Do my brothers know where I am? Didn't you get the hint not to fuck with us when Wynter shot you?" She crosses the room, rounding the table until she comes toe to toe with me, her neck craned back to look up at me.

"Why don't we have a seat?" I gesture to the two plates full of food, one at the head of the table and the other to the left. My hand twitches to touch her, the pull almost too great for me to fight, but I quickly shove my hand back into my pocket.

"If you think I'm eating anything on that plate, you're fucking insane." She stamps her foot like an angry toddler, and I allow a chuckle to slip from my throat.

"You're going to do as you're told if you want any answers." I shrug, stepping around her and taking my seat at the head of the table. If she wants answers badly enough, she's going to sit her pretty ass down and eat the damn breakfast Mrs. Chambers prepared for us. I won't have her going without food, so if she decides not to eat, I will be forced to make her.

I train my eyes on my plate, picking up my knife and fork as I survey the bacon and eggs covering the plate. Mrs. Chambers makes a mean breakfast. It was one of the only good parts of my childhood. Every time my father or uncles hurt me, she was there to clean my wounds and make sure I was fed. Even when they locked me in a closet for a week after I refused to kill someone when I was ten, she always made sure I had food, even if she was risking her own life by giving it to me.

A few minutes pass, and I start to think she's not going to sit down, but then she appears in my peripheral vision, and she drops into the chair beside me. "Okay, I'm sitting. Now answer my questions."

"Uh, uh, uh. The proviso was not you sitting, it was you eating some breakfast. It's not good for you to skip meals."

She rolls her eyes. "I don't normally eat so much in the morning. Usually just a smoothie or some fruit."

I nod. "I'll make sure Mrs. Chambers knows for tomorrow morning. But today, you're going to eat what's on your plate if you want to get the answers to your questions." She'll likely get them regardless, seeing as I need to have her call Storm soon if I don't want the whole Saint James family burning my house to the ground, but she doesn't need to know that.

She tentatively picks up her own knife and fork and takes a bite of her eggs. My eyes track her every movement, right down to the way her lips wrap around the fork and how her throat bobs when she swallows. She groans in appreciation, and my hands tighten around my cutlery. Perhaps I hadn't totally prepared myself for how tempting my little Snowflake would be.

"Storm knows you're here," I tell her.

"What?" she squeaks in surprise.

"You're going to call him shortly to tell him you're safe and that we're taking good care of you."

She drops her knife and fork, and they clatter when they hit the plate. The defiance in her eyes is almost my undoing, but I keep my features neutral. "I will do nothing of the sort," Snow hisses.

I sigh, placing my own cutlery down and dragging her seat closer to my own before she can think to jump out of it, not stopping until her knees are flush against my leg. "I think you're a little confused about how this is going to go, so let me spell it out for you. You are not here as some kind of revenge plot against your family, and your brothers did not hire me to teach you a lesson for always sneaking away from your security team. You are here because I want you to be, because you belong to me, and you have for the last ten years. You are going to do as you're told and call your brother, or I will start thinking of creative ways to punish you. Given that level of transgression would likely lead to your entire family trying to take you away from me, I think the punishment for that would be harming someone you care about. So it's up to you, Snowflake. You're either a good girl and do what I tell you, or you're bad, and someone you love gets hurt." I shrug but make no move to return her seat to its former position.

Having her close to me is intoxicating, and if I have it my way, I'll never give her an inch of space from now on. She belongs here. She belongs to me.

Snow's eyes flare with a mixture of fear and anger, but her mouth remains pressed in a hard line. I at least expected an argument, but then again, her biggest weakness is her love for others. I never wanted to threaten someone she loves because by harming them, I would cause her immense pain, and I don't want that, but I'll do whatever I have to do to keep her here.

"He won't believe I'm here of my own freewill," she finally says.

"He will if you're convincing enough. I know you can do it. I've watched you play the part of the good girl moments before you sneak off and let your wild side run rampant. I have no doubt in my mind that you can lie to your brother just enough so he's not bashing down my door in a few hours' time."

She huffs, her eyes tearing away from mine at the same time she crosses her arms over her chest defiantly.

A smile tugs at the corners of my lips, but I quickly replace it with the mask I've worn my whole life. I can't allow her to see my weakness for her yet. She can't know how I feel until there's nowhere for her to escape.

"Now, would you like to call him now, or do you want to

finish your breakfast first?" I ask, nodding toward the barely touched meal in front of her.

"I'll do it now." She sighs.

I don't like the way she's not fighting me on this, and there's something about her acceptance that isn't sitting right with me. I'm under no illusions that this is going to be an easy transition for her, and the fact she isn't screaming and yelling and throwing shit is disconcerting.

I nod once and tug my phone from my pocket. When I took it off *Do Not Disturb* this morning after sneaking out of her room, I had ten voice mails from Storm, all of which were filled with strings of profanities. He's mad, perhaps understandably so, but that doesn't change the reality of our situation.

Snow reaches for the phone, but I quickly pull it from her reach.

"Ground rules. First of all, you should know that I have been following you for a very long time, so I know all about the codes you have if you get in trouble and need help. If you even think of using one of them, I will make good on my promise. Do you understand?"

Her mouth drops open in surprise and understanding flickers across her features. That's why she isn't mid-tantrum right now, she didn't think I would know if she called for help. "I understand," she whispers.

"I thought about writing you a script but figured Storm would see through it if he thought you were reading from something, so I'm going to tell you around about what I want you to say, and you're going to say it. Okay?"

Snow nods, her eyes dropping to where her hands are bundled in her lap. I hate seeing her so dejected, but this is just how things are going to have to be for the moment.

"Good girl. Now, I want you to spin some story about how we've been sneaking around since we made the alliance, and you are so deliriously happy here with me that you want to spend some time exploring our relationship."

"Absolutely not," she snaps. "We do not have any kind of relationship. I don't know what the fuck you think it is that's going to happen here, but it sure as hell isn't a fucking relationship."

There she is.

Eleven

Snow

Elijah Russo is fucking insane.

I've known it since the first time I heard his name uttered when I was a kid. Everett used to tell us stories about his cousin who liked to play with knives and fire, two things I knew you were meant to stay away from.

We've had encounters over the years, usually from afar, and usually I don't pay him a lot of attention. I'm surrounded by men who could end a life in five seconds flat and not blink an eye, I don't need anymore, but there was always something about him that I couldn't put my finger on.

Perhaps it's the way his moss-green eyes captivate me each time they meet mine or the way his dirty blonde hair looks both perfectly styled and like he just rolled out of bed at the same time. Or maybe it's how each time I'm around him, my body feels a pull I've never felt before. There are so many reasons that's fucked up, but I don't have the time to debate that in my own mind at the moment.

I have to deal with the much more pressing issue of him thinking he has some fucked-up claim over me, and I don't quite know how to deal with that. He seems dead fucking serious about every word he's saying, but surely he doesn't expect me to call my brother and lie through my teeth.

Elijah sighs, his hands moving from where they caged me in up to my thighs. His touch is electric, sending shock waves through my body. "We will have plenty of time to discuss our relationship and what it means, but right now, we need to deal with your brother. I do want to make something abundantly clear though, we do have a relationship. That's why you're here."

The blood drains from my face, and my mouth drops open. He cannot be serious. Please, God, tell me he's not serious.

"What are you going to say to Storm?" he asks.

I stare at him, unable to put words together as a new level of panic rages through my veins. I have to tell Storm I'm in danger, I need him to come rescue me, but I don't think I can tip him off without Elijah knowing.

"Snowflake, I'm going to need an answer."

"Why do you keep calling me that?" I whisper.

The corners of his lips tip up in a smile as his thumbs brush across my thigh, the contact making my heart race. "Because snowflakes are beautiful. On the surface they seem fragile, but in order to make it from the sky to the earth, their strength is tested. And when they land, they hold their shape."

"And that's how you see me?" I ask.

"Everyone thinks you're fragile, but really you've always been stronger than any of them have been able to see."

My heart does a painful somersault in my chest, the compliment unexpected. I'd like to blame the fact that I've been constantly underestimated for the last twenty-three years of my life, but there's something in the back of my mind telling me that's not why I'm preening under his attention. Perhaps it's self-preservation. The longer I can keep my captor happy, the safer I'll be, but then again, he has to have taken me for a reason, and how safe can anyone really be when they're locked up by one of the most ruthless men in the city?

"I'm going to tell Storm that we've been seeing each other for a few weeks, and I'm staying with you for a while to make a go at it. I'm going to say that having a security team is unnecessary while I'm here because you have your own, and it's just doubling resources that could be used elsewhere." The words slip from my lips, but I'm almost not conscious of them. He's not giving me any other option than to do what he's telling me, and how much sway do I really have with the crazy man who's torn me from my life?

A pleased smile tugs at his lips, and he nods slowly. "Good girl." He hands me the phone already unlocked with my brother's name on the screen. "Remind me what happens if you decide to do something stupid?"

My stomach drops, and my eyes rise from the phone to his green ones. "You'll hurt someone I love," I whisper, afraid my voice will crack if I speak the words too loud. Our family has been through so much, I can't put them at risk again. Emerson is still recovering from the trauma Elijah's father and uncles put her through, and Wynter was held captive by a sociopath only a month ago. I don't want them to have to endure anything else.

"Exactly. See, you're starting to see how this is going to go. Now, I want you to put the phone on speaker so I can hear all the delightful things your brother is going to say when you tell him we're dating."

I take a deep breath and steel myself for the words I'm about to say. "I'm going to do this regardless, you're not really giving me a lot of choice, but I hope you know that no matter what I say on this call, no matter how convincing I am, my brother is going to show up here to take me home. Rayne and Storm have never let me date, and the only way I've ever had any semblance of normalcy is when I sneak out."

Elijah's eyes flash with something resembling pity, and I fucking hate it. "That's why I'm going to be right here, and if he gets too mad, I'll take the phone so you don't have to deal with it, okay?"

I roll my eyes. "I'm not a fucking child. I can deal with my brother being an overbearing asshole. I've been doing it all my life. I'm just saying if I were you, I would be expecting one, if not both, of my brothers and probably your cousin on the doorstep within hours of me making this call."

He shrugs. "Then you'll have to convince them how happy I make you in person."

My mouth drops open, and I stare at him for long moments. I thought reasoning with Storm was difficult, but Jesus, Elijah is a whole other kind of unreasonable. "You're insane," I mutter, my finger hovering over the screen. Can I really do this? Can I really convince my brother I'm dating someone we considered an enemy up until a few weeks ago?

"You don't know the half of it," Elijah says.

I ignore his comment and press Storm's number. If I don't do it now, I'm just going to keep putting it off, and the longer I do that, the worse it's going to be.

"Elijah, I swear to God I'm about two minutes from—"

"Storm, it's me," I whisper.

He breathes a sigh of relief and some of the anger dissipates from the line. "Snow, are you okay? Where are you? Everett's been working on your location all night, but that psycho has you hidden pretty well."

I close my eyes and steady myself before bringing the lie to the surface. "I'm fine," I tell him. "I'm here of my own free will." The lie is bitter on my tongue, and my body screams at me to tell the truth, but he hasn't left me a lot of options.

"You what?" he growls.

My eyes move to Elijah who's watching me carefully, a knowing smile plastered across his full lips. In all the times we've met, I don't think I've ever seen him seem so… dare I say it, happy. "Elijah and I have been seeing each other for a few weeks."

Silence meets me on the other end of the phone, but I wait for his reply. All my life, my family has been disappointed in me, but this will be a new low, even for me. "Come again," Storm's words are so deep and angry I almost can't reconcile it with the man I've looked up to my entire life.

"We bumped into each other at a bar not long after we made the alliance, and we've been seeing each other ever since. It's still new, but I really want to explore it."

"You have got to be kidding me, Snow. Out of all the bullshit you've pulled for attention, this has got to be the worst."

I flinch at his words.

"You cannot date Elijah Russo. Just because we have an understanding doesn't mean he can be trusted. I barely trust him with his word, let alone my baby sister."

The phone is wrenched from my hand, and my eyes go wide when he brings the phone closer to him. "That's enough," he barks into the phone. "Snow is old enough to make her own decisions, and I am not going to allow you to treat her like she's an inconvenience in your life."

Deafening silence greets us on the other end of the line, and my fingers tangle together in my lap. Logically I know I'm telling a lie to keep my family safe, and the last place I want to be is locked up here with Elijah, but the way my brothers always assume the worst of me, always assume every time I act out is because I want attention, only makes me want to defy them more.

"Put my sister back on thc phone," Storm finally demands.

"No," Elijah replies. "You've already upset her, and I'm not going to let you continue to do so. When you're ready to have a civilized conversation, let me know and we'll organize another time."

"Why is her phone off?" he asks.

"Because I knew you were going to be like this," I say, nothing but strength and resolve in my voice. I may not want to be locked up in Elijah Russo's fortress, but right now, I'd take it over being anywhere near my brother.

Twelve

Elijah

I've always known my Snowflake has claws. No one else sees past the good girl exterior to the lioness beneath. She's been overlooked and underestimated her entire life, but not anymore. Being with me will give her the strength to be the woman she was always meant to be. She'll no longer stand in her sibling's shadow, instead she'll be by my side, exactly where she belongs.

Fire flames to life in her eyes as she stares at the phone in my hand. I'll be honest, I planned for a lot of different eventualities when she made this call, but her getting mad at Storm for telling her what she can and can't do is not one I expected.

"Snow—" he starts.

"No. You listen to me, Storm. I'm an adult. I am completely capable of making my own decisions." She pauses, and her eyes move to mine, anxiety playing behind the pools of blue. She's trying to decide the answer to an age-old question, is she better off with the devil she knows, or the one she doesn't? "If

I was dating a normal guy who didn't understand the safety implications, then I would understand your stance, but if there's one person in this whole fucking city that gets it, it's Elijah."

We stare at one another as the silence drags out. She doesn't want to be here, that much she has made abundantly clear in the short time she's been here, but if the anger flickering in her eyes is anything to go by, I don't think she wants to be at the estate either. Which is a good thing because that's no longer her home. Her home is here with me, and that's a reality she's going to have to get on board with relatively quickly. I'm not a patient man, and my allowances for her outbursts are only limited.

Storm sighs on the other end of the line. "Fine, you can stay there for a while longer. But you will be coming home."

"This is her home now," I say and can't help but smirk at the anger that flares to life in her eyes at my words.

"No, it's fucking not," Storm snaps. "I'm trying really fucking hard to be understanding, but don't fucking test me. I will not hesitate to put you in the ground beside your father and uncles." Menace drips from his words, but I can't shake my smile.

"I'll come home when I'm ready to," Snow offers.

My smile falters and I glare at her, but she just shrugs, turning her attention back to the phone in my hand.

"Is that her?" Wynter's voice fills the other end of the line and then a moment later there's an obvious change in hands. "Snow?"

Snow squeezes her eyes shut, tears pooling at the brim. Talking to Storm was one thing, but her sister is her best friend, lying to her is an entirely different thing altogether. "Hey Wyn." She forces the words out through thick emotion.

"Are you okay? We've been really worried."

"I'm fine, I'm… with Elijah." My name on her lips is like a fucking symphony. All these years I've dreamed of how it would sound in her sweet voice, but every time she says it, my cock gets impossibly harder.

"Elijah Russo?"

"Yes."

Wynter doesn't respond for a few moments, and I imagine her and Storm having a silent conversation. "When are you coming home? I have some news."

Snow's eyes lock with mine, question dancing behind them. She knows she's not getting out of here without my say-so, and I hold all the cards right now. "I'm not sure at the moment. Can you tell me over the phone?"

"Not this kind of news. That's okay. I'll hold off until I can see you. Just don't scare me like that again!"

I give Snow a nod, and she lets out a little sigh of relief.

"I won't, I promise."

"Elijah," Wynter chimes.

"Yes, Wynter."

"If you so much as lay a hand on my sister that she doesn't

want, I promise I won't miss when I shoot you this time."

I chuckle. While I've always been obsessed with the youngest Saint James, I can see what my cousin sees in her. "I understand."

We say our goodbyes and when the line goes dead, Snow stares at me, unasked questions floating across her gaze. She doesn't understand why any of this is happening, and to be fair, I haven't offered her any answers.

"Why am I here, Elijah? Are you sure this isn't some fucked up way to get back at my brothers? Because I'm not going to be a pawn between you and my family." She crosses her arms across her chest defiantly. Her knees brush against mine, the contact making me want to bend her over the table and fuck her until she can't breathe without feeling me.

"I already explained this, Snow. You're here because you're mine. You've been mine for a long time, and you will continue to be mine from now on."

"Don't I get a say in this at all?"

"No."

"So you're just as bad as my brothers then? I've just been moved from one prison to another, is that it?"

I growl, my patience wearing thin. She's pushing my buttons, and she fucking knows it. Before she can think to move, I rise from my chair and bend until our faces are only an inch apart. Her nervous breath whispers across my cheek and I swallow down the groan that claws its way up my throat. I promised myself I wouldn't force anything on her, that while I'm a monster, I don't want to be that kind of monster, but I underestimated how fucking hard it would be to be close to her.

"Right now, you might feel like a prisoner, but I don't trust you at the moment. If you want freedom, you'll have to earn it. You'll have to show me you're not going to run back to your family and tell them I took you against your will. You'll have to prove to me you're not going to run from me."

She lets out a nervous breath as if having me so close has taken the anger from her body and replaced it with fear. "Why?"

"Why are you mine?"

She nods in response, and I reach forward to brush my thumb across her cheek. The softness beneath the pad is intoxicating, but then I always knew she was going to be impossibly soft. An angel tainted by my darkness.

"Because the first time I laid eyes on you, I knew you belonged with me. Everything I've done for the last ten years has been to get ready for a time when I could have you, and now you're here, you're not going anywhere." I push off the chair and stalk away from her. The longer I spend breathing the same air as her, the more likely I am to do something I shouldn't.

Snow's chair scrapes back across the floorboards as she follows me. "So, you've decided that I'm yours. You've decided I'm going to spend my life with you, but what if that's not what I want? Are you going to take me against my will? Because that's the only way you're ever touching me."

My head snaps around and before either of us realizes what I'm doing, I'm backing her into a wall, knocking the wind out of her lungs on impact. I press my body against hers, making sure to angle my cock against her belly so she knows how her fire affects me. I wrap my tattooed hand around her neck and almost groan at the sight. Good and evil. Light and dark. An angel and her devil. That's what we are together, and what we'll always be. I tighten my hand just enough that she can drag in a breath, but she can't speak. What I have to say to her doesn't require a response.

"Make no mistake, Snowflake. This is happening. You are my woman, and you are going to be my woman for the rest of our lives. There's no running from me, because I'll fucking find you no matter where you go. There isn't enough money or power on this earth that could keep me away from you. I'm not going to take you against your will. I'm going to tease and deny you, and when you can't take it anymore, you're going to beg for me to fuck you. You're going to beg for me to take away the ache, and the moment you beg, the moment those words leave your pretty red lips, you'll have made a deal with the devil."

I tear my body from hers before she can respond and walk straight out of the dining room toward my office. She got under my skin. But then I expected that. That's what Snow Saint James does, but this time it will be her own downfall.

THIRTEEN

SNOW

I stare at the empty doorway long after Elijah walks through it and a door down the hallway slams shut. My breath is uneven, my body shaking with what I can only assume is fear because the alternative is so wrong I can't even bring myself to think it. I did not like it. I didn't like his hands on me, or the way his tattoos looked against my creamy skin, or how his green eyes flared with lust as he made it impossible for me to say a word, or how he was barely able to drag himself away from me, his restraint fraying at the edges.

"Are you okay, dear?" Mary asks, her brows furrowing when I startle.

It takes me a moment to get my thoughts straight and to find my voice before I can reply, "Yeah, of course."

She watches me for another moment before moving to the table and gathering our barely touched plates. "Did you have enough to eat?"

"I'm not that hungry. I think it's whatever he drugged me

with," I mumble, using the wall behind me to support my weight. Part of me feels bad for lying to her, but she told me she wouldn't stand for Elijah hurting me, and if I can make her think he's not treating me well, maybe she'll help me escape. Hell, I'll settle for her giving me a phone to contact my brothers to come get me.

Mary moves toward me, her hand moving to my forehead. "You don't feel warm, but I don't want to take any chances. I want you to hop back to bed and have a nap. I told him those drugs take too long to work their way out of the system." She shakes her head, her hand wrapping around my arm and guiding me from the room.

My eyes dart around the hallway, trying to place which door he disappeared through, but they all look the same and there's no sound coming from behind any of them. I need more time to explore. The more I know about this place, the more likely I'll be able to escape, and right now, that's the only thing I can think about. Because if I allow myself to be swallowed by the feeling of his body touching mine and how his words affect me like no one else's ever have, I don't think I'll ever be able to drag myself from the depths.

Two days pass, and I haven't seen or heard from Elijah once. In fact, the only person who I've seen is Mary, and as much as I'm starting to like the older woman who reminds me of my mother in so many ways, I'm going out of my goddamn mind. I've never been so bored in my life. Growing up with three siblings and having Everett around from when I was ten meant I was never without some kind of company at home, so spending forty-eight hours alone, in my room, with only the occasional visit from Mary, I'm going out of my damn mind.

The first night the door was left open, I ventured out to get a feel of the house. I tried every external door, but all of them were locked up tight. I riffled through every drawer in every room I have access to, and there wasn't a single key in any of them. In fact, the only key I could find was the one hanging outside my bedroom door. It's like a cruel fucking joke, taunting me with the threat of locking me up in this room again.

But then, what would the difference be? I'm already a fucking prisoner, and my jailer hasn't even done me the courtesy of checking on me. The nagging voice in the back of my head tries to tell me the reason I'm mad is because he said all those things to me, and now it seems they're broken promises, but that's absurd. The only way that would be the reason I'm upset is if I wanted Elijah, and that's the furthest thing from the truth.

Mary strolls in at the same time she has the last two mornings, a bright smile on her face as she makes her way to the other side of the room to draw the blinds. I haven't bothered to get out of bed this morning, instead choosing to stay in the big comfortable bed. It's where I've spent the last forty-eight hours. What's the point of leaving it if I'm just going to end up back here again?

"Time to get up, dear," she chimes.

"I'm not feeling well," I mumble, tugging the blankets up higher.

Mary moves to the end of the bed and puts both hands to her

hips, her eyebrows raised. "I know this is an adjustment for you, Snow. I know this isn't something you've chosen for yourself, and Elijah isn't helping by keeping himself locked up in his office rather than trying to make this transition easier on you, but the more you wallow, the harder it's going to be for you in the long run."

I sigh and burrow my face deeper into the pillow. "What's the point of getting up, Mary? Just so I can sit in another room in this house? Might as well stay here where it reminds me of home." The last few words slip from my lips without my permission. I assume every room in this place is bugged, including this one, but then again, if Elijah hasn't bothered to come out to see me for two days, why would he bother to listen to what I'm saying?

Mary moves around the bed until she's sitting beside me, her hand gently brushing through my hair like my mom used to when I was sick and my heart hurts thinking about her. I miss her so much it hurts. All the moments I'm going to miss, that all my siblings will, some days it's more than I can handle. Today is one of those days. "I can imagine this is very difficult for you, Snow. I'm sure you're feeling hopeless and like all you want is to go back to your family. But if there's one thing I can tell you about Elijah, it's that once he sets his mind to something, he makes it happen. I can tell you that this plan has been in motion for a long time. Much longer than anyone in his life realized, including myself. And now that he has you, he's not going to let you go anywhere. I'm sorry if that's not what you want to hear, but I don't want to lie to you."

"Please leave," I whisper, a flurry of emotions hitting me all at once and causing my chest to ache.

The idea that I could be locked up in this house for the rest of my life has nausea settling in my stomach. I close my eyes and try to imagine I'm in my room at the estate. The sound of Wynter and Everett bickering down the hallway and Storm reprimanding them. Emerson's giggle as Rayne chases her up the stairs. The time we've spent there since our parents died has given us something we'd all but forgotten we needed. Each other. Before we would see one another at work or at family events but living and grieving together has strengthened our relationship and made us inseparable. What if I never get to see them again? What if Elijah cuts me off from my family, and all I have left is him and Mary? The possibility makes my stomach flip uncomfortably.

"You need to eat, Snow."

I shake my head against the pillow, not bothering to open my eyes. "I'm not hungry."

She sighs. Her presence hangs over me for a few more seconds before soft footsteps retreat from the room, the door clicking shut quietly behind her.

The fucked-up thing is I almost wish she would lock the door again. At least when I was locked away, I knew where I stood. I was a prisoner. Now Elijah Russo has claimed me, told me I will always be his, and then proceeded to lock himself away for days at a time.

I don't want to belong to anyone, but certainly not him, and yet some part of me is hurt that he's done this and that I haven't seen him. How am I supposed to make his life hell if he isn't around for me to do it? Elijah may think the youngest Saint James is easy to manipulate and control, but he has another thing coming. He's just met his match.

FOURTEEN
ELIJAH

Mrs. Chambers makes her way from Snow's room straight to the office without missing a beat. The moment she denied food, I expected our housekeeper to be at my door, and here she is with annoyance written all over her face.

The moment the door swings open, she's storming in, her finger jabbing into my chest. "You told me you were going to take care of her, Elijah. You promised she would not be harmed while she was here."

"I haven't harmed her." I shrug, moving back behind my desk where I can see my Snowflake. She hasn't moved from beneath the blankets, and I don't think she will until I go move her.

Mrs. Chambers sighs and collapses into the seat across from me. "Just because you haven't physically hit her doesn't mean you haven't hurt her. You've stolen her from her family, deprived her of the outside world, and left her with only a few short conversations with me each day while you've been in here. I agreed to this because you told me she's the one, but so far, you've spent twenty minutes together."

I drag my eyes away from the screen and look across the desk at the woman who raised me. She cleaned my wounds when my father hurt me and fed me even when she wasn't supposed to. She hid toys when I was young so I wouldn't miss out on being a child. She's the closest thing I've ever had to a mother, and as much as I hate to admit it, she's right. I've done everything to bring Snow here, years of planning, moving chess pieces and waiting for the right time, and now that she's here, I haven't spent any time trying to convince her this is the best thing for the both of us.

"If you don't make her trust you soon, she's going to run. She's going to find a way out of this house and she's going to run as far as she can from you. You've given her no reason not to. You have to give her a reason, Elijah."

I scrub my hands down my face and sigh. She's right. Snow's been sneaking around the house at night looking for a way out, but she's not going to find one, at least not where she's looking. But she's crafty, and at some stage, she's going to work it out. She's been escaping from places and people she shouldn't have her whole life, and no matter how many measures I put in place to avoid it happening, she'll do it again.

"I'll talk to her."

"She's not eating. She barely ate dinner last night, and she's flat out refusing to eat this morning. You need to fix this before I make good on my promise and get her out of here." She stares at me pointedly, resting both hands on her hips like a disappointed parent.

"You will not," I growl.

"Oh, but I will, Elijah. That poor girl lost her parents a few months ago, you held her sister hostage only a month ago, and now you've taken her from everything and everyone she knows."

"That's why I made her room like the one at the estate, so she would feel at home here." I brush my thumb across my bottom lip. I've never been the best with people, I don't understand them and I've never wanted to before. But I want to understand Snow. It's what I've been trying to do from afar all these years. But there's only so much you can learn about someone from the shadows. Now it's time I step out into the light.

Mrs. Chambers's eyes soften. "I know, dear, but you have to remember this isn't a choice she's made, and you have to be patient with her."

"I'll make sure she eats something."

"Good. There's food on a tray in the dining room for her. It's everything you told me she likes."

When you've watched someone as long as I've watched Snow, you get to know all their favorite foods, scents and little things not even the people closest to them know, and so I made Mrs. Chambers a guide to all things that make up Snow Saint James. I meant it when I said I want her to be happy here. Because this is her home now, and while she's here, regardless of her feelings about it, her feelings matter to me, even if no one's ever had before.

Mrs. Chambers leaves the office without another word, and I drop my head into my hands. I don't have time for this. As much as I want to spend time with my Snowflake and help her settle in, the business is taking up a lot more of my time than I anticipated, and as much as she wants to think the reason she hasn't seen me is because of our altercation the other morning, the reality is much less exciting. I need to promote someone enough they can take some of this shit off my plate.

I push myself up from my desk and move into the dining room to pick up the tray. True to her word, a decadent selection of French toast and fruit smothered in maple syrup is ready for me to take to her. While she mainly eats fruit and smoothies in the morning, this is her favorite. It's the treat her mother used to make her when she was sad and what she makes herself when the world gets to be too much.

When I push the door open to her room, I can't help but stop and stare for a moment. The room smells like her. The perfume she wears, the shampoo she uses, it's mingled in the very structure of the room after only a few days of her being here, and I'm addicted to the scent. She's curled up in a ball in the center of the bed, her blonde curls surrounding her. She looks so fucking beautiful as she lets out a little snore, and I find myself gravitating toward her.

I place the tray down quietly on the table beside the bed, making sure not to wake her. Before I consciously make the decision, I kick my shoes off and carefully lay beside her. Close enough that her breath whispers across my cheeks, but far enough that she doesn't realize I'm here. I wish I could say this is the first time I've climbed into bed beside her without her knowing, but that's far from the case. Every time I broke into her apartment at night, unable to keep myself away from her for another moment, I would do just this. I'd never sleep, not when she could wake up and find me there, but just being close to her calmed a part of me that was always wild. The caged animal could finally breathe.

I should wake her so she can eat something, but she won't let me this close while her eyes are open. Not yet. Mrs. Chambers was right about one thing, if I don't make her want to be here, she's going to run, and while I'll always bring her back, always bring her home, she's not going to appreciate being hunted.

All the times I've done this in the past, I haven't wanted her to catch me. Being there wasn't ever part of the plan, but now she's here, in my house, at my mercy. It doesn't matter if she knows I have a proclivity for watching her sleep. She can finally know how truly obsessed I've been with her all these years.

I reach out and brush my fingers across her cheek, her skin so soft I barely contain the groan clawing its way up my throat. It makes the baser part of me scream to throw the sheets back and ravage her body, taking what has always been mine, even if she didn't know it. But I promised her I wouldn't take her against her will, and I meant it. Unlike most of the men in my family, I don't enjoy when a woman struggles beneath me or the way she screams at the invasion of her body, and I certainly won't be doing it to Snow. But that doesn't mean I'm not going to touch her. She'll never know what she wants if I don't show her, and I'm going to show her just how good we can be together.

FIFTEEN

SNOW

Ever since I was taken, I've known I'm being watched. Every moment of every day, there are eyes on me. Whether I can see them is a whole other story, but I know they're there, watching my every move.

But as consciousness comes back to me, there's something different about the way I'm being watched. At first, I keep my eyes closed, not wanting to draw attention to the fact I'm awake, but the moment something touches my cheek, my eyes fly open, and a scream tears from my throat.

Before I've fully realized it's Elijah lying beside me, his green eyes assessing my every move, he rolls me to my back and settles his weight over me, a small smile playing on his lips.

"I like it when you scream for me, Snowflake." The way my name rolls off his tongue is like a holy man saying a prayer. Reverence and heat in every letter.

"What are you doing?" I whisper as fear grips me around the throat and makes it impossible to drag in a breath.

"A little bird told me you're not eating."

"So? What do you care?" I should push him off me, or at the very least make some attempt to get away from him, but I'm frozen in place, like the moment he rolled on top of me, I lost all ability to fight.

Elijah sighs, annoyance flickering across his gaze. Rationally I know I shouldn't antagonize one of the scariest men in Chicago, perhaps only surpassed by Tommy and his love for blood and death, but I can't help myself.

"I thought I'd been quite clear with you about all this, Snow. You are here because you're mine, and I take care of what belongs to me, even if you're not willing to look after yourself."

I stare up at him, trying not to allow myself to relax beneath his weight. His warmth is comforting despite him being the reason for my anxiety in the first place. "I'm not hungry."

I turn my head until my cheek hits the pillow. It's easier to deal with men like Elijah when you don't have to look them in the eye. It's why when I pick a fight with my brothers, I always do it over the phone.

His fingers grip my chin in a harsh hold, and he pries my face back to his. When our eyes clash, there's heat and anger behind his gaze. "I don't care if you're hungry, Snow. I care if you're healthy. Mrs. Chambers said you barely ate last night, which means if you miss breakfast, you would have missed two meals in a row, and that's unacceptable."

I glare up at him. How dare he speak to me like I'm a petulant child? I'm old enough to choose if I want to eat or not. Who the hell does he think he is?

"Mrs. Chambers made your favorite." He nods toward the table beside my bed, and I follow his gaze, the smell hitting me the moment my eyes fall upon the plate. How did I not notice that before?

My mouth drops open and my head snaps back to look at him. "How the fuck do you know about that?" I hiss, using all my strength to shove his chest, but he barely budges. The only sign I hit him is the slight exhale and grunt he makes at my feeble attempts. He moves so quickly I barely catch the movement as he releases his grip on my chin and bundles my hands in one of his, pinning them above my head and rendering me completely at his mercy.

"I can see we're getting off on the wrong foot here, Snow, so let me spell this out for you, so you understand. I know everything there is to know about you. Your favorite food, the shampoo you use, the flavor of ice cream you reach for after a bad day. I've been getting to know you from the shadows since the day I laid eyes on you."

I stare up at him for long moments, completely immobilized by the way he's handling me. His torso reaches over mine, and even with all the strength in my legs, I wouldn't be able to throw him off. I think back to the self-defense classes Wynter dragged me to and almost sigh out loud. This position right here, this is the position they told us never to allow ourselves to get into, because it's not as simple as throwing your assailant off you. It's so much more complicated than that. Even if I were able to get out from under him, and that's a very big if, what then? There's nowhere to run. I'm locked in this house, this prison, and no matter how much I try to convince myself otherwise, I'm in a lot more trouble than I've ever been before.

Elijah sighs at my silence, annoyance flickering across the green of his eyes, but words escape me. What do you say to a man holding you against your will? One who is so clearly unhinged and obsessed with you at that?

"Why me?" I whisper without thinking. It's not the first time the question has flitted through my mind since I woke up here, but it's the first time I've thought to ask the man holding me captive.

A small smile tugs at the corners of his mouth. "The first night I saw you, I thought you were an angel," he muses as he softens his hold on my wrists, not so much I can escape, but just enough to make me more comfortable. "It was right around the time Everett moved in with your family. I was always so jealous he got away from them and I didn't, but he never belonged there. We'd grown up as enemies of sorts, despite being cousins. We were constantly reminded that one of us would take over for Angelo one day, and we were always in competition for who that would be, even when we were children and didn't understand what our uncle did.

All night I was looking for him, my father wanted me to hurt him for abandoning the family in favor of the enemy, and I would have done it, but then I saw you. You were so beautiful, so carefree and happy, and I was fascinated by you. I followed you around all night, completely forgetting about what my father had asked me to do, completely oblivious to every other person at that party except for you. For the first time in my life, there was light in the darkness I called home, and when the night was over, and you left with your family, I knew I couldn't return to the dark, somehow I had to have your light in my life, even if I had to steal it."

This time when my mouth drops open, it's in surprise rather than horror. His words are almost poetic, the way he speaks about me like I'm the only good he's ever known, but surely that's not the case. Even though Rayne and Storm grew up in a Mafia family, they've always been loved, and there's always been some light in their hearts. But then, I can't imagine any of the Russo men had an ounce of good in them.

"I want you to want to be here, Snow. I've done everything I can to make sure you're comfortable, but you're staying here even if you don't want to. This is happening, we are happening, and there's nothing you can say or do that's going to change that reality."

"How long?"

"How long what?"

"Am I here? I assume you're going to get bored and send me back at some stage. So how long? Or will you kill me and dispose of me the way your father and uncles used to when they were done with women?" Even as the words fall from my lips, I regret them, but I've never been that good at restraining myself and the things I say.

SIXTEEN

ELIJAH

There was a moment while I told her about the first time I saw her that I thought I was finally making some progress with Snow. At no point did I think this was going to be easy. I was, after all, stealing her from her life and everything she loves, but what I didn't prepare myself for was the fact that she sees me as nothing more than another Russo man, and the anger beating through my blood right now is barely contained. In fact, if it weren't for the fact her body is pressed against mine and the soft skin of her wrists are bundled in my hands, I would be tearing apart this whole fucking house.

"Come again," I growl.

"At the end of this, are you going to let me go, or are you going to dispose of me like yesterday's trash like your family is so good at?" Snow asks calmly, like she doesn't realize she's poking a bear who could easily snap at any moment. But she knows. There's no doubt in my mind that my little Snowflake is testing the waters and how much she can get away with before I'll snap, how much I'll let her push me before I'll push back, and she's reaching that limit very fucking rapidly.

I close my eyes and let out a breath, trying to contain the angry beast pushing against my chest to be let out. The one I was trained to be, the one I am in every other part of my life but this one, the one I can never allow Snow to see. She's trying to make me snap. She wants me to be the monster in her closet at night, but I'm not, and at some point, she's going to have to accept that. Before I register my own movements, I'm tearing the blanket down between us, her hands still held in one of mine as I flip her onto her stomach.

The hitch in her breath tells me she's scared, but she makes no attempt to throw me off. She could escape if she really wanted to. I've seen Snow fight, seen her and her sister spar when Wynter forced her to go to self-defense classes a few years back. But even though she's scared, even though her pulse beats quickly against my fingers, she doesn't fight. I'm not sure what to make of it, to be honest. I've stolen her from everything she loves and locked her up in what even I can admit is a creepy duplicate of her childhood bedroom, she should be making every attempt to rid herself of me, but each time I've touched her, each time I've pressed my body to hers, she's stilled and allowed it to happen. Does my Snowflake feel it too? Does she feel the pull I felt all those years ago? The invisible tether that held us together even when she had no idea I existed in the shadows.

I settle my weight across her back, my legs straddling her perfect ass, and my cock immediately hardens at its proximity to her tight holes. But it's not time yet. Not until she begs for my cock. I lean down until my lips brush the shell of her ear and she shivers at the touch.

"Let's get something clear, Snowflake. This arrangement is not temporary. When I took you, it was with the intention of keeping you. Not for a few days, or a few weeks, or even a few years. No, the intention is to keep you forever. You and I will get married, sooner rather than later if I get my way. So no, I will not be killing you and disposing of your body like trash. Because you are the greatest treasure I've ever had. I am not my father, and I am not my uncles. I will not treat you like all your worth lives between your legs, but I would suggest you stop comparing me to them because you will not like the consequences if you keep that shit up. Do you understand?"

Snow nods against the pillow, her breath coming in hard and fast.

I grind my hard cock against her ass, making sure she feels every inch of hardness. "I need your words, Snow."

"Yes, I understand," she pants, the slightest edge of lust masked just beneath the fear.

"Good girl," I rumble.

Being so close to her, having her addictively sweet scent so close, it's almost impossible for me to drag myself from her warmth, but I meant when I said I wouldn't force myself on her. Slowly, I drag my body from hers before pushing myself off the bed and taking a few steps to where her French toast is getting cold. I glance over my shoulder to make sure Snow hasn't picked up anything heavy to hit me with. I find her sitting up with her knees pressed to her chest and her eyes darting around the room, still trying to find an escape from her new reality.

Once I'm sure she's not going to attack me from behind, I

busy myself with preparing her plate and bringing it to the bed. I expect her to flinch away from me when I kneel on the edge of the mattress, but she remains perfectly still, her eyes tracking each of my movements. I place the tray down beside her and sit back against the headboard.

"What are you doing?" Snow whispers.

"Making sure you eat." I nod toward the untouched food.

She sighs loudly and unfolds herself, making sure to inch farther across the bed away from me. The movement is so slight I'm sure she doesn't think I would have noticed, but soon she'll see that every move she makes is one I see. There's nothing she can do without my knowledge. She watches me closely as she reaches for the knife and fork and tentatively cuts off a piece and brings it to her lips. The moment the food passes through her lips, she lets out a groan of appreciation and my cock reacts immediately to the sound.

"This is so good," she moans and takes another bite. This time her eyes close and another happy sound erupts from her throat.

Fuck me. I should have left. I shouldn't be sitting here watching her eat like what she's tasting is better than any sex she's ever had. "I'll make sure to tell Mrs. Chambers you enjoyed it."

She watches me carefully as she chews another piece of French toast, as if she's trying to figure out how to ask something. "Why do you call her that?"

"Who?"

"Mary. She asked me to call her that and she hates that everyone else calls her Mrs. Chambers, so why do you call her that?"

I consider my answer for a moment because I don't know why I've refused to use her first name for all these years. Or maybe I do know, but I'm not sure if being so vulnerable with the woman I'm holding against her will is the best choice. "Mrs. Chambers raised me. I suppose it's the same way you don't start calling your mother by her name. She'll always be Mrs. Chambers to me." I shrug.

Snow's eyes soften as she takes her next bite. "I suppose I can see that."

"She really wants to make you feel at home here and to make your adjustment as easy as she can on you."

Snow sighs. "What exactly did you expect when you stole me away from my family and my life? Did you think I was going to lie down and take it? Because you claim to know me so well, and if that's the case, you should know there's no way I won't fight until my dying breath."

I chuckle, my head dropping until my chin brushes my chest. "No, Snowflake. I knew you were going to fight. In fact, I counted on it. But you can fight all you want, it's not going to make a difference to the end result. This is happening, and there isn't a thing you can do about it. The sooner you accept your fate, the easier it's going to be on you."

Without waiting for a response, I push myself from the bed and cross the room without looking back. Spending any amount of time on a bed with Snow Saint James when I can't take her the way I want is a bad idea, and I need to get back to work. The sooner I find someone to take some of my responsibilities, the sooner I can start putting the rest of the wheels in motion so Snow has no other choice than to be mine for the rest of her life.

SEVENTEEN

SNOW

If I didn't already know I needed to find a way out of here after my altercation with Elijah yesterday, I certainly know it now. And not entirely because he's a raving lunatic who stole me from my life with crazy expectations that we're going to get married and live happily ever after.

No, the reason I need to get the fuck out of here is because when he touches me, he sets my body on fire. There's something about having his hands on me, hands that have killed people, who have torn people's lives apart without so much as a thought, that takes the air from my lungs and makes my heart beat so hard it hurts.

Perhaps it's my self-destructive nature talking, or maybe it's more than that, but regardless, I need to run.

Lucky for me, Elijah presented me with the perfect opportunity this afternoon. He walked straight into my room and told me we're going to have dinner with my family, and then he left without another word. I can only assume we're going somewhere public and not to the estate where I would have the upper hand but seeing as we've spent a total of half an hour together since I arrived here, I'm quietly confident my siblings will be able to see through the charade he's trying to portray and rescue me.

So instead of fighting everything he says as I have with everything else he's ordered me to do over the last few days, I set to getting ready. I'm almost overwhelmed by the number of dresses I have to choose from and the number of beauty products he bought me before I arrived, but I go through the motions of primping to the utmost degree. After days of being locked up in this room, I'm almost excited to step foot out of the house and to converse with people who aren't a raving lunatic and his dutiful housekeeper, but it's all the unknowns that eat away at that excitement.

Elijah has to know I'm going to try something to escape tonight, and I almost wonder if this is a test, if he's setting me up to fail. But it doesn't matter what his intentions are for tonight. All that matters is that I'm going to be leaving with my family, never to see Elijah Russo again.

"You look breathtaking," he says from behind me, making me jolt in surprise. He's so light on his feet I swear he's part cat, not that I would ever say that to him. Something tells me comparing a big bad Mafia leader to a cuddly kitty cat probably isn't the best life choice. He stands in the doorway behind me, a tailored suit making him look every bit as handsome as it does terrifying. It's the big bad wolf in sheep's clothing you have to worry about. His eyes lock on mine in the mirror, making no move toward me as he waits for my reaction to his words.

"Thank you," I murmur, reaching for the necklace I have set out on the vanity in front of me.

Before I'm able to unclasp it, large, tattooed hands envelop mine and take the delicate jewelry from me. His heat against my bare back makes it impossible to breathe, and for the first time since I picked my outfit, I wonder if the mid-length, backless crimson dress I chose was the best choice. Perhaps I should have chosen something more conservative, like jeans and a sweater.

His coarse fingers brush across my neck as he winds the gold chain around my throat, never breaking contact with my eyes in the mirror in front of us. An involuntary shiver makes its way across my skin at his gentle touch, so at odds with the man he is.

Elijah doesn't pull away once the clasp is fastened, instead his fingers run down my bare arms. I question my decision to wear my hair up in a messy updo when his breath whispers across my bare neck. His eyes flame with desire, taking my breath away.

"Before we leave, I wanted to run over the ground rules," he rumbles.

"Okay," I whisper, not trusting my voice to be steady with his proximity.

"I organized this night for you because, contrary to what you believe, I do not want to tear you from your life or your family. Being locked up in the house is a temporary measure until I'm sure you're not going to run, and then you will be given some of the freedom you're accustomed to. Tonight is the first step in me allowing you some of those liberties. If you try to tip your siblings off to our circumstances, I will whisk you out of there so quickly you won't be able to finish your sentence. If you try to run, I will chase you, and I promise you *will* be locked in this room indefinitely. And if any of your attempts happen to be successful, I will not hesitate to make good on the promise I made you the first morning. Do you remember?"

I close my eyes to push down the bile rising in my throat. "Yes, I remember."

"Eyes on me, Snowflake."

My eyes snap open and I meet his in the mirror again. For someone who claims to have had their feelings repressed their entire life, his eyes are so expressive I can see what he's feeling before any other part of him shows signs of that emotion.

"Good girl." His eyes finally break contact with mine as they track down the bare flesh of my neck. "Your heart is beating so hard. Are you nervous?" His hands tighten around my forearms, holding me in place as if predicting I might try to move out of his grasp, but honestly, the thought hadn't occurred to me.

"No," I lie.

Every moment Elijah is close is another moment I live in fear of what he might do, and what I might allow him to do.

Elijah chuckles, his fingers moving back up my arms and resting on my shoulders, rubbing the bare flesh beneath the spaghetti straps in comforting circles. "You forget I've been watching you for ten years, little Snowflake. I know you better than anyone else ever could."

"You know that's creepy, right?"

"I'm very aware that my obsession with you is untraditional, but that doesn't change anything. If you're a good girl for me tonight, you'll be rewarded. But if I so much as suspect you're up to something, I can promise you will not enjoy the consequences."

"Just so we're clear, if I don't behave, you'll hurt one of my loved ones?"

"Exactly." Elijah smiles widely as if pleased we're on the same page and not at all concerned by the fact he's blackmailing me into compliance.

I take a steady breath, calming myself for the words about to slip from my lips because I don't know how he's going to interpret them, and although historically my favorite thing to do is poke the bear, Elijah is a whole other kind of unpredictable that makes me hesitate.

"They're going to know. We've told them we've been… dating, for lack of a better word, for a month, but in reality, we've spent less than an hour together, and most of that time has been spent with you threatening me. There's no way they're going to buy this." What I don't say is that I hope they see through the farce and whisk me back to the safety of the estate.

His grip on my shoulders tightens, and he brings my body back until I'm flush with his front, and his very obvious hard-on presses against my ass. The first time I felt that thing against me, I hoped I was imagining the size, but I wasn't. He brings his lips right to my ear, the softness brushing against the shell of my ear and causing an involuntary shiver throughout my body.

"I can assure you they'll believe I'm infatuated with you, little Snowflake. You just need to convince them you're equally so with me. Shouldn't be too hard for you, you're constantly leading everyone to believe you're something you're not, isn't that right?"

"No," I hiss, attempting to move from his embrace, but he holds me tightly, his hands moving around my torso and anchoring me to him.

"Little liar." He nips at my ear, the sting only making my anger simmer hotter. "You want everyone to believe you're the spoiled little Mafia princess trapped in your ivory tower. You allow them to believe the mask you portray in front of the world, the partying rule breaker, the black sheep of the family, if you will. But in reality, you're so much more. You were meant to lead just the same way your siblings do."

I stare at him in the mirror, his eyes barely blinking as his gaze remains on mine while I assess him. If I thought I wished I was wearing more before, that's doubled, hell even tripled now because I may as well be naked. I've never felt so seen. No one has ever called me out like this, and my brain screams for me to move, but my body is powerless to move away from the man who seems to know me better than I do myself.

Eighteen

Elijah

Perhaps I should have kept my mouth shut. The moment the words rolled off my tongue, Snow retreated into herself, and she hasn't said a word since. It's not that I wanted to point out her shortcomings, because that was never my intention, but she's so embroiled in the life she leads and the way she leads it that without someone pushing her in the right direction, she's always going to play the part of the littlest Saint James who doesn't compare to her siblings.

We sit in the back of the SUV I usually use to get around in. My driver Pete, whose name I finally learned, dodges a mess of traffic and pedestrians. I chose to bring her out on a Saturday night because it would be busy. Most would say it's a security nightmare, and they wouldn't be wrong, but if she chooses to make a scene, which certainly isn't off the table, I can claim a security breach and whisk her out of there before she can finish her plea for help.

Snow stares out the window, her hands tangled together in her lap as she watches the city go by. She didn't even complain when I placed a hand on her bare thigh when we climbed into the car, and she's made no attempt to remove it. Perhaps that should have been my first sign that my words affected her so much.

Pete turns a corner before coming to a stop outside Snow's favorite restaurant. When I sent the invite to Wynter this morning, it won me some points for knowing her sister so well, but I left out the part where I've been stalking Snow for the last ten years. That definitely wouldn't have won me any favors.

I squeeze her thigh. "We're here."

Her head snaps around, almost as if she didn't realize the car had stopped moving. "Oh, this is my fav…" She trails off when her eyes meet mine, and she realizes her mistake. Of course I know it's her favorite. I know everything there is to know about her.

"Come on, let's get inside." I smile and take one of her hands in my much larger one.

I nod to Pete once we're on the sidewalk and quickly tug her toward the door. The bitter Chicago wind whips around us, and I pull her closer to shield her as best I can. The coat she picked up on the way out of her room is doing nothing to protect her, and her body trembles from the cold.

Warmth and the scent of authentic Italian food envelop us the moment we're through the door, and Snow lets out a little sound of contentment.

I scan the restaurant for threats despite the fact I had two security teams do a sweep before we arrived. It's a habit more than anything else, but you can never be too careful, not when all the surviving members of the two families of Chicago's underworld are in the same place at the same time.

I catch Storm's gaze across the room, his gray eyes filled with anger as he stares me down, but he won't intimidate me. I haven't been planning a life with Snow all these years without factoring in her overprotective brothers. They were never going to be happy about their enemy dating their sister, but if they want to continue being in her life, they're going to have to get used to the idea.

I hold his gaze as we weave through tables of people to the one in the back corner, the one I purposely requested so no one could sneak up on us. The moment Wynter sees her sister, she flies out of her seat and crashes into Snow, who immediately tears her hand from mine to wrap both arms around her sister.

"I missed you!" Wynter mumbles. "If you're going to take off with a new boyfriend, can you at least give me some heads up?"

Boyfriend… the word doesn't seem like enough considering the gravity of my feelings toward Snow, and the fact I was willing to risk absolutely everything to have her. My business. My life. My family. I've put it all on the line so I can have my Snowflake, and the word boyfriend just doesn't feel like enough.

Snow pulls back slightly, her eyes filled with tears. "I'm sorry, I should have told you. It's just so new, and I didn't want you to tell Rayne and Storm. And you did shoot him not that long ago." She scoffs and I can't help but chuckle as well. It wasn't the first bullet I've taken, but it's the only time I've ever been shot by a member of a family I intend to marry into.

Wynter's head drops back, and her laugh fills the already loud restaurant. "Okay, I guess I see your point."

She pushes us toward the table, and Snow immediately sits beside her, leaving me at one end of the table and Storm at the other. On my other side, Rayne glares at me, his arm wrapped tightly around Emerson's shoulders as if my only reason for being here tonight is to harm her. Everett's eyes track my every move from the other side of Wynter, but his gaze doesn't hold the same hatred as the other men. And perhaps it should, seeing as I helped to orchestrate his girlfriend being held against her will and being held at gunpoint.

The moment Snow spots the full glass of white wine in front of her, she reaches for it with shaky hands and takes several large sips.

"I'm glad you could all make it." I smile, looking around the table.

"Thank you for organizing this. Snow and I aren't used to being apart." Wynter half laughs, but it's true. The two of them are like two peas in a pod, and by me taking her, it's left them both missing a piece of themselves.

"Why are we really here, Elijah?" Storm asks, his elbows resting on the table in front of him.

"I don't know what you mean. You said you wanted to see Snow, and Snow and I are together, so here we both are." I shrug, reaching for the glass of water and taking a sip.

His attention turns to Snow. "And you thought that dating the enemy is such a great idea? You can't see how any of this puts our entire family in danger?"

Some of the color drains from Snow's face, and I immediately take her hand in mine. It's not a conscious movement, not something I've done to remind her of the consequences of not doing as she's told, but I'm sure that's how it looks for her.

She takes a breath and lets it out slowly. "Elijah isn't the enemy anymore. Our families are working together. I don't see the problem."

"Of course you don't. You never see the fucking problem with your actions, Snow. We're always picking up the goddamn pieces of your reckless decisions," Storm snaps.

Before I realize I'm doing it, I'm pushing my chair back, ready to show him no one can speak to my woman like that when Snow squeezes my hand to tell me to stay put, and for some reason, my ass remains planted in its seat.

"I didn't come here to be berated, Storm. I'm an adult, and I make my own decisions. Your concern is noted but not necessary." Snow leans into her sister while taking another sip of her wine to settle her nerves. "You said on the phone you have news?"

"Yes!" Wynter turns to Everett, grabbing his hand on top of the table and squeezing it. His eyes finally tear from mine and look down at her with pure adoration. "We waited to tell everyone until we could all be together."

"We're getting married." Everett grins, tugging Wynter into his lap and resting both hands on her stomach. "And we're having a baby."

The entire table erupts into what I can only describe as complete chaos, and the waitress, who had been heading toward us with her notepad in hand, turns on her heel in the opposite direction. Probably for the best.

Snow throws her arms around both Wynter and Everett on one side with tears streaming down her cheeks, and Storm does the same on the other. Rayne and Emerson are out of their seats and joining the group hug full of happiness. When they disperse, all the animosity they hold for me is almost forgotten, and nothing but excitement is abuzz.

I push my seat back and stand, walking around behind the happy couple. "Congratulations to both of you, that's wonderful news." Unlike everyone else, I hold my hand out and offer it to my cousin and his future bride.

Everett takes my hand, his other still spread across Wynter's stomach protectively. "Thank you."

Wynter beams and jumps up, throwing her arms around me. "I can't wait to tell him or her about the time I shot their uncle."

"It's a her." Everett rolls his eyes.

To most people, the comment would seem innocent, especially seeing as Everett is my cousin. We are each other's only living family, and as far as everyone at this table is concerned, I'm dating a Saint James. But to me, the man whose family never showed them even a moment of kindness, it means everything, and some of the ice in my veins begins to melt.

NINETEEN

SNOW

I've never seen my sister look happier than she does right now. The complete joy radiating from her is so bright it's almost blinding.

Even when she returned to her own seat, Everett didn't release Wynter from his hold even for a moment, and for the first time in my life, I find myself longing for what they share.

I've never been one to want to find my soul mate or to have a happily ever after, but if it can make my sister, who has been through hell so ridiculously happy, who wouldn't want that for themselves?

I drag my eyes from their happiness and reach for the wine that was refilled while the entire table was fussing over Wynter. Elijah catches my eye, his gaze locked on me as the rest of the table discusses wedding and baby plans. The excitement I felt when they first told us has started to fade, and now I'm left with an aching sense of dread. It seeps into my pores and makes my heart heavy. This is what he's threatening. If I don't do as I'm told, he could tear me away from my family permanently. He could keep me from my sister's wedding and out of my niece's or nephew's life. All the plans I had to escape, to tell someone I'm being held against my will, it all goes out the window as the potential consequences settle over me.

I push my seat back and excuse myself from the table. I need to put some distance between myself and my sordid situation so I can catch my breath before the gravity of everything suffocates me.

The moment the bathroom door comes into view, my entire body shakes with the force of the emotions pouring over me. Everything I've held inside, hidden away, since the moment I woke up and realized I had been torn from my life rises to the surface and a loud sob breaks from my throat.

By the time I'm within reach of the sink, all the air has left my lungs and it's impossible to drag in a breath past the blinding panic ravaging my body. I may have been playing my situation off as a minor annoyance, but suddenly it's anything but minor. Elijah Russo holds my entire future in his cruel, scarred hands.

The door swings open behind me, but I don't bother to look up. If it's Wynter or Emerson, I'll have to lie through blinding panic, and if it's a stranger, I'll probably be on the front page of the tabloids tomorrow morning for my public meltdown. Wouldn't be the first time.

Arms wrap around my middle, and I'm tugged back against a hard body. The way Elijah moves can't be described as anything other than elegantly stealthy. He moves with silent grace like a cat in the night, and perhaps I should have known it was him before he ever touched me.

"Breathe, Snowflake," he murmurs into my ear. "I need you to breathe."

I shake my head, broken sobs break from my chest, leaving agony in their wake. People say when they die, they see their lives flash before their eyes, but what about when you're living a life you don't want to live? If Elijah is going to tear me from my family and force me into a life I never wanted, is that fate any kinder than death?

"Snow." The command in his voice has my eyes meeting his in the mirror.

The two of us are a perfect contradiction. I'm petite and broken, all blonde hair and pale skin, and Elijah is muscular, tattooed from head to toe as far as I can tell, and he exudes nothing but confidence and raw power.

"You're going to make yourself sick, and you know how I feel about anything harming you, including yourself. So I need you to breathe for me."

For some reason, staring into his green eyes in the mirror makes it easier to drag in a breath, and then another, and another after that. His calm but ruthless demeanor captures my attention and holds it hostage while my body fights off the panic.

"That's it, good girl," Elijah praises and my heart skips a beat. Being praised by him is unexpected, but I welcome it.

I reach for the paper towel dispenser, my face a mess of black tear stains, but he's faster. His body barely leaves mine for a second before he's back and spinning me to face him. Elijah dabs the course towel on my hot cheeks, wiping away the evidence of my meltdown. He stares down at me thoughtfully, but he doesn't say a word as he cleans my face.

There's something inherently intimate about the moment, maybe because you wouldn't expect someone as ruthless and cold as Elijah Russo to be able to be so gentle, or maybe it's having him so close without wanting to scream in his face. For the first time since I realized who had taken me, all the anger and resentment has faded, and all that's left behind is hopelessness.

"What's going on in that pretty head of yours, Snowflake? You were so happy when Wynter and Everett shared their news, and then something changed." A man like Elijah shouldn't be so observant. Something tells me I'm never going to be able to hide anything from him, and that's definitely not a good thing.

"Please don't keep me away from them," I choke out. "Please don't take them away from me. I don't want to miss Wynter's wedding, and I want to be a part of my niece's or nephew's life. Please don't take them away." Fresh tears fall against my cheeks as I beg the man I swore I would never allow to see me break.

Elijah wraps me up in his arms and holds me tight, not a breath of space between us as he rubs my bare back comfortingly. Idly, I wonder if he's ever comforted anyone else in the past, or if this rare moment of compassion is just for me, and I find myself hoping it's the latter.

"Shh, little Snowflake," he whispers into my hair. "You know the deal. If you're good for me, if you don't try to run, then you'll have anything you want. If you want to see Wynter and the baby every day, then that's what you'll do."

He thinks his words are comforting, but they're anything but. The man is giving me an ultimatum. Either I do as I'm told and hand myself over to him, or he takes it by force along with everything I love. That's not a choice because he knows there's only one option that I'll take. There's a reason Storm doesn't date, and Rayne didn't until Emerson came along. Having loved ones is a liability, and my family is mine.

TWENTY

ELIJAH

I've watched Snow cry so many times I've lost count. When her parents told her she couldn't go to Mexico for spring break with her friends, she cried. When boys broke her heart in high school, she cried. And when her parents died, she cried for days on end. Her tears have always been fascinating to me, and at times I've imagined them rolling down her cheeks as I fuck her pretty lips. But there's something about holding her as she sobs and being the reason for her tears that makes the cold, dead place where my heart should live hurt.

I've never given much thought to other people and their emotions, the concept of which never resonated with me, but holding Snow right now, her broken sobs vibrating through our bodies as she begs me not to tear her away from the people she loves, an unfamiliar feeling washes over me. Guilt.

Carefully, I grasp her shoulders and push her back just enough so I can look at her. Dark smudges under her eyes and black streaks down her cheeks make it obvious she's been crying.

Snow looks up at me through soft blue eyes, the plea in them not lost on me. I'm not one to bend for anyone, not even my own family. I was born to lead, born to kill, and born to take what I want when I want it. But right now, looking down at my woman, I want to bow down and give her the whole fucking world.

"Marry me." The words fall from my lips before I can think them through. I never intended to ask her, never intended to give her a choice, and therefore, why would I bother asking the question?

"What?"

"Marry me. Marry me, and I won't ever keep you from your family."

Her mouth drops open and anger fills the normally calm blue, a storm raging behind them. "It's not really a choice then, is it?" she hisses, bringing both hands to my chest and shoving me away. When my body gives her a whisper of space, she slips from my arms and moves to the paper towel dispenser before stepping up to the mirror and dabbing at the dark marks beneath her eyes.

"You're asking me to give you something, so I'm asking for something in return." I shrug, keeping my distance from her for the moment. What she doesn't realize is that I don't compromise. When I decide something, I don't back down from it. What I'm offering her is a rare moment of compassion… well, my version of it anyway.

"That's not a fucking choice, Elijah. Jesus fucking Christ, you're an asshole."

My jaw tightens as anger washes over me. Can't she see I'm trying? Can't she see I'm giving her something where I don't have to? I hold all the cards, every single fucking one. She's mine regardless. I'm marrying her regardless of whether she agrees to it or not. But I'm offering her something I never intended to. Unlimited access to her family.

I prowl toward her, the heat of anger washing over my normally calm demeanor. There's something about Snow that gets under my skin the way no one has ever done before. She has a power over me that's dangerous, one that could lead to my own demise, but I don't care. There's no option where I don't have Snow by my side, and soon enough, she's going to accept that.

By the time she notices me behind her, it's too late, there's no time to dodge what's coming. I grip her waist in both hands and spin her to face me, lifting her from the ground and perching her on the edge of the vanity, and step between her legs. The position is intimate, almost too much so. My cock aches behind the zipper of my pants, begging to be allowed closer to Snow's sweet cunt, but it's not time for that yet.

I bring my hand to her chin and lift it until our gazes meet. Defiance flares behind the blue and only makes my cock harden further. She doesn't understand yet, but her brattiness only makes me want to bend her over and fuck her so hard she can't breathe, let alone talk back.

"Your brothers despise my very existence. They are going to constantly try to take you away from me, and I can't risk that. You're mine. You've been mine for the last ten years. I gave you that time to live your life and do whatever the fuck you wanted to do, but now it's my turn. The only way you get unlimited access to your family is with a ring on your finger because that's the only way your brothers will stop trying to take you from me."

Annoyance hovers behind her eyes. "Let me down," she demands.

"No."

"Elijah, I swear to God I'll scream so loud this whole fucking place hears and your little plan will be over so quick, you won't be able to blink."

I chuckle. "Oh, sweet Snowflake, if you think anything could keep me away from you, you're sorely mistaken. Even if your brothers whisked you away and sent you to the other side of the world to hide, I would find you and bring you home. There isn't a corner of this earth I wouldn't find you, that I wouldn't scour to bring my woman home."

"I'm not your woman," Snow hisses.

"Oh, but you are, Snowflake," I growl, a sinister smile tipping up the corners of my mouth. "I am not a good man, nor am I a reasonable one, but this is my version of a compromise. I suggest you think long and hard about your choice."

I turn on my heel and stalk out of the bathroom before I can do something stupid like bend her over and spank her bratty ass.

By the time I take my seat at the table, every single set of Saint James' eyes settle on me. Wynter's curious, Everett questioning, but every other person at the table is furious.

"What the fuck are you playing at, Elijah?" Storm snaps from his seat at the other end of the table.

"I don't know what you mean."

"Don't play dumb with me. Why the fuck are you going after my sister? The alliance wasn't enough for you, you want to take an insurance policy as well?" The barely contained anger behind his words would make a lesser man quake with fear, but lucky for me, I've faced much scarier men than Storm Saint James.

I take a breath, settling the need for violence simmering barely beneath the surface. The combination of Snow and her brother makes it hard to keep the mask I wear in public in place, hiding the ruthless man I am when no one else is watching. "I have been interested in Snow for a long time, much longer than she has known I exist," I admit. "I made my move as soon as my father and uncles were out of the picture for her safety. I would never put her in danger, never allow any harm to come to her. I'm sure you don't believe my intentions are pure, however, they are as pure as a man like me can offer. I can assure you that this is not some kind of revenge plot for you taking out my family. It's not a way to unite our two families. This is real."

Typically, I don't like explaining myself. Perhaps it's the Russo blood running through my veins or the lifestyle I've become accustomed to, but deep down, I know I have to offer them some kind of explanation, because without one, they're going to try to take her from me, and I'm not going to allow that.

The moment Snow steps out of the bathroom, I turn in my seat. She's done a good job of fixing her makeup, to the point I'd be surprised if anyone bar Wynter notices she cried at all, but it's the venom in her gaze as it settles on me that has my cock twitching in my pants.

She takes measured steps toward the table, never faltering as she weaves her way through the tables of people.

Movement to her left draws my attention away from my angel, and I'm out of my seat and barreling toward her before I can take my next breath.

TWENTY-ONE

SNOW

From the day I learned to walk, I was taught to be aware of my surroundings. Growing up the way that I did, in a family that walks the line of high society, and the underworld is dangerous on both sides, and so I was taught to always be on the lookout for threats.

But as I walk back to the table in a daze, returning to what seems to be the future I never wanted for myself, I'm oblivious to the world around me. My thoughts are plagued with an ultimatum that doesn't have a good option and a man who both terrifies and intrigues me.

When I lock eyes with Elijah, his seat shoved back as he launches himself to his feet, my brows pull together in confusion up until the sound of the safety of a gun clicking off catches my attention.

A masked man stands between tables, terrified diners huddle together beside him, shielding their loved ones from the scene playing out in front of them. His arm is raised, and he holds a heavy, black gun in his palm. It's not the first time he's done something like this, not with how calm his demeanor is, but it's the first time for one of us. I've never had a gun pointed at me.

"Snow!" Elijah shouts as he dodges past a terrified couple sitting between us. The fear in his eyes is unexpected. Elijah Russo doesn't strike me as someone who's afraid of much of anything, but right now, he's terrified. "Get down."

But I'm frozen in place. No matter how loud I scream at myself to move, my own fear takes over and makes it impossible to do much of anything other than stare at the brown-eyed man holding my life in his cruel hands.

"She said you were the idiot of the family, but she didn't mention you have no survival instinct. I guess your family has coddled you too much." He chuckles, his finger squeezing the trigger until the slightest movement is the difference between the bullet remaining in its barrel and it coming right at me. "Enjoy hell, bitch."

The moment the busy restaurant is filled with a startling bang, I'm whisked out of the way and knocked to the ground. The air leaves my lungs the moment my back hits the ground and a hard body lands on top of me, covering every inch of my body, protecting me from the gunman.

When I finally drag a breath in, and my eyes focus on the person keeping me pinned to the hard ground, moss-colored eyes meet mine.

Elijah.

He saved me. He put his own life at risk to protect me.

"I've got you, little Snowflake," he murmurs. "Your brothers are taking care of it." But he makes no move to remove himself from me. There's something in his gaze I can't place, something that doesn't belong on this ruthless man.

I make no attempt to get up, finding the weight of him above me oddly comforting. Having a gun held on me, the idea that my life could have been over in the blink of an eye, it's overwhelming. My heart beats painfully in my chest, and the only thing holding the sob lodged in my throat from breaking free is the warmth the man above me emits.

Elijah tears his eyes from mine to look over his shoulder, checking on the situation around us, but my eyes remain locked on him. They wander to his neck, the intricate design I've only ever admired from afar so close I can make it out. Black vines curl up around his neck, peeking out from beneath his tailored shirt. The darkness wraps around his throat, and the level of detail can only be admired when you're as close as I am.

I find myself completely entranced with the intricate design that I almost don't notice when people surround us. It's only his weight lifting from my body hesitantly that brings me back to the here and now.

"Oh god, Snow. Are you okay?" Wynter drops to her knees beside me, her eyes moving across my body as if looking for visible injuries, but there aren't any. The pain coursing through my body isn't physical.

"I'm okay," I whisper, but I make no move to get to my feet, quite satisfied to remain flat on my back in the middle of the busy restaurant.

She looks up on the other side of me in the direction the gunman was, but when her brows knit together, I know what she's about to say. "I think he got away. But don't worry about it. We'll get them," she promises me.

"Are you okay?" I nod to her stomach, the evidence of her pregnancy not yet visible.

Her eyes follow my gaze and a small smile tips her lips up as she brings her palm to rest on her flat stomach. "Yeah, we're okay. Everett put me under the table the second he saw the gun."

I breathe a sigh of relief. I couldn't live with myself if something happened to her during an attack that was meant for me. Suddenly it occurs to me that Elijah has moved away from us, and I look around frantically, finally prying my body from the cold, hard ground.

"He's talking to Storm," Emerson tells me, dropping down beside Wynter and taking my shaking hand in hers.

"He saved me," I whisper.

Wynter smiles sadly. "Elijah won some points with our brothers tonight. Putting his body between a bullet and you, proves he's loyal and in it for the right reasons."

It's on the tip of my tongue to tell them that's not exactly the case, but what good will it do? The man just threw himself in front of a bullet to protect me, knowing full well he could be hit. As crazy as he and all the things he's done are, I can't argue with the fact that he cares about me, perhaps more than I realized.

Elijah looks over at me, our eyes locking, and before Rayne

can finish whatever he's saying, Elijah is crossing back to me, kneeling beside me and brushing my hair from my face.

"I'm going to take you home and have the doctor come check you out," he tells me.

"I'm fine. I don't need a doctor."

Elijah sighs, frustration flaring in his face before being replaced with something softer. "Snowflake, please let me make sure you're okay."

I stare at him for another moment before nodding. It's not in my nature to concede so easily, usually I'll fight to the death about things I don't even care about, but the way he looks at me, the pure fear in his eyes looking so out of place on someone like him, I can't deny him this.

"Thank you," Elijah murmurs right before he lifts me effortlessly from the floor, his arms wrapping around me protectively.

As badly as I want to bury my face in his chest and hide from the world, I turn to my sister. "The media."

"It's okay, I've got it. You go home and get some rest. Text me with what the doctor says and call me in the morning," Wynter says.

I nod, my eyes barely stopping their roll before it can begin. Being the baby in the family has always meant they've coddled me, but this time, I can't be mad at them for it. They all just watched a masked man hold me at gunpoint and pull the trigger. It's understandable for them to be a little overbearing.

Storm, Rayne, and Everett watch with interest as Elijah weaves around tables with me bundled in his arms, the warmth of his body too comforting for me not to lean into.

His grip on me tightens as soon as we step into the street. Cold wind whips around us in the moments it takes to cross to the car where Pete holds the door open for us.

The driver's eyes drop to where I'm burrowed into his boss's chest, and concern fills his features. "Are you okay, Miss Saint James?" he asks.

"Depends which one of us you ask." I try to laugh, but nothing comes out. As much as I want to make light of this situation, it's not possible. There's nothing light about it.

Elijah shakes his head as he climbs into the back of the SUV, never loosening his grip around me, and I find comfort in his arms. It's strange to think a few hours ago, I was fighting tooth and nail at the idea of being forced into a marriage I didn't want, but maybe marrying Elijah wouldn't be the worst thing in the world.

I'd get to see my family whenever I wanted, I'd have a life of luxury, and although I don't return the feelings, my husband would be protective enough of me that he would throw himself in front of a bullet to keep me safe.

It's that thought that allows me to close my eyes and lean into the warmth, my body suddenly bogged down with exhaustion. Maybe if I just close my eyes for a little while.

TWENTY-TWO
ELIJAH

The moment her body relaxes into mine, I know she's asleep. The soft snores that follow allow me to breathe a little easier, reminding me she's still here with me.

A man like me doesn't feel fear. There's nothing on this earth that scares me, except losing Snow. That scares the fucking shit out of me, and tonight it was a very real possibility. Somehow, a man was allowed into the restaurant wearing a black ski mask and holding a handgun that he subsequently aimed at my woman.

Storm is looking into how this could have happened with three security teams on the premises, but I have a feeling the guy came through the kitchen. It's the only way he could have got in without us knowing about it, and I curse myself for not having a team through the staff areas. I know the owner, and he would have understood the need to keep my woman safe.

But it's too late for could have, would have, should haves.

It doesn't take long to make it back to the house, most of the traffic from earlier cleared. The moment the car comes to a stop, I'm climbing out with Snow held securely against me. I don't know how I'm ever going to let her out of my arms again. I need her to be safe, and the only person I trust with her safety is myself.

Mrs. Chambers stands at the open door, her eyes locked on the small bundle in my arms. Snow's out for the count, the exhaustion allowing her to hide from the reality of tonight for a little while. I'll allow her to sleep until the doctor arrives, and then I'll need to wake her so they can assess her.

"What happened?" she whispers.

"Someone shot at Snow," it's all I can manage. If I spend too much time thinking about what could have happened tonight, I'll lose it, and I can't do that while I'm holding Snow. She's already frightened, she doesn't need to be afraid of me on top of that.

Mrs. Chambers gasps, her hand covering her mouth as she closes the front door behind us. "Is she okay?"

"I think so. The doctor will be here shortly to check her over."

"Take her into her room. I'll bring her some tea and get her a change of clothes for when she wakes."

"She'll be in my room tonight." And every other night from here on out. I could have lost her tonight, and I'm not willing to waste another moment. She's mine. And therefore, she should be in my bed with me every night. I gave her time, more than I wanted to in fact, and now it's time she takes her place by my side.

Mrs. Chambers makes a sound, but she doesn't say a word

as I take long strides toward my bedroom. The space is dark and masculine, but I suspect I will have to concede on some changes to keep my queen happy. She can do whatever the fuck she wants as long as she spends every night in this bed with me.

I lay her down carefully and the moment her body isn't pressed to mine, I'm tempted to pick her up again. Snow rolls to her side in her sleep, curling up into a small ball, holding herself tightly. I'm not the only one who was afraid tonight. No, my little Snowflake was terrified. Whether she admits that is likely an entirely different story.

Mrs. Chambers walks in behind me, her eyes focused on my sweet Snow curled up around herself, the worry clear in the older woman's eyes. She's very fond of our newest resident, and I suspect she likes having another woman in the house. For so long she looked after ruthless men, it must be a change to have Snow here.

Her hands are full of things for Snow. A cup of tea which she places on the nightstand, a pile of clothes and the bathrobe I've seen my sweet captive wear as she wanders the house late at night, all of which she puts at the end of the bed. "I'll get her changed before the doctor arrives."

"I'll do it," I tell her, reaching for the silk pajamas in the pile. They're a simple light pink shorts and camisole duo, but I already know it's going to be hard to keep my hands off her tonight.

"I don't know if…" she starts.

"I almost lost her tonight," I snap. "I'm done being patient, so from here on out, I'll be the one to coddle her when she needs it." I don't mean to sound so harsh, but my patience is wearing thin tonight, and all I can think about is wrapping myself around my woman and reminding myself repeatedly she's okay.

Mrs. Chambers looks as if she's about to say something, but instead she nods curtly and turns on her heel. If I were a normal man, perhaps I would feel guilty for my tone, but she should know better than to argue with the men in my family. We don't take kindly to being questioned.

I turn my attention back to Snow and frown. Her tiny body shakes, her head moving from side to side like her dream has taken a turn. I reach for her, brushing her blonde locks from her cheeks.

"Snowflake," I murmur quietly, perching on the edge of the bed beside her.

Snow's head thrashes from one side to the other and her body tightens at whatever images her mind is conjuring.

"Snow," I say a little louder, not wanting to startle her from her nightmare.

Her blue eyes fly open and meet mine. There's something behind them that seems to settle when she sees it's me beside her, but perhaps that's wishful thinking.

"Where am I?" she whispers, her eyes taking in the new space she's in. My bedroom is one of the only rooms in the house that I've kept locked since her arrival, not for any other reason than I suspected she may try to kill me at some point and didn't want to make it easy for her. But my captive has been more docile than I expected.

"My room," I tell her. "Let's get you out of this dress and into something more comfortable."

She stares at me for a moment before her eyes drop to what she's wearing and then to the change of clothes I'm holding. "I can do it." She reaches for the shorts in my hand, but I quickly move them from her grasp.

"I know you *can* do it." I drop the silk to the bed beside her and begin pushing her satin gown up her legs before she can argue. "But I'm going to do it for you."

Her eyes track my movements, the skin beneath my hands pebbles the higher I push her dress. Is my girl turned on? My lips twitch at the idea that despite her better judgment, she feels the pull I've felt the last ten years, but her eyes remain glued to my hands.

"Elijah," Snow whispers, the worry in her voice evident.

I sigh, stopping my movements to touch my fingers to her chin and lift it until our eyes clash. "I'm not going to take advantage of you. I told you I wouldn't touch you until you begged for it, and I meant it. Just relax and let me take care of you."

She worries her bottom lip between her teeth, considering me for a moment before she nods slightly.

I drop my hands back to the hem of her dress and move it up over her thighs. She lifts her ass just enough I can push the tight dress past, and then I whip it over her head.

My mouth dries when I allow my gaze to fall upon her perfect body. All milky white skin and hard rosy nipples. The only clothing remaining on her body is the tiniest thong I've ever seen in my life, and it's making it difficult to keep my promise. It's not the first time I've seen her naked, or close to at least, but this is different. This time she's right in front of me, her soft skin within reach.

Snow's body is a temptation I can't refuse.

TWENTY-THREE
SNOW

Elijah's looking at me like he wants to eat me alive. His moss-green eyes are full of heat, to the point I wonder if anyone has ever looked at me like this before. I'm almost certain they haven't, because surely I would remember my skin burning beneath someone's gaze.

His eyes slowly drag down my body, taking in every inch, every curve he's uncovered until they fall on my face again. His breathing has changed since he removed my dress, but I don't comment on it, not wanting to break the spell he's under.

The man who rules with an iron fist looks ready to fall to his knees in front of me.

Elijah swallows heavily, his hand whispering across my thigh, gliding across my stomach until his knuckle brushes across my hardened nipples. I wish I could blame the cold for how hard they are, but it's not the temperature in the room that has my body humming. It's the look in his eye and how tense his shoulders are underneath his suit. He's barely holding on to control.

A small moan drops from my lips as his knuckle circles my other nipple. As much as I want to tell the man who holds my fate in his hands I'm not interested, that's just not the case, especially after tonight.

I drag in a shaky breath, words I never thought I would say sitting at the tip of my tongue. Maybe it's the trauma and fear from the night, or something else entirely, but my body screams at me to beg him to touch me, but I manage to swallow the words. If I'm going to make that choice, I'm going to do it with a clear mind.

The doorbell chimes through the house and tears our attention from each other. The spell we were under is broken, and Elijah immediately reaches for the shirt he dropped earlier and wastes no time slipping it over my head and helping my arms into it. Before I can say anything, he drops to his knees in front of me and carefully drags the shorts up my leg, tapping my thigh when he wants me to lift my ass. He reaches for the robe resting at the end of the bed and helps me to slip my arms in before wrapping it tightly around me and tying it around the waist.

I've never allowed anyone to dress me, not since I was a kid, but there's something almost intimate about the moment. Maybe it's the way we're both breathing a little too heavy considering we're doing such a menial task, or maybe it's because ever since I opened my eyes, Elijah has been looking at me like his entire world begins and ends with me.

"The doctor is going to take a look at you and make sure you're not injured."

"I'm fine," I whisper, not trusting my voice not to break.

"That may be, but I want to have a medical professional confirm that."

Before I can respond, the door opens, and Mary appears in the doorway with a very angry Doc standing beside her. The man who I've known for years looks around the room with murderous intensity in his black eyes. When his stare falls on me, he seems to relax slightly, but that moment of calm is gone almost as quickly as it came when it lands on Elijah standing slightly in front of me, as if putting his body between me and a threat.

"What the fuck are you doing with her?" Doc thunders, taking long steps toward us until he towers over Elijah. He's not a short man, not by any means being well over six foot, but Doc would tower over anyone. He's six foot seven and made of pure muscle. Plus, he has the whole, covered in tattoos thing going on that adds to how intimidating he is.

"She's mine," Elijah manages through gritted teeth. He's barely holding on to his composure, and something tells me if one more person questions our relationship, if that's what you want to call it, he's going to snap.

Doc's eyes flare with anger and in the blink of an eye, he's dropped his medical bag and wrapped his fist around Elijah's throat. "What's your game here, Russo?" he growls.

"Doc," I whisper, curling my legs underneath me on the bed. I'm trying not to focus on the fact I'm in Elijah's bedroom for the first time and his sheets smell like him. If I allow myself to focus too hard on that, I'm at risk of melting into a puddle and never moving again.

His eyes snap to mine, the intensity of the blackness almost makes me flinch, but I remain perfectly still.

"Elijah and I are dating. We have been for about a month," the lie slips from my tongue with such ease that I almost believe it myself. It's not as if I've spent much time practicing, but for some reason, the words are easy right now.

Doc doesn't loosen his grip on Elijah's neck, and I'm surprised to find my captor watching me closely. Not because he's telling me to tell the lies he's forcing me to live, but because he didn't expect me to defend him.

"Doc, please," I murmur.

He watches me for a moment, looking for the lie in my words, and I hold my breath. He's going to see right through us. He's going to realize I don't want this, or at least, I didn't want this. But tonight has me second-guessing myself and second-guessing everything I thought I knew.

Slowly, Doc releases his grip on Elijah, never tearing his eyes from me. Maybe he's still looking for the lie, or perhaps there's something else here that I don't understand. One of the only things I know about the man is that he hates the Russo family with a burning passion, and I think it's safe to say that hatred extends to Elijah.

"What happened?" he asks.

"A man held me at gunpoint and Elijah threw himself on me to protect me." My eyes dart to the man in question, but he's not wearing the smugness I expect. "I'm fine, but my overprotective boyfriend over there wanted to make sure." I scoff more at the word I used to describe Elijah than anything else. The word boy and the ruthless man who took me from my life shouldn't find themselves in the same sentence, but what else am I supposed to call him?

"How the fuck did a man with a gun get near you?" Doc snaps, his attention turning back to Elijah. "She shouldn't be here if you can't keep her safe."

"Storm and I both had teams at the restaurant," Elijah grinds out, barely containing the rage hovering beneath the surface. "He shouldn't have got anywhere near her, but our current theory is he came through the kitchen."

I reach for Doc's arm, careful to make sure he sees the movement coming. I've made that mistake before and found myself pinned to a wall, winded from the force he slammed me into it with. Something in his past made him averse to unseen touches, and I've never been in a place to pry. "He saved me, Doc. He threw himself in front of a bullet for me. Cut him some slack." I never thought I would defend Elijah Russo, but here we are.

He lets out an annoyed huff before turning his full attention on me, blocking the other man from his eye line. "Okay, let's have a look at you."

It's an hour before Doc leaves, convinced I'm not badly hurt and that Elijah isn't going to change that the moment he walks out the door. When the two men leave the room, heading for the front of the house, I push myself to my feet and pad across to the door. Now he knows I'm okay, I'm sure he'll want me to go back to my room. He wouldn't have decorated it exactly like my room at the estate if he didn't intend for that to be my home while I'm here.

As soon as I step over the threshold and I'm no longer enveloped by his scent, I miss it. His masculine smell calms me, and when it no longer surrounds me, some of the panic returns. I could have been shot tonight. I could have died. I've been so worried about Elijah keeping me away from my family that it never occurred to me that my life has been in constant danger since the day I was born.

I'm distracted as I trudge back toward my lonely room, my prison, and more than ever before, I crave my siblings. I was never alone growing up, but that's all I ever am now. All by myself in this huge house, and that's the life that waits for me as well.

An arm hooks around my waist and tugs me back into a hard body. I let out a surprised squeak, but panic doesn't grow as I expect it to.

"Where do you think you're going, my little Snowflake?" Elijah breathes against the shell of my ear.

"Going back to my room," I whisper into the dark hallway, the only light coming from his room behind us.

"Your room is back the way you came."

My body stills. What the fuck is he talking about? Is he taking away the only refuge I have here? The only piece of home I have in the prison I'll be locked in for the rest of my life?

Twenty-Four

Elijah

When her body stills in my arms, I know she's about to fight me, but I don't give her a chance, quickly scooping her up and carrying her back to my room before she can draw out her claws.

"I don't understand, I thought…" Snow looks up at me with confusion and worry etched into her features.

"What did you think, Snow? Did you think I would have a wife who would sleep in another room?" I ask, placing her in the middle of the bed and tugging the tie of her robe open.

"I haven't agreed to that," she whispers.

I shake my head, making no attempt to hide the smile that tugs at the corners of my lips. "Didn't you say in the bathroom it's not really a choice at all?"

She glares at me. "I did. And then I had a man hold a gun on me, and now I'm kinda reevaluating things. That kind of thing happens when your life flashes before your eyes." She crosses her arms across her chest to stop me from undressing her any further, but she should know if I want her naked, that's exactly how I'm going to have her.

I sigh and massage the bridge of my nose. Every time I think we've made progress, she takes three steps backward, and it's incredibly frustrating. "I know you've had a challenging evening, but I almost lost you tonight. You almost died right in front of me, and that's moved up the timeline. You are my woman, and therefore, you will sleep in my bed."

She considers me for a moment, and then she does exactly as I expect. She rolls off the other side of the bed and shakes her head. "Nope. Not going to happen. You said you wouldn't force yourself on me, and this feels a lot like that."

"I am a criminal, Snow. I lie for a living."

Fear crosses her features, and her eyes dart to the door, looking for an escape that doesn't exist. "There's nowhere in the house you can hide from me, nowhere in the world, for that matter."

"I'm not sleeping with you," Snow whispers.

"I'm not asking for sex, Snow. That will come, but tonight you're sleeping in this bed, with me, whether you like it or not."

"Or what?"

"There is no or what. Either you get your pretty ass between those sheets, or I'm going to tie you to the bed until further notice. Which option do you like better?" I raise an eyebrow.

"I don't believe you."

I laugh, the sound almost foreign to me, it's so rare. Slowly, I reach for the bedside table and pull the drawer open, keeping my eyes locked on hers while I fish around to find what I'm looking for. I meant it when I said she wasn't going to like the result of defying me. My fingers brush across cool leather and a small smirk settles on my lips as I bring the item into view.

Snow's eyes fall on the leather handcuffs I'm holding, and her mouth drops open. "Elijah," she warns.

"Get in the bed, Snow. One way or another, you're sleeping in here tonight. I suggest you choose the right option."

After another moment of consideration, she sighs and steps back toward the bed, slowly pulling the sheets away so she can slip between them. Even as the words occur to me, I know I shouldn't voice them, I shouldn't push her any harder than she's already been pushed tonight, but I can't help it and the words slip free before I can stop them.

"You're wearing too much."

She looks down at the robe and quickly pushes it off her shoulders, discarding it on the chair by the window.

"Still too much."

Snow's mouth drops open and her eyes flare with a mix of understanding and anger. "I am not sleeping naked with you," she snaps.

I sigh, holding up the cuffs again. "Either you strip down to those tiny little panties, or I'll do it for you." She's trying my very thin patience, and if she were anyone else, I would have already thrown her in the bed and tied her up so she couldn't run. But she's not just anyone else, she's the woman I intend to force to marry me as soon as possible, and therefore a certain level of restraint must be shown.

The defiance that flares to life in Snow's blue eyes only makes my cock harden in my dress pants. I haven't had a chance to change from dinner yet, and my dick begs to be set free. With one last sigh, Snow pulls the camisole from her body, her perky tits bouncing slightly when the fabric brushes past them. Next, she bends over and shoves the shorts down her toned legs until she's standing in nothing but a black thong that leaves nothing to the imagination.

"Happy?" she snaps.

"Delirious."

Snow mutters something under her breath as she climbs between the sheets and pulls them up to cover her naked body, but I don't question her. Instead, I start to undress myself. I slip my jacket off my shoulders and watch her closely as I unbutton my shirt. She's trying not to watch me, looking anywhere but where I'm standing at the base of the bed, but every now and then, her eyes dart past me. She's not as unaffected by me as she would like me to believe.

I push the shirt off my shoulders and allow it to drop to the floor before moving my hands to my belt.

Snow's eyes finally settle on me, giving up her attempt to keep them off me and what I'm doing, and her mouth drops open slightly as I shove my pants down my legs and all I'm wearing is a pair of boxer briefs. The outline of my rock-hard cock is clear through them, and I can't help but tease her by squeezing it once.

"Do you like what you see, Snowflake?"

"Aw, Elijah. Do you need your ego stroked? I'm afraid you've come to the wrong girl if that's the case."

"My ego isn't what I need stroked, Snow, and I suggest you keep that pretty mouth shut if you don't want me to fuck it."

She crosses her arms across her chest, which only pushes her breasts up and considers me for a moment. "You promised you wouldn't do anything until I begged you, and I don't recall begging you for that."

I smirk as I drop my boxer briefs, leaving me completely naked. Her eyes drift across every bit of skin, tracking across the dark tattoos as if putting together the pieces of the puzzle her mind has been trying to since she saw the ones on my arms. Slowly, almost too much so, I place each knee on the edge of the mattress and prowl toward her. It's not the first time I've likened myself to a predator hunting my prey, but it's the first time Snow has been my target.

"Do you know what the good thing about being in charge is, my little Snowflake?" I murmur as I close the distance between us until our faces are just an inch apart. "I can change my mind any damn time I please."

TWENTY-FIVE

SNOW

I barely have enough time to take a breath before Elijah pulls us both off the bed and shoves me to my knees. The soft carpet scrapes across my bare legs and burns, but all I can focus on is the panic raging through my veins. He promised he wouldn't violate me, he promised he would wait for me to beg him, but he lied. I don't know what I expected from a man like Elijah. He's a pathological liar and expecting him to be anything other than that is my own mistake.

When my eyes clash with his, the darkness behind the normally light green almost startles me. His hand moves to fist my hair, tugging the strands back painfully until I'm sure my scalp is bleeding with how raw it feels.

"You can't expect to poke the bear and not get mauled, Snow," Elijah says as he brings my face closer to his hard, veiny cock.

It's bigger than any I've ever seen in the past, and I'm not entirely sure that's a good thing. For one, if he shoves it in my mouth, which at this point seems like a given, he's going to choke me. Two, if and when I relent and allow him into other parts of my body, it's going to hurt, and not just the delightful little burn you have when you're so full it takes your breath away. No, this thing is going to tear me in half.

"Elijah," I whisper, half plea for mercy, half breathy moan for more.

My mind and body are clearly not on the same page. I should be kicking and screaming and doing anything I can to escape his grasp. But I'm not. I'm kneeling at his feet with his monster cock so close to my face his musky scent has my mouth watering. Yeah, my mind and body aren't even in the same book anymore, let alone the same page.

"Open your mouth."

As if my body has all the power here and my mind is just along for the ride, my mouth drops open of its own accord, and a moment later the broad head of his cock touches my lips. A bead of precum smooths across my bottom lip tearing an involuntary groan from my throat.

Elijah's eyes flare with fire, my reaction to him exactly as he had hoped it would be. "You're going to take everything I give you, Snow, and you're going to do it without teeth. Do you understand?"

"Please."

"Please, what? Please stop, or please fuck your mouth like I threatened?"

I push my legs together in the hope it will ease the ache between them, but all it does is cause my panties to brush across the wetness pooling there. How can I be so turned on and so scared at the same time?

"You don't have to do this," I whisper.

His head drops back and a loud chuckle fills the room. "Open your mouth, Snow."

For a moment, I consider defying him, but what good will it do? I'm his prisoner and denying him tonight will only make the next time worse. I allow my jaw to relax and my mouth to drop open.

"See, you can be a good girl," Elijah taunts a moment before his cock slips into my mouth, stopping any retort I may have had. He groans long and loud as he slides deeper until he hits the back of my throat and retreats slightly. He's being surprisingly gentle so far, but I have a feeling it's going to be short-lived. "Fuck," he curses. "Your mouth is so fucking good. I knew it would be. I knew every single one of your tight holes would be its own paradise."

His words make me press my legs together harder, needing any kind of relief I can get. Despite my mind screaming at my body that this is wrong and that he's taking this without our full consent, the hussy is taking matters into her own hands and dripping for him.

"Is your little pussy aching for me?"

I stare up at him, his cock moving slowly between my lips as he guides my face where he wants me.

"I think it is," Elijah taunts. "I think your cunt is aching for me to sink deep into your wetness. But not tonight. Tonight I'm going to teach this smart mouth a lesson."

The gentle strokes of his cock quickly come to an end, and a moment later, his cock is battering the back of my throat in quick, sharp motions that are so at odds with how he treated me earlier.

His grip on my hair tightens as he thrusts between my lips, and my hands fly out to grip his thighs. Ever since I arrived here, I've tried to keep my distance, never touching him if I can help it, but right now, I need all the balance I can get.

My throat burns with each thrust, and hot tears run down my cheeks. The next time his cock hits the back of my throat, he doesn't stop, he doesn't retreat, instead he pushes forward, hitting my gag reflex and causing my entire body to lurch.

"Let me in, Snowflake. I want to fuck your pretty little throat." Elijah grips my throat from the side, rubbing his fingers gently into the flesh as his cock surges forward again.

I squeeze my eyes shut, trying to stamp down the panic of not being able to breathe brings on, but it doesn't help.

"Open your fucking eyes, Snow. I want them on me as I fuck your face," he snaps, and I focus back on him immediately. I've never been attracted to dominant men, probably because every man in my life has thought they could walk all over me, and I don't want one to do that in the bedroom. But the more control Elijah pries from my hold, the more the ache between my thighs grows.

Tears rolled down my cheeks, making the image of Elijah above me blurry. I can't tell where the tears from gagging end and the ones for my loss of freedom begin. We're on a slippery slope now. First he takes a blow job. What part of my body is he going to take against my will next?

The hasty, irrational part of my brain screams at me to bite him, to make him hurt the same way he is me. But that will only cause me more pain in the long run. After all, Elijah holds all the cards.

The moment he pulls his cock from my mouth, I gasp for air, choking as I inhale a mixture of my own saliva and his sticky precum. Elijah grips the base of his manhood, squeezing as he runs the length across my tear-stained cheeks. "I don't normally like seeing you cry, but when it's for my cock, it only makes me harder."

"Fuck you," I hiss.

"Don't tempt me, Snow," he growls. Before I can think to respond, he's shoving himself back into my mouth and doesn't stop when he hits the back of my throat. "Swallow for me, dirty girl. Swallow my cock."

I try to shake my head as my body heaves with the power of my choking. Panic grips me, and I shove at Elijah's thighs with every bit of strength I can manage, but it doesn't make a bit of difference. His grip on my head is firm and unwavering making it impossible to pull away to drag in a breath.

Elijah's eyes remain locked with mine, the lust flaring in them should unsettle me further, but seeing as he threw himself in front of a bullet for me a few hours ago, it doesn't seem like he wants me to choke to death.

I want to close my eyes to escape the depths of his eyes, but I can't do it. Something tells me if I look away it's only going to make him angrier, and right now I don't think my throat can handle that.

"Swallow," he demands.

The panic still claws at me, but I take comfort in the likelihood that he doesn't want me to choke and die and force my body to relax. The grip I have on his thighs relaxes, my body molds into his hold, and I allow my throat to grant him access, swallowing heavily around his thick length.

"Good girl," Elijah groans out in a sound that doesn't even sound human. He holds himself there for a moment, his grip in my hair loosens slightly and his fingers brush through my hair.

I don't want to like his praise, not when he's actively depriving me of oxygen, but the low rumble in his chest and the small smile on his lips only make me want to please him.

Is that fucked up? Maybe it is, and hell, maybe it's the start of Stockholm syndrome or whatever it's called, but if I'm going to be stuck here indefinitely, I might as well sink into the feeling.

Twenty-Six

Elijah

I've imagined this moment a million different ways over the years. I've jacked off in the shower to the image of Snow on her knees, my cock so deep in her throat her nose touches my abs. I've thought about how hot and sweet her mouth would feel, and what it would be like to hold her head and fuck her face just the way I like it.

But I never imagined it would be like this. The warmth of her mouth is almost enough to bring me to my fucking knees. She fought it at first, and I'm just fucked up enough that I enjoyed every second she tried to escape her fate, but I saw the moment she made the decision to comply, and every moment since then has been so sweet. Even though I'm obsessed with her fire, her submission is all I've ever wanted, and when she hands her body over to me and relaxes into my hold, I can't help but praise her.

I withdraw my cock from her throat and she gasps in heavy breaths. I didn't intend for this to happen tonight, but I'm fucking glad it has. Snow needs to realize who's in charge, she needs to understand her life is in my hands, and if she's not going to get with the program, I'm going to have to take matters into my own hands.

I brush the head of my cock along her pouty lips, barely containing the need to shove myself back into her wet hole while she's still trying to catch her breath. "You're so pretty with my cock in your mouth, Snow. So fucking pretty," I murmur, smearing the mixture of precum and her saliva across her cheek.

Conflict dances in the ice of her eyes. She doesn't know if she should keep fighting or hand herself over completely, but what she needs to realize is that both options have the exact same outcome. She is mine, and I will take whatever I want, whenever I want from what belongs to me.

"Are you going to be a good girl and take my cum down your throat, Snowflake?"

She draws her bottom lip between her teeth and nibbles on the abused flesh for a moment, considering her options before nodding.

"Oh no, I'm going to need your words," I tell her, barely keeping the smile from my lips as I resume rubbing my head across her lips. "*Beg* me for my cum, Snow."

A bead of precum gathers at the tip of my cock and I smear it across her plump bottom lip. Snow's pink tongue darts out and gathers the salty treat despite the distaste in her eyes.

I groan at the sight. My sweet Snowflake looks like a fallen angel kneeling at my feet, but I want to hear her beg. I want the words on her lips so I can fuck them right out of her. I tighten my grip on her hair, tilting her head back until she's forced to hold my gaze.

"No," she whispers.

"Wrong answer, Snowflake," I growl, crouching down in front of her until our eyes are at the same level. My grip moves to her chin and I hold her tight. "Do you want to try again?"

"I don't want this."

I chuckle, the sound more evil than I intend, but that's exactly how the world sees me. Evil as the devil himself. With my free hand I reach between her legs and shove my fingers into her panties. Immediately, her legs press together trying to ward off my invasion, but she should know by now I'm stronger than her, and I'm going to take anything I want from her body. When my fingers brush through her folds, I find exactly what I was expecting. She's fucking soaked. Her mind may be fighting me, but her body loves everything I've done to her. "See, I think that's a lie, little Snowflake." I pull my fingers from her soaking wet panties and hold them up in the dim moonlight coming through the window. Her juices glisten on my fingers and her cheeks turn the most delectable shade of pink. "Your sweet pussy is telling a different story to your pretty pink lips."

Snow's mouth drops open when she sees how wet she is, but immediately clamps it closed. She can't defend what I'm showing her because I'm telling the truth. She's not willing to admit it yet, but Snow wants me almost as badly as I want her.

"Either you beg for my cum, or you don't come for a month."

"You can't do that," Snow snaps.

I laugh. "I can and I will, Snowflake. I can do whatever the fuck I want, do you know why?" I pause for a moment as if I'm actually asking her. "Because I'm in charge here. You are mine. Your body. Your mind. Your soul. It all belongs to me, and I'm going to use you any way I please. If I don't want you to come, you're not going to come. It's as simple as that."

"You're not here all the time, you can't possibly police that." She underestimates me. She doesn't realize just how deep my obsession runs, but she will.

"There are cameras that cover every single inch of this house. If you so much as touch your pussy without my permission, you'll find yourself chained to the bed anytime I'm not around. Is that what you want?" I raise my brow.

"No," she whispers.

"That's what I thought." I smile smugly. "Now, I think there was something you were going to ask me for, or perhaps beg…" I trail off.

The fire in her glare only makes my cock twitch, but I remain crouched in front of her, waiting for the words to leave her pouty lips. "Can I please have your cum?" she mumbles.

"Not good enough," I growl, bringing my face close to hers until we're breathing the same air. "Try again, and each time you get it wrong is an orgasm I'm going to take from you."

Snow's mouth drops open but immediately snaps shut again as if she's afraid I might shove something else into it. There's only one thing I want to sink into her wet mouth, and that's going to happen regardless. She lets out a defeated sigh. The more time she spends here with me, the more she realizes her free will is gone. Whatever I want is going to happen, and then what she wants may or may not happen depending on my mood and her behavior.

"Please Elijah, please give me your cum." The words come out sweet, but there's a hatred behind them that I will need to work on, but not right now. Right now, my sweet Snowflake is going to choke on my cock until she's drained every drop from my balls.

I stand, gripping the base of my dick and rub it across her cheeks. "There, that wasn't so hard, was it?"

The moment she opens her mouth to snap back, I shove my cock all the way to the back of her throat, tearing a groan from my chest. Fuck, her mouth is perfect. I could spend the rest of my days buried right here and never come up for air.

I withdraw slightly before pushing back until I hit her gag reflex. "Let me in, Snow," I murmur, moving my free hand to her neck. "Swallow for me."

Tears gather at the corners of her eyes, but she's in no position to argue and the moment her throat relaxes around my cock, I slide deep and it almost brings me to my knees. "Good girl," I praise, brushing my fingers through her hair as I snap my hips in short strokes, never breaking eye contact.

The familiar tingling at the base of my spine tells me I'm getting close, and although I want to spend the rest of my fucking life right here with Snow at my feet, I can't go another moment without the release I've needed since the day I took her.

"I'm going to come, Snow," I warn. "Be a good girl and take

every drop."

When I erupt straight down her throat, stars play at the corners of my vision, and I barely keep my feet beneath me at the intensity. Every nerve ending sings with my release, the one I've been dreaming of for the last ten years. The first time I would fill one of Snow's tight holes.

One down, two to go.

TWENTY-SEVEN

SNOW

Shame burns at the edge of my consciousness.

I just allowed the enemy to use my body for his own pleasure. And what's worse? I enjoyed it. Everything he did made me ache for him. His rough treatment only made me want more. The way he praised me made my heart skip a beat. And the rapture in his eyes as he came down my throat, holding my hair so tight I'm sure he tore chunks from my scalp, it was like art. That's the only way I can describe the way he fell apart above me, allowing himself to be vulnerable.

I was so mesmerized by the moment that I almost choked on his hot sticky cum before I finally swallowed it down.

As soon as his grip on my hair loosens, I pull away from him, scooting back until I hit the wall before bringing my knees up to my chest. I can't believe I let him do that to me. I can't believe I was so stupid to think he meant it when he said he wouldn't force himself on me. But then I've always been the stupid Saint James. The expendable one even. Storm is the leader, Wynter is always so poised and perfect, and Rayne is the strong one. They each forged a role in the family, and I never did. Even the tabloids know it.

I've lost count of the number of articles the trash newspapers in the city have written about me. Every time I step out of the house, I've done something wrong in society's eyes, and there's always someone there to capture my mistakes. Except of course when I needed the paparazzi to be there the day Elijah stole me from my life and everything I love. The only time in years they've missed something notable happening, and it just so happens to be me being kidnapped by the cruelest man in the city. How convenient.

For long moments my breathing comes in fast and hard pants. Panic claws up my throat but it's too overbearing for me to fight, and so I allow it to drag me down with it.

Tonight I was held at gunpoint and I thought that was the worst thing that could ever happen to me, but God, was I wrong. The worst thing that could happen to me was having my freedom taken from me, and on top of that, my freewill.

Elijah has taken everything from me. Every fucking thing. But I can't allow him to take anything else, not without fighting like my life depends on it. Because if he lied to me about this, he's sure to have lied to me about other things. Like what will happen to me when all of this ends.

"Snow?" Elijah's voice startles me. It's closer than it should be. I left him a few feet away and didn't hear him move, but then again, I've often thought he moves like a silent assassin, it shouldn't surprise me anymore.

I don't look up at him, too ashamed of what I've allowed him to do to my body. Instead, I tighten my arms around my knees and bury my face as deep as I can into them. I can't allow myself to fall apart in front of the man who holds my entire fate in his hands, even if I now know there's nowhere in this house he can't see me. Nowhere I can fall apart.

Rough hands brush up my bare legs and although my mind tells me to pull away, my body remains rooted in place. "Snowflake," he whispers my nickname like a prayer. His hands disappear for a moment and the way my heart sinks at the thought of him leaving me after what he just did only adds to the shame tearing me apart piece by piece.

A moment later my body is lifted from the ground and my side rests against his chest. He presses a gentle kiss to my temple as he takes a few steps to the bed, carefully sitting back and keeping his arms wrapped around me. It's just another one of the times I should fight like hell, but I don't have any fight left in me. Not tonight at least.

Tears roll down my cheeks in heavy drops, mourning the loss of the life I thought I would lead. I thought I would eventually meet a nice man, probably one of Storm's contacts, and he would treat me well enough. We would have two point four children and a dog and a white picket fence, and I would be happy. Maybe not in the way I was when I was wild and free, but happy enough. I'll never have that chance now.

Elijah has taken all my choices away, everything I always thought my life would be is gone, and now my future looks very different. The wife of a Mafia king, forced to bear his heirs, and then when he's done with me, when I start to age and there's no use for me, he'll kill me. If I'm lucky it will be quick and painless, but it depends how alike he is to his uncles.

His arms hold me so tightly I almost allow myself to pretend it's not him, that it's someone who genuinely cares for me and my feelings. He holds me for so long and so tight that the tears eventually dry, and all that's left is the shame he forced upon me.

Elijah shifts beneath me and my fingers cling to him. As fucked up as it sounds, he's the only thing holding me together right now, even though he's the reason I'm falling apart in the first place. "I'm not going anywhere, Snowflake," he murmurs against the top of my head. "Let's get you into bed."

He doesn't wait for me to say anything, instead he lifts me carefully from his chest as if I weigh nothing and lays me beside him in the middle of the bed. Immediately I curl into a ball, as if the movement can protect me from the events of the night. But even I know there's no protecting myself from my new reality.

The bed dips beside me and his overheated body curls around my back. I should pull away and lay as far away from him as the bed will allow, but the monster behind me is all I have now, and the sooner I accept that, the easier it's going to be for me in the long run.

"We're getting married next weekend. I'll have someone come to help you plan everything. You can have anything you want, I don't care how much it costs, but you will be my wife." There's no room for argument in his tone, nothing I can say or do to change his mind. All I can hope for is that I can make his life even an ounce as awful as he's going to make mine.

"Okay," I whisper.

"You're going to be happy here, Snow." One of his arms snakes beneath me and rests on one of my bare breasts, while his other forces my legs apart enough that it can cup my pussy. "So wet and needy for me," he murmurs, pressing a kiss to the place below my ear. "Are you ready to ask me nicely for what you need?"

"I don't need anything from you."

He chuckles, his breath whispering across my skin. "Little liar."

Twenty-Eight

Elijah

A man like me has demons. So many I can't count them, but when I close my eyes at night, they come for me. All the sins of my past, the lives I've taken, the things that brought me to this point. But holding Snow as she sleeps soundly, her body relaxing into mine despite herself, it allows my body to relax and sleep to take me.

When I wake up, I'm not sure what woke me at first. There's no sound in the house, the sun is still hiding below the horizon, and Snow is still curled up safely in my arms. Her sweet pussy has soaked my hand, but I'm careful not to give her any stimulation. I meant it when I said she would have to beg for my cock, and I won't be making her come until I'm balls deep in her cunt.

Something vibrates across the carpet, and I groan. It's my phone. I forgot to get it out of my pocket when I undressed last night and perhaps that's the biggest indication of how much of a distraction Snow truly is. I've never put anything, or anyone, above my work. Even when I spent all my free time stalking her, I still dropped everything when work came calling, but it's different now she's here with me.

I disentangle myself from her warm body and carefully climb from the bed, trying not to disrupt her. She had a hard night and I only made it worse, she deserves a few hours of sleep before she has to start planning our wedding.

I fish my phone out of my pocket and creep into the hallway, closing the door behind me, paying no mind to the fact I'm stark naked. Mrs. Chambers goes home to her husband at night, and security doesn't patrol within the house when I'm home. Honestly, they wouldn't step foot in the house at all if I could help it. I hate the idea of other men being near Snow. But it's unavoidable.

When I look at the screen on my phone, the backlight like the sun in the dark hallway, I see Storm has tried to call me four times. Immediately, I tap his name and hold the phone to my ear. He doesn't chase anyone, and for him to have called so many times something must be wrong.

"Elijah."

"Storm, you called."

"How's my sister?"

"I'm sure Doc told you she's fine physically. But she's a bit shaken as you can imagine. She's asleep right now. What did you find out?"

"Nothing. The guy's a fucking ghost. Everett managed to pull a photo of him as he was slipping the mask on out the back of the restaurant, but he doesn't exist. Not in any country, any database, nothing."

"How is that possible?"

"I don't know. He said he's never seen it before. But that's not why I'm calling. At the same time as the gunman was holding Snow at gunpoint, we had a shipment go missing. Happen to know anything about that?"

I tip my head back and barely hold back the growl of frustration. Of course I know they don't trust me yet, why would they? I've been their enemy for as long as we've all been walking this earth, and that's before adding everything I was forced to do to my cousin growing up. They have no reason to believe that I want to be allies rather than enemies, and that's what I tell my temper as it threatens to flare. "No, Storm. I don't know anything about a missing shipment."

He's quiet on the other end of the line for a few moments, considering my answer before he sighs. "I need you down at the docks to meet Rayne and Everett."

I turn to face my bedroom door where Snow sleeps soundly on the other side. I don't want to leave her like a thief in the night, but if I want this alliance to work, and if I want the Saint James family to agree to me marrying their sister in a week's time, I need to jump through whatever hoops they tell me to. "I'll be there in twenty."

"Good," he says before ending the call.

I creep back into the bedroom and can't help but stare at the lump in the bed. In all the years since I bought this place, I've never had a woman here. When the need for a tight wet hole got too much, I would fuck one of the girls at the strip clubs we owned quick and dirty. There was never a reason to take things slow with them, but it's different with Snow. She's going to beg for my cock, I know she is, but the longer I have to wait for those words to fall from her lips, the harder it is to control myself around her.

As quickly and quietly as I can, I dress in a pair of black sweatpants and a matching sweater before crossing to the bed where Snow is burrowed into my pillow. My lips twitch into a smile, her consciousness is at a constant battle with what her subconscious wants, but even in her sleep she seeks me out.

I drop a kiss to her cheek and quickly jot a note on the pad on the bedside table to let her know where I've gone. She doesn't need to know what I'm doing, but while she's learning to trust me it's best I'm as open and honest with her as I can be.

When I turn back to the door, I can't bear another glance at the bed. My body screams at me to return to her warmth, but business has always come first, and now that I'm in bed with the Saint James family, both metaphorically and literally, I need to play their game until they trust me.

The cold Chicago air whips off Lake Michigan and surrounds me, causing me to shiver. It's cold as fucking shit out here, and more than ever I wish I was home with Snow, her sweet body pressed against mine as she snores softly beside me.

I've been out of the house for two hours and I've already checked the camera in my room three times. The pull to Snow only grows stronger every day I have her in my grasp, and now that I've allowed myself a taste of her, my need is only going to grow stronger.

"Did you find anything?" Everett asks, tearing my attention away from my phone. We've been at this for far too long, but they won't call it. Whoever pulled this job is a professional. They haven't left so much as a fucking cigarette butt, which is perhaps the most suspicious part of this whole thing. The docks are full of smokers. In my experience, there's something about this type of work that breeds smokers, and for there not to be one discarded cigarette for a mile, they must have had one hell of a clean-up crew.

"Not a fucking thing."

He eyes me warily, watching me for the telltale signs of a lie, but he's not going to find anything. Even if I were behind this, I've been besting Everett since we were kids, and that's not likely to change now. But I'm not, and this loss of shipment impacts me just as much as it does them. If there's a new player in town, it means we both have something to worry about.

"Anything on the cameras?"

He shakes his head. "Nothing. They hacked into the feed and had old footage playing over and over which is why our security team didn't pick anything up."

"Anyone you know of with that kind of access?"

"Only you," he replies pointedly, the accusation in the words obvious. He's not trying to hide his disdain for me or my involvement with his family, but he's barking up the wrong tree.

I sigh, slipping my phone back into the pocket of my sweatpants. The sun is poking out of the horizon, the slightest bit of natural light streaming across the docks. It won't be long before Snow wakes up without me there, but there's not a lot I can do about that right now. "I fired everyone who worked for the Russo family before the hit. My team is so depleted there's no way we could pull off a job of this size and to this extent in the time they did," I tell him honestly. "I'm afraid with all likelihood this is much worse than you have allowed yourself to consider. There's a new player in town, and they're taking our alliance as an invitation to start making moves."

TWENTY-NINE

SNOW

Consciousness returns to me slowly, the thick sheets wrapped around my body allowing me to hide from the world for longer than I normally would, and Elijah's woodsy scent brings me a comfort I can never allow him to know about.

It only takes a few seconds for me to realize he's not here, and with each moment that passes the shame creeps back in like a parasite seeping into every pore. He used me and then he left. I'm nothing more to him than a whore who will eventually bear his children, and that thought is depressing as hell.

Sounds down the hallway draw me from my self-sabotaging mind. There's no clock in here, but by the way the sun lays low on the horizon it can't be much later than seven and Mrs. Chambers was here late last night, only leaving when she showed Doc out.

Curiosity gets the better of me and I slip out from between the sheets and pad to the doors across from the bed. I can only assume one of them is the bathroom and the other the closet, but who knows with Elijah, one could very well be a dungeon he intends to lock me in when he doesn't get his own way.

I check the door on the left first and find the bathroom. When my eyes lock with my own in the mirror, I cringe at the sight before me. I never go to sleep with makeup on, and perhaps with the madness of the evening I assumed I had cried so much it wasn't necessary, but staring at myself with flecks of black under my eyes, the shadows of tear tracks down my pale cheeks, and dried saliva around my mouth from Elijah's rough treatment tells me that wasn't the case.

My jaw aches from taking his huge cock and I can only imagine when the time comes for him to force himself into my unwilling body, my pussy will feel just as tender afterward.

The space is dark and masculine, with all the surfaces a gray concrete that matches my captor. Cold. Unfeeling. Hard.

I don't allow myself to linger for long, quickly stepping into the shower and washing my hair and body as fast as I can while trying to ignore the fact I now smell like Elijah, and every time I move today it will be his scent that overpowers me. As if being stuck in this house isn't reminder enough of the man who holds my future like cards in his hands, now I have to smell like him as well.

Rationally I realize I could have gone back to the room where all my favorite things are stocked up and smell like myself, that I'm leaning into the victim complex I've always played to my advantage, but I ignore that voice. I deserve to throw myself a pity party, after all, I'm mourning the loss of my life as I know it.

Once I've cleaned last night away from my skin, spending extra time scrubbing as if it can wipe me clean of the memories, I pad out into Elijah's room and look around at the dark walls and abstract art. He would like bullshit like this. The things no one else understands would be the ones Elijah Russo finds fascinating.

I don't allow myself to linger for long, searching for the clothes I was wearing last night and coming up empty aside for the fluffy robe folded over the back of the chair by the window. I slip my arms into it quickly and take off toward the sounds I heard when I woke up.

The dim light filters through open doors as I pad down the hallway with my arms wrapped tightly around myself. Although I've come to see some of this house's charm, it's also creepy as hell at times. Every time I've gone looking for clues like a cat burglar, I've always ended up back in my room with the blankets wrapped around my neck waiting for the monster that doesn't exist to come and get me.

As I wander up the hallway, I find the kitchen light on, and I hold my breath as I duck my head in. Is it likely that there's someone in the house that could harm me? No, the likelihood of Elijah having anything less than a state-of-the-art security system doesn't seem high. But is that fact calming to my paranoid mind who in the last week has been kidnapped and held hostage, and held at gunpoint by a masked man intent to kill me? Absolutely not.

"Miss Saint James, I didn't expect you to be up so early," a voice penetrates the quiet room, and my breath halts in my lungs. I should have stayed in bed, at least there I was safe, or I could pretend to be.

I round the corner and my eyes fall on a well-dressed man with a mug in his hands leaning against the counter. My eyes track from his freshly polished shoes, up his tailored pant legs, to his fitted suit jacket, until they fall on a breathtaking pair of deep brown eyes. The color of chocolate seems amused as he watches me, a small smirk tugging at the corners of his lips.

"Who are you?" I ask, pulling the tie to my robe just to give my hands something to do. I've always been a sucker for a well-dressed man, and something tells me Elijah wouldn't want another man touching what belongs to him.

The moment the idea pops into my head I try to squash it down. But the brat in me loves to break the rules and hates being told what to do. What if I didn't touch the guy? What if I had a little fun, made Elijah a little mad, and showed him what his future is going to look like if he forces me into this marriage, because while my siblings would never break marriage vows, I won't hesitate if I'm in a loveless marriage. Does that make me an asshole? Yep. But I'm being forced to take vows with a man who will likely grow tired of me the moment I develop crow's feet and send one of his men to dump me in the bottom of Lake Michigan, so I'm allowed to be a bit of an asshole.

"Dwayne. I work for Mr. Russo."

I nod slowly, taking a tentative step farther into the kitchen. "What do you do for Elijah?" I ask, reaching above the bench for a mug. Usually Mary brings me my coffee in the mornings, not because I don't try to do it myself, but because it seems like the woman can read my damn mind. Every time I get up to get something, she's already walking down the hallway with whatever I was heading to the kitchen for.

"Security."

I'm used to vague answers, I've been dealing with men just like Dwayne since I was born. They think because I'm a woman I can't possibly know the truth about what happens behind closed doors.

I pour the coffee into the mug, keeping my back to him as I slowly stir cream into the dark caffeine. At least there's good coffee here, otherwise I would have gone insane by day two. I'd give up every single material thing in my life long before I'll give up good coffee.

I turn and lean against the bench. The kitchen is big enough that although we are directly across from one another, there's still an appropriate amount of space between us.

The idea dancing at the edge of my mind will only make things worse for myself in the long run, but it would be fun. It's been a long time since I've seduced one of the guards just for the hell of it and to incite a reaction from the men in my life. For the first time since I was taken, a glimmer of my old self peaks out from behind the broken woman I've become. After all, I don't want Elijah thinking he's marrying someone he can walk all over. That's not the woman my parents raised me to be.

Dwayne takes another sip of his coffee, his chocolate brown eyes holding mine over the rim of his mug. He's assessing me, trying to decide if he trusts me or not.

"You know your boss has me here against my will, right?" I finally say. Silence has always made me uneasy, but there's something about Dwayne that unsettles me. I should listen to the little voice in the back of my mind begging me to turn my ass around and go back to binge watching *Gossip Girl*, and yet my legs don't move. The thrill of the chase is intoxicating.

"I'm aware."

I crack a smile. "Of course you are. I suppose I'll add you to the list for when my brothers figure out I'm not here because I want to be," my tone is soft and playful, but there's no mistaking the meaning behind my words. It's a threat clear as day, except Saint James don't make threats, we only make promises.

A booming laugh fills the kitchen, bouncing off the cool tiles beneath my feet and causing me to startle. Not enough that Dwayne will notice, but just enough for my heart to skip a beat. "It's cute that you think a man like Elijah will ever let you go."

I shrug. "Even powerful men have their weaknesses." I don't bother telling him that I haven't quite worked out Elijah's yet, but it will come. Men like him and my brothers like to think they're invincible, when in reality they just have so much more to lose. "If I were you, I would be wary of the side you choose." I place my mug back on the counter and move toward the door. I've said all I have to say, and I've placed the threat exactly where it needs to be. Now it's just a matter of who Dwayne is loyal to. Elijah, or himself. If he's smart, he'll do as I've indirectly asked him to, and if he's an idiot, which, let's be honest, is more than likely the case, he'll tell Elijah about our little chat.

"Do you think I don't know what you're doing?" His heat is at my back, so close his breath whispers across my neck. Where I expect to feel excitement, the usual thrill of poking someone in just the right way to incite a reaction, fear grasps my lungs and holds on tight. What the hell was I thinking? All those times I played games with security I had a safety net, I had my parents or my brothers to come save me. But who do I have now? Elijah? He'll probably hang me out to dry just for the fun of it. Just to see me suffer.

"I don't know what you're talking about," I say, forcing my voice to remain even despite the thundering of my heart.

One moment I'm standing in the doorway, ready to make a run for my bedroom, and the next there's an iron arm around my middle and I'm being yanked back into a hard body. "I think you know exactly what you're doing, Snow." He steps us forward until my front is pressed against the wall in the hallway, his rock-hard member pressed against my ass.

For the first time since I walked into the kitchen, I remember I'm dressed in nothing more than a robe. One flick of his wrist and he can have me untied and naked as the day I was born.

"Now you're going to do exactly as I tell you, and maybe I won't tell Elijah what a little whore his woman is," he hisses in my ear.

THIRTY

ELIJAH

Dealing with shit at the docks takes longer than it should, but that's probably only because the people I'm working with don't trust me as far as they can throw me. But every moment I'm away from the house I grow more and more uneasy.

I never thought I would be one of those men who constantly needs to know where his woman was and what she was doing, but Snow changed me the moment she crossed the threshold to the house. For the first time in my life, I have something to lose, and that fact is terrifying.

"I have stuff I need to do," I tell Everett when the sun crosses the horizon. I've already been away for too long and the nagging feeling only grows with each minute that passes. "What do you need from me? I have a few guys I can have work alongside your guys the next time you're expecting a shipment if you need."

Everett watches me for a moment, assessing the offer but then simply nods. "I'll let you know."

Before he can say another word, I'm on my way back to the car. I don't have time for him to ask me anymore questions about my intentions, or to start poking around in my relationship with Snow. At least not until I have a ring on her finger and there's no way they can take her away from me.

I drive well above the speed limit all the way home. No cop in this city is brave enough to pull me over, because they know they won't walk away with their life. The Russo name still holds just as much fear as it always has, even with the death of the rest of my family.

The closer I get to the house, the more uneasiness eats away at my usually calm demeanor. Although now I have her, I wouldn't give Snow up for the world, I understand what my father always said about women being liabilities and feeling anything toward them making you weak. But I don't give a fuck. If anyone in this city wants to challenge me for my woman, they won't be walking away with their heart in their chest.

The brakes screech as I come to a stop, throwing the door open before the car is stationary. I take the front steps two at a time, giving a curt nod to the guards on duty. One of them is missing. What's his name again? Darrell? David? I know it starts with a D.

My thoughts stop in their tracks when I open the door and find said security guard with my woman pushed against the wall, the robe she's wearing barely covers her ass, and his hands are traveling up her thigh toward what I assume is her bare cunt.

Snow's hair is still wet from her shower, and when her ice

blue eyes clash with mine a mixture of fear and relief dance behind them. Her body shakes beneath his touch, but not in the same way she does when I have my hands on her, and if it weren't for the searing rage boiling in my veins, perhaps I would be smug about that.

The guard follows my girl's scared gaze and his eyes clash with my own but he makes no attempt to remove his hands from what belongs to me.

"Boss," he regards me as if we're about to have a casual conversation. As if he doesn't have his filthy hands all over *my* woman.

I take measured steps toward them, keeping my eyes fixed on the guard. If I allow myself to watch Snow I'll snap, and I can't risk her getting caught in the crossfire, not with how deep my anger beats with my heart. "I suggest you remove your hands from my woman before I remove them from your body," I growl, and the sound is barely human. Snow brings out every primal part of me, and I'm barely controlling the monster from tearing him apart.

"I was escorting Miss Saint James back to her quarters," the lie slips from his lips with such confidence most people would believe the words, but when you lie for a living, you see through everyone's bullshit.

"You were not," Snow snaps, shoving at his arms but he has her in a vice grip.

"Shut up, bitch," he snarls, pushing her harder into the wall until she lets out a squeak of pain. The small sound cracks my usually composed mask, and my body moves of its own accord. I grip him around the neck and tear his body from

Snow. He matches me in almost every way, size, weight, muscle, but there's one very important difference between us. My woman has been threatened, and that means I'm more unpredictable and savage than usual and seeing as I've made my name killing people in cold blood, that doesn't bode well for him.

Snow falls to her knees and the front of her robe pulls open as she hits the ground.

I whip Dwayne's body to the side. "Close your fucking eyes because I will not hesitate to gouge them out if you see my woman's tits." The venom in my words makes Snow flinch, her trembling hands rushing to tug the ties closed, but she remains on the ground and pushes herself back until she hits the wall. It's not often Snow shows outward fear, but in the last twenty-four hours I've seen it twice, and I fucking hate it. My woman should fear nothing because she should know that I will never let anything hurt her.

For the first time since his eyes landed on me coming through the door, Dwayne shows his first outward sign of uncertainty. It's only small, a slight shake in his hands when they grip at my arm, trying to pry it away from his neck, but it's there, nonetheless. It's also the first sign this guy never should have been working for me in the first place. To work for me, you need to be cold and ruthless, able to stare death in the face and take a step forward, but this motherfucker would run in the opposite direction if I gave him half a chance.

"She was flirting with me. She wanted me to tell her brothers she's here against her will."

I almost laugh. Perhaps I would if the anger wasn't threatening to tear my body apart. Of course my little spitfire tried to orchestrate an escape, tried to make an alliance with someone on the inside. Hell, I would be surprised if she didn't because if I were in her shoes, I would do the exact same thing. People like us, people who grew up the way we did, we know what needs to be done, and how to appeal to people's baser instincts, including their need to survive.

Snow brings her knees up to her chest, resting her cheek on them as she watches the scene quietly. If that weren't the case, she would rush to correct him, but she remains quiet.

"That may be the case, Dwayne," his name tastes bitter on my tongue, the sound of it only causing the rage to boil higher. "But that does not give you permission to touch what doesn't belong to you." I kick his knees from behind, forcing him to fall to them, but I don't release my grip around his neck. The gun in my waistband burns into my skin, begging to be used to end this asshole's miserable existence.

"Elijah," Snow whispers and when my eyes snap to meet her, I can't tell if she's pleading with me to kill him or spare his life. There's conflict in the ice, as if she isn't sure of that herself. My Snowflake hasn't seen the violence the rest of her family has, but she's about to see what crossing a man like me leads to.

"Hush, Snow. I'll deal with you in a minute."

Her eyes flare with a mixture of fear and arousal, but I don't allow myself to dwell on it for even a second. The man kneeling before me needs to be taken care of before I punish my naughty Snowflake for her attempts to run from me, although clearly not well executed, she still needs to know it will not be tolerated in the future.

"She was begging for it, coming into the kitchen wearing nothing but a robe. I can't be held accountable for that shit."

I dig my forearm farther into his neck, causing the last few words to come out garbled and unclear. If he knows what's good for him, he'll shut the fuck up before he digs himself a shallow grave. But he's an idiot. He thinks I'll side with my men over my woman, and he's dead wrong.

There's only one person in my life who isn't expendable, and she and everyone else are about to find out just how true that is.

THIRTY-ONE

SNOW

I've always been reckless. Call it youngest child syndrome, or the result of growing up in a Mafia family. Call it whatever the fuck you want because it's probably true. I've taken off on international trips with men I met half an hour before departure and danced on tables in dangerous bars. I've flirted with danger more times than I will ever admit to any member of my family, but something tells me I've never been in more danger than I am right now.

Elijah is feral with rage, his moss-green eyes flaming with his anger, and with each moment that passes, his grip on Dwayne only tightens.

The large man's body seems small in my captors embrace, despite them being the same size if they were standing side by side. His eyes dart to mine, the silent plea in the distaste. He thinks I'm going to save him, but if he doesn't realize Elijah has already made up his mind and not even I could change it, he's truly as dumb as he looks.

"Snow," Elijah rumbles, tearing my attention back to his face. His jaw is tightly set, the muscles in his neck flexing under the pressure of his anger. "Go into my office, open the top drawer of my desk and bring me the contents."

There's no room for argument in his words, and while it's in my nature to fight every instruction I'm ever given, I find myself sliding up the wall and padding down the hallway. Since the second night I was here I've assumed this door is always locked, but when I turn the handle and the heavy wood swings open, my chest falters. Surely he hasn't left this open every day I've been here? Surely I haven't had the key to my escape at my disposal and I didn't know it.

I take quick steps toward the desk, not allowing myself to look too closely at the room. If I fall down this rabbit hole now and leave Elijah waiting, something tells me that would be an even bigger mistake than trying to talk my way out of here.

The desk drawer is heavy as I tug it open, the dark wood cracking. The moment my eyes fall on the items along the bottom, I almost slam it shut and walk right out of here. But that would mean poking the psychotic bear, and I don't think that's a good idea. With a deep breath, I lift the gun, knife and rope from the drawer and quickly make my way from the room. I've held weapons, I've even shot guns, but never one that was about to murder someone in cold blood.

When I step back into the hallway my eyes dart to the men still in the same place I left them. Elijah standing with his arm wrapped around Dwayne's neck, restricting his breathing. The sight shouldn't turn me on. It shouldn't make me want to drop my robe and allow Elijah to have his way with me, but there's something inherently sexy about a man being willing to kill for you.

I take measured steps toward the men, keeping my eyes on Elijah because something tells me he's barely holding on to his composure, and if I allow my eyes to wander to the man kneeling at his mercy, he's going to lose it.

He tracks my every move, not taking his gaze off me as I cross to where he's standing, walking against the wall as I pass Dwayne in an irrational gesture of fear. He can't hurt me, not with Elijah holding him by the neck and restricting each breath he's dragging into his lungs.

"Good girl," Elijah praises as I step toward him. "Hand me the rope first." He holds his palm out expectantly and I quickly move to obey. A smirk of approval tugs at the corners of his lips but his attention quickly turns to the task at hand.

I step back until I hit the wall, my hands still held out in front of me with the weapons. My fear of them is irrational seeing as I know how to use them, but it's different when it's a real-life situation and not target practice.

Elijah works methodically to tie Dwayne's arms behind his back and then hooks the knot around his ankles to ensure he can't run. "What did you think was going to happen when I found out you touched my woman?" he asks, the venom in his voice would make even the bravest of men tremble, but Dwayne is holding strong, I'll give him that.

There's only the slightest amount of fear in his eyes, and if I hadn't spent most of my life manipulating the people around me, I probably wouldn't notice it.

"She's the enemy's whore, I didn't think you'd care who touched her so long as she wasn't knocked up."

My stomach churns painfully at the words. What if Elijah didn't come home? What if I was held at his mercy without anyone to come to my rescue?

Elijah lands a heavy punch to his stomach, the wind audibly knocking from his lungs. The man slumps forward, his torso hitting the carpet and making him groan. The way he's tied allows no room to escape, no way to protect himself, and a sick part of me likes it. My brothers have never allowed me to see them hurt anyone, always doing it behind closed doors out of sight of my curious gaze, but this is going to happen in front of me. Elijah's nostrils flare as he circles Dwayne, like a caged animal circling his prey. I'm sure it's not the first time he's been likened to a predator, but something tells me it's the first time the brute who lays bound and immobile has ever been compared to little more than someone's dinner.

"Let me get this straight. You thought that the woman I stole from her family, the one I've been stalking for ten fucking years because my obsession with her runs so fucking deep, you thought she was some disposable piece of meat I would let any of my men take a ride on?" Elijah's words are barely human, the anger beats heavily against the walls to the point I wonder if the neighbors can feel it. Can they feel the chaos that descends upon us?

His words make me flinch, because there's a good chance that's exactly what Dwayne thought. I know how the Mafia normally works although my family has always been different, and more than that, I know how the Russo family works. Women are little more than baby makers and a trophy to wear on your arm, who cares what happens to them when they're not doing one of their two duties?

Dwayne pales slightly as if it's only just occurring to him that maybe things aren't going to go the way he thought they would. "She's not even your wife yet, thought you might like her broken in on your wedding night and we both know that slut is anything but a blushing virgin." His eyes capture mine as I look on with horror, my back pressed so tightly to the wall the cornices dig into my shoulder blades to the point of pain, but the pain keeps me grounded, it reminds me I'm safe… well, as safe as you can be while watching the man who's about to force me to marry him kill another man for daring to lay a hand on me.

The loud crunch that fills the hallway turns my stomach even before I realize what has happened. Elijah's heavy boot retreats from Dwayne's ribs and the next thing I know I'm watching kick after kick land as the other man lays helpless, his screams of agony tearing through the house. Each blow is louder than the last as Elijah descends into the brutal man I know him to be. There's none of the softness I see in his eyes when he looks at me. No, he's like a crazed man craving blood, taking everything he has and delivering it in harsh kicks.

"If you thought you could *ever* be good enough for *my* woman, you're sadly fucking mistaken, and you're going to pay for that mistake with your life."

"I'm sorry, I didn't realize," Dwayne gurgles, lines of blood dripping from his lips.

"You didn't realize she belonged to me?" he bellows, the sound bounces off the walls and echoes through the house. "You didn't realize that not all men are willing to share their belongings?" Another blow and a stomach-churning crunch fill the space. The weapons lay heavy in my trembling palms, and I wish for this to end. My eyes fall on the pistol in my hand, a thought dawning on me.

I'm holding the key to my own escape, so what the hell am I waiting for?

THIRTY-TWO

ELIJAH

I'm known for violence.

The underworld in Chicago bleeds with the evidence of my victims, and even the strongest men in the city cross the street when they see me walking toward them.

But I've never known the thirst for blood like what's beating through my body right now. The motherfucker must have a death wish because that's the only way he would be talking like this about my woman.

Part of me wants to put a bullet between his eyes and rid the earth of his filth, but the other part, the part of me that craves blood and cruelty, wants to drag his death out for hours, maybe even days, making each form of torture worse than the last.

I land another harsh kick to his ribs, making sure to hit the same spot over and over again. It hurts more that way, makes my victim wish for death even though he should know he won't get away with it that easily.

Movement in the corner of my vision tears my gaze from the man crumpled at my feet, and when I bring my eyes up to meet icy blue, my cock twitches in my sweatpants. I'll be the first to admit to being turned on by some fucked-up shit, but this is the first time I've ever had a hard-on while looking down the barrel of a gun.

The corners of my lips quirk up at the sight of Snow holding the weapon in shaky hands, her wide stance is perfect, and her grip on the trigger should worry me, but it doesn't.

She's not going to shoot me. She might think she will, she might even try to, but when push comes to shove, she's going to come to her senses and realize what I knew the moment we locked eyes all those years ago.

We belong together.

It's a simple thought, one that I've been trying to show her, but she's fighting it, and hell, I'm enjoying every ounce of her hesitation. It will only make my victory that much sweeter.

"What are you doing, my little Snowflake?" I ask, my eyes holding hers.

"Let me go," she whispers.

"Or what? You'll shoot me?" I chuckle, taking a step toward her.

Snow flinches at my movement, her back pressing into the wall. If I thought she was capable of pulling the trigger before, I'm sure as hell not now. She's scared of the weapon she's holding, and that just won't do. I can't have my woman afraid of the thing that might be the difference between life and death one day. "Yes."

I nod, taking another step closer to her, my hands held at my sides where she can see them. Although I don't think she'll shoot me, caged animals are capable of all kinds of things when they're trying to escape, and I need to remember I've taken everything away from her. I've torn her life from her grasp and she's not going to go down without a fight. And let's face it, it's her fight that's always kept me on my toes. "Give me the gun, Snow."

"No." She shakes her head, tears pooling at the corners.

I take a breath, allowing some of the rage to fall away as I take another step toward my fractured Snowflake. "So, I let you go, and you don't shoot me, is that the deal?"

Snow nods, the gun shaking slightly as she trembles from the weight of it.

"I see. And you think that I would just allow you to walk away like that? You think I'll just let you go after obsessing over you for ten years?"

What little color she had in her cheeks drains away and her reality settles upon her shoulders. She needs to know there isn't anywhere on this earth she can hide from me. I'll hunt her down like a lion stalks its prey, and when I have her back within my sights, she'll be given none of the freedoms I'm currently willing to afford her.

"If you ever want true freedom, my dear Snowflake, you'll have to kill me."

Her eyes widen at my words, the meaning of them settling over her and doubt crosses her face. Snow isn't a violent person. She doesn't have it in her to be cold and unfeeling like her brothers and me. She's the guiding light that sees me through the darkness of my own soul, and although the only way she will ever truly be granted freedom is by killing me, she's not capable of it.

"So what's it going to be?" I ask, closing the distance between us until the cool barrel presses into my chest. "Do you want your freedom badly enough that you're willing to kill for it? Are you willing to dirty your soul for the sake of escaping me?"

Snow swallows, fear flashing through her eyes. She had to have known I was going to call her out, that I would never believe she was going to pull the trigger and end my life.

"Give me the gun," I demand, my voice soft but there's no mistaking how serious I am.

"No." She shakes her head.

"This only ends one way, Snow. You know there's no escape. You know you can't pull the trigger and you know if you don't, I'll hunt you to the end of the earth."

Tears fall against her pale cheeks, her grip faltering for just long enough for me to grip the barrel and move it away from my chest. Although I'm confident she couldn't pull the trigger and end my life, especially when I've seen the glimmers of affection for me, I would be remiss to underestimate a Saint James, even one as innocent as Snow.

The moment the gun is pointed away from me, I draw her into my arms, holding her fragile body against me as rough sobs claw from her throat. The fear and sadness pour from her like rain on a cloudy winter's day, and she relaxes into my hold, taking the comfort I offer her.

She grips the gun in one hand and my shirt in the other, anchoring herself with her own internal war. She hasn't allowed herself to admit it yet, but she doesn't want me dead, she doesn't even really want to leave here, she just isn't ready to accept it yet. She will though. She'll see just how happy she can be here, how happy I can make her.

Slowly, I move us closer to Dwayne. She needs to be punished for threatening me, and for trying to escape, and I have the perfect way to do it.

"She makes you weak," the bound man gurgles, the corners of his mouth leaking with crimson red. "Your father and uncles understood how a woman should be treated."

"The way they treated women is one of the many reasons they're dead," I growl, pulling Snow from my chest and turning her until her back presses into me. My arm steels across her torso so she can't move away from me. "And now a woman is going to be the one to take your miserable life."

Snow's body stills in my grasp, her breath hitching as my words settle over her. She may not have been able to pull the trigger on me, but she will be ending a life tonight.

THIRTY-THREE

SNOW

His words settle around me, the meaning of them stealing the breath from my lungs. I don't know why I ever thought I could kill Elijah, or that he would let me go if I threatened him for that matter. It was a stupid idea, one I'm sure I'm going to be punished for, one that has led to this moment.

Elijah holds me tightly against his chest, his hard length pressing into my ass. The fabric of the robe is barely long enough for it to cover me, but that's the last of my worries right now.

"I can't," I whisper. My fingers grip the gun so tightly they ache from the pressure. My entire body trembles with a mixture of fear and adrenaline, and more than anything I wish I had stayed in bed this morning. I wish I curled up in Elijah's scent, enjoyed the warmth and safety he gives me even if I'll never admit it to him.

"Yes, you can, Snow," he says, his chin dropping to rest on

my shoulder. The feel of his body pressing into mine makes it hard to think, hard to remember all the reasons I shouldn't want to be here. Elijah's other hand moves to wrap around my wrist, angling the gun until it's pointed at Dwayne's head. "He would have raped you, Snow. If I didn't get here when I did, he wouldn't have hesitated to take your little cunt, no matter how much you screamed, how loud you begged for his mercy, he wouldn't have given it to you."

His words seep into my pores and dread washes over me. He's right. He wouldn't have thought twice about violating me, in fact, he would have *liked* how hard I struggled. I came so close to having something I wasn't willing to give taken from me, but I can't take a life. I'm not capable of that kind of violence. Even if the situation was life or death, I think I'd have a hard time choosing between me or them.

"Please," I murmur, the plea in my words needy and afraid. Begging Elijah is pointless, he doesn't show anyone mercy, and certainly not someone who just held a gun on him.

He grinds his hard cock into my ass and I barely hold the groan from tearing from my throat. Being with Elijah is a contradiction if there ever was one. I don't want to want him. I don't want to want his touch, or his words, or his body, but I do, and perhaps that's the scariest part of this whole situation. I want the monster to take me, and no matter how hard I fight against those instincts, how much I kick and scream against my own thoughts, there's nothing I can do to escape it.

"One way or another, you're going to pull that trigger, Snow. You will end his life for what he planned to do to you."

"I really don't think I can."

He *tsks* in my ear, the disapproving sound grips me around the neck and something inside of me screams to obey him. Maybe it's the Stockholm Syndrome kicking in, or maybe there's something else entirely at work. "From the moment I saw you across the room at that party, I knew you were destined to stand by my side, to rule beside me. And ever since then, I've watched you from the sidelines. I've watched you laugh and cry, I've watched you yell and scream, and I've watched you watch your siblings with jealousy in those pretty blue eyes. Being the youngest always means you're the one everyone underestimates. When it came time for Storm to name a successor, I bet you didn't even get a look in. It was always going to be Rayne or Wynter because you've always been kept away from the dirty part of your family, so why would they put you in charge of it?"

His words sting more than I'll ever admit, but he's right. Every word he's spoken is the truth. I am jealous of my siblings for their roles in the family while I've always been little more than the pretty face at the back of the family portrait.

"This is your chance, Snowflake. You have the chance to rule beside me, to take all the things you always craved within your own family and make them your own. But to do that, you need to spill blood. Your brothers have done it, even your sister, but they've kept you in the dark, away from the violence, and away from your true potential."

My fingers tremble around the cool metal, the barrel pointed right at Dwayne who watches me quietly. He doesn't think I'll do it either, he sees me as the weak little girl the rest of the world sees me as, but that's not me. I'm stronger than anyone has ever given me credit for, I just don't know if it will pull me through killing a man.

"Do it," Elijah says calmly, his breath whispers across my cheek and causes a shiver to force its way through my body.

I shake my head, it's too much.

"Do it," his words are louder than before as one of his hands wraps around my wrist, making sure my aim on the bound man at our feet is just right.

I take a deep breath and hold it, unable to allow my body the freedom of breathing when I'm about to do something so heinous. It seems completely irrelevant that this man deserves to die, or that if I don't kill him, he could attack another woman just the way he attacked me.

"Do it," Elijah yells. The anger radiates from his body, the heat of his fury enough to take my breath away. "Fucking do it, Snow."

The loud bang echoes off the walls of the hallway before I even realize I've pulled the trigger. The moment I realize what I've done, the gun slips from my fingers and hits the ground in a heavy thud. I just killed a man. I took his life in a moment because the man who holds me captive told me to.

Tears pool at the corners of my eyes as I bring both hands up to cover my mouth. How could I have done that? It makes me nothing more than the monster I shared a bed with last night.

Elijah's arms wrap around my waist and hold me tightly, as if he can feel how close I am to falling apart.

"Why did you make me do that?" I whisper. I'm not sure why they're the first words I think to say after murdering the man who almost raped me, but they slip from my lips before I have the chance to catch them.

"Because you need to see yourself the way I see you, Snow."

"So you see me as a murderer then?" I hiss. "Good to know." I shove my elbows back into his torso, hoping it will be enough for him to let up his grip around me, but if anything, he holds me closer.

"No, Snow. I see you as a warrior. I see you as the only woman on this earth worthy of standing by my side. You think I want you to be the weak little woman at home that I'm going to toss away one day, but that's not what I want. That's not why you're here." He spins me so quickly my churning stomach protests and a moment later, I'm pinned against the wall with his hard body pressing into mine, holding me in place. "You're here because I need a woman with a strong stomach and the strength to lead. I saw it in you the first day I saw you, even when you were young you were so much more than anyone ever gave you credit for, and now you can prove them all wrong. You can prove to everyone who thought you were the weak Saint James that that's the furthest thing from the truth. You were born to rule, just the same way I was. And together, we will be unstoppable."

THIRTY-FOUR
ELIJAH

Her eyes are wide and her mouth slightly open as she stares at me like I've lost my mind. Little does she know when you grow up the way I did, you're always going to be at least a little unhinged. And I've always leaned into the more psychotic tendencies that call to me.

Snow's entire body shakes like a leaf, to the point I worry she may be cold, but it's just the adrenaline coursing through her veins, taking over every fiber of her being. Although I have taken more lives than I've cared to count, I can appreciate how hard this must be for her.

My dear Snowflake has lived a sheltered life. Her family has kept her away from the more unsavory parts of their legacy, and she's managed to escape a lot of the usual realities of a Mafia princess. But if she's going to stand by my side, if she's going to rule our kingdom with me, she needs to get very familiar with those sides of the business.

I brush my fingers down her cheek, cutting through the tears as they fall. She's beautiful when she cries. Her vulnerability only makes my cock harden further and knowing she's naked beneath her robe only makes me want to pick her up and slide right into her wet heat.

She closes her eyes, breaking the contact and a rough growl claws up my throat. She's hiding from me, trying to put up walls so I won't see her fall apart. But I want to see it. I want to tear Snow apart until she's nothing, and then build her up until she's the queen I know she can be.

"Snowflake," I murmur, my fingers trailing down until they wrap gently around her throat. Her eyes pop open as if remembering she shouldn't turn her back on the monster who keeps her captive. "I'm sure you must be very upset right now—"

"Upset?" she squeaks, her arms squeezing between us in an attempt to shove me away. "You think I'm upset? I just killed a man. I just ended someone's life. He could have a wife and children! He probably has parents who never got to say goodbye to him. I'm much more than upset."

The fire burning in her eyes makes it that much harder to stop myself from pulling my sweatpants down and slamming into her cunt. She looks like she's ready to punch me in the face, and I wish she would. I crave the pain, need it even, and having it dished out by Snow would only make it that much better.

I fight the smirk tugging at my lips, hoping my amusement isn't too clear in my eyes.

"I hate you," Snow yells, the venom in her voice like a slap to the face. "I fucking hate you. All you've brought me is pain.

You stole me from my life. You're threatening to keep me from my family if I don't marry you, and you just forced me to kill someone. I hate you so fucking much."

This is the Snow Saint James I crave. The one who is so angry at the world, angry at everything, and that shows it without thinking to hide that part of herself. I've seen snippets of this version of her over the years, small moments where I saw the window into her soul. Underneath all the beauty and the image she portrays to the world is the most vibrant and extraordinary woman I've ever seen. She's strong and confident, full of fire and passion, and she's the woman I want by my side for the rest of our lives. She's the woman I want as the mother of my children.

One of her hands snakes out from my hold, and a moment later her fist connects with my cheek. The way her face twists in agony I wouldn't be surprised if she's broken her hand, but the movement is hot as hell and before I can think twice about it, I'm tightening my hand around her throat and grinding my rock-hard length against her. The robe rises with each grind, and I'm tempted to tear the thing from her body and claim her the way I've craved since the moment I slid the needle into her neck and she lost consciousness in my arms. But I manage to hold on to my carefully crafted composure.

"Is that how you want it, Snow?" I growl, my fingers biting into the soft flesh until I'm sure my fingerprints will be burned into her skin.

"I *want* you to let me go. I *want* to go back to my life. I *want* to go back to a time before I knew what it felt like to murder a man. Those are all things I want," she hisses, her voice croaking from the pressure on her throat. If I had it my way she would be on her knees putting her mouth to better use, but right now I have a better idea. If she wants to see me as a monster, that's exactly what I'll be.

I shove her back toward my office, her feet tripping over themselves as she stumbles in front of me. Her body stiffens in my hold and her fear permeates the air. I can almost hear her thoughts. Have I pushed him too hard? Is he going to kill me?

No, my sweet Snowflake. I'm not going to kill you. I'm going to claim you. I'm going to stake my claim on every bit of your delectable body and allow the baser parts of me to come out to play. And you're going to love every single second of it.

THIRTY-FIVE

SNOW

All the anger I felt moments ago, all the rage that built up inside me and mingled with the guilt of my own actions, drains from my body and all that remains is terror. I've pushed him too far. I've pushed and I've pushed, and then punched him. I punched the scariest fucking man in this city and thought I was going to walk away from it?

I've done some dumb shit in my life, but honestly, this might take the cake. Elijah Russo is not a man to be messed with. He's not someone you hit and walk away from, and why would I be any exception? He claims to care for me, claims to have real feelings for me, but that affection can only run so deep before his brutality takes over.

The moment he bends me over his desk, both hands bound behind my back with what feels a lot like a tie, I know my time is almost over. All the false bravado I've shelled out withers away and all that remains is the pathetic princess everyone has always accused me of being. But there's no one to save me now, no one to swoop in and pluck me from the bad situation

I've found myself in. It's just Elijah and me.

Quiet sobs tear from my throat despite my attempts to swallow them. I don't want him to think I'm weak. If I'm going to die right here with my bare ass in the air and my arms bound behind my back, I at least want to do it with some dignity. Tears roll down my cheeks and drip onto the papers beneath my face, but Elijah doesn't seem to care about the contents on his desk. In fact, I can't tell what the hell he's doing behind me. He hasn't said a word since he hauled me in here, and the deathly silence is beginning to weigh on my frayed nerves.

When warm fingers brush across the top of my thighs, my robe doing nothing to keep my modesty intact, I jump. Where I expected his touch to be rough, it's gentle, and I idly wonder whether he's trying to lead me into a false sense of security.

A man like Elijah probably enjoys playing with his food before he eats it, toying with it until it can't take it anymore, and then pushing even harder. It's the game of cat and mouse I thought I could play and win, but I've come out the other side nothing more than a lion's next meal.

Elijah's hands travel up the backs of my thighs until they reach my bare ass, and the groan that tears from his throat almost isn't human. The sound is as if he's in pain, like the sight of my almost naked body spread out across his desk is painful for him to see, and maybe it is. Maybe he's coming to terms with the fact he has to kill his plaything. That's all I've ever been to him, a toy for him to stalk until the time came to start playing with me in person.

"I may be a monster in this city, Snow. I may kill people without a second thought and demand respect everywhere I go. I may rule with an iron fist and torture those who wrong me. But when it comes to you." He pauses, as if he isn't sure the words he's about to utter are a good idea. "You make me consider things I've never considered before. I don't like to see you in pain or upset," he admits, and my heart does a somersault despite my better judgment. I'm still fairly confident he's leading me into a false sense of security, giving me time to calm down, talking me off my paranoid ledge only for him to throw me back over when I least expect it. But try telling my heart that. The battered organ that no one has ever cared about rejoices at the idea of someone, anyone, caring about us in a way that isn't purely one-sided.

"Then why did you make me do that?" I ask, swallowing the lump in my throat just enough for me to force the words out.

"Like I told you, Snow. You're my woman, you will bear my heirs, and I need you to stand by my side. I'm not a good man, and I've never claimed to be. So I need you to be able to swallow the darker sides of me and my life, and spilling blood is a part of that." His fingers slip beneath the front of the robe, gently tugging the ends of the tie until it parts. If my wrists weren't bound behind my back, I would tug it closed again, trying to save some of the modesty Elijah keeps stealing from me.

There's movement behind me, but I don't bother lifting my cheek from the wooden desk. I'm powerless, and fighting will only make it hurt more. All I can hope for now is that whatever he has planned won't kill me or leave me permanently scarred.

The sound of a magazine clipping into a gun fills my ears and causes my body to flinch. I'm not sure I'll ever be able to be near a gun again without wanting to throw up from the memory of what I did. When the cool metal brushes across the back of my thigh, my stomach lurches painfully. One minute he's saying I'm going to be the mother of his children, and the next, he's caressing a gun over my bare skin.

"You never seemed scared of guns when you were learning to shoot with your brothers," he muses and my stomach flips uncomfortably. How does he know that? Wynter and I learned to handle guns at the estate, there's no way an outsider should know so much about the intricate parts of my life behind the gates of our family home.

"How do you…" I trail off, thinking better of questioning the man who holds all the cards while I wait for him to show me his hand.

"How do I know?" The cool metal moves up until it's pressed against the curve of my ass. An involuntary shiver brushes across my skin, and I honestly can't tell whether it's from the adrenaline, fear or something I'm not willing to entertain, but Elijah's quiet chuckle tells me he notices the small bumps that appear across my backside, and he's satisfied with what he sees. "I feel as if I keep telling you how deeply obsessed I have been with you from the moment I saw you, but I don't think you're truly understanding what I'm telling you, my sweet Snowflake."

The gun moves back to my thigh, brushing across the sensitive flesh on the inside, so close to my core that my breath catches in my throat. His words settle over me. Just how closely was he watching me all these years? Of course it's occurred to me that at some stage, he had to have been at the estate to know so much about my bedroom, but it never occurred to me that he was a constant fixture in my life from the shadows. A constant presence I was never aware of.

When the cool metal makes contact with my folds, I lurch forward, the fronts of my hips slamming into the corner of the desk in a move that makes me hiss in pain.

Elijah's hand clamps down on my lower back, his fingers dig into me so hard I'm sure there will be bruises there later. "Stay still, Snow. You'll only make it hurt if you struggle."

A fresh wave of tears fall against my cheeks as fear grips me by the throat. I almost can't breathe through the panic that claws at my insides to the point of pain.

"Elijah," I whimper.

I'm not in the habit of begging for anything. Even in the bathroom at the restaurant when I begged him not to keep my family from me was a moment of weakness, but right now, I'm ready to drop to my knees and plead for my life. I'm not ready to die. I don't want to miss out on Wynter having a baby and getting married, and I don't want to miss those things for myself either. It's not my time yet.

"Please don't kill me," I whisper the words before I can think better of them.

"Oh, little Snowflake. I'm not going to kill you," he says, his other hand moving to rub my back in comforting circles. It's almost enough to soothe me, but when he starts to speak again, I know I'm not going to like what he's about to say. "What I am going to do is make you come all over this gun, and then I'm going to claim you the way I've been craving since the moment I laid eyes on you."

THIRTY-SIX

ELIJAH

As soon as the words leave my mouth, a tremble of fear and anticipation forces its way through Snow's body. She's stiff as a board bent over my desk, her cheek pressed into the cool wood and her hands bound behind her back.

I drag the barrel of the gun through her wet folds. I'll admit, I didn't expect my little Snowflake to get off on being fucked with a weapon, but if her pretty cunt is anything to go by, she's craving my touch in any way I give it to her.

Her wetness coats the barrel, and I can't help but groan at the sight. Who would have thought my innocent little Mafia princess could murder a man in cold blood, and then be aroused almost immediately afterward.

I press the tip against her tight opening, placing a hand on her lower back to hold her in place. She can't get very far anyway, not with me right behind her and her hands bound, but I want complete control. I want her every move to be dictated by me, her every breath to be with my permission. It's what I crave and what my little Snowflake will learn to give me.

"Elijah," she breathes. My name on her lips is like a quiet prayer, halfway between a plea and a moan, and if I heard it over and over again every day for the rest of my life, I would die a happy man.

The moment the barrel slips past through her entrance, we both let out a groan and a smirk tugs at the corners of my lips. She *likes* it. Once the gun is seated inside her, I hold it still and say, "Beg."

Snow's body stills beneath mine and her breath catches in her throat at the command. If I didn't already know she wasn't used to dominant men in the bedroom, every time I've issued a demand since she was carried into this house would have told me everything I need to know.

A violent tremble overtakes her tiny frame and even my rough grip on her back doesn't do anything to calm her. The part of me that's obsessed with her and would kill anyone who dared to harm her wants to bundle her up in my arms and hold her until she stops shaking, but the savage man I've always been, the one who takes whatever I want, whenever I want, and doesn't give a fuck about anyone else, pushes his way to the front.

"I said beg, Snow," I growl. "Don't make me ask again."

A quiet sob fills the room, her tears falling against her cheeks and dripping onto the papers beneath her face.

"Elijah," she cries, and it almost breaks my resolve, but I stand my ground, the monster holding on to us both without regard. "Please." The word is so quiet I almost miss it, but it's enough. It won't always be the case, but I've already pushed her so far today, I can't keep pushing without being willing to bend a little.

Slowly, I withdraw the gun until only the tip is inside her, and then I'm pushing it back into her tightness. Watching her tight cunt wrap around the barrel is almost enough for me to abandon this entire plan and fuck her within an inch of her life, but that will come. We both need to show a little patience.

Snow whimpers as I push the barrel deeper into her, the foreign feeling of metal clashing with her own need has her hands clawing at one another around the tie Mrs. Chambers put in my desk drawer in case of an emergency. It's the first time it's come in handy.

"Does my dirty girl like having a gun in her cunt?" I grind out.

She shakes her head against the desk, but by the way her pussy grips around the gun and her arousal coating the inside of her thighs, she's only lying to herself.

"Little liar," I murmur, releasing my hand from her back and moving it to the sensitive bundle of nerves between her legs. The moment my fingers brush against her clit, Snow lurches forward. "You're going to come around the gun, Snow, and you're going to do it exactly when I say so. Do you understand?"

"I can't," she whispers, the words almost completely absorbed by her sobs.

"You can and you will, Snow. It wasn't a question, it's an order," I growl. I start drawing gentle circles into her clit, the motion at complete odds with the way I'm abusing her pretty pussy with the gun, but the combination of hard and soft only seems to make her drip more. I'll never be able to use this gun again, never be able to wash her sweet scent from the metal or taint it with blood and death. I'll keep it as a trophy, a reward for the first time I fucked my Snowflake. Maybe I'll even frame it and show it to people when they visit. Now there's an idea.

A broken sob cracks through and her body shakes with the violence of it, but I don't relent. She's going to do as she's told, and she's going to do it when I tell her because my patience is wearing thin. All I can think about as I watch the barrel disappear through her soaking wet folds is my cock doing the same thing, and it's my own personal version of torture.

My eyes roam over her luscious curves, feasting on every bit of creamy skin I've uncovered. Her back and arms are still covered with the robe, but I'll rectify that as soon as she comes. I want her naked body splayed out in front of me like a sacrificial offering. The thought only makes me more impatient to get inside her tight body.

"Come right now, Snow. Come all over the gun and then you can have my cock."

"Elijah," she murmurs.

"Right the fuck now, Snow," I demand.

The moment her orgasm takes over her body is the most beautiful fucking thing I've ever seen in my life. I've seen her come plenty of times, more times than I'll ever admit to her. Sometimes at her own hand, sometimes at the hand of others, but the way her pussy grips the barrel in a vice grip and her body tightens with ecstasy, it's the most intoxicating thing

I've ever seen. Nothing has ever been as beautiful as Snow falling apart in front of me.

As soon as her body relaxes, spent from the power of her orgasm, I withdraw the gun and place it on the desk beside her head. Snow's exhausted eyes watch my movement and widen the moment she sees the clip is missing.

She must think pretty poorly of me to think I would endanger her life by shoving a loaded gun in her cunt. The unspoken accusation makes my nostrils flare with anger. I keep telling her what she means to me, and yet she continues to think the worst of me. It's not altogether surprising, I have killed more people with my bare hands than any other man in the city, but it still has rage beating through my veins.

As if noticing my anger, Snow flinches when I reach for the tie at her wrists and it only makes my jaw clench harder. After all the things I've told her, how can she think I would harm her physically?

I growl long and low, the sound escaping my throat despite my best efforts to swallow it. The moment her hands are untied, I scoop her up and carry her from the office, leaving the well-used gun on the desk to deal with later.

"Elijah," Snow whimpers, fear flashing across the ice blue of her eyes. I hate that I scare her, but it has its advantages. She's always more compliant when she's afraid.

I don't respond, simply carrying her through the house until we reach our bedroom. I kick the door closed behind me, the paintings on the walls rattling with the force of it. I prowl toward the bed and throw her in the center, watching as her robe falls open, exposing one of her breasts. The rosy peak at the center tells me all I need to know. Snow is turned on by her fear. I knew it when I made her blow me last night, I knew it as I fucked her with my favorite weapon, and I know it now as I stare at her.

My little Snowflake is every bit the deviant I hoped she would be.

THIRTY-SEVEN

SNOW

The way Elijah watches me can only be described one way.

A predator stalking his prey.

That should terrify me. I should be running as fast as I can and fighting like my life depends on it, which, let's face it, it does. And yet I'm rooted to the bed, unable to make a move. I'm vaguely aware of my robe falling off my shoulder, but when his eyes track down my body and feast on my bare breast, I can't find it in me to cover myself. He's seen it all before anyway. Considering the number of times he's referred to stalking me. I'm sure he's seen them a whole bunch of times.

"Robe," Elijah says simply. He doesn't need to say another word for me to know what he's asking, and before I can really think through what I'm doing, I slip it off my shoulders and allow it to pool around me. When cool air hits my heated skin, goose bumps assault me, and a shiver brushes down my spine. "Good girl."

My skin heats at his praise, a flush spreading from my chest up to my cheeks and he seems to like what he sees.

Slowly, so fucking slowly it almost hurts, Elijah reaches for the back of his shirt and tugs it over his head to reveal his perfectly sculpted chest. This man is a work of art, but when you take a moment to take in his tattoos as well, Jesus Christ, God was doing some of his finest work the day he made Elijah Russo.

The intricate lines spread across his vast chest, down his toned abdomen, and disappear into the waistband of his sweatpants. The images inked into his arms are so beautiful they almost look like the art on the wall. Gods and goddesses cover every spare inch of skin and it's on the tip of my tongue to ask what inspired him to have himself permanently marked with mythological beings. But I can't bring myself to ruin this moment, to break the trance we're both held in.

Elijah takes a step toward the bed. His abs flex with the movement and I press my legs together to ease the ache. How can a man so large and savage move with such grace? It almost seems unnatural.

"Do you like what you see, Snowflake?" he asks, his voice a low rumble.

My breath catches in my throat. I'm still not convinced he's not going to hurt me for holding a gun on him and giving him an ultimatum, but the way he looks at me with pure fire and lust, there's something in the way his eyes roam across my body that tells me if he was going to hurt me, he would have done it already.

"I asked you a question, Snow. I'm not a patient man, don't

mistake me for being one."

"Yes," I murmur the answer into the quiet room, the only sounds are our heavy breaths mixing together as he gets closer to the edge of the bed. My pussy aches from his rough treatment and the hardness of the gun. I've never had anything that wasn't meant to be used for fucking in my pussy before, and the burn is a constant reminder of what he just did to me.

The entire time he was thrusting the weapon into me, I was expecting it to go off. Part of me thought when I came would be the moment he pulled the trigger and ended my life, like some kind of fucked-up poetic justice. But when I realized it was never loaded, it was like I could breathe again after being held underwater for so long I thought I might drown.

A deviant smirk tugs at the corners of his lips, and a moment later, he's pushing his sweatpants down his muscular thighs and discarding them across the room. He's not wearing anything underneath, and when I focus on his hard cock, I can't help but swallow in a combination of need and terror. He's huge. Way bigger than any other guy I've ever been with, and not by a small margin. My jaw still aches from when he fucked my mouth, I can't imagine my pussy is going to fare any better.

The way he moves toward me is predatory. It doesn't matter if this isn't what I want, or if I kick and scream until my lungs give out. Elijah is going to take exactly what he wants, and right now, that's me. I'd be lying to myself if I said I didn't want this. Despite my better judgment and all the reasons I *should* fight, I don't want to. I enjoy the way my skin heats when his eyes rake down my body, and the way a tingle of need spreads through me every time his fingers brush across my skin. I'm addicted to how I feel when I'm with him, including how fucking terrified I am at how unpredictable he is. Perhaps that's part of the appeal. I've always craved going against the grain, breaking the rules just for the sake of it. And what's considered more of a broken rule than fucking the enemy?

"If you keep looking at me like that, Snowflake, I'm going to start thinking you want me to fuck you," he rumbles. The deep tone of his voice makes my legs press together of their own accord. Despite my recent orgasm, I need relief almost as badly as I need my next breath.

When his muscular thighs meet the edge of the mattress, he pauses and watches me for long moments. Every movement I make, from the slight quiver of my lip under his scrutiny to the way my body trembles with a mixture of fear and need, his watchful gaze only seems to escalate it. My heart beats so hard in my chest I'm afraid it's going to leap across the room, and if I didn't know better, I would think Elijah can sense it. But he's too far away to see my pulse beating in my neck.

Elijah chuckles, his knees digging into the mattress one at a time as he crawls toward me. The moment his body brushes over mine, a shiver makes its way up my spine. He's right, I do want this. I want it so badly I can barely breathe through it, but I'm not ready to admit that to him yet, not when he's been able to best me at every turn.

"Is your pussy craving my cock, little Snowflake?" he murmurs, his head dropping until his lips whisper across my neck and leave goose bumps in their wake.

"No," I lie.

Elijah sinks his teeth into the soft flesh of my throat, and I hiss at the sudden pain. "Don't lie to me, Snow. I've made a lot of allowances for you, more than I ever would anyone else, but I will not tolerate you denying what we both know."

My breath catches in my throat. How does he always know? Every time I've lied to him, even when I've merely kept something from him, he's known.

"Now, try again. Is your sweet little cunt craving my cock? Do you want me to fuck you so hard you forget your own fucking name?"

"Yes," I whisper into the space between us. His face is so close to mine it would be easy to press my lips to his, but I fight against the pull.

"That's what I thought." He smiles smugly, pressing his knees forward until my thighs are wrapped around his body and his cock is nestled at my entrance. "Now I'm not going to make you beg, although you are so pretty when you do. But you will ask nicely."

I stare at him blankly for a moment, thinking he must be joking since the two things are so similar, but when there isn't a trace of amusement dancing in his green eyes, I know he's as serious as he is about everything else. My mouth dries at the idea of asking for something I swore I would never want, but who am I to deny my own pleasure? And even if I were strong enough to do so, Elijah Russo isn't a man who takes no for an answer.

THIRTY-EIGHT

ELIJAH

Snow's breaths are coming in hard and fast and I haven't even touched her. Watching her chest rise and fall with sharp desperate pants is almost enough to send me off the edge of my restraint and sink so deep inside her sweet pussy that she feels my cock in her throat. But something tells me that won't do me any good right now.

Her arousal is thick in the air, her thighs damp with the evidence of her need, but she's fighting with herself. The conflict in her eyes would normally only make me want to take what I want more, but Snow is the only person on this planet that makes me pause before doing things. Her feelings, her safety, what she wants, it all matters to me where it's never mattered in the past. Hell, I was relieved when my entire family was slaughtered because it saved me from having to do it myself.

Her pink tongue darts across her lips, but her eyes never move from mine, watching my every move. She's smart to keep her eyes on the monster in the room, but when I decide to strike, there will be nothing she can do to temper my need for her. She takes a deep breath, only barely settling her rapid breathing enough for words to form. "Please fuck me," she murmurs as if she doesn't trust her own voice.

I barely suppress the growl that claws up my throat. The words are like the sweetest victory I've ever had, but it's not enough. I need more. I suspect I'll always want more from Snow. No matter how much she gives me, I'll take and take, and when she has nothing left to give, I'll demand it anyway.

"I know you can do better than that, my little Snowflake," I force through gritted teeth. My entire body screams at me to touch her, to reach out and wrap my hand around her throat and show her who's in charge, but I remain perfectly still, waiting for her to do as she's told.

She drags her bottom lips between her teeth, the soft pillow disappearing as she considers her next words. "Elijah, please fuck me." The plea falls from her pouty lips like a prayer, and I almost snap, almost pin her down and slide into the paradise between her legs, but she isn't finished. "I need you." The admission is so quiet I would have missed it if I hadn't been watching her as closely as I am.

A moment later, I close the distance between us, her body spreading out beneath me as I cover every inch of her. She seems so tiny when we're like this. My body covers the entirety of hers with plenty to spare.

"See, look at the rewards you get when you behave," I murmur as I press kisses to her neck. I slide my cock through her wet folds, careful not to allow myself too close to her entrance just yet.

"I don't have your cock, so I wouldn't call it a reward just yet."

I huff out a laugh. If any other woman said that to me, if they even dared to think it, I would have them over my knee and punish them for their transgressions. But not Snow. As much as I relish the thought of her bent over with a red ass, I find her sass amusing, and perhaps that's just another sign that I've found the woman who is meant to stand at my side. "Touché."

I wrap my palm around my cock and slide the head through her wet heat. Fuck, it's like heaven and I haven't even felt her tightness yet.

"Is my Snowflake feeling impatient?" I rumble. The more of her wetness that coats my length, the harder it is to hold myself back from sliding deep into her tight cunt.

"Just fuck me already." She lifts her hips from the mattress, watching me with hooded eyes as she angles her hips to line me up with her entrance.

I close my eyes for the briefest of moments to collect my control. She tests me at every turn. Every bit of discipline I've learned over the years, every bit of carefully crafted control that was forced onto me as a child, it all crumples the moment Snow's sweet scent and perfect body are near. "What have I told you about trying to call the shots?"

Snow smirks, her perfect mouth turning up in a genuine, unfiltered moment. The cracks in her armor become more obvious with each day that passes, and none more than right now. Her body is so wound up that her mind can't tell her how bad an idea this is. For the first time since she arrived, she isn't thinking about the life I stole from her, or how I've threatened to keep her from her family, or about the man I just forced her to murder. No, all Snow can think about right now is my cock, and that knowledge only makes it more difficult to control myself.

"I'm not sure. You might need to remind me." The words are full of lust and it's all I can do not to give into the monster trying to tear his way from my chest, craving the treat laid out in front of me.

I shake my head, giving my rock-hard cock a few quick strokes. I've never been this turned on before. I've never needed to fuck more than I do right now. "You're poking the bear, Snow."

"Good, maybe he'll eat me."

Another laugh tumbles from my throat, and the sound almost startles me. In a life like mine, full of anger and pain and evil, there isn't much opportunity for laughter. In fact, it was always frowned upon. Any emotion makes you vulnerable, it shows your enemies exactly where they need to hit to hit you the hardest, and a Russo can't risk that. But Snow brings out the man I never had the opportunity to be.

The moment my cock notches at her entrance, we both let out an impatient moan. She doesn't realize this, and although she was never leaving before, the moment I sink into her will be the end of any chance she had at continuing in the life she used to lead. The sooner my ring is on her finger and my baby is growing in her belly, the better.

"Elijah," she whines, the need in her voice almost enough to break my composure. "I asked nicely."

I drop my head forward and chuckle, fuck, this woman keeps

me on my toes. Every time I've ever thought I had her figured out, she surprises me with a new layer of herself.

"That you did," I murmur, pressing my hips forward just enough for her to stretch around the head of my cock. Feeling her wrapped around me has a feral growl clawing up my throat, and this time I can't hold it back. The sound is primal, as if the monster inside me knows we're about to claim our woman.

It's on the tip of my tongue to tell Snow that this is it, that once her cunt has wrapped around my length for the first time, there will be no escaping her fate. But I'm a selfish bastard, and I know all telling her will do is make her fight me while I take what belongs to me. I like it better when she's compliant, when she looks at me with hooded eyes and asks me nicely to fuck her. My eyes lock at the place where we're barely joined. Just the tip of my cock breaching her tightness, but it's the single most erotic thing I've ever seen in my life. It's like her cunt was made for me, as if somewhere along the way, her body was crafted just for me to claim.

I take a deep breath and push forward through her folds, a long groan breaking from my chest as I sink farther into her until I'm fully seated inside her.

"Holy fuck," Snow breathes, her body trembling beneath mine.

There are no words for the pleasure shooting up my spine or how perfectly she takes me. I hold myself still for long moments, desperately trying to grasp on to the composure I hold in every other aspect of my life. But I should know by now that Snow challenges everything I've ever known and everything I've ever been.

THIRTY-NINE

SNOW

The moment Elijah starts moving again is like I can finally draw in a full breath. Like my body doesn't know how to breathe without him anymore.

Elijah's jaw is tight as he thrusts forward in sharp snaps, the force of which makes me ache. He's not gentle, but then I didn't expect him to be. It's not like the first time I've fucked any other guy, there isn't the slow start as we try to figure each other out. No, Elijah seems to know everything about my body without me having to say a word.

"Your cunt is squeezing the hell out of me," he grunts the words through clenched teeth. The man who's always in control looks ready to throw caution to the wind and fuck me like I crave, but I've already conceded too much to him. I've already begged him to fuck me with a gun and played right into his hands by asking him to claim me.

I can't allow myself to give him anything else or to let him know just how much he affects me.

I press my head back into the mattress, dragging my eyes from his in an attempt to stamp down the intimacy of the moment. I've never done anything close to making love. In fact, I've laughed at people who use that phrase on a regular basis. But what Elijah is doing to me right now and the way my body is reacting… it's as close as I've ever been. My heart beats heavily in my chest, each thump more painful than the last.

"Eyes on me, Snowflake." The rumble of his voice startles me into doing as he says before I've consciously thought about what I'm doing. He's pleased by my submission, and I want to hate it. I want to fight against him and tear my eyes from his, but I don't.

Elijah moves with measured strokes, his hips meeting mine with each thrust, his hands planted on either side of my head. We're too close. His heat is almost suffocating. Being surrounded by him makes it hard to breathe, and yet I know the moment he pulls away I'll gasp for the air he provides.

I wrap my legs around his waist, unable to hold back my own desperation for him. My hips raise to meet his, and his eyes flare with a fire I've never seen before. I've seen him angry, I've seen him turned on, and I may have even seen him happy on a couple of occasions. But I've never seen him lose the control he holds on to.

"Fuck, Snow," he groans, his pace picking up into a wild rhythm of skin slapping together and the sound of my wetness filling the room. Perhaps I would be embarrassed by the sound if it were anyone else plowing into me, but by the way Elijah stares at me like my pussy is made of gold, I can't find it in me to be anything other than turned the fuck on.

For the first time since I've been here, I reach for him. I reach for Elijah and trail my fingers down his bare chest, committing every tattoo, scar, and hard muscle to memory. Perhaps he means it when he says that I'm it for him and there's nowhere for me to run, but I've been the disappointment my entire life. Why would this be any different? It's only a matter of time before Elijah realizes that, and if he allows me to live, I want to remember every last second of this.

"Touch yourself," he demands.

I immediately snake my hand between our bodies, seeking the bundle of nerves that will inevitably throw me over the edge of the cliff into an oblivion I'm not sure I'm ready for.

"You're much more compliant with my cock inside you," Elijah muses between thrusts. "Perhaps I'll need to keep you impaled at all times so you're always a good girl for me."

My cheeks heat at his words, and I expect anger to overwhelm me, but instead my pussy pulses around him and drags a long moan from both of us.

"Do you like that idea, Snowflake? Do you want my cock inside you all the time?"

"Yes." The word tumbles from my lips as I approach my orgasm. The power of his thrusts mixed with my own petting brings me to the brink and I hover there, dragging my bottom lip between my teeth as I fight against the power of it.

A snarl forms on his lips as if he's barely containing the other side of him, the one the rest of the world sees. "You'll get very good at controlling your orgasms, Snow, but right now, I want to feel your cunt come around me."

I suck in a breath, barely holding myself back from doing as he wants, but there's something in the back of my mind that keeps my orgasm just out of reach. Perhaps it's the fact that the moment I fall apart in his arms, I'll never be able to put myself together again without him. But I can't focus on it for more than a second before the pleasure tears me back to my body.

"Now, Snow. Don't make me ask again." His words come on a growl, his jaw set so tight I'm worried it might snap.

As if my body can't deny him, every muscle tightens, and then all at once, release, taking me over the edge into an oblivion I've only ever read about. The intensity has my lungs seizing in my chest, unable to drag in a breath around the pleasure holding my body hostage.

Elijah's thrusts are brutal but measured, each one drawing ecstasy from me like it's his personal mission in life.

When I finally start to come down, my body limp with exhaustion, his eyes flare with the need to consume me.

"Fuck, Snow," he groans. "That was the sexiest fucking thing I've ever seen in my life." He doesn't slow, not even for a moment, his hips pistoning into me as he chases his own release.

That thought brings me back to a sobering reality, and all the mellow I felt only seconds ago drains from my body, leaving behind nothing but dread.

"Stop," I say, immediately pushing at his chest. But he doesn't budge, so unaffected by my demand that he doesn't slow for even a second. "Elijah, I said stop," I yell.

"I don't think so, Snowflake." He moves one of his hands

from where it was planted beside my head to rest at my throat. There's no pressure under his hold, but it's a warning. He's telling me without words that there's nothing I can say or do that will make him change his mind.

"You can't come inside me."

A self-satisfied grin crosses his face and his thrusts speed up. "I can and I will, Snow."

The blood drains from my face, my entire body shaking at the meaning behind his words. Tears form at the corners of my eyes and trickle down my cheeks, my chest constricting with terror. I'm not on any birth control—and he knows it.

I don't know how he knows I was meant to get my next shot the day after he took me, or that I was already three weeks late because I lost track of time around the wedding and losing my parents, but it's clear he does.

As if stealing me from my family, forcing me to stay here with him, and making me murder a man wasn't bad enough, now he wants to hit me with the ultimate blow.

He wants to get me pregnant, and there's not a damn thing I can do about it.

FORTY

ELIJAH

The look of horror on her face is almost enough to make me pause. Almost, but not quite.

The primal need to mark her is more than I can argue with, and when I feel the tingling in the base of my spine that tells me I'm about to coat her sweet cunt with my seed, I speed up and fuck her harder.

Tears fall against her cheeks and make my release that much stronger. She doesn't see it yet, but everything I'm doing, I'm doing for us. I'm doing it for our future. She's fighting me at every turn, making everything harder than it needs to be, but the moment her belly grows round with my baby is when she'll accept everything I've been trying to tell her since I brought her here.

I collapse on top of her once my balls are drained. Her chest rises and falls in gentle sobs. She's upset now, but she'll see. Soon she'll understand why I had to take this choice out of her hands.

"I need to clean up," Snow whimpers, her palms pressing into my chest in an attempt to move me.

"No, you don't."

"Yes, I do," she argues, pushing me harder as the anger takes hold. The rage in her eyes makes my semi-hard cock twitch inside her, eliciting a moan of surprise from her throat.

I shake my head slowly, a smirk of satisfaction playing on my lips. If I wanted, I could take her again right now. My cock is ready to go again, hardening with each tear that streaks down her cheek. I could slam back into her and plant another load in her sweet pussy.

But I won't. Not because I don't want to, or even because she *doesn't* want me to. No, I won't take her again so soon because every time I move inside her, she winces just a little. Between my rough treatment with the gun and how I just fucked her with nothing but brutality, it wouldn't be fair for me to fuck her again so soon, especially seeing as I will never be soft and gentle. Those are two words that don't exist for a man like me.

I keep her pinned beneath me for long minutes, my cock aching to keep fucking her and her gentle sobs only make me want to mark her over and over again. I always knew the day I finally fucked her would be the start of the end, that leaving the bed ever again would be near impossible. But eventually I will have to get back to work, especially with a new threat on the horizon.

Carefully, I withdraw from her tender pussy and meet her gaze. She isn't angry, scared perhaps, but there's no anger flickering within the ice of her eyes. This is hard for her, and that's something I'm willing to accept, and willing to make allowances for. After all, she is right when she says she didn't ask for this. She was quite happy living her life as the baby Saint James that everyone underestimated. But that's not who she is to me, or who she has ever been.

The moment my body no longer touches her, the warmth she provides stolen away in the blink of an eye, I almost can't stand it. I grew up without physical touch, and every sexual partner I've had, I've tied them up and fucked them from behind because I'm not familiar with physical touch or emotion. But having Snow in my arms feels so fucking right. Like all the pieces in the puzzle have fallen together.

I bundle her up in my arms and slide off the bed, holding her close to my chest. Snow burrows her face into my chest, her tears rolling down my bare pecs, and I barely control the growl that climbs up my throat. Even through her distaste of what I've just done to her, her body instinctively leans into me for support.

When we reach the bathroom, I immediately reach to turn the shower on, making sure the temperature is right before stepping in with my Snowflake still in my arms. There's something about carrying her around that feels so right I don't dare to question it.

The warm water hits her pale skin, and she lets out a groan of happiness. I can't help but smile down at her in my arms.

Fuck. How am I ever meant to leave her to work? Marking her has only made my obsession grow deeper, the need I have for her grow stronger.

"Better?" I ask.

"Yes."

"You did good today, little Snowflake."

Her eyes darken, the first glimmer of anger since we left the bed evident. "Which part, Elijah? The part where I tried to get one of your men to help me leave? Or the bit when he almost raped me? Or how about when you forced me to kill him and then fucked me with a gun? Or could it be the part where I begged you not to come inside me and you did anyway?" The fire in her words would burn a lesser man, but she should know by now I'm not going to bow like every other man she's been with. Snow pushes against my chest with closed fists, and this time I allow her out of my embrace, carefully lowering her to the ground. "You had no fucking right, Elijah. That's not a decision you take out of someone's hands. I've just lost my parents, everyday I'm here, I'm losing my life and my family, and any day now you're going to force me to march down the aisle and become your wife. You should have given me this one choice." Hot, angry tears roll down her cheeks and a ragged sob breaks from her throat, her chest heaving with the force of it.

Snow's entire body trembles despite how warm the water is as her back hits the tiled wall. She wants to put distance between us, but I'm standing between her and the door.

I reach for her, unable to hold my protective instincts at bay despite the fact I'm the one who caused her this pain, but she shies away from my touch. "Don't fucking touch me," she snarls.

I almost snap back, almost revert to the cold, brutal man I've always been, but it won't win me any favors with my Snowflake, and although it goes against everything I am, I have to try to be what she needs right now.

"Snow," I say, my voice low and calm. "I'm sorry I've upset you, but you have to understand this is your life now. I know you're still adjusting to the idea, but I've known this is where we were headed since the day we met. Everything that has come since then was merely a detour on our journey."

She wraps her arms around herself as if the gesture can protect her from me and my words, but as I've tried to tell her over and over again, there isn't a damn thing on this earth that can keep me away from her, and that's a reality she needs to grasp sooner rather than later.

"I was only a teenager," she yells. "How could you know I was the one you were meant to spend the rest of your fucking life with?" Her shouts bounce off the tiles and echo.

If I wasn't already glad I gave Mrs. Chambers the day off because of the dead body in the hallway, I would be even more so right now. If she saw Snow like this, I have no doubt in my mind the older woman would be getting her the hell out of here, regardless of the consequences.

"Because I knew." I shrug, taking a small step toward her. "I need you to breathe for me, little Snowflake. You're going to hurt yourself, and I don't accept anything hurting what belongs to me, including yourself."

"I don't really care what you want, Elijah," she snaps. "I don't even fucking care if you kill me at this point. Because death would be a kinder future than whatever you have planned for me."

Her words are like a knife to the throat, the sharpness slicing into my skin and leaving a gaping wound in its path. She's angry. I understand that, but I will not allow anyone, including her, to speak to me like this.

I prowl through the warm spray toward her, not stopping when she cowers against the wall, her body shaking like a leaf on a windy day. Snow is about to find out what happens when she doesn't behave, and she's not going to like it.

FORTY-ONE

SNOW

Anger flares in Elijah's eyes as he stalks toward me, the monster the world sees dancing at the edge and threatening to consume me.

But he's not the only one with fury beating through his veins. I've never been angrier than I am right now, because not only has Elijah taken everything for me, but he also now thinks he has the monopoly over my body as well. I don't fucking think so.

His body is imposing as he towers over me. His hard lines and menacing tattoos cause my body to tremble despite itself. I don't want him to see my weakness, but he sees everything.

Elijah has been watching me for a decade, and I suspect there isn't a thing I could get past him.

When his hand lifts toward my face, I can't help but flinch, my heart lurching into my throat at the motion. His arm freezes in midair, horror crossing the moss green of his eyes.

It's the first time I've ever seen Elijah look so… hurt. That's the only word I can come up with to describe the way he's staring at me.

We stare at each other for long moments, neither of us moving a muscle, and then he's surrounding me.

His body is imposing as it envelops mine in his warmth. The moment his arms wrap around me, everything I've been trying to hide from him, all the emotions I've been stamping down, it all breaks from my chest at once and a painful sob tears from my throat.

Elijah lifts one of his hands to the back of my head and holds it to his chest. The water beats down on our skin, the combination of his warmth and the steam makes it hard to pull in a breath, but I'm not willing to drag myself away from the comfort he's providing me.

As if he can tell I'm overheating, he reaches for the faucet without a word and shuts off the spray.

He keeps one arm wrapped around me, and reaches for a towel, folding it around my shoulder and gently patting the droplets from my skin.

His silence is unsettling. I've spent my entire life around men like Elijah, and I know the quiet never means anything good. The tension in his chest and shoulders vibrates through his body, but his touch is nothing but gentle, despite it being at complete odds with his nature.

He dries me without a word, using one hand to quickly pat some of the water from his naked body before lifting my towel-covered body from the cool tiles and carrying me straight through the room.

He doesn't release me for a moment, not when he crawls onto the bed, droplets of water seeping into the sheets as he positions us with me cradled in his lap, and not even when he pulls the sheets up around us, making sure my whole body is covered.

Silence envelops us, and I lean into it. The only sounds are our combined breathing. We're quiet for so long that my heartbeat starts to come down, the tears rolling down my cheeks begin to slow, and the heaving in my chest begins to calm.

Elijah's hand moves to the back of my neck, holding me securely against him so there's nowhere I can go, and honestly, I don't want to go anywhere. I need him right now, no matter how fucked up that is, how much I should want to run a mile from the man who has taken everything from me, I don't want to.

"I will never hurt you, Snow." Elijah's deep rumble startles me slightly, but I allow myself to relax back into his warmth. "I'm not my uncles, and I don't think you're dispensable. You are everything." He pauses for a moment, as if finding the right words for whatever is coming next. "When we met, my father immediately noticed how I looked at you. I was still young, and I hadn't quite figured out that my family were bad people. I was kept isolated from other children growing up, aside from Everett of course, and I guess even him to a certain extent. It never occurred to me that I should hide my affection for you from them."

I shift slightly, trying to look up at him. It's clear that whatever he's about to tell me is meaningful, and I want to be able to look into his eyes as he tells me the story. But when he steels his arms around me, holding me in place, I don't fight him. It's not in his nature to be vulnerable, and if he's going to lay all his cards out on the table for me, I need to respect his boundaries, even if he hasn't shown me the same courtesy so far.

"They saw it as a way to attack your family. I'm sure you're well aware of our complicated shared history and throwing in that Everett chose your family over his own… it made things tense. They thought that if I got close to you, perhaps they would have the in they always needed to bring everything down from the inside."

Why is he telling me this? The thought strikes me that perhaps this entire thing has been a ruse to avenge his family. That maybe the alliance, taking me, marrying me, it all feeds back into some revenge plot that I've found myself the center of.

Elijah brushes his fingers down my spine, silently telling me to relax, and I can't help but comply. "I had to get sneaky about how I watched you and had to throw them off the scent. One day my uncle Angelo came over with this woman." He shakes his head, the movement jostling my body slightly, but I make no move, remaining perfectly still so as not to interrupt. "I was about seventeen at the time, I think, and I'd never really found members of the opposite sex that appealing. Apart from you of course." He tightens his grasp around me, and I almost believe it's to remind him I'm here and that I'm real, even if the circumstances that brought me here weren't above board. "I was forced to lose my virginity at the same age Everett was, to become a man, they said, but after that, it just wasn't something that interested me that much, especially because the women my father and uncles would have around, were there against their will. I wasn't into it."

It's on the tip of my tongue to remind him that I'm here against my will and that he doesn't seem to have a problem with getting off on keeping an unwilling woman locked up in his house, but I manage to swallow down the comment.

"But this woman Uncle Angelo brought around to the house one afternoon was a test. I knew it the moment she walked in the door because of the way he watched me. They wanted me to prove what I said about you was true, that I had no interest in the littlest Saint James. They wanted to catch me out on a lie because if it was you who I was truly interested in, they would use it, and me, to bring your family down from the inside."

Elijah is quiet for long moments, but his body vibrates with the unspoken words, and even without him saying another word, it's clear this story is going somewhere dark, and after all I've been through in the last twenty-four hours, I'm not sure I can handle it. But I don't move. I remain perfectly still, leaning into the warmth he emits and finding comfort in the soft circles he draws into my bare back.

"Her name was Serena," he tells me. "She was taken from her family in France, stolen away in the night, without so much as a goodbye. From what I could tell, her father owed Uncle Angelo some money, and when he didn't pay, he took something else in return for his generosity. Although the Russo family name doesn't extend as far as yours, there's a reason we are known for the atrocities that we are."

My body stills at his words. I've always known the Russo family were involved in some bad shit, way worse than any of the pies my family have our fingers in. But to take someone's daughter, to steal them away without so much as a thought, it gives me room for pause.

Serena and I are not alike. Our situations may as well be worlds apart. Elijah has taken me from my life, that much is true, but it's not because of some revenge plot, or because my family owes him money. It's because he wants me, and if I'm really honest with myself, if I allow myself to put all the reasons this situation is fucked up to the side, I want him too.

When we come together, it's like thunder and lightning. Two forces that move in a symphony despite themselves.

The revelation has my heart stalling in my chest, but I force myself to remain relaxed as Elijah continues. "She was a nice enough girl, intelligent. She would have had a great future if she'd been given the opportunity. But being taken by Angelo Russo may as well have been a death sentence. Hell, death would have been far kinder than the fate Serena met."

I squeeze my eyes closed, tears pooling behind the lids that I can't allow to fall against my cheeks. If he realizes how much the story is upsetting me, he might stop, and my morbid curiosity is getting the better of me. Whatever he's about to tell me, whatever his uncle did to this poor girl, was caused by me. Regardless of whether I knew it or not, I played a part in someone else's pain.

"What happened to her?"

Forty-Two

Elijah

The story playing on loop in my mind isn't one I ever thought I would think about again, let alone tell another living soul. They say there are great defining moments in life that shape who you're meant to be, and this is one of mine.

Perhaps if I had walked away from my family before this point, just the way Everett did, I would be able to be saved. Perhaps there would have been some part of my soul that was redeemable, but not after the things I saw and the things I was forced to do. No soul can survive that much darkness.

I press her harder against my body, using her to weigh my own down. The reminder of her warmth, of her presence, is enough to keep me grounded. From the way she tensed, I know she's realized this could have just as easily been a story about her, and although it makes me an even shittier person than I already am, I'm glad I have my little Snowflake safely in my arms.

It doesn't matter how she came to be here, or that she still hasn't accepted her place at my side. All that matters is that she walks this earth, that she breathes the same air I do. For that, I will always be grateful.

"Uncle Angelo presented Serena to me as if she were a gift. She was so young, and so broken by the time she got to me. For the most part, I was kept away from the trafficking side of things. Not really for any other reason than it wasn't something dad had a lot to do with, and therefore my exposure was minimal. She was bruised from head to toe, and she looked as if she hadn't washed for at least a week. Her hair was matted, and she had this look in her eye." I pause, trying to put my finger on exactly what it was about her eyes that had even the blackest of souls hurting. "She looked dead inside. It was like when she looked at me, there was no one behind the gaze. I don't know what they did to her before she was presented to me, and honestly, even I don't like to think about it."

The memory slams into me like a steam train that has lost control. So much that I saw as a child and as a teenager was dark and gritty, but the way this girl was used, as a pawn in a war she had nothing to do with, even I can admit it was fucked up.

"My father told me that I was to make a decision. Either I married Serena, or I killed her. I'd never killed a woman before, only men who I was told deserved it, but at the time I didn't think there was anything a woman could do that would lead to such a punishment. The look of resignation she gave me as they laid out my options, neither of them were better than the other for her. One would lead to her becoming a plaything for the men in my family, and eventually bearing my children, and the other would put her out of her misery, even if it meant never taking another breath."

Snow's breathing picks up. She keeps saying I've taken her from her life, but if this story is teaching her anything, it's that that's simply not true. Not in the way she likes to think it is. Despite the fact I kidnapped her, I've allowed her access to her siblings, she's been allowed to leave the house at times, and I didn't take her until I knew she wanted it, until her body craved me just as deeply as mine does her.

"What did you choose?" Her words are barely above a whisper, as if she's afraid of the answer.

I squeeze my eyes shut as I bury my face into her neck, breathing in her sweet scent. It pulls me back to the present as my mind threatens to drag me into the darkest corners of itself. "I told my father I needed time to think about it. I'd barely made sense of my attraction to you, and I wasn't prepared to give that up. I always knew it would take a lot to get you here, that you'd fight me with every last breath, and I couldn't do that with a wife. But I wasn't prepared to kill an innocent woman who had done no wrong aside from having a father who borrowed money from the wrong man.

"None of the men in my family are patient, so they only gave me one day to decide. I snuck out that night to watch you. I broke into your family's estate and settled outside your window. It was the middle of winter, and I remember it so clearly. You and Storm were arguing about something, and when you came into your room you slammed the door with the fury and fire that only served to foster my obsession." It's not in my nature to be so candid, and although I always knew she would be here with me one day, I never thought I would be telling her about the night I knew she would become my everything. "I sat there all night in the snow, and when snowflakes fell against my skin, I realized there was no way

I could go ahead with marrying Serena. She would never be happy with me, and I would never be happy with her, even if it was the best way for me to get my father and uncles off my scent when it came to you."

She tries to lift her head from my chest, but I hold her still, unable to see the look in her eye when I tell her about the moment I lost my humanity to keep our future alive. I never wanted her to know what I lost for us to be together, but perhaps it will be enough for her to stop fighting me at every turn.

"But when I got home and I was faced with the broken girl who had done nothing wrong, I wanted to have it both ways. I wanted to save her, and I wanted to pursue you. So I told my father I would try to feel something toward her. More than anything, I wanted to make sure you were safe. You were always my priority, just as you always will be. You, my little Snowflake, are where my life begins and ends, because a man like me doesn't care about anything but their queen." I pause to allow her to swallow the pill I've just shoved down her throat. "It worked for a little while. Serena was so fucked up from whatever my uncle had done to her before he handed her over to me that she barely got out of bed, and I spent all my time following you around, my obsession only growing deeper the longer I watched you. But after seeing what Angelo did to Serena, I couldn't risk him doing the same to you, or worse because of your family, I knew I had to start working toward their demise because it was going to be a slow process to take them down from within."

"You were trying to take them down?"

"From the day I laid eyes on you," I confess. "They would

have always been a threat to you, and that's not something I was willing to risk. I couldn't have you until they'd taken their last breath."

The words carry more meaning than I intend them to, but when Snow curls around me, it's clear I'm winning some points, no matter how short-lived it will be.

"I didn't expect them to interfere so soon. I thought I had more time before they would want proof that I was treating Serena the way the Russo name required me to. But one day I came home from watching you at the art gallery with your friends, to find Serena on the exam table with her legs in stirrups. At first I didn't understand what was happening, but when I saw her face and how scared she was, I knew it couldn't be good."

"They were checking if you'd been fucking her," Snow offers, and I'm almost relieved I don't have to say the words myself.

I nod. "Yes."

"And you hadn't been?"

"No."

Snow sucks in a harsh breath, her cheek pressing harder into my chest. "What did they do?"

"I'll spare you the details of what I had to watch them do to that poor girl, but in the end, I was handed a gun and she begged me to end her life. She'd known nothing but pain for so long that she couldn't bear another moment of her own heart beating."

"You killed her." She doesn't pose it as a question because we both know the answer.

"I did," I confirm. "The reason I tell you this, Snow, is because I need you to understand that while I am a monster, I am not the same as my father and uncles. I do not enjoy hurting women, and I've gone to great lengths to bring us together. I would not do anything to jeopardize that, and I will never lay a hand on you in anger."

Silence descends over us, but she makes no attempt to move from where she's sprawled across my chest. There have been few times over the years where I have been able to quiet my racing mind, where I have been free from the plotting and scheming, where death hasn't lingered over me like a cloud. But as I hold Snow, her gentle breath whispering across my chest, there's nothing but her filling my mind, and I could really get used to the quiet.

FORTY-THREE

SNOW

Warmth surrounds me so completely that I almost can't tell what tugs me out of my comfortable slumber. Arms are steeled around me, holding me tightly against a hard body. After Elijah's confession and earnestness in his words, I allowed myself to fall into a deep sleep in the safety of his arms. He never did strike me as the cuddling type, but every time I tried to roll across the bed to escape the furnace, he tucked me right back against him.

I lay for a few moments, keeping my body still while I try to pick up on any noise in the house, but it's completely silent apart from Elijah's soft snores behind me.

It's another few minutes before pain spreads through my lower belly and takes my breath away. Oh no.

As quickly and quietly as I can, I pry myself from his grip and scurry across the room, not bothering to pick up my robe from the floor on my way back to my bedroom. I stop in the doorway and lean against the frame, pain radiating down to the tops of my thighs and taking my breath away.

I've always had bad periods. Ever since my first one when I was twelve. Most months, I spend two or three days in my room feeling sorry for myself because I physically cannot get out of bed, and by the way the cramps take hold, this one doesn't seem any different.

I must have lost track of my cycle since being here, but the arrival of my period does allow me to breathe a little easier. Although anything can happen, it's unlikely I would get pregnant at this point in my cycle. If nothing else, I need to find a way to get on birth control without Elijah knowing it, even if it only buys me a few months.

I'm not ready to be a mother, and I'm certainly not ready to bring a child into the world while we're at this impasse. We're still trying to find a way to make things work, and for the most part, I'm still pushing him away every chance I get. Why would I want to bring a baby into a situation like that?

I do feel comforted by his promise to never raise a hand to me, which means he probably won't kill me when my usefulness expires. It may be naive of me to believe him, but there was something in his tone that told me he was being sincere, and it gave me the opportunity to rest.

I burst into my bathroom and quickly slam the door behind me, turning the lock immediately. I'm sure there's a camera in here somewhere, but the illusion of privacy is enough for me right now. And if Elijah decides he wants to get nosey, it'll be his fault when he sees something he isn't ready for.

Another cramp hits me just as I lower myself onto the tiled floor by the toilet, the pain so intense it makes my stomach protest painfully. I've done this enough times to know the throwing up isn't far away. My hands fall to my lower stomach and tears escape the corners of my eyes.

I need to put some clothes on, but the cool tiles on my overheated skin is like heaven. Plus, I'm not sure I can get up off the ground without assistance, and I'm sure as hell not allowing Elijah to see me like this.

When I'm sure my stomach isn't about to lurch its way up my throat, I crawl across the tiles to a stash of underwear I hid in here so I didn't have to get dressed in a room I knew had cameras. Now I know all of them do, it seems redundant, but at least it's handy in times like this.

Next I make my way to the vanity, praying that whoever stocked it had the foresight to prepare for menstruation, and breathe a sigh of relief when a box of tampons catches my eye. Oh, thank God. The thought that I may have to ask the scary Mafia man, who has killed more people than I've probably met in my life, to go to the store and buy them makes me blush and scoff at the same time. Lord have mercy on the shop assistant that would have had to assist him.

Before I can force myself to my feet to take care of business, the sound of my name booming down the hallway startles me. I don't want him to see me like this, not when we've just started to find our way. But if I don't answer him, it will only end badly for me.

"I'm in here," I groan, not sure my voice will carry through the door and into the hallway.

Hot tears stream down my cheeks as my body begins to heave. There's nothing in my stomach, between everything that happened before Elijah and I fell into bed and slept the day away, I never had a chance to eat anything, but that doesn't stop my body from trying to expel the contents of my stomach.

The door handle moves, but the lock doesn't allow him to get any further, and a loud knock ricochets off the tiles.

"Snow! Why is this door locked?" he demands, his voice full of anger. I'm sure he thinks I'm hiding from him, hiding from how vulnerable we were with one another.

"I'm sick. Go back to bed." I barely manage to get the words out before my body heaves out nothing but clear bile.

There's silence for a moment and I almost think he's doing as I asked, but when the sound of metal on metal fills the room, I realize I'm about to have company.

"Please don't come in here, Elijah," I plead.

Instead of a response, the door swings open, and a very naked Elijah meets my gaze.

I must look a sight. Hunched over the toilet, naked, with tears streaming down my face as I clutch my stomach.

He takes me in for only a moment before he's kneeling on the tiles beside me. "What's wrong?" His eyes are gentle as he gathers my hair in his fist and pulls me back into his hard body. His warmth comforts my shivering body, and I can't help but relax back into him.

I shake my head. This is mortifying. As if being taken by the enemy isn't bad enough, I've then proceeded to start to like him, and now I have to talk about my period? Absolutely not.

Elijah tenses at my silence, but his hold on me remains soft. He doesn't strike me as someone who has ever looked after someone like this, but he's surprisingly good at it. "I need you to tell me what's going on, Snowflake. I can't fix it if you don't tell me."

"You can't fix it anyway," I croak right before another cramp grabs hold and a spasm shoots down my leg.

"I'll burn the entire world down for you, Snow. I can have a doctor here in ten minutes, but I need to know what they're treating to make sure I get the right one." His words are strained, and I almost wonder if he's struggling to see me in so much pain. The man who causes grievous bodily harm and murders people for a living, doesn't like seeing me like this, and that makes my heart do a flip in my chest.

"A doctor can't do anything for me. Plenty have tried, but this is just how it is." The admission only makes me feel sorrier for myself. This has happened every month for the last thirteen years, and no medication, or birth control, has even begun to mellow out the symptoms, some of them even made them worse.

Elijah lets out a breath and nods against my back. "Your period." It's not a question and I almost roll my eyes at myself. Of course he knows. Of course the man who has stalked me for the last decade knows about my long sordid history with every doctor in the city. It shouldn't come as a surprise, and yet it does.

"Yes," I murmur.

Silence falls over us, and I find myself relaxing more and more into his warmth. Elijah brings a sense of calm to my usually active mind, and it's nice to lean into the quiet for a little while, especially as my body revolts against itself.

"Are you still feeling sick?" Elijah asks quietly, his breath whispering across my bare shoulder. I'd all but forgotten I'm naked because he's been keeping me warm.

"No." I shake my head, barely able to move even to do that.

"Let's get you in the shower. The warmth might help." He stands carefully, never allowing my body to leave his, before lifting us both from the ground altogether.

The moment my eyes lock with a small patch of blood on the pail white tiles, my entire body heats with embarrassment. I've never been more mortified than I am right now, and I've done some pretty embarrassing things that have ended up on the front page of the Chicago Times.

Elijah's gaze follows mine and a chuckle rumbles in his chest. "Little Snowflake, I kill people for a living. Do you really think a little blood is going to gross me out?"

"It's different," I mutter against him.

He uses his free hand to tip my chin up until my eyes meet his. "No, it's not. It's natural, and you don't have to hide these things from me. We're a partnership, and if one of us is in pain, or not feeling well, the other is always going to want to help in any way they can. If that means I have to clean up a little bit of blood, so be it. I'd do it a thousand times over if it meant it would help you."

I open my mouth to respond, but no words come out. I'm completely speechless. No man has ever been willing to use the word 'period' around me, let alone buy sanitary items or even see me naked during that time of the month, and yet Elijah takes it in his stride, and more than that, he wants to help. He wants to make me feel better while I'm at my lowest, and as if it were ice in a river, some of my resolve to hate the man who has taken me from my life cracks.

Elijah Russo is nothing like the man I thought he would be, and I'm beginning to think that maybe he was right. Maybe ten years ago when he saw me across a crowded room and decided that someday I would be his, perhaps he was right about it all. Because if I'm honest with myself, my heart is starting to beat in time with his cold, dead one.

FORTY-FOUR

ELIJAH

I stride through the front doors of the Saint James estate with Snow's hand wrapped around mine. Her excitement is bursting from her, barely contained by her tiny body as she looks around with the biggest smile I've seen on her face since I brought her home.

When I told her we were coming here today so I could talk business with her brothers and she could do some wedding planning, I thought she was going to cry with joy. To me it didn't seem like that big a deal, but I have to remember that aside from the one night for dinner, Snow has been cooped up for almost two weeks without much contact with the outside world, and her only company being from myself or a sixty-year-old woman.

She needs this.

It's been two days since I found her on the bathroom floor crying from the pain of her cramps, and ever since then she's been much more pliable with me. She still argues when I tell her to do something, but there's none of the disdain I've grown accustomed to seeing in her eyes. She fights now because she thinks she should, not because she wants to, which means we're making progress.

It was hard for me to see her in so much pain but caring for her came naturally to me. I've never looked after another human being in my life, never cared about their comfort or their pain, but I shouldn't be surprised that Snow is different. She's the exception to every single one of my rules.

"Snow!" Wynter beams as she sprints down the hallway toward us. I'm used to seeing her in business attire, but today she's wearing a pair of leggings and a gray sweater that swims on her.

"Dove!" Everett bellows from behind her. "No running."

She rolls her eyes and slows to a walk. "I'm pregnant, not broken," she chimes. "Plenty of women run marathons well into pregnancy."

Everett shakes his head, massaging the bridge of his nose to ease the ache.

"I think you're going to make his head explode." Snow giggles.

"Maybe then I'll be allowed to leave the house without a small army escorting me around."

Everett scrubs his hand down his face before meeting my eyes. "We're this way."

I hold on to Snow's hand for another moment, quietly telling her to behave. I'm putting a lot of trust in her by allowing her to be alone with her sister, knowing she could spill the metaphorical beans and tell them I've been keeping her against her will for the last two weeks.

Snow looks up at me with a smile, and for some reason, I trust that she's not going to make a run for it. Everything changed that night in the bathroom, including her feelings toward me.

I release her hand, giving her a gentle kiss on the cheek before following Everett. Tearing myself away from her is harder with every day that passes, and the need to get a second in charge grows more urgent.

I glance into the living room as I pass it, a small smirk capturing my lips. The plan for that night went from bad to worse so fucking quickly it was barely long enough to blink.

I was meant to take Snow that night amongst the chaos Charles created. I was going to smuggle her out, but then Wynter shot me, and all my plans went out the window. I should have known better than to underestimate a Saint James woman. They never do what you expect them to, and perhaps that's part of the appeal.

It worked out for the best if I'm honest. Taking her while we have an alliance in place means they couldn't retaliate the way they may have previously, even if she was playing along like she is now.

When I meet Everett a few steps later, he's only just tearing his eyes away from where the girls are chatting excitedly. It's not until they're standing side by side that you truly notice how similar they are, in more than just their looks. Their mannerisms are so alike that some may mistake them for the same person if they were looking at that alone.

"That woman is going to give me a fucking heart attack," Everett mutters, turning to guide me down the hallway. This is the first time I've been inside the house with an invite, but I know the layout almost as well as the people who live here.

"Imagine if you have a daughter," I scoff. It's strange to talk to my cousin like this, like we haven't spent our entire lives being forced to compete and beat the shit out of one another.

Everett's eyes widen. "Jesus."

I chuckle as I follow him through the house. It's ostentatious and old in its decorating, reminding me of Uncle Angelo's home. It must be a requirement when you become a Mafia boss to hire interior designers from the eighteenth century to decorate your house.

I expect to stop at Storm's office and my step falters when Everett continues down the hallway past the door. If I'm not meeting them in there, where are we going?

"Any news about the shipment?" I ask. Snow and I have been living in our own little world the last couple of days, and apart from having one of my men talk to some people on the street, I haven't looked into it at all. I told Storm as much when he called this morning, and he didn't seem particularly happy, but while we may have an alliance, I don't work for him. I'm still a Russo and he's still a Saint James. Our businesses are completely different, we deal in different shit, which is why we can coexist in the city and work together when needed.

It's the moment Everett opens the door that leads to the basement that I know I wasn't called here to talk through wedding plans or theories about who may be targeting shipments.

I glance at my cousin, not letting on that I know there's something amiss, and notice the slightest of tics. His fingers fist together and release over and over again. Some may think it is the tell of a man who was trained to fight the way we were, but perhaps I'm the only one who can see past it because I was raised the same way.

I have no option but to walk down the steps ahead of him when he gestures for me to do so. I didn't bring any security into the house, because I didn't think I would have to. It would have looked like I didn't trust the Saint James family, and that's the last thing I need when I'm marrying their sister in a few days. And yet the moment a fist meets my cheek, I realize I've been played.

FORTY-FIVE

SNOW

When I step into my room, there's none of the same relief I expect to feel. All the way here, I was imagining what it would be like to finally be home, to have my own belongings surrounding me, and to be with my family under the same roof. But all the relief I expected is absent.

The room is missing something, but it takes me long moments to figure out what it is.

Elijah.

Although it's identical to the one at home, it's missing his scent, his presence. The realization makes me stop in my tracks, stopping in the middle of the room as reality washes over me.

I've come to think of Elijah's house as my home, and I can't quite put my finger on when that happened. The estate I grew up in, and even my apartment in the city, they don't feel like mine anymore.

It could be Stockholm syndrome. Maybe my mind has accepted there's nothing I can do to escape the man who stole me away, but something tells me that's not the case. There's a niggling feeling deep in my gut that tells me I'm exactly where I'm meant to be.

Maybe it's some of Elijah's confidence rubbing off on me. When he tells me about how sure he was from the first moment he laid eyes on me, the conviction and all the things he did to make it a reality, I can't help but believe him.

"Are you okay?" Wynter's voice breaks through my thoughts, tearing me back to the moment.

"Of course," I tell her, continuing into the room and perching on the edge of the bed. Even the mattress doesn't feel quite right, but then again, I've spent the last few nights with Elijah, and I don't think any bed he's not in will ever feel right again.

She watches me carefully, uncertainty crossing her features as she rests her hand absentmindedly on her barely there baby bump. Of course she looks perfect while pregnant, because Wynter takes everything in her stride and looks like a supermodel doing it. I'm sure even when she's in labor, she'll be ready to step out onto the runway.

"This wedding is very rushed," she finally says, crossing the room to where I'm sitting.

I nod slowly and shrug. "It is, but when you know, you know."

She lets out a slow breath and I can almost hear the words on her tongue before she speaks them. "You've always been the free spirit in the family, and I love that about you. I love how brave you are, and how willing you are to go against the grain of what's expected of you. I just can't help but wonder if perhaps this may be a case of you going against Storm." She chooses her words carefully, making sure to not say what she's thinking. They think this is just another case of me rebelling.

"This is what I want, Wynter." It's a lie I've practiced over and over again, because I knew this conversation was coming. Except, as the words roll off my tongue, I find it's not a lie. Not anymore. I do want to be with Elijah. The realization slams into me and knocks the air from my lungs just the way the first one did. Holy shit.

She watches me for long moments, looking for mistruth in my words, but when she doesn't find any, she lets out a soft sigh. "I just want you to be happy, and if he gives you happiness, he's okay in my books."

I smile and reach for her, wrapping my arms around her. "You're going to be the best mom, Wyn."

She lets out a laugh, the feeling vibrating through our embrace. "I hope so. And hey, maybe you'll give him or her a cousin soon too!"

I hold on to her tighter for a few moments and squeeze my eyes shut to ward off the tears. This is the thing that keeps dragging me back. I'm not ready to be a mother, and I'm certainly not ready to bring a child into the world with Elijah. I may want to be with him, but the idea of having a baby with such a brutal man, scares the life out of me.

Wynter doesn't seem to notice the dull panic that erupts in my belly at the thought, and for that I'm grateful.

"I'm just going to go to the bathroom," I say, quickly standing from the bed and crossing the room before she can say anything.

When I slip into the bathroom and close the door behind me, I immediately drop to my knees in front of the cupboard. My heart beats heavily in my chest as I rummage behind the bottles and makeup products until I find what I'm looking for and relief washes over me.

A few months ago, Doc gave me three months' worth of a contraceptive pill to try to regulate my periods, and I never got around to starting them between everything else that was going on. I've never been more grateful for his foresight and my forgetfulness as I am right now.

I shove the small packets into my bag with a fleeting hope that Elijah doesn't go through whatever I want to take back with us. I don't think he will, I think we're past the point of him thinking I might kill him, and me thinking I might want to. I've already killed one too many people.

I flush the toilet I didn't use and wash my hands idly. Wynter is suspicious enough without me doing anything else to tip her off. And hell, she should be suspicious. Her sister who has never expressed a desire to get married, who never played with bridal dolls as a child, is getting married in a few days, with not enough time to plan, to a man who has always been a mortal enemy of our family. I'd be fucking suspicious too.

When I walk back into the room, my sister is pacing back and forth across the room, worry etched into her brow. Wynter isn't much of a stressor, normally the calm and collected one as the rest of us go into varying levels of panic, but she looks about ready to tear her own hair out.

"Everything okay, Wyn?" I ask.

She stops in her tracks, turning to look at me as she worries her lip between her teeth. Her brows are pulled together. Whatever is troubling her is causing her real stress. "I need to tell you something."

"Anything. You know that." I take a few steps closer to her, but when she steps back my stomach plummets. There's something wrong.

She takes a deep breath and lets it out, rubbing her stomach a few times as if it will give her some kind of strength. "Storm and Everett think Elijah is double-crossing us. They think he's the one who took the shipment the other day and that orchestrated the attempt on your life."

Blood roars through my ears and I barely remember to breathe. The memory of having a gun held on me is still too raw, too fresh, for me to think about, and the reminder has a cold sweat breaking out on my brow.

"They invited you both here under the ruse of planning the wedding, but I think they have other plans."

My eyes snap up to meet my sister's which are so similar to my own. "What do you mean?"

"I mean, I think they might hurt Elijah."

I'm running for the door before his name finishes rolling off her tongue. I need to stop this. They can't hurt him, not when I'm finally starting to feel things for him, not when I'm finally starting to understand the connection he's felt for a decade.

I'm down the stairs and sprinting toward Storm's office before

I can even think to ask where they are, and when I find the room empty, I know exactly where they'll be.

The basement.

I continue down the hallway, not slowing down despite my lungs screaming at me to do so. I've never been much of a runner, and my body isn't accustomed to this much physical exertion, especially after being locked in the same house for two weeks.

Without thought, I burst through the basement door, taking the steps two at a time. Muffled voices and groans of pain fill my ears, but I don't stop.

I don't stop when I see Elijah tied to a chair with blood running down his face.

I don't stop when Rayne throws another punch, landing it in the middle of his torso.

And I certainly don't stop when Everett catches a glimpse of me marching toward them.

"What the fuck do you think you're doing?" I demand, inserting myself between the three men and the man I'm coming to care for.

"Snow, this has nothing to do with you," Storm says slowly. Anger vibrates off him, but he won't hurt me. None of the men standing before me would lay a finger on me, and that's the only advantage I have right now.

"This doesn't have anything to do with me?" I shout, backing up until Elijah's knees brush against the back of my own. "You have my fiancé tied to a fucking chair, beating him?

Which part of this has nothing to do with me?"

"This is business," Rayne tells me.

"Right." I nod as if that's the answer to all my questions. "Well, we're leaving. And you can all consider yourselves uninvited from our wedding. I don't want any of you there. You clearly can't respect my choice of husband, and I won't have you there ruining my day." The words come out cold and callous.

"Snow—" Storm starts.

"No." I put my hand up to stop him. "I don't want to hear it."

"We had a shipment go missing the night you were attacked, and all signs point to Elijah," Everett tells me.

I let out a breath, barely holding on to my temper. "The night I was attacked, Elijah didn't leave my side for a moment. If he was going to pull off a job like that, don't you think he'd have to make a call or two at the very least?" I raise a brow in question. I know men are capable of anything, especially men like Elijah, but something tells me he didn't do this. I move behind Elijah and start working at the rope binding his wrists together. Beneath the scratchy material there are angry red marks from where he fought them, and my anger intensifies.

I've never been a particularly angry person, feisty yes, but not angry. Except for right now. Right now, the rage boiling in my blood blinds me, and I'm barely containing my need to pick up the baseball bat I'm certain they had planned to use on the man I'm about to marry and beat all three of them within an inch of their lives.

"Snowflake," Elijah murmurs groggily.

"I'm going to get you out of here."

"You're not taking him anywhere," Storm snaps.

I drop the rope to the ground and stand, glaring at my brother. "Yes, I am. I'm taking my fiancé home."

Rayne steps forward and I move my body between him and Elijah protectively, a snarl on my lips. I'm not the same woman I was a few weeks ago, and if they think I'm going to back down, they have another thing coming.

FORTY-SIX

ELIJAH

I've seen many sides of Snow over the years I've followed her.

I've seen her sweet side and her sassy. The woman she hides from the world, and the persona she puts on in front of strangers. I've seen her happy, sad, excited, scared, and every other emotion under the sun.

But this is new to me.

Fiercely protective.

And what's more, it's me she's protecting.

I shouldn't have allowed them to get the jump on me, not when I figured out what I was doing here before I even made it into the basement, but I couldn't be the one to draw first blood, not when my Snowflake was caught in the middle.

Rayne's eyes widen in shock as he watches his little sister put her body on the line for me. If it was anyone else, I would reprimand her for putting herself in danger, and hell, I might still do that, but the men in this room would rather die than hurt her, and I find comfort in that fact.

She looks at me over her shoulder, worry etched into her brow as her eyes move across my face. Blood drips down my cheek from a cut in my eyebrow and from the corner of my mouth. I don't want to be the one to tell her I've had beatings far worse than this one in my lifetime, and I'm sure there is far worse in my future.

I drag my stiff arms from behind me, barely swallowing the groan that claws up my throat. It was beaten into me as a child to never show weakness to anyone, but especially not my enemies.

"Can you walk?" she asks quietly, although her voice carries through the large basement.

I nod once, pushing myself to my feet despite every muscle screaming at me. The three of them hadn't gone easy on me, each one taking their turn to try to make me talk. My only saving grace is that Tommy wasn't here to do even more damage. I've seen that crazy fuckers work, and I don't want to be his latest victim.

Footsteps on the stairs draw our attention to the door where Wynter stands, fire flaring in her eyes. Apparently, my Snowflake isn't the only one who's angry at the men in their lives. "What the fuck?" she demands.

Storm scrubs a hand down his face and Rayne takes a step back from us, as if it's occurring to them for the first time that maybe they were wrong about me. "He's our enemy," is all the defense Storm can muster.

"No, he's not," Wynter snaps. "Our sister is marrying him. He's about to be our goddamn brother-in-law. Would you do this to Emerson or Everett?"

"Of course not," Storm replies at the same time Rayne growls, the thought of his wife being in harm's way enough to bring out the beast within. I can relate to that, because the monster lurking inside me will tear anyone who dares to lay a hand on my woman into shreds.

Wynter descends the stairs, pushing her way past the other men until she's standing in front of me. "I'm sorry, Elijah. I knew they suspected you of orchestrating the shipment being stolen. I should have warned you."

I force a smile to my lips. "It's not your fault, Wynter." I turn my attention to the rest of the room, carefully wrapping an arm around Snow and tugging her back into me. "If there is still question about my involvement in the missing shipment, I would like to assure you that I had no part in it. I do not currently have a second in charge, nor do I have the manpower to pull off such a seamless operation. As I'm sure you're aware, when you had my family killed, I took out a lot of the people who worked for us to prevent them from retaliating. There were many loyal men who would have taken any opportunity to get back at you for what happened to my father and uncles, but I was sincere when I said I wanted an alliance." I take a deep breath and barely withhold a wince at the shooting pain in my ribs. "Perhaps it was too soon to propose such a thing."

"You're not going anywhere with him, Snow." Rayne steps between us and the exit.

Snow steps toward her brother, her stance wide as if she's going to battle, and I almost can't stop my face from morphing into a smile. "I'd like to see you stop me."

If he even thinks about putting his hands on her, regardless of his relation to her, I will break them without hesitation, so he needs to choose his next moves very carefully.

"Rayne, stop it," Wynter snaps, inserting herself between her siblings.

Everett reaches for her, trying to pull her out of the thick of the conflict, but she slaps his hand away.

"It's like you three haven't learned a goddamn thing over the last few months. Just because we're women doesn't mean we are incapable of making decisions and looking after ourselves. If Snow wants to marry Elijah, then that's what she's going to do. Just the way Emerson was able to choose to marry you, and I'm able to choose to marry Everett."

Silence echoes through the space, and before anyone can say anything else, Snow grabs a hold of my hand and pulls me with her through her siblings. She doesn't stop when we hit the top of the stairs, or when we reach the front door. It's not until we reach the car that she dips her hand into my pocket, tugs the keys out and walks around to the driver's side without a word.

Anger vibrates through her as she revs the engine, and a moment later, she's taking off down the driveway like a bat out of hell.

"Snow," I warn, keeping my voice low and non-confrontational.

"Shut up," she snaps, turning out onto the main road faster than I would have liked in the car that cost me half a million dollars, but I'm not game to fight her right now. After being the siblings everyone always underestimated, she's finally taking back her power, and I don't want to become collateral in her rampage.

She speeds back to the house as if she's been there a thousand times, when in reality, I've only taken her out twice since she arrived.

The tires squeal as she slams on the brakes out the front and powers off the engine, finally releasing her death grip from the steering wheel. Her knuckles are stained white as she rests her hands in her lap and lets out the breath she's been holding.

"Where did you learn to drive like that?" I finally ask.

She scoffs, shaking her head slightly. "Don't you already know everything there is to know about me?" She smirks at me.

I drop my head back and chuckle, barely swallowing the groan of pain. While I never doubted Snow's ability to stand by my side, to be the fierce leader she needs to be to survive in my life, today she proved herself. She stood tall and strong, defending me even though it meant going against her family.

"Rayne did effective driving, his words not mine, training with us a few years ago after someone followed me one night and I couldn't lose them."

I chuckle. "Well, that's one less thing I need to worry about with you. I don't think any of my men can drive like that."

She flashes me a smile, but it quickly drops when her eyes narrow on my injuries. Worry replaces the amusement and she closes her eyes for a moment to school her emotions. "Let's get you inside and cleaned up."

FORTY-SEVEN

SNOW

Elijah's face is a mess. Whatever was happening in the basement before I stormed in must have been bad. His eyes are swelling by the minute and purple bruising ripens against his cheeks.

The front door flings open the moment I carefully pull Elijah from the low sports car, and I barely stop myself from cursing the car. Driving home has calmed me, but the anger raging through my blood is still palpable.

I've never felt such contempt for my family as I do right now.

Mary flies out the door, both hands held over her mouth as her eyes sweep over Elijah's injuries. Once her initial shock wears off, she hurries down the steps, meeting us at the bottom. He's allowing me to support some of his weight, but I have a feeling it's more for my benefit than his. He walked himself out of the estate and got himself into the car without any complaint, so I'm certain he could do this himself, but I'm not willing to allow him to try.

"What happened?" she asks, her brows pulled together with concern.

I look to Elijah to answer, and he does the same to me. There are a few seconds of silence where we each wait for the other, but when understanding dawns on me, I sigh. "We ran into some trouble with my family."

She watches me for a moment before looking to Elijah. "Are they not pleased about the wedding?" she asks.

"We'll talk about it inside," I say, wrapping my arm around Elijah's waist and tugging him forward carefully.

He doesn't struggle on the way up the stairs or as we walk through the house toward our bedroom, and by the time we reach the bathroom, I've all but stopped helping him. He doesn't need it and there's only so much a man like Elijah is going to allow me to coddle him.

Without a word, I reach for the first aid kit he keeps above the basin and point for him to sit on the edge of the bath. I'm not sure if I want to scream and let out the anger, or if I want to cry from all the emotions whirling around inside me.

I've never felt so out of control.

"Snowflake," Elijah murmurs, and I realize I've been staring at the contents of the first aid kit for long enough to warrant his concern.

I take a deep breath and turn to him, brushing my eyes down his face before looking back to the kit. I pull some cotton and antiseptic from the pouch and set it on the edge of the basin. "Take your shirt off."

Elijah scoffs. "Do you want me to strip for you, Snow?" he drawls.

I huff out a sigh, barely holding on to my composure. The rubber band inside me only stretches so far, and I'm so close to snapping I won't be able to control myself if it does. "Just do it."

"Since when do you call the shots?" Elijah cocks his head to the side, challenging me. He knows what he's doing, and he wants to see me detonate.

"Since you just had the shit kicked out of you," I snap.

A smirk tugs at the corner of his lips, the movement so slight most people wouldn't notice it, but I do. I notice everything Elijah does, and that's part of the problem. The longer I'm here, the more I fall for him. And the more I fall for him, the harder I'll hit the ground when it's all over.

I'm not so naive to think something like this can last. A romance founded on obsession that started when he kidnapped me. That's not the makings of a successful marriage, and although I am going to go ahead with it, I'm going in with my eyes wide open.

"If I were a betting man, I would think you were worried about me," he muses.

"So what if I am?"

"Well, my little Snowflake. If you're worried about me, that means you care about me."

I close my eyes and take a deep breath, centering the anger beating in my chest. "Is there a point coming?" I hiss.

Elijah reaches for me, and while I should pull away from his embrace, I need it right now, and I'm not ashamed to say, I need *him* right now. His arms wrap around me tightly, his head resting on my breasts as he holds me against him. His warmth radiates through me, bringing me comfort I didn't think would be possible. The rage that vibrated through my veins calms, and his presence brings me a reprieve I so desperately needed.

"That's better," he murmurs.

"I need to check you over," I whisper, holding him to my chest despite my words. I'm not ready to give up what we're sharing yet, but I know what I need to do. Blood seeps from the open wounds of his face into my white blouse, the red a direct contrast to the silky fabric. It's not the shirt I'm worried about though. No, it's the injuries I can't see. My brothers and Everett are fucking machines when they want information, and I don't need to have ever seen them interrogate someone for me to know that.

"I'll make you a deal," he mumbles into my breasts, my nipples hardening against my bra despite the layers between his face and the hard peaks.

"I'm not making a deal with you, Elijah. You're letting me patch up your wounds."

He draws back and looks up at me through amused eyes. He's getting too much enjoyment out of this considering how messed up his face is. I'm surprised he can still open his eyes at all, and I suspect the swelling will soon take over. "I'll let you clean me up if you do it with my cock inside you."

My mouth drops open and I quickly snap it shut. He's the only person to ever render me speechless, and I don't like it. I've always been quick-witted and snappy, but not with Elijah. He knows exactly which cord to strike to have all the words in my mind disappear.

"So do we have a deal?" His green eyes peer up at me despite the swelling.

"No, we absolutely do not have a deal," I snap, pulling my body away from his only to be tugged right back in. "Elijah, let me go. That is not happening."

He tilts his head and stares at me, as if he doesn't understand the meaning of the word no, which actually makes a lot of sense. The number of times I've said the word to him since I got here and he's completely ignored it seems to grow by the day.

I take a deep breath, allowing some of the anger in my chest to roll off me. I shouldn't clean his wounds while I'm angry, I could end up hurting him more. "I am barely holding on to my composure right now, I still have my period, and sex is literally the furthest thing from my mind." The words come out low, but the anguish behind them is clear.

There are so many reasons I don't want to have sex right now, starting with all the blood he's coated with, and ending with the deep ache in my chest because I won't have one member of my family at my wedding. Everett won't let Wynter come without him, and I don't want him anywhere near the church on Saturday, just the same as my brothers. The emotional pain burns in my heart, and the more my adrenaline calms, the harder it is to stop the tears behind my eyes from falling down my cheeks. Sex won't help anything. All it will do is make me more vulnerable than I already am.

"If you do it, I'll call that as your punishment and we'll be even."

"Punishment?" I cry, pulling away from him and stumbling back. "What the fuck am I being punished for? I saved your ass!" All the rational thought I had a few moments ago has gone out the window.

Elijah stands to his full height, his injuries barely making his movements slow before he stalks toward me. For each step I take, a larger step he takes toward me until my back hits the cool tiles of the shower and he crowds my space. "You put yourself in danger today, Snow. You inserted yourself between me and a threat, and you could have got seriously hurt," his voice is low and menacing, and the blood in my veins cools under them.

"They're my brothers! They would never hurt me!" I move my hands to his chest with the intent of pushing him away, but he quickly bundles them into one of his and holds them above my head, rendering me completely helpless, just the way he likes me.

FORTY-EIGHT

ELIJAH

Having Snow at my mercy is my favorite thing on this earth. There's nothing better than holding the woman of my obsession and seeing an intoxicating cocktail of fear and arousal mingling in her heavy gaze, and I can't get enough.

The pain in my ribs is excruciating, but it doesn't stop my dick from hardening the moment I had my face resting on my woman's tits, and hell, if I'm honest with myself, the moment she stood between me and a threat like a lioness protecting her pride was the moment my cock stiffened painfully in my jeans.

But she put herself in harm's way, regardless of who the threat was, she never should have put herself between me and it, and that's something she can never do again, because next time it might not be her brothers. Next time it could be someone who could really hurt her, and the thought of that makes me homicidal. I would tear the world apart for my Snowflake, and anyone who dares to lay a hand on her will meet their maker before their next breath.

"You *never* put yourself between me and a threat, Snow. Never," I growl. "Rayne could have hurt you unintentionally."

"He wouldn't—" she starts.

"Never, Snow. Never." The words come out harsh and she flinches, turning her head away from me to get any space she can. She should know by now that there will never be any space between us, and it's something she needs to get used to. "If you ever do that again, I promise I will spank you so hard you won't be able to sit for a week, and then I'll keep you locked in our room for a month so I know where you are and that you're safe."

"You can't do that."

"On the contrary, my dear Snowflake. I can do whatever the fuck I want because you're *mine*. Every single part of you belongs to me, and if you ever put yourself in that kind of danger again, I will not hesitate to punish you, and it will not be as kind as the one you're going to get today."

She stares at me for long moments, as if she's trying to process the words I've said. She needs to realize that her safety is everything to me. If something were to happen to her, I would tear this city apart and slaughter every last person who ever dared harm my Snowflake.

I wait patiently for her to respond, for her to understand just how much she terrified me today. It didn't matter that it was her brother, or that I know no one in that basement, myself included, would ever harm a hair on her head, the thought of Snow in any amount of danger has the monster inside clawing at his cage, begging to be set free.

"I'm sorry I scared you," Snow says finally, her tongue darting out to wet her lips. "I saw you tied to the chair, and I..." She pauses to choose the right words. "I acted on instinct. I won't do it again in the future, I promise. But I'm not going to sit on your dick while I assess your injuries. You're hurt enough as it is, and I won't be a party to you hurting yourself more."

She's skating around admitting that I wasn't the only scared one today. She has real feelings for me, but she's still processing them and that's one thing I can't push too hard on. She needs to come to the conclusion I came to ten years ago on her own.

We belong together.

"You'll do as you're told, or you'll find yourself tied to our bed on the edge of an orgasm I'm not going to give you."

"You can't do that."

I chuckle, shaking my head slowly before bringing my face to hers. "Oh, but I can, my little Snowflake. I can do whatever the fuck I want, and you'll love every single second of it."

"Elijah," she hisses my name, and my cock presses harder into her lower belly. I love when she gets like this, when the fire burns bright and the flames flicker at the edge of her temper. "You are hurt. You are in no condition to be sticking your dick anywhere. Not to mention the fact that I'm still out of business." The way she avoids speaking about her period only has the corners of my lips tipping up more. It's cute that she thinks it will gross me out, but soon she'll understand that there's not one thing she could do that would turn me off from fucking her, especially not a little blood.

"That's irrelevant."

"It is certainly not irrelevant," she screeches, tugging at the hand that restrains her.

I sigh. "I'm not arguing about this anymore. You will do as you're told, and I won't hear any more arguments. The next protest out of your mouth better be to tell me not to stop, because anything else will result in a red ass and me withholding your orgasms. Do we understand one another?"

"You're impossible," she mutters.

"Was that an argument I heard, Snow?" I raise a brow.

"No," she says quickly.

"Good." I smile, pressing a gentle kiss to her cheek before releasing her wrists and turning to stride back across the bathroom.

Before I can start stripping off, a knock at the bedroom door pulls both our attention, and a moment later, Mrs. Chambers appears with a tray of items, her brows knit together with worry. She's always been like this. She hates seeing me hurt, and I suppose I understand why. The number of times she's had to patch me up over the years is almost enough for her to have become a fully qualified nurse.

Snow lets out a breath, as if she thinks having someone else in the room is going to rescue her from her punishment. I decide not to correct her right away, it's more fun to make her think she's safe, just to tear the sheet out from under her.

"I brought you some ice. I wasn't sure how much you would need, so I emptied both freezers."

I lower myself back to the edge of the bath, positioning myself to cover my rock-hard cock. She doesn't need to know I'm a few minutes away from sinking into Snow's tight little cunt. That's something she can remain blissfully unaware of.

Snow opens her mouth to say something, but I quickly cut her off. She forgets I've been obsessed with her for a decade, I know her better than she knows herself, and I know exactly what the words she was about to speak were going to be. "Thank you, Mrs. Chambers. Why don't you take the rest of the afternoon off? Snow and I will be having a quiet night going over some wedding plans, and we can order in for dinner."

"Oh, are you sure? I can help to tend to your injuries. Should we call the doctor?" She turns to Snow, directing the question at her.

"I'm quite sure, Mrs. Chambers. I'm sure Mr. Chambers would like to have you home early."

She looks between us a few times, her eyes surveying the situation in front of her. Snow still stands against the wall in the shower, her cheeks flushed and her body tense. Then she looks to me, my posture calm considering I had the shit kicked out of me not that long ago, but that's where her understanding starts to click into place.

Mrs. Chambers has seen me like this a thousand times in the past. Covered in bruises and blood, and God knows what else, and each time I've been angry. I've been ready to take to the streets and kill every last person who dared to question my authority. But I'm calm. Calmer than I ever was before Snow was carried through the front doors and became a permanent fixture in my life. "I see." She nods. "Very well. I'll be going.

I'll see you both in the morning."

She gives us one last quizzical glance before turning back toward the bedroom. The moment the door clicks closed I'm stalking back across the bathroom to where Snow stands, her hands bundled together in front of her as she considers what her next move is going to be.

"Time for your punishment, little Snowflake."

FORTY-NINE

SNOW

Is he fucking serious?

Sometimes I wonder if I agree to things, or if he just shocks me and through that shock, I end up agreeing to whatever crazy thing he wants me to do. That's the only logical explanation for all the things I've conceded on since I woke up here and have barely been allowed to leave.

But that's not my reality. I willingly hand over decisions, even if I do fight them to begin with. Elijah is the only person who has ever been able to sway my choices, and maybe that should make me run in the opposite direction.

But with a man like Elijah, you have no other choice than to run toward him and hope he catches you.

His eyes are feral as he approaches me, and I have nowhere to go. The cool tiles at my back send a shiver down my spine, my need for him evident as wetness grows between my thighs. I shouldn't want him. I shouldn't be in the mood after what just happened, but something I'm beginning to understand, I always want Elijah. Even when my head says no, my body says yes.

Before I can think to move, he lifts me from my feet and throws me over his shoulder. The air leaves my lungs as I make contact with it, and by the time I'm capable of speech, he's lowering the both of us onto the edge of the bathtub.

It's not until I'm back on solid ground that I'm capable of speaking. "Elijah," I screech. "You're injured. You could have hurt yourself even more!"

He chuckles, making quick work of unbuttoning my jeans and shoving them down my legs, closely followed by my underwear and his own pants. "There's only one part of me hurting, Snowflake, and it wasn't your brothers that caused it."

My mouth falls open at his words and a blush spreads across my cheeks like wildfire. This man. Lord.

When his hands curl around the backs of my legs, ready to lift me into place, my mind finally clicks into action and I manage to back away just enough that he can't get a grip on me. "Wait!" I hold both hands up as if reasoning with a bull in a China shop. Hell, dealing with Elijah when he wants something fits that description to a tee. "I still have my period. I have a tampon in," I whisper shout as if it's something to be ashamed of. Elijah has just spent the last two days nursing me back to health, holding me while I cry, carrying me to the bathroom because I haven't been able to get out of bed, and standing in the shower with me for an hour because the heat gave me some relief, and yet I'm still ashamed of the most natural thing my body does, like breathing and my heart beating.

"Well, take it out and get over here. I need you to nurse me back to health." He smirks.

"Absolutely not. Nope. Not happening." I shake my head emphatically. Period sex is at the very bottom of the things I've wanted to try in the bedroom, and I don't intend to move it up the list.

Elijah sighs, frustration flickering in his eyes for the first time since we entered the bathroom. "Snow. Either you remove the tampon and climb up onto my cock, or I'm going to do it for you, and you won't like that option very much because it doesn't involve you having any orgasms."

I huff out a sigh and glare at him. He's never heard the word no, I'm sure of it. "Turn around," I snap.

"No."

"For fuck's sake, Elijah. I'm already mortified. Can you just give me a second of fucking privacy?" Hot tears pool at the corners of my eyes, and a moment later, they spill against my heated cheeks. All the emotions I've been trying to stamp down hit me all at once, and my legs wobble beneath me until I'm sure they're about to give way.

Except, when they do, strong arms wrap around me and lower us both to the ground. As soon as the cold tiles make contact with my bare legs, I flinch, but Elijah's warmth soothes me immediately. He carefully positions me in his lap, both of us only dressed from the waist up, and I idly wonder what Mary would think if she walked back through the door right now.

He presses his hand to the side of my head, holding my face to his chest and I take comfort in the beating of his heart. Until now, I haven't allowed myself to consider what could have happened today. If Wynter hadn't told me what our brothers and Everett suspected, I wouldn't have gone to the basement. I would have obliviously planned my wedding while Elijah was turned black and blue, and maybe even killed. I would have been blissfully unaware of my own flesh and blood killing the man I…

The moment the word crosses my mind, all the air leaves my lungs, and panic claws at my throat. Oh no. Oh no, no, no. I can't feel that for him. I can't allow myself to feel that emotion for a man like Elijah Russo. No matter what he says, or how many times he promises me he isn't going to use me as a baby farm and kill me when I'm no longer useful, I can never allow myself to fall for the monster.

A ragged sob tears from my throat as I realize I'm no more capable of controlling my emotions for him than I am controlling the weather. He's like the perfect storm, and it doesn't matter how much I fight it, how hard I push back, he's always going to blow me away.

Elijah holds me against him so tightly, and for so long, that his warmth lulls my tears, and my body stops trembling with the mixture of adrenaline and terror I've felt today.

"I'm sorry," I murmur against his still-covered chest. His white button-down shirt is stained red from the blood dripping from his face, and it matches my own from where he was resting his head.

"You have nothing to be sorry for, my little Snowflake. I pushed too hard." The admission falls easily from his lips, like the words don't mean a thing, but they mean everything. Elijah Russo is not a man who admits his shortcomings. He's a man who takes what he wants, when he wants, and he makes no apologies for who he is. But not with me.

A vibrating sound startles me, and we both look up at where Elijah's phone is moving around the cabinet. "Ignore it," I whisper.

He chuckles and reaches for it, quickly bringing it to his ear. "What?" he snaps, immediately moving into work mode. The direct contrast of who he is around others, and the man he allows me to see under the hard exterior is startling.

I listen for the other end of the call, but I can't make out their hurried words, only the fear lurking behind them. Whoever is on the phone is terrified of Elijah, much like the rest of Chicago, I suppose.

"What do you mean they're missing?" he growls, pausing as he listens for their response. "David, six dealers don't just up and disappear in one day. Where the fuck are they?" Another pause and the voice on the other end of the line sounds even more panicked than before. I can't say I would like to be the one to deliver bad news to Elijah.

He scrubs his hands down his face, anger vibrating off his body, but his hold on me remains firm but gentle, never allowing the rage to touch me. Is he aware he's doing it? Does he know he's still drawing soft circles into my back as if he's trying to calm us both.

"Fuck. Okay. Round up the rest of the dealers and see if they know anything. I want to know if anyone out of the ordinary approached them, if they made any sales that seemed out of place, and I want them all off the street until we get to the bottom of this," he barks out the order and abruptly ends the call before David can respond.

“We gotta make this quick, Snowflake,” he says, quickly moving me from his lap and onto my hands and knees. I barely have time to take a breath before he’s behind me. “I need your tight cunt.”

My protests die in my throat, and before I’m conscious of my own movements I’ve removed the tampon, a deep blush coating my cheeks as I quickly dispose of it, and before I can think to say anything, he’s seated himself inside me. The stretch burns so much that it steals the air from my lungs. He’s a big man, and without the right preparation, sex can be painful, but I allow him to take what he needs from me.

“Your injuries,” I rasp.

“Your sweet pussy makes it all better, Snowflake.” His hips slam into me at a rapid pace and my knees dig painfully into the hard floors. But the bite of pain mixed with the way his cock hits my G-spot at the perfect angle causes an intense orgasm to tear through my body.

Elijah grunts behind me, his cock pulsing inside my tender pussy. “Fuck, Snow,” he growls a moment before he buries himself deep inside me and his release takes hold. His fingers dig into my hips to the point of pain, but I love it. I love everything Elijah gives me, and perhaps that should terrify me, but it doesn’t. It just makes me want to see what else the terrifying man can throw at me.

Elijah doesn’t withdraw right away, staying deep inside me for long moments after his orgasm subsides. His fingers draw soft lines in my hips, my ass, my lower back, and I start to wonder if he went too hard and hurt himself.

"Are you okay?" I whimper as he slides out of me, the evidence of his release immediately dripping between my thighs.

"Exactly what the doctor ordered." He chuckles as he lifts me from the ground. "Now, I need you to call your brothers and get them over here."

"What?"

"It seems more than just a shipment has gone missing, which means we may have a common enemy."

FIFTY

ELIJAH

Snow paces restlessly up and down my office. She hasn't stopped moving since she sent the message to Wynter an hour ago, and each time I move to comfort her, she sends me a glare I'm not brave enough to question.

If you told me a month ago that Snow Saint James would have me wrapped around her little finger, I would have put a bullet in your brain for suggesting such a thing, but that's exactly what's happened. The fierce woman I want to stand by my side could rule our kingdom without any questions being asked, and that thought alone has my cock hardening again.

After we finished in the bathroom, I carried her to the shower and kept her distracted as the water washed away the evidence of our quick fuck. I'm a dick for taking her like that, especially when she's only barely over the agony her period put her through, but I needed her.

Just another reason to get her pregnant as soon as possible. She won't have to be in that amount of pain for at least nine months. For two days I couldn't bear to be away from her, not when she was bedridden, often crying from the intensity of the pain she was in.

"Snow, you're going to wear a path in my carpet, and Mrs. Chambers is going to kill me."

She stops in her tracks, turning her brutal stare on me. "I just stopped my brothers from killing you, and then you invited them over for a casual afternoon of Mafia wars. Please tell me in what possible universe I wouldn't be freaking the hell out right now?"

If it were any other woman yelling at me, she would be locked up until she learned to speak to me with the respect I deserve. But not Snow. Her fire makes me hard as a rock, and I wouldn't have her any other way.

"Mafia wars?" I raise a brow.

"What else would you like me to call it?" she snaps at the same time the doorbell rings through the house, and her body stills in its place, terror crossing her features. "Are you sure we don't need to bring in some extra guards?"

I smile, slowly rising from the desk and crossing the office to where she's standing still as a statue. When I reach her, I tug her body into mine, forcing down the grunt of pain when her body collides with my likely broken ribs, and tip her chin up to look at me. "It's going to be okay, Snowflake. I don't want you stressing about this, even if I do like you being worried about me." I smirk.

"Don't let it go to your head." She rolls her eyes, but the ghost of a smile plays on her lips.

I press a kiss to her temple, relishing in the way our scents mingle together after we've fucked. Even after a shower, I can smell our mutual release on her skin, and it takes every ounce of restraint in my body not to throw her over my shoulder and fuck her against my desk like I long to do. But I can't leave her family standing on the doorstep, even if their presence is only going to make Snow more uncomfortable than she already is.

I drag myself away from her, pointing at the chair I placed beside my own at the desk. If she's going to rule by my side, she needs to do it from the right side of the table.

I don't chance another look over my shoulder, not with how wound up I am and how close I am to dragging Snow back to our room and not letting her leave until I've had my fill, which if my constant need for her over the last decade is anything to go by, isn't likely to ever happen.

By the time I reach the door, I've slipped into business mode. I swing the double doors open and find Storm and Rayne standing on the top step, each with a mask just like my own in place. Behind them, Everett has Wynter tucked under his arm, worry etched into her brow.

"Where's my sister?" Storm snaps.

"Waiting for us in the office. As you can imagine, she's nervous about your visit after the… compromising position she found us all in earlier." It's not like me to beat around the bush or avoid conflict, but I'm trying to conserve as much of our fragile relationship as I can. Although in another time, I would have retaliated for a stunt like the one they pulled this morning, that isn't an option right now. Not only because they're Snow's family, but because I won't hurt her like that.

I push the doors wider and step to the side, silently inviting them into the house that has only just started feeling like a home.

"This way," I say as I start up the hallway. When I reach the office, she's sitting in her chair and her face shows none of the anxiety she displayed only a few minutes ago. She has one leg crossed over the other, her tight black jeans hugging her shapely legs. She looks calm and collected when her eyes meet mine, and my obsession with her grows to a new high.

Snow is utter perfection.

I take my place at her side, a feeling of rightness crashing down on me. I knew from the moment I saw her that she would be my wife one day, but I always hoped she would be more than that, and to see that come to fruition is more than I ever could have imagined.

Snow's face is stony as each of her siblings filter into the room, taking a seat across the desk from us. The air in the room is thick with tension and unspoken words. Just a few hours ago, they were beating me black and blue, but none of them seem remorseful for their actions.

"What are we doing here, Russo?" Storm finally asks, leaning back in his seat as if he would rather be anywhere but here.

"Storm!" Wynter hisses. "We talked about this."

"We talked about being civil, and that's what I'm doing."

"No, we talked about being nice so we don't miss out on our sister's life because of your pigheadedness."

Storm sighs, irritation seeping from him. "Fine. How can we

help you, Elijah?" He turns his attention from me immediately to look at his sister, as if asking if that was better.

"I had a call from the guy that manages my dealers. I haven't had a chance to choose or train a second in charge, but this guy was doing it for my uncle and had no allegiance to him after he died, so I kept him on." I'm giving more detail than I need to, but only because I'm hoping it will show I'm being genuine. "Anyway, he called after Snow and I got home, and we've had six of our dealers go missing in the last few hours. He does a check-in with all the dealers three times a day depending on the times they're working, and when he didn't hear back from them, he went to check on them and none of them were where they normally work."

"Did you ever think maybe they just fucked off with the drugs?" Rayne asks.

"Normally I would think that, but these guys that are missing have families. They wouldn't put them at risk for a few grand of coke and some pills."

Silence falls over the room as they consider my words and what they could mean. To me, it seems like someone is targeting both families and hitting us where it hurts. In terms of targets, we are the two biggest ones in the city, so it's ambitious, but it makes the most sense. Our biggest trade has always been drugs. Angelo wanted it to be trafficking, and that side of the business was very lucrative, but it wasn't as steady as drugs. You have to wait to get girls. You can't just break down the doors in villages and steal women from their homes, and then stick them on a plane to the USA, no matter how much he would have liked to have done that.

The Saint James family sells weapons, technology, and a bunch of shit I don't even pretend to understand. That's always been Everett's domain, and I don't want to stick my nose in where it doesn't belong. If we wanted to hit them, it was always to take a shipment, even when we had no idea what to do with the shit we stole because it wasn't our domain. It was always an easy dent in their armor.

"Was it you?" Snow asks, her eyes trained on Rayne and her hands folded in her lap. Her tone is firm but casual. "Seems awfully convenient that you decided Elijah took the shipment on the same day six of our dealers went missing." The people across the desk have underestimated Snow, her entire life, but today is her chance to show them the leader she was always meant to be, and I'm not going to take that opportunity away from her.

"Our?" Storm rumbles. "Are you forgetting who your family is?"

Her eyes move to mine, surprise hidden in the icy blue. She's shocked by her own words, but I'm not. The moment the word left her pretty pink lips I knew she was in this just as deep as I have been for the last ten years.

I give her a small nod, telling her this business is just as much hers now as it is mine.

"Elijah and I are getting married on Saturday," she reminds them. "Now, answer my question."

"No," Rayne answers. "We've had our sights on figuring out who took the shipment. All our men have been on that or on security to make sure we couldn't be hit again while we were working out who the threat was."

"What was your tip off?"

"Tip off for what?"

"What pointed you in Elijah's direction? What made you assume your sister's fiancé, who you recently agreed to an alliance with, was the one who took the shipment?"

Rayne hesitates, his eyes darting to Everett beside him for an explanation.

"The job was too clean for anyone else. No one else has the experience or the resources you have access to, and there were telltale signs of some of the previous missing shipments that pointed us in your direction," Everett explains, holding Wynter tightly in his lap. He feels the same intense protectiveness for her as I do Snow, and if I didn't know our family were cold, heartless killers, I would think perhaps it was hereditary.

"Are you serious?" Snow snaps. "You three beat my fiancé black and blue, and your evidence was that the scene was clean?" The anger in her voice burns through the room, and I don't miss the way her brother's eyes widen.

"Will you stop calling him that?" Storm growls. "You are not marrying a Russo."

FIFTY-ONE

SNOW

"Come again?" I hiss. I've never felt anything but love for my siblings, but right now, I could kill my brothers. My fingers itch to reach for the gun I know Elijah hides under his desk, the one my knee brushed when he fucked me with another one.

The memory assaults my senses and takes my breath away, but I keep my eyes narrowed on my brother. The audacity of these men never fails to amaze me. Where do they get off telling me who I can and can't marry?

"You heard me." Storm leans back in his seat. "I've indulged you and have allowed you to have your fun, but you will not be getting married on Saturday. In fact, why don't you go pack your shit and you can come home with us."

A growl beside me has me reaching for Elijah's hand before he can leap across the desk and tackle him.

"You try to take my woman out of this house, and I will not hesitate to put a bullet between your eyes." The anger coming off him is like nothing I've ever felt from him before. He was angry when he found Dwayne with his hands on me, but not like he is right now. He's so tightly wound that I'm certain if my hand wasn't holding his tightly, he would be in a violent rage right now and my family likely wouldn't be walking out the front door.

Storm stands abruptly, his chair screeching across the hardwood flooring. "She is my sister, and I am the leader of this family. If I say Snow is leaving, then that's exactly what's going to be happening."

"Storm," Everett warns, carefully moving Wynter to her own seat in preparation to jump in if things get out of hand.

"No. I've had enough of these games. Elijah is a Russo through and through. He brought us here this afternoon to flaunt the fact our baby sister is sitting by his side playing king and queen with him, and I've had enough. I bet none of your dealers are missing at all."

"Enough," I shout, standing from my seat to lean forward over the desk. My palms brush across the mahogany, the smoothness under my hands enough to keep me grounded as rage beats through my blood with every beat of my heart. "You are acting like a child, Storm. Yes, you are the leader of our family, and you do the job well, but you need to remember that I am not a child, and I should have the autonomy to make my own decisions. Wynter is marrying Everett, who is every bit a Russo as Elijah is. Just because they don't share the name doesn't make him any less related to Angelo."

"Everett is our brother," Storm growls.

"Yes, he is," I agree. We may not have been born to the same parents, but Everett is just as much a brother to me as Storm and Rayne, however that doesn't make my words any less true. "I'm marrying Elijah on Saturday, regardless of what you think. I respect you, and I respect your authority within the family, but this is not a family decision. This is me, for the first time in my life, making a decision for myself and not rolling over when a Saint James man says I should. I know what I want, and I want to marry Elijah."

"Well, Snow, we don't always get what we want," Storm retorts.

A laugh claws its way up my throat, and I can't help but allow the vindictive sound to fill the room. "No. You all get what you want. Rayne got Emerson. Wynter got Everett. You got to lead the business and do whatever the fuck you want. *I* got nothing. I got told what I could and couldn't do all my life. I got underestimated and doubted."

"So you admit you're only doing this to push our buttons."

"No. I didn't say that. What I said is, for once in my life, I'm taking what I want. I'm doing what I want, regardless of what you say. Elijah and I are happy, and I feel more whole than I've ever felt in my life."

Wynter stands from her seat and dodges Everett when he tries to wrap his arms around her and keep her where he deems it to be safe. She moves to Storm and places a hand on his shoulder. My heart aches at the sight of my sister, my best friend in the whole world, taking his side and allowing him to dictate my happiness. But I don't know why I expected anything else. Of course, she's loyal to Storm. She is his succession plan after all. It's only right that she stands on the side that she may lead one day.

But a moment later, she takes measured steps until he's standing beside me. What the fuck is she doing?

"Wynter," Everett rumbles.

"I will not stand on the side that doesn't allow my sister to marry who she wants to marry. She's right. Everett is a Russo just like Elijah, and he's been a part of our family since day one. Why can't we accept that our sister is happy and give her fiancé a chance?"

"You shot him a few months ago!" Storm reminds her.

She lets out a small laugh, and I can't help the small smile that pulls at my lips. There's definitely a funny side to all this. Maybe one day I'll be able to laugh about how preposterous this conversation has been. "You're right. I did. He threatened my safety, and I took the shot I had to take. But that doesn't mean he's not capable of change. That doesn't mean he's not suitable for our sister. She's right. You have always barked orders at us, and we've always jumped. If there is anywhere in this city that Snow is as safe as she is with us, it's here with Elijah."

"You cannot be serious."

"I'm deadly serious, Storm. Either you get on board with this and stop threatening our sister's fiancé, or I'm out. You can find someone else to take the reins if something happens to you." She shrugs as if the thought of abandoning our family doesn't have her breath picking up and panic raging through her veins.

"You would leave us just like that?" Storm asks incredulously.

"I would do what I need to do to make sure my little sister is given the same opportunities we've been given."

I turn my attention to Elijah, who almost seems amused by the back and forth. The anger he displayed only a few minutes ago has dissipated. "As amusing as this display of familial bickering is, I'd like to bring it back to the issue at hand, and while I appreciate your good intentions, Wynter, you can take a seat back with my cousin before he decapitates me with his mind. Snow will not be leaving this house, and I hazard you against trying to take her, sway her feelings, or attempting to tear us apart, because I will not allow it. For the last time, Snow and I will be getting married on Saturday, and if you don't like it, you don't have to attend the ceremony. However, I know it would mean the world to Snow to have you there by her side." He gives me a small smile as he reaches across the space between us and takes my hand in his. The silent support is almost enough to settle my racing heart as I watch Wynter move back toward Everett. Once she's close enough, he wraps his arms around her waist and tugs her into his lap carefully. He whispers something into her ear, and a deep blush stains her cheeks.

"How sure are you that your dealers didn't just take off?" Rayne asks. It's unlike him to be quiet for this long during these kinds of discussions, but I have a feeling he is much more understanding of matters of the heart now he has Emerson.

"Ninety-nine percent," Elijah answers immediately. "These guys have wives and kids. One of them is a single father. I had my guy check where the families are, and his little boy wasn't picked up from school this afternoon. He sat on the step for an hour before one of the teachers noticed him and called child services. I've known this guy for a lot of years and he wouldn't do that to that kid. He's his entire world."

Wynter sucks in a breath, her hand falling protectively over her swelling stomach, but I can't allow the emotions to crash over me, not when I need to establish my role within the organization. I need to show the same amount of strength Elijah does.

Rayne nods slowly, his eyes meeting Everett beside him. "Where's the kid?"

"I had one of my guys pick him up and take him home, where my housekeeper, Mrs. Chambers, met them. She's warm and nurturing, exactly what he needs to distract him from his dad being missing."

"It looks like we have a common enemy," Storm says, his eyes moving to meet mine.

"So what are we going to do about it?" I ask.

"We're going to wait for them to make their next move, except this time, we're going to be ready for them."

FIFTY-TWO
ELIJAH

All the times I imagined Snow becoming my wife, none of them involved doing so in part to draw out our enemy. But that's how the chips have fallen and something we'll both have to learn to live with.

When the Saint James family left our home the other day, Snow jumped into wedding planning. She had dresses brought in to pick from. She had the best wedding planner in the city on our doorstep an hour after she called. And she hasn't stopped since.

Part of me wonders if she's walking down the aisle for the right reasons, but as long as she takes my name after all is said and done, I don't give a fuck what the driving force is.

No matter how hard I try to focus on my laptop in front of me, tracking the movement of our drugs and dealers, I can't keep my eyes off Snow as she flicks through the last of the decisions we have to make. The seating chart, the programs we give out at the church, and the menu are the last things we have to finalize before we get married the day after tomorrow.

Her blonde hair falls around her face, acting as a shield between us, and I can barely handle it. I can barely keep myself in my seat rather than striding across the room, bending her over the arm of the couch and fucking her so hard she'll be feeling my cock until she becomes my wife.

As if she can read my mind, her eyes move from the papers in front of her and meet mine, a slight blush brushing across her cheeks. "Do you need something?"

I chuckle. "Careful, Snowflake. Watch your mouth, or I'll put it to better use."

"Promises, promises." She smirks, peering over at her phone beside her. I returned it to her after her siblings left. She's not a flight risk anymore, and the way she stood up to her brothers with fierce determination is all the evidence I needed of that. The look on her face when I handed over her phone and a new laptop, as well as a set of keys to the house and her new car, was the best gift I could ever receive. Apart from her of course.

"Don't tempt me, Snow."

She laughs, her head falling back against the arm of the couch. "I need to talk to you about something, and I want you to listen to me before you jump in and lose your mind."

I place my laptop beside me and shuffle to the edge of my seat. "Go ahead."

"I'm going to stay at the estate tomorrow night—"

"Absolutely not," I growl. The idea of her being out of my

sight, let alone in another house, with the people who have repeatedly tried to take her away from me, makes me want to chain her to our bed and throw away the key.

She rolls her eyes and sighs heavily. "That's not letting me finish, Elijah."

"You don't need to waste your breath, it's a no, and there's nothing that could come out of that pretty mouth that would change my mind."

She groans. "Can you just listen to me for a minute and stop being such a stubborn ass?"

I raise my brow, the ghost of a smile playing on my lips. If anyone else spoke to me like this, I would kill them before they could take another breath, but not Snow. No, I find her sass and constant defiance charming. "Go on then." I lean back in my seat, spreading my arms out across the back of the couch as I wait for her to deliver her argument.

"I know we're using this wedding as a ploy to draw out whoever is messing with our families, but I would still like to follow the traditions. If this is the only wedding I'm going to have, then I want to do it right."

I narrow my eyes on her, anger simmering under the surface that I barely manage to tamp down. "Of course this is the only wedding you're going to have," I growl.

"So let me do it right! Let me have the freedom to choose to spend the night with my sisters, and to get pampered and primped and for you to see me for the first time as I walk down the aisle. If this marriage is going to work, I need you to trust me to make these kinds of decisions for myself." The earnestness in her voice disarms me. Will I ever be able to say no to her? Will I ever be able to deny my Snowflake a thing she wants when she looks at me like this?

I close my eyes and blow out a long breath. This woman is going to be the death of me. "What about Wynter and Emerson come stay here for the night? I'll make myself scarce and make sure we don't see one another before the wedding."

"There are cameras in every room in this house," she counters. "And there's no way Rayne lets Emerson step foot in this house."

"Then you just have Wynter, and I turn off the cameras." I shrug.

Snow groans, frustration radiating off her. "I don't want just Wynter. I want both my sisters. And even if you turn the cameras off, I know you well enough to know you will just turn them back on again the moment I turn my back."

She's not entirely wrong about that. The need to have eyes on my woman is so strong that the moment she walks out of the room, I'm itching to turn my screens to the camera feed and watch her as she makes her way through the house.

I sigh. "Come here." I pat my knee.

She watches me for a moment before placing the things on her lap to the side. She crosses from her seat to where I'm sitting and carefully lowers herself into my lap. The moment her body makes contact with mine is like I can breathe again. I thought my obsession with her ran deep before, but now I know what it's like to feel her skin on mine, to hold her through the night, and slide into her sweet pussy, that obsession only grows deeper by the day.

"I understand what you're saying, but I don't think I can have you out of my sight at the moment, not when there's someone targeting both of our families." I'm not a man who concedes on anything, but I find myself wanting to give her anything her heart desires.

"The estate is one of the safest places in the city."

"I know, but what about when you're going back and forth? What about when people are coming in to do hair and makeup? How can I be sure your family's security will check every pocket in their bags to make sure there's nothing that can harm you?" The thoughts whirling in my mind have anger thrumming through my veins, but I force my body to remain calm.

"You're overthinking this, Elijah."

I move her so quickly she lets out a squeak of surprise as I position her so she's straddling my lap. One hand moves up her back and gathers the hair at the nape of her neck in my fist. "When it comes to your safety, there is no such thing as overthinking. I will overthink every single decision that impacts your health and safety for the rest of our lives, and that's just something you're going to have to learn to live with."

Snow sighs, her eyes dropping closed as her mind wanders to another solution. But there isn't one. Her only option is to spend the night here with me, and she'll be lucky if I even allow her to sleep in another room within the house, let alone in a house across the city.

"I know this is hard for you, Snowflake, and I'm sorry our wedding can't be everything you dreamed it to be, but once this is all over, I'll make up for it, okay?"

She nods slowly, tears gathering in the corners of her eyes that I quickly wipe away.

"Please don't cry," I murmur.

"There will never be time," she whispers. "You forget that I know how this life works. Just because one threat is neutralized, it doesn't mean the rest are. We will never be safe. I will never have the freedom I crave, because you will always be overprotective and overbearing." Before I can stop her, she moves herself from my lap and strides across the room, slamming the door on her way out.

In almost any other circumstance, I would likely find her outburst amusing. But the reality is, she's right. It's been this way my entire life, and it will be the same until the day I die.

When you're part of a Mafia family, you're never safe, and that's a painful reality we've both had to grow up with.

FIFTY-THREE

SNOW

Like every little girl I know, I spent most of my childhood imagining the future I would have. I had dolls that I pretended were my children and friends I swore I would have by my side for the rest of my life.

But there was one day I played over and over in my mind, dreaming up everything I could ever hope for, and then some.

My wedding day.

Visually, the church is exactly what I envisioned. My dress is the princess style I always wanted, my hair is curled down my back as I imagined it would be, and my sister is just as radiant in her deep crimson dress as I knew she would be.

On paper, my wedding is exactly what I dreamed of all those years ago. But my reality is something else entirely.

All the nights I spent dreaming of my wedding, I never thought I would have a gun strapped to my thigh, or a knife sewn into the boning of my dress. I never thought I would be marrying a man who my family has always considered to be the enemy. And I certainly never imagined my wedding would be used as a ploy to draw out whoever is fucking with both families.

And yet here we are.

The soft lace and harsh boning digging into my ribs are such a direct contrast it holds my mind in the here and now each time it starts to wander. All the things that could have been. The fact my father isn't the one walking me down the aisle, and my mother isn't here to give me last minute pieces of advice. The fact my brothers were almost uninvited altogether and now hover nearby, as if waiting for the penny to drop and Elijah to pull out some nefarious scheme.

Wynter readjusts the back of my dress for the tenth time since we took our place behind the door at the end of the aisle. The veil my mother wore on her wedding day is delicately draped over my face and having something of hers so close to me allows me to feel like she's here with me.

"Stop fussing over her, Wyn. You're making her nervous." Emerson takes one of my hands and squeezes, a gesture of silent support. While she's only been in the family for a few months, I consider her to be every bit as much a sister as Wynter, and she has each of us so perfectly worked out, I almost can't believe it some days. "How are you feeling?"

I close my eyes and let out a shaky breath. I could lie to her, but she'd know. It's her job to know when people are lying or skating around the truth. "Nervous," I admit.

She nods, sympathy shrouding her emerald eyes. "I was sure I was going to need to stop halfway up the aisle and throw up when Rayne and I got married." She smiles affectionately at her husband.

"She was basically hyperventilating by the time she made it to me." He chuckles, taking long strides across the small space and bundling his wife up in his arms.

I meet Storm's thunderous eyes by the door and offer him a small smile. It's not much, but it's all I can give him. We've always had a strained relationship. It comes with the territory I suppose but it's never been more so than it is now. The fact I'm going against his wishes and marrying Elijah is seen as a betrayal, and I don't entirely disagree with his logic. If you told me six months ago that I would be standing here in my dream wedding dress, about to walk down the aisle and marry Elijah Russo, I would have laughed in your face. Even now, the idea is preposterous, but it feels right.

Even through all the planning and fear, the closer I came to this moment, the more settled in my choice I was. Something inside tells me I was meant to be with Elijah, and I've never been one to argue with my gut before.

I take a breath and take another look at my family. Both my sisters, and all three brothers. A family forged through trials and tribulations, and we're about to gain another member, even if half of them aren't happy about the choice. "I know you think this is a huge mistake, and you think I'm only doing it as a way to get a rise out of you, but I can assure you that I'm not that big of an idiot. I wouldn't tie myself to another person for the rest of my life unless I was absolutely sure it was the right choice, especially not someone in a family like ours. I'm well aware that the only escape from a Mafia marriage is death, and I quite enjoy breathing." I half laugh at my attempt at humor and glance down at my dress again. It truly is a work of art. The designer pulled it together so quickly I'm truly not sure how it was even possible, but I don't question how they got it done.

Storm sighs, his eyes softening as he follows the same path my own had a moment ago. "I don't think you're an idiot, Snow. I think you're a bright, incredible, beautiful young woman who has their entire life ahead of them, and I don't want you to make any mistakes you can't take back." He pauses, something I don't recognize crossing his gray eyes. "All I ever wanted for you and Wynter is for you to be happy, and you were… right the other day when you said I shouldn't judge Elijah based on who his family is because we've never done that to Everett. I am still hesitant about this arrangement, but I will no longer interfere."

I smile and hold my hand out to him. He takes it immediately and tugs me into an embrace that, for once, doesn't feel foreign. It feels right. "Thank you for being here," I whisper.

"I wouldn't miss your big day, Snow."

Music fills the church on the other side of the door and panic fills my lungs, taking up all the space air would normally occupy. Am I really doing this? Am I really marrying a man I considered to be our enemy a month ago? And am I really going to do it with a threat hanging over our heads?

There's so much security in this church it seems like the impossible mark, but if I've learned anything growing up in a Mafia family, it's that nothing is impossible. There's always something, or someone, lurking in the shadows ready to strike.

"You ready?" Wynter flashes me a bright smile, and her excitement settles my nerves enough for me to nod. She gives me a quick hug and rearranges my dress again. "You look so beautiful, Snow. Mom and Dad would be so proud of you."

"Thank you," I choke out.

Emerson and Rayne stand by the doors, their arms linked as they listen for their queue. Wynter and Everett are behind them, and Storm links his arm with mine. When I asked him to walk me down the aisle, I wasn't sure he would say yes. Not with how he feels about the man I'm marrying. But it was one of the rare moments I've seen him speechless.

"You've got this, little sis," he whispers to me as the doors push open and all eyes turn to Emerson and Rayne. They take measured steps toward the altar, and I try to get a glimpse of Elijah, but there are people blocking my view.

The church is packed. We invited everyone we both know, making for an interesting assortment of high society and the criminals of the city. There are the most decorated police officers and the most fucked up, deranged men who call Chicago home in the pews, and the irony of it isn't lost on me.

"We've got you, Snow." Storm gives me a small smile, and then we're moving.

The moment my eyes lock with Elijah's at the other end of the aisle, something inside me settles and I let out the breath I didn't realize I was holding. Perhaps it should worry me just how deeply my feelings for him are ingrained, but right now, all I can think about is how sexy he looks in his three-piece suit clinging to every hard muscle. It looks like the thing was made for his body, and considering the price we paid for it, I might actually believe it was stitched right onto his body this morning.

His face is set in impenetrable stone, but there's a hint of adoration in his eyes only I can recognize, because I'm the only one who has ever been on the receiving end of it. He wears a mask for the rest of the world, but I can see through it to the man he is behind closed doors. The man he is just for me.

When Emerson and Rayne reach the altar, he gives her hand a squeeze and they separate. He stands behind Elijah while she moves to where I'll stand across from him. He's hesitant to let her out of his reach, but we planned for every eventuality. If something goes down, Emerson, Wynter and I will make a break for the door behind the altar and we're to wait there until the coast is clear.

Wynter and Everett follow the same patterns, and then there's no one between me and my soon-to-be husband.

Storm stops a few feet from Elijah and draws me into his arms for the second time today. His grip on me is tight and certain, and I don't dare pull away for fear he might never do it again. "I'm proud of you." He releases me before I can respond, his eyes finding Elijah's as he steps down toward us, his hand extended to take mine. "Take care of my baby sister," Storm rumbles.

"With every beat of my heart," Elijah says, not bothering to drag his eyes away from me. "You are a vision, my Snowflake."

I wonder if he can see the intricate details I had added to my gown to represent his nickname for me. The individually sewn snowflakes weaved within the lace and tulle. When I asked the designer to add them, I was met with dead silence on the other end of the line and I imagined her rolling her eyes at the request. She probably thought it was some melodramatic nod to my unusual name. But no. It's a nod to my almost-husband and the way he became obsessed with me.

I take Elijah's hand and allow him to help me to the altar, his eyes never leaving me.

The pews quieten and silence falls throughout the church. My breaths come in quickly as my eyes scan the crowd. They're here. I can feel it. There's something in the air that grips my throat and danger rings through my body.

"Relax," Elijah murmurs, his fingers moving to my chin and pulling me to face him.

The moment our eyes meet, the worry is replaced with a calm only he can bring me. I allow myself to lean into his warmth, soaking up the comfort he offers. I don't care if there's a church full of people staring at us. I don't care if for this moment the world sees me for who I am, not the person I've portrayed all these years. All that matters is Elijah.

"Good girl," he whispers, and a moment later, the priest's voice rumbles through the church, but neither of us can drag our eyes away from one another.

The priest's words barely register as he engages his audience. We chose not to write our own vows, worried it would show our weakness, and on top of that, we haven't actually spoken about how we feel about one another. It's clear Elijah is obsessed with me. I knew it the moment our eyes met across the dining room that first morning. But obsession and love aren't the same thing, and the feelings that have seeped into my heart and make it hard to breathe when he's not around is much closer to the latter.

It's not until Elijah quirks an eyebrow at me that I finally tune into the words being said around me. "Do you, Snow Elizabeth Saint James, take Elijah Anthony Russo to be your lawfully wedded husband? To have and to hold, in sickness and in health, in good times and bad, for richer or poorer, keeping yourself unto him for as long as you both shall live?"

"I do," I reply immediately, the words falling from my lips so quickly I barely register them.

Elijah smirks, the corners of his lips quirking up so slightly no one but me would notice.

"Do you, Elijah Anthony Russo, take Snow Elizabeth Saint James to be your lawfully wedded husband? To have and to hold, in sickness and in health, in good times and bad, for richer or poorer, keeping yourself unto her for as long as you both shall live?"

"I do," he says evenly.

"By the power vested in me by the state of Illinois, I now pronounce you husband and wife."

Elijah and I are embracing before he can finish the words, our kiss feral and driven by need and fear, and all the other emotions running rampant through our bodies. I've never needed someone so badly I couldn't breathe without them, but that's what it's like with Elijah, and I'm in no position to argue.

When he finally breaks our kiss, he pays no mind to the crowd of people cheering for us. Instead, he rests his forehead on mine, and we take a moment to allow it all to soak in.

"I lo—" Before Elijah can finish, a loud bang at the front of the church drags our attention from one another, and a moment later, chaos reigns down on us.

Fifty-Four

Elijah

Gunfire fills the church, and before I realize I'm doing it, I shove Snow behind one of the large speakers at the front of the altar and use my own body to shield her.

I knew this was a bad idea. I knew nothing good could come from using our wedding to bait whoever is fucking with us, and yet I allowed her to continually reassure me.

"Stay right here. Do not fucking move until myself or one of your brothers tells you to."

Snow nods frantically. Her hand slips up the skirt of her dress and reveals a gun. Where the fuck did she get that from? "I'll be okay," she promises.

I watch her for another moment, but a loud explosion to the left of the building pulls my attention away from my bride. One of the exits has been destroyed, and guests are panicked as they try to escape the chaos.

"Elijah!" Storm shouts from behind one of the other speakers, and I quickly make my way to him. Stray bullets fly around me, but I don't have time to try to dodge them right now. I have to get my wife the fuck out of here and figure out who the hell is doing this to us.

"Where are Wynter and Emerson?" I ask quickly, my eyes locking on two men in full combat gear as they push through the crowd. Without so much as a thought, I aim at the first one and fire, hitting him in the throat, the only bit of skin not covered with gear. Quickly, I move my aim to the other one and fire. The moment the bullet penetrates through his forehead, he drops to the ground like a sack of potatoes.

"Rayne took them out the back. You should get Snow out as well."

I glance at the back exit and then at Snow across from me. Her dress is still immaculate despite the rubble around us. She's been far enough away from the explosions and gunfire that she hasn't been tainted by it yet. "I have a bad feeling."

"What do you mean you have a bad feeling?" Storm snaps. "Get my sister the fuck out of here."

"Not through that door."

Almost as if my words summoned them, the door swings open and three men in the same gear as the rest of the attackers walk through with guns drawn.

Snow's face pales as their sights set on her, and dread seeps into my chest.

"Where the fuck are our guys?" I shout.

"I don't fucking know. We're outnumbered by a long shot!"

Panic isn't something I ever expected to hear in Storm's voice, and I expect if we make it out of this church alive, I likely won't hear it again. "Where the hell is Everett?"

I glance over the speaker, scanning the church until my eyes lock on my cousin above the crowd in the upstairs pews, a rifle trained on the men approaching Snow.

Storm follows my gaze and I swear he lets out a relieved breath. "We need to get her out of here."

"All the exits are covered, and I'm not risking walking her into a gunfight."

"As opposed to sitting in the middle of one?"

I glare at him, but my focus is back on my wife. I have to get to her, but bullets are flying everywhere and there's no way I'll make it back without being shot.

"Grab the girl, and let's get out of here." One of the men nods toward Snow and her eyes widen.

Panic assaults my senses as she lifts the gun to point at one of them. Her hands are steady and sure despite the fear in her eyes.

The men look at one another, their faces covered with balaclavas, and then they start laughing. As if the idea of Snow being the one who shoots them is preposterous. Her eyes narrow on one of them, she takes in a deep breath, and then she pops off three shots in succession and they drop like flies.

Storm lets out a shocked breath as pride fills my chest. My little warrior.

"Get her out of here, Elijah."

I look up to where Everett is picking off the men who come into his range. I need to draw his attention to cover me while I get to Snow, but he's too focused on taking out the enemy.

"Elijah, don't," Snow shouts from the other side of the altar, her eyes wild with fear and adrenaline. If it was any other time, I would be finding somewhere to bend her over and fuck her until she couldn't breathe, but sex should be the last thing on my mind right now. All that matters is getting her out of this building.

Everett finally looks down at me just as I push myself off the speaker and leap toward Snow, and he immediately starts picking off the men aiming at the stage. There are so many of them, easily four dozen, maybe more. Who the fuck has this much firepower behind them? As far as I know, the Russo and Saint James families have been running this city for the last twenty years without so much as a whisper of challenge, so where the hell has this new enemy come from?

Pain radiates through my side as I hit the ground, and by the terror in Snow's eyes as she scrambles toward me, I know I've been hit.

"Stay where you are," I growl and point my gun toward the pews, scanning for the motherfucker who shot me.

"I'm not leaving you," Snow snaps, crawling across the altar in her ridiculously large dress. I should have insisted on the bodice being made from bulletproof material, but when I suggested that and had Snow and the dress designer stare at me like I'd lost my damn mind, I backed down.

"Snow, if you don't get back behind that speaker right this minute, I'm going to spank you every night for the next year."

"You can only follow through with that threat if you don't bleed out first." She wraps her arms around my upper body, the contact immediately settling the part of me that runs rampant when she's outside of my grasp. But it's no time to feel settled, not when she's in danger, and certainly not when it seems she's the one they've come for.

"There she is!" a voice to our left yells, and we both turn to see five men surrounding us.

My eyes dart to Everett, except he's not in the top pews anymore. He's not anywhere. I turn my attention to the other speaker I left Storm behind to see two men holding him down, his face pressed into the rough carpet of the altar.

We're surrounded.

We're surrounded, and there's no escape.

I put my woman in danger. I allowed our wedding to be a trap. And because of that choice, we're going to lose everything. And worse than that, I'm going to lose Snow. That's a far worse punishment than death. A life without her, without my Snowflake, it's not a life at all.

I can't let that happen.

A burst of adrenaline shoots through my body, and I burst to life. I train my gun on one of the men and shoot him right between the eyes before moving to the guy beside him. But the others don't slow their advance. If anything, they close in on us quicker.

“Elijah,” Snow whimpers, her body trembling.

“It’s okay, Snow. I won’t let them take you. I’ll never let anyone take you away from me.” I’m not sure which one of us I’m trying to assure of that, but neither of us appear any less tense after the words leave my mouth.

“Just give her up, Russo. Give her to us and we’ll leave,” one of the men reasons.

My entire body screams at me, but I force myself to my feet, all but forgetting that I’ve just been shot. “You’ll take her over my dead body,” I growl, stepping in front of her to shield her from them.

“That can be arranged.”

A gunshot fills the church, so loud and so close I could have sworn it was from one of the men standing before me, but they seem just as surprised by the sound as I am. Our heads whip to the side collectively, looking for the source, and when I find a lone gunman in the middle of the pews, the gun trained behind me, my stomach drops. Before I can turn around, Snow falls to the ground, red staining her white gown.

Fear and agony morph together across Snow’s face and a bloodcurdling scream claws up her throat. The sound sets something off inside me, something primal bites at the edges, the monster I hide from the world tearing through to the surface.

Burning red clouds my vision, rage beating through my veins with every beat of my heart, and then, as if my body has a mind of its own, I draw my gun and take aim at one of the men approaching Snow. I fire shot after shot at each of the men and revel in the sight of them falling to the ground until there are none left standing over my woman.

"Elijah," Snow cries, her focus behind me where Storms surrounded.

"All you have to do is let us take the girl and you can get back to your lives. Isn't that what you want?" one of the men asks, his pistol pointed at Storm's head.

His eyes flare with anger as he shakes his head ever so slightly as if I would ever consider giving my wife over to whoever these assholes work for.

"How about this," I muse, barely forcing the growl back from my throat. "You tell me who the fuck you work for, and maybe I'll let you walk out of here alive."

The man who spoke before laughs, and my finger tightens on the trigger, even if I can't put a bullet in his head yet. There are three of them on Storm, one on his back pressing him into the carpet. Another has a gun pointed at his head. And the other, the one I'm itching to wipe off the face of the earth, he's standing between us. "We're not some tiny bug you can wipe from the city. You have no idea of our reach. And you can make us go away by giving us your little whore. Seems like an easy choice to me."

An inhuman growl forces its way from my throat and I barely catch myself from throwing myself forward and tearing him apart with my bare hands. How dare he speak of my woman like that. "You will not be taking her from this church, and I will destroy anyone that tries." The words come out strained, the anger bubbling in my veins is barely contained. I thought I'd felt anger before. I thought I'd felt rage. But none of those moments compares to the emotions slamming into me with each second that passes.

My woman is bleeding behind me, but I can't get to her without taking my eyes off the threat. Every single fiber of my being screams at me to go to her, to throw my gun down and get her the fuck out of here. But we wouldn't make it. There's no chance there aren't more of their men at every exit. If we're going to get out of here, we need to play it smart, and that means going against every instinct I have and allowing my woman to bleed without me.

I glance out at the pews, thankful when I see there are no other gunmen in sight, and it seems as if all the guests have escaped or been killed. I should care that people have died, our guests at that. But all I care about is getting Snow out of here safely, and any collateral damage along the way is worth it.

"Then you'll all die." He shrugs.

A loud explosion fills the space, and the ground shakes beneath our feet. Dust surrounds us, almost pulling my attention away from the men threatening my now brother-in-law. The men surrounding Storm look up for just long enough for me to take aim at the guy with the gun pointed at his head, and shoot, the bullet hitting him in the side of the head. Blood spurts from his wound, but I can't take the time to enjoy the bloodshed like I normally would.

I quickly aim at the man on Storm's back and unload a bullet in his head and then finally take aim at the leader before he can even register what has happened. He made a mistake when he underestimated us. They should have expected us to fight with everything we have. But then I suppose from the outside looking in, this looks like an arranged marriage. After all, they are common in the Mafia world, often used to seal alliances.

But that was their fatal mistake.

The moment he falls to the ground, I drop my gun and drop to my knees beside Snow, immediately pulling her into my lap. "I'm so sorry, baby," I whisper.

"It's not your fault." She winces.

My eyes trail down her body until they lock on the red spot that seems to get bigger by the second and a fresh wave of panic hits me, knocking the air right from my lungs. How much blood has she lost?

"It looks worse than it is," Snow hisses out.

I glare at her. "Don't lie to me, Snowflake. You know I can see right through it." Her weight settles in my lap, and even though I need to get her the hell out of here, I'm not sure I should move her.

Her eyes flutter closed, her breathing shallow and harsh. "Elijah," she whimpers.

"It's okay, baby. Just stay with me, okay? I'm going to get you out of here and get you some help as soon as I can, but I need you to hold on just a little longer. Can you do that for me?"

Snow nods, but the muscles in her neck barely hold the weight of her head. She's fading fast.

"How is she?" Storm asks, crouching down in front of us.

"We have to get her out of here."

Storm glances down at his phone and frowns. "I'm waiting on

confirmation that we're not walking into a fucking war zone when we get out there."

"Make it happen," I snap, brushing Snow's blonde curls from her cheeks and cupping her face in my hand. "Just hold on for me, Snowflake. I waited too long to get you, I can't lose you when you're finally mine." My voice cracks, but I don't give a fuck if these people know Snow is my weakness.

"It hurts." Tears roll down her cheeks, and each one that falls has another crack forming in my heart. The organ I thought was dead for so long, beats for the woman bleeding in my arms. Without her, there is no sense in living, because the sun can't rise and fall without the moon.

"I know it does, Snowflake," I whisper, holding her tight against my body. "Just hold on for me."

The front doors of the church burst open and I'm in motion before I even realize I'm doing it. I move my back to the threat, holding Snow tightly against me to make sure she won't bear the brunt of an attack.

"It's Rayne. Let's get her out of here," Storm says, his eyes watching us curiously, as if he's seeing us together for the first time. Up until now, he believed I was only with Snow as a bargaining chip, but now he sees it. Now he sees that my feelings for his sister transcend infatuation.

FIFTY-FIVE

SNOW

Agony tears through my torso and radiates in every direction. I never gave much thought to how it would feel to be shot, but I never thought anything could hurt like this. It's like the bullet still travels through me, ripping through flesh and muscles and organs as it forces its way through them.

"I'm going to get you out of here, Snowflake," Elijah murmurs, his eyes sweeping over me for what feels like the hundredth time. I think he's checking over and over that I'm really hurt, like he thinks he can pinch himself and wake up from this nightmare. Believe me, if that was an option, I would have already done it.

"There's an ambulance waiting out the front," Everett says as he approaches us, his brows knitted together as he takes in the sight.

"We can't take her to a hospital," Elijah snaps. "That's exactly what they'll expect us to do and there are too many things that can go wrong, too much time, I won't be able to be with her."

Storm sighs and rubs his hand over his face, wiping away some of the dust and debris that had settled on his skin. "I know, but we don't have much choice. Doc doesn't have the facilities for the level of care she needs, and I'm not willing to risk my sister's life because we were too stubborn to take her to a real hospital." His words are calm, but just beneath the surface is seething anger. When you grow up as close as we did, you get to know the tiny tells you each give off.

"Absolutely not." Elijah tightens his grip on me, and I hiss out in pain. It's not him, not really, my entire body hurts. Every inch of my skin is in agony, my insides are on fire, and every breath is like a searing hot poker is being driven through my lungs. The sound of my exhale gets his attention and guilt flashes through the green of his eyes. "Fuck, I'm sorry, Snow."

"It's okay," I wheeze.

"She needs a hospital, Elijah." Everett approaches us carefully, as if he's approaching a wild animal. "I've already called ahead, and I've already arranged for an entire floor to be vacated, I've called in every security company in the city for every spare guard, and I've paid off the doctors and nurses to allow one of us to be present for all treatment, including surgery if she needs it. She's going to be in good hands, but we need to get her there as soon as possible to make sure the bullet doesn't do any extra damage."

Elijah considers him for a moment before turning his attention back to me. "I'm going to make it better, Snow. I promise I'll make it better." The conviction in his voice is so deep, so sure of his words, and I can't help but believe him. "Every single person involved in what happened today will lose their life for hurting you, and when I find their leader, I'll bring you their heart as a trophy."

A tear slips down my cheek. I hate that he's hurting. I hate that my pain is causing him pain. And I hate that we haven't had the chance to tell each other how we really feel. Before I can respond, a wave of nausea hits me, and I pry myself from Elijah's arms just enough to throw up beside us. The heaving causes heavy sobs to break through my chest and agony to shoot through my body. I've never known pain like this, and I hope I'll never have to experience anything like this again.

"I've got you, Snow," Elijah murmurs. "I've always got you."

The next few minutes are a blur of movement and pain. Elijah cradles me against his chest as he walks us out of the destroyed church. I can't allow myself to process the fact that this is where my parents were married, or the fact that my wedding day will always be associated with the day I was shot, or even that whoever is coming for us is clearly a lot more connected than we gave them credit for. We were cocky. We thought there was no way whoever this is could have more firepower than we have between us. But we were wrong. God, we were so wrong.

"Just place her down on the gurney," the paramedic says, stopping it in front of Elijah.

"No," he replies, quickly dodging it and striding toward the ambulance without missing a step.

"Uh, sir. You need to allow us to do our job."

"And I will. But you'll be doing it with my wife in my lap." There's no room for argument in Elijah's tone, and he carefully steps up into the ambulance, barely jostling me in the process.

"That's not… that's…"

"That's how it's going to be."

"Elijah," I whisper. "Please let them do their job."

His eyes meet mine and soften immediately. If I didn't already know how deep his feelings for me run, this look is all I would need to tell me everything I need to know. When it comes to me, Elijah doesn't care if the rest of the world sees he's not the unfeeling monster he's always portrayed himself to be. All he cares about is making sure I'm safe and happy. He gives me a small nod and presses a kiss to the top of my head.

The paramedic watches us for a moment before taking a breath. "What about if you sit on the gurney with her on your lap?" His eyes move down to where blood seeps through the lace of my dress, drenching the snowflakes in dark crimson. "Sir, have you been shot as well?"

"It doesn't matter," Elijah rumbles. "All your focus needs to be on my wife. I'll get seen to as soon as she's okay."

I sigh and close my eyes. The pain is excruciating, and the nausea continues to crash into me in waves. This isn't how my wedding day should have been. I should have had my dad to walk me down the aisle, and my mom to give me some last-minute pieces of advice. I should have walked toward my almost-husband without a gun strapped to my thigh, and I should have married him without a gunfight breaking out in the church. I should have celebrated our union with our friends and family, and when that was done, I should have had Elijah take me home and ravish me through the night.

But all I've managed to get out of today is a new last name

and a gunshot wound.

"Elijah," I say quietly. "You need to let them look at you. At least to pack the wound so you don't lose too much blood."

"Fine, but not until you're taken care of."

Tears gather in the corners of my eyes the moment the doors slam shut and Elijah settles us on the gurney. Everything hurts. My arms, my legs, my head. Every single inch of me aches like the bullet exploded inside me and pieces have spread throughout me. "Are Wynter and Emerson safe?" I ask quietly, afraid my voice will break under the weight of the emotions pressing down on my chest.

"Yes. Rayne was able to get them to safety before the back door was seized. They're at his penthouse in the panic room until Rayne and Everett can return to them."

I let out a breath, but instead of feeling relief, the confirmation is an invitation for the emotions to slam into me all at once. A heavy sob breaks through my chest, and I turn my face into Elijah's chest, desperately seeking out his warmth. I've never needed another human being like I need him. Hell, I've never needed anything like I do Elijah. Not air or water or food. It's like my heart doesn't know how to beat without him anymore.

"I've got you, little Snowflake. Let it all out, give me all your pain," Elijah murmurs into my ear.

The paramedic watches us with interest, but there's fear in his eyes. He knows who we are, and even if some of the rumors about our families are true, he knows one wrong move could end badly for him. "I'm going to start a central line so I can administer some painkillers," he explains, his eyes flicking between us to assess our reactions.

"Do whatever you need to do," I tell him between sniffles. "And don't worry about my husband. His bark is worse than his bite." The joke falls flat and I find myself nestling farther into Elijah's warmth.

"I like hearing that word on your lips, Snowflake."

"What word?"

"Husband."

FIFTY-SIX

ELIJAH

"Where is she?" Wynter looks around frantically the moment she steps out of the elevator.

I've been pacing up and down the hallway for the last two hours, each step I take hurts, but the pain reminds me of everything I could have lost today. I could have lost my entire reason for existing, and I deserve to feel the pain because I allowed this to happen.

I should have protected her. I should have made sure she got out when Wynter and Emerson did. But I didn't, and I deserve every ounce of pain on this earth for that. My gunshot wound was only a graze and didn't hit any major organs or arteries. But Snow is a whole other story entirely.

"She's in surgery," I tell her, not stopping my pace. If I stop, I have to deal with the fact my woman is hurt, and I can't fix it. There's nothing I can do for her, and I have to put her care in the hands of strangers. Well, not all strangers, I suppose.

Doc is in there with her. Originally I wanted to be the one who kept an eye on the doctors to make sure they didn't harm her further, but when Everett suggested Doc, it made a lot more sense. He would know if they were doing something wrong, whereas the rest of us would be clueless.

"Is she okay?"

"Wyn, let's just sit down. The doctors will come out and tell us what's going on when they can," Everett says softly, leading her toward a row of chairs I'm yet to sit in. The only time I managed to sit still was when we were in the ambulance, and that was only because Snow was in my arms, her warmth reminding me she was alive and that's all I could hope for after what had just transpired at the church.

Wynter tugs her hand from Everett's and follows me up the hallway, quickening her steps until she falls in stride beside me. "Are you okay, Elijah?"

I close my eyes and take a breath, shoving down the self-loathing and anger that threatens to tear through. "No, I am not okay. My wife is in surgery, no one has told me anything, and I don't trust any of these motherfuckers after today." I keep my voice even, not wanting to frighten her, because none of this is her fault.

Wynter hesitates for a moment before she reaches out and takes my hand in hers, giving it a gentle squeeze. "Snow is a fighter. She's going to pull through just fine, and then we can focus on finding out how the hell today happened." Her other hand rests on her growing stomach, absentmindedly rubbing it. She's changed out of her dress into a pair of yoga pants and a sweater, but her bump is becoming more prominent each time I see her.

"Thank you, Wynter," I say quietly, holding on to her hand for a few more seconds before dropping it.

Storm paces up and down the reception counter like a caged animal at mealtime. He's just as close to losing his shit as I am, and I'm not sure which of us is closer to snapping. I'd like to say me, but I have a feeling Storm is feeling the weight of the world right now. He's the only thing standing between us and a full-blown war with an enemy we don't know, an unseen presence who seems to be two steps ahead of us at every turn.

I'm in no position to be managing the fallout from the wedding, and the responsibility is falling on Storm for both of us. I've never regretted not appointing a second in charge as much as I do now.

My phone buzzes in my pocket and I let out a growl under my breath as I reach for it. What part of uncontactable do these fucking morons not understand?

"What?" I snap.

"Boss, I'm sorry to bother—"

"What do you want, David?"

He lets out a breath on the other end of the line. "The warehouse has been raided by the cops."

I stop dead in my tracks, my eyes meeting Storm's on the other side of the waiting room. "Come again?"

"The Feds rocked up an hour ago and detained everyone in the building before taking all the drugs we had. They've cleaned us out."

I rub my hand down my face. "The cops in this city know better than that."

"Like I said, it was the Feds. I have the warrant and it came from DC. Whoever ordered this isn't local."

"Fuck."

"I know you said not to bother you, but I thought you might need to know this."

"Keep me updated." I end the call without another word and take long, measured steps to where Storm has stopped to watch me. "My warehouse was just raided by the Feds."

He doesn't reply immediately as he considers my words, but the fury burning in his eyes is hot enough that a lesser man would take a step back. "While we were too distracted with the church fiasco…" He trails off.

"They'll likely hit you next."

He nods. "That does seem like the most logical next step." His eyes dart to where Wynter is perched on Everett's lap and sighs. "Fuck, I hate her being involved in this shit while she's pregnant."

The corners of my lips quirk up, but I can't quite manage a smile. "Wynter is probably the calmest of us under pressure."

Storm scoffs. "The most level headed, absolutely. The calmest, I'm not so sure." He hesitates for another moment before crossing to where they're sitting. "We have a problem."

"You mean aside from my sister currently being on an operating table after her wedding was hijacked by a bunch of gunmen who we have no idea who they work for? Apart from that?" Wynter's voice is even despite the slight ounce of hysteria under the surface.

Everett rubs her back soothingly, whispering something in her ear that makes her shoulders relax and she leans into him for support. "What's going on?" he asks.

"Our warehouse has just been raided by the Feds," I explain. "And I think they're likely to hit you next."

"The wedding was a decoy..." Wynter groans. "We need to figure out who the hell is coming after us, and we need to do it soon."

"Once Snow can go home, we'll throw everything we have at figuring it out," Storm says, his eyes watching me closely. "I'll call my guy at the FBI and see what he can tell me and if we can get at least some of what they seized back."

"Thanks," I sigh as the doors behind the reception desk swing open and all four of us turn our attention to Doc strolling out.

Unsurprisingly, he glares at me before turning on a megawatt smile for Wynter. If he wasn't one of the only people I trusted with Snow's health, I would put a bullet between his eyes.

"How is she?" I ask, unable to wait for him to grace us with the answer in his own time.

"She's stable. But there were some complications."

"What do you mean, complications?" I snap. I don't have the time nor the patience to play games with him, and the idea that Snow will have to live with any kind of lasting effects from this has a deep ache piercing through my heart.

"The bullet damaged one of her ovaries, and it had to be removed. She also had severe blood loss which made it really touch and go for a while there."

I suck in a breath and close my eyes to get a handle on my emotions. It's not the time to lose my cool. Not when my Snowflake is lying in a hospital bed. "Can I see her? When can she be transported home?"

"You can see her, but I don't think it's a good idea for her to leave just yet. With the kind of blood loss she had, there can be unforeseen things that come up during recovery. It's better she remains here for at least a day or two for observation before being transported."

"She's coming home today," I growl. I don't trust any of the doctors or nurses here. No matter how much I pay them, I can't guarantee their loyalty. They could already be working for whoever is coming for us, and I can't risk that.

Storm clears his throat and looks from me to Doc and back again. "Elijah, I know we don't see eye to eye on much, but I think we should do what he says. How would you feel if you take her home and something goes wrong?"

"Then Doc can come home with us," I say.

"Uh, I don't think so." He shakes his head. "I'm not the kind of doctor she would need if shit goes sideways. I would feel a lot more comfortable if she stays here."

A growl works its way from my chest, anger raging through my veins. I can't leave her here. Doesn't he understand that Snow is my entire life and I won't feel better until she's behind the walls of my home where she's safe?

Storm steps toward me. "I don't like this any more than you do, but why don't you go in and see her? You don't want her to wake up alone."

I close my eyes and let out a frustrated breath. He's right. I want to be there when she opens her eyes to tell her everything is going to be okay and I will kill every motherfucker with any involvement today, because anyone who dares hurt my woman deserves to meet the devil himself.

FIFTY-SEVEN

SNOW

A warm hand tugs me out of a dreamless state, but my eyes refuse to open and my body won't move no matter how hard I try to force it. Unfamiliar sounds fill my head, beeping, voices through a speaker, something heavy being wheeled down what seems to be a never-ending hallway.

Where the hell am I? And why does my throat feel like the desert?

The hand that holds mine squeezes, the warmth they omit is familiar, but my disorientated mind can't muddle through to who it is.

I force my body to take a deep breath, and it gets caught in my throat when the pain hits me. So much pain that it forces my eyes open and I'm immediately blinded by blaring lights. Jesus Christ, this room is lit up brighter than a Christmas tree. The scent of disinfectant assaults me and the pieces finally start to click together as to where I am. Hospital.

"Snowflake?" a voice rumbles from beside me, and I

immediately turn my head to face them. My head protests and stars dance in my field of vision, blinding me for long seconds. Fingers brush down my cheek and when my eyes finally focus, Elijah is staring back at me, worry clear in his gaze. "Thank God you're awake."

"What happened?" I croak. My throat feels like I've just been on a three-day bender and finally allowed myself to sober up.

"You don't remember?" he asks, his eyes searching the table beside him before bringing a cup with a straw to my lips.

I drink greedily, the water slipping down my dry throat and through to my tender stomach. I shake my head as I continue to drink, not willing to give up the water to speak.

"You were shot." He flinches at his own words, something dark crossing his face before he pulls the straw from between my lips. "That's enough, I don't want it to upset your stomach." His words are softer than any he's ever spoken to me, and I find myself craving the darkness he usually exudes.

My brows pinch together as memories crash into me. The church. Our wedding. The gunmen. The explosions. It all hits me all at once and takes my breath away.

"Snow?" The concern in his voice is evident, but I can't tear myself away from the images assaulting me one after another. His fingers brush down my cheek and carefully brings me to face him. "Come back to me."

It's only now I realize my breaths are coming in hard and fast, panic washing over me like waves in the ocean and threatening to drag me out to sea. It's all too much, and the memories mixed with the pain is too much for me to handle.

"Snow," he commands, and my eyes snap to his, his demanding tone getting my attention and pausing the panic in its tracks. He gives me a satisfied smirk and leans his face until it's just a breath from my own. "That's better. I need you to stay calm for me, Snowflake. You had to have fairly extensive surgery, and I don't want you to hurt yourself any more than you already have."

"Surgery?" I croak.

He nods, his eyes closing for a moment as he releases a breath. "The bullet did a bit of damage, and you lost a lot of blood."

"How much damage?"

He pauses, watching me for long seconds before letting out a heavy sigh. "They had to remove one of your ovaries."

I stare at him, like surely there has to be a punchline, surely what he's telling me has to be a joke, because I don't think I can handle the alternative. But it never comes, instead, Elijah watches me carefully, waiting for the moment his words sink in and I break in his arms.

"I don't want you to freak out about this. It doesn't mean anything, Doc said your other ovary is still perfect and it shouldn't impact your ability to have children down the road."

This is karma. I did this to myself. The moment I started taking birth control pills without telling Elijah, in fact, I blatantly hid it from him because I wasn't prepared to face him to tell him I'm not ready for children, I set the wheels in motion for this to happen. By going behind his back, the gods decided to take the choice out of my hands altogether and punish me for my lies.

"Snowflake," he murmurs, brushing his thumbs across my cheeks, wiping wetness away. I didn't even realize I was crying, but the moment I do, the tears come hard and fast. Elijah's eyes are panicked, he doesn't know how to deal with my tears, and I don't know how to stop them. His eyes dart to the door and then a moment later, he's carefully scooping me up from the bed, his hands gentle as he lifts me and positions himself on the bed with me in his lap. "It's okay. I'm here. I've got you."

I don't deserve his comfort, but I lean into it, nonetheless. I have to come clean. It's not fair on him if I don't. "I'm sorry," I sob, turning my face into his chest and allowing my tears to stain his shirt. He's still wearing his bloody clothes from the wedding, the red a stark contrast to the white fabric.

"You have nothing to be sorry for, little Snowflake. None of this is your fault," he murmurs into my hair.

"You don't understand." A loud choke fills the room and burns through my chest. "This is all my fault."

"No, it's not, Snow. You didn't ask for this to happen. You didn't ask to be shot. But nothing is ever going to hurt you again. I will keep you safe from anything that ever threatens you or our family."

His words only make the tears come faster. The family I probably can't give him anymore. What use is a Mafia wife who can't provide heirs?

Thoughts swirl around in my mind, none staying for long enough for me to focus on it. At least Elijah seems to be attached enough to me that he probably won't kill me. If I'm lucky, he'll drop me back at the estate with some annulment papers, and that will be that. If I'm unlucky, I'll find myself at the bottom of Lake Michigan with concrete tied to my ankles.

"I need you to settle, Snow." Elijah's voice is firm, but it only makes the tears come in harder and faster. "You're going to hurt yourself and I do not tolerate anything hurting my Snowflake."

"I deserved this," I cry.

"What did you just say?" Elijah growls, his body tensing beneath mine despite his hold on me remaining gentle.

I take a few calming breaths, enough that I can look at him and see the thunder in his eyes. "I deserved this. It's karma," I whisper, not trusting my words to come out even.

"What the hell are you talking about, Snow?" he snaps. His patience is wearing thin, and I almost want to ask him to put me down while I tell him this because I don't know how he's going to react.

"I was taking the pill," I murmur. "I had a few packets at the estate and I started taking it the day the dealers went missing. I wasn't ready for children, and you were so against the idea of birth control," I sob. "This is my karma."

Elijah is quiet for long moments, so long I begin to wonder if he's going to reply at all. Some of the tension in his body has eased, but there's still something vibrating through his body, begging to be let out to play. He sighs and his breath whispers across my cheeks. "You didn't deserve this, Snow. I can see how I was a little… heavy-handed and may not have taken what you wanted into account, and for that, I am sorry. When you're ready, we can start trying for children, and Doc said if we do have any issues, we could try IVF. Or we could adopt. There are plenty of kids in this city that need a loving home."

I stare at him, trying to make sense of the words he's saying. Adopt? What Mafia boss has adopted children? Could he pass the family down to them?

"I can see that pretty little head racing a mile a minute, but you need to relax before you hurt yourself. This is not something we need to worry about right now and I don't want you making yourself sick." He presses a gentle kiss to the top of my head before resting his chin there. He holds me so tight and for so long the tears begin to settle and the ache in my chest starts to ease.

But there's still a nagging thought in the back of my mind that he's just saying this because he feels guilty I was hurt, and if that's the case, I don't know how long it will be before he snaps and leaves me.

FIFTY-EIGHT

ELIJAH

The only time I can bring myself to work is when Snow sleeps.

It's been eight days since our wedding and three since she was allowed to come home, but I haven't spent more than a few minutes away from her. I can't. I came too close to losing her, and anytime she's out of my sight, panic claws up the back of my throat and holds on until I see her again.

She's been withdrawn since I brought her home, not the same Snow I became obsessed with all those years ago, and I hate it. I miss her fire. I miss when she argued with me about everything. I miss her. But she's healing and I can't expect her to be jumping for joy after being shot. I have to be patient with her.

"Storm," I answer my phone as I slip into the hallway but keep the door cracked open so Snow is still in my line of sight.

"How's Snow?"

“Still quiet. She sleeps most of the time, and when she’s not sleeping, it’s almost like she’s checked out. I don’t know what to do for her,” I sigh. I never thought I would be talking to someone who is meant to be my mortal enemy about my relationship, but it’s funny how these things play out.

“It’s only been a week, I’m sure she’s just working through it all.” His words do nothing to comfort the ache in the pit of my stomach that maybe I’ve made a mistake. I’m starting to think I never should have stolen her from her life, never should have taken her from her family and kept her. She wouldn’t have been hurt if I had stayed in the shadows. She’d still be her lively self who I’ve obsessed over for the last decade.

“I know.”

“We’ve had another shipment go missing,” he sighs.

“What? How?”

“I have no fucking idea. We had so many men at the docks we were bordering on suspicious, but when they went to do the count, everything was missing.”

I lean on the wall opposite the bedroom door, my eyes brushing over my Snowflake as she sleeps. Watching her allows my mind to work better, as if when she’s around, all the worry I feel and measures I have in place to protect her disappears, and my business mind starts firing. “They’re hitting it before it docks,” I say.

“What?”

“They must be intercepting the ship somewhere. That scene was too clean the last time, and there’s no way they got past your guys this time, so the only explanation is that they have to hit the ship during its journey, not after it docks."

Silence greets me on the other end of the line and I pull the phone from my ear to check he hasn't hung up on me. "Those motherfuckers," he growls. "We have guards on the ship though, and cameras. Surely someone would have seen an entire shipment of guns get unloaded to another ship."

I nod, thinking through how I would have approached this back when I would run jobs for my uncles. "The cameras are easy, they would have hacked in and had a loop play over and over again so you wouldn't be suspicious."

"But the guards?"

"That I'm not too sure of." It's been too long since I've had a complex problem to solve and too long since I've been out of these four walls, but I won't leave Snow. I don't trust anyone who works for me, and I certainly don't trust anyone in Storm's ranks. The only people I trust with her safety are me, and her brothers, and I'm still not convinced they won't try to take her back from me the first opportunity they get.

Storm sighs, the sound of ice on glass filling the line. "Wynter wants to come see Snow," he tells me.

I brush my eyes down my fragile Snowflake curled up in the middle of our bed and allow my head to fall back against the wall. "Give her a few more days. I don't think Wynter would intentionally upset her, but she's fragile right now." I hoped that after her admission in the hospital, some of the guilt would disappear, but if anything, it gets worse with each day that passes. She's convinced this is karma, that by taking birth control without my knowledge, she set a series of events in motion that led to her losing an ovary.

Nothing I say or do seems to ease her worries and seeing her in so much emotional turmoil makes my cold, dead heart ache.

"You can't hide her away forever, Elijah. And you can't personally guard her for the rest of her life. At some point, you're going to have to hand her safety over to someone else, at least for some of the time."

"No," I growl. He may be right, but I'm not ready to hear it yet. I need more time. More time to watch her, to bring her back to me, to prove to us both that I can keep her safe from any threat that comes at us.

A knock at the door draws my attention away from Snow, and I watch as Mrs. Chambers makes her way to the front door, wiping her hands on her apron. I watch as she looks through the peephole and pauses for a moment, a frown tugging at her brow before she unlocks the door and opens it.

David, the guy who distributes the drugs to the dealers, falls through the door. His face is bloody, so much so, I doubt he can see through the swelling and blood. His clothes are torn and soiled, and by the way he collapses in the entry, I can only imagine there are other injuries I can't see.

"Elijah?" Storm says on the other end of the line.

"Get over here," I snap and end the call. I chance one more look over my shoulder at my Snowflake sleeping before tearing my attention from her to the more pressing issue. The half dead man in my hallway.

Mrs. Chambers jumps into action, quickly making her way to the cabinet where we keep an emergency first aid kit for times just like these.

I stride toward the large man. Once I reach him, I kneel beside him and push him onto his back.

A strangled groan erupts from his chest, and his eyes squeeze together before he forces one open. The other is swollen shut and I doubt he'll be seeing out of it anytime in the next week. I've had my fair share of black eyes, and this one isn't going to heal quickly.

"What the fuck happened?" I ask as Mrs. Chambers presses cotton pads onto his wounds to soak up some of the blood.

"They're coming," he chokes, a bloody cough tearing from his throat, splatting red across the carpet.

"Who are?"

"They're coming for her."

"Who, David?" I snap, looking up at Mrs. Chambers's worried eyes. She doesn't need to say anything for me to know he's about to die, because I've seen death so many times, in so many different ways, that it will never come as a surprise to me again.

He tries to say something, but he dissolves into a coughing fit, more and more blood pouring from his mouth. His time is coming to an end. Any second now, he's going to die, and not only will I have lost the only person who knows distribution like the back of his hand, I'm no closer to figuring out who is coming for us.

When David's body stops straining to cough and his head lulls to the side, there's a moment of eerie silence. It's been the same in every death I've experienced, as if time slows down ever so slightly and the outside world quietens for just a second as death takes his latest victim.

“He’s dead,” Mrs. Chambers says quietly. She collects the cotton pads she was using and carefully pushes herself to her feet. For such an innocent-looking woman, she doesn’t flinch at the sight of death, and for that I admire her. She could just as easily pass out, or start panicking, but instead she takes it in her stride and gets on with it.

Fifteen minutes later, a knock at the door drags my attention away from the dead body in my hallway. Mrs. Chambers cleaned him up as much as she could, and I’ve called the cleaner, but there’s nothing else I can do but wait.

I reach for the knob and open the door to find Storm and Everett standing on my stoop. Their eyes both narrow on the dead man in the entry and collectively sigh.

“What the fuck happened?” Storm asks, closing the door and surveying the scene in front of him.

“I don’t know,” I tell him honestly. “But he said that someone is coming for Snow.”

“Who?” Everett kneels beside the body and carefully turns David’s head from side to side, like all the answers to our questions can be found on the body.

“He didn’t say. He died before he could give me anything more than, ‘they’re coming for her.’”

Repeating the words leaves a sick feeling in my stomach, because the idea that anyone could be hunting Snow, that someone could try to take her away from me again… it’s unacceptable. I can’t allow any more harm to come to her.

Storm nods, his eyes flicking to Everett's and then back to me. "Why don't you and Snow come to the estate for a few nights? It's safer there, more security, panic rooms. I'm sure you'll feel better having her somewhere safe."

"She's safe here," I growl.

Everett sighs, pushing himself to his feet. "That may be so, but your security relies on people. The estate doesn't. Not anymore. We don't know who we can trust right now, and I have to agree with Storm. You would both be safer there."

I close my eyes as I breathe through the rising anger. As much as I want to be selfish, for once, I can't. This isn't like when I stole her away from her life and her family, or when I forced her to marry me, or when I refused to use birth control. All of those things made me a selfish bastard, but for once, I have to put someone else's needs ahead of my own.

"She needs to go with you," I murmur.

"You can come too?" Storm's eyes narrow. "I know we've had our share of issues, but we're family now. The estate is open to you if you need it."

I shake my head. "No, I have to stay here. If I go with you, it will look like we're hiding behind the big gates. You need to take Snow and keep her safe until this is all over."

"How do you think she's going to feel about that?" Everett asks.

"I don't care. As long as she's safe, she can hate me all she wants."

FIFTY-NINE

SNOW

Voices in the hallway carry through the house and pull me from my restless sleep. Every time I close my eyes, I see a gun pointing in my face and immediately want to open them. But that's not the worst of the nightmares.

Each time I close my eyes and my body relaxes enough to fall asleep, I dream of a future I could have had. Elijah running around with our kids while I'm sitting on the sidelines laughing at the big bad Mafia man playing so freely with his children. Somehow I know that's the kind of dad he would be. I have nothing to base it on, especially seeing as he's so ruthless in every part of his life, why wouldn't he approach parenthood the same way? But I know he would be soft and kind, and I'm sure one day he'll find a woman who can give him that.

I roll over to face the window and tug a pillow over my head. The house has been deathly quiet for days. No one is brave enough to make a sound that might frighten me because they think Elijah will lose it, but I doubt that's the case. He's just counting down the days until I'm well enough to send back to the estate. He hasn't touched me since we've been home. Each night he sleeps in the armchair beside the bed, saying he doesn't want to accidentally hurt me in my sleep. But I see right through his farce.

A gentle hand runs up my bare arm, and I pretend to be asleep. I don't want to deal with whatever they've come in here for, so maybe if they believe I'm getting some much-needed sleep, they'll leave me alone. But my hopes are taken away a moment later when the pillow is gently lifted from my head.

"Snow?" Elijah says softly.

"Go away," I murmur, attempting to turn away from him, but his hand comes out to rest on my shoulder, holding me so I can't escape.

He chuckles quietly. "I need you to get up, Snowflake. Storm and Everett are here, I need you to go back to the estate with them where you'll be safe."

I force my eyes open and meet the forest green of his eyes. He isn't looking at me like he's about to break my heart and stomp on it, but then again, he doesn't know I love him either. I've never been able to work up the nerve to tell him. Partly because I don't think he's capable of such an emotion, and partly because I'm scared he'll reject me.

"What?"

"There's been a threat made against you, and Storm and I think you would be safer at the estate. Mrs. Chambers is packing your things. Is there anything in particular you're going to need?"

Tears spring to my eyes as I look up at him. I thought I had more time. I thought he would at least wait a few weeks before he sent me back, but that's not really his style. Why not rip the band-aid off while the gaping wound is still fresh?

"It's okay, Snow." He gives me a small smile, kneeling at the edge of the bed so we're at eye level. "It's just until the threat has passed."

"Why can't I stay here if it's just a threat?" I ask quietly.

"Because Storm and I don't trust my men. At least at the estate, it's an iron fortress even without guards."

"You broke in," I remind him.

"You're right, I did. But Everett was telling me about the upgrades they've done, and I don't know anyone stupid enough to go up against them."

I squeeze my eyes closed to push the tears back. I can't cry. I can't fall apart. After all, what else did I expect when I fell in love with a monster? His lack of regard for human life, for my life, should surprise me, but it doesn't. This is who he is, and I knew that before I walked down the aisle and became his wife.

"It's not forever, Snow," he tells me gently, but I can read between the lines.

I don't need to hear the words to understand what this means. Sure, it's not forever right now, but it will be. With a little time away from me, he'll decide this is for the best. He'll realize a wife who can't bear heirs is useless, and then the divorce papers will arrive. I've read enough books and watched enough TV to know exactly how this goes.

I nod once and push myself up from the mattress. I almost can't bear the idea that this is the last time I'll sleep in this bed, surrounded by the scent of Elijah even when his warmth isn't near. But I can't allow myself to focus on that right now. I have to focus on putting one foot in front of the other without falling apart. I'll do that when I'm safely back in my bedroom at the estate, and he can't see just how much he's broken me.

Elijah reaches out to help me stand, but I flinch away. Him touching me could break my resolve, it could be what opens the floodgates and allows the tears I'm barely swallowing down to burst from me. His face drops as his hand does.

The sadness in his eyes hurts my heart more than the poor battered organ already does. Even as he breaks me, I can't bear the thought that he's sad. Isn't it funny what love does to us? It builds us up to the highest of highs, just to drop us the moment we reach the top. I was an idiot to think Elijah Russo could give me happiness. As soon as I let my guard down, I lost everything, and I didn't even know it at the time.

My legs shake beneath me, but I force myself to stay standing, taking careful steps toward the bedroom door. I catalog everything to memory. The furniture, the scent, the bed where Elijah took me for the first time. Everything about the room goes into the memory bank, because this is the last time I'll ever be here.

I take measured steps down the hallway, trying not to think too hard about the times I've had within these walls. I try not to think about the man I killed in this hallway, or the way I allowed Elijah to tie me up and fuck me with a gun in his office. I don't think about how I planned the wedding that was destroyed or felt true happiness for the first time in my life.

And I certainly don't think about how I healed here. Little by little, the shattered pieces of my heart melded back together, just for it to be destroyed again.

I meet Storm's gaze at the end of the hallway, concern tugging at his brows. I'm surprised he's going along with this, but I guess this is what he always wanted. He wanted Elijah and me to fail, he didn't want to be tied to the Russo's for the rest of his life, and now he won't have to be.

I barely spare the dead body in the middle of the floor a glance before slipping on my boots by the door and carefully pulling my coat around my shoulders. "Let's go," I say softly, giving Mrs. Chambers a kind smile as I reach for the doorknob. I think aside from Elijah, I'll miss her most about this house. The kindness she showed me in those early days, the way she went out of her way to make me smile, to make me feel at home.

Everett steps in front of me as the door opens, his eyes surveying the empty street before wrapping his arm around my shoulder and guiding me toward a black SUV.

As I take each step away from Elijah, a new crack in my heart appears.

SIXTY

ELIJAH

Sending Snow away was the hardest thing I've ever had to do. As she walked down the hallway and from the house I built with her in mind, her shoulders slumped more and more, and the dejection in her eyes as she flashed one last look at me tore my cold, dead heart from my chest.

She thinks I'm leaving her, and I can't bring myself to correct her. Because if I were a good man, or had an ounce of a conscience, I would do just that. I'm a monster, and she deserves someone who can give her light, not someone who can only give her darkness.

Since the moment she stepped foot back into the estate I've had eyes on her. The cameras I installed all those years ago are still operational despite the security overhaul Everett did a couple of months ago. She hasn't left her room in three days, and each day I watch her wallow, is a day closer I am to going to get her. She won't take my calls, each time my name lights up her phone she watches it ring out.

Out of all the times I've wished I could read her mind, this is the first time I've been afraid of what she's thinking. I know her well enough to have a good idea, but the reality of those thoughts would make me see red, and I have enough of that without adding Snow's inner musings to the equation.

"Are you even listening to me?" Storm snaps and I finally drag my attention from the screen and settle on the man sitting across the desk.

"Sorry, what were you saying?" I fight the urge to look back to where Snow is curled up in her bed, the covers pulled up around her neck.

Storm sighs and rubs his hands down his face. He's tired. The black stains beneath his eyes get darker each time he visits and match the ones I see in the mirror each morning. We're no closer to figuring out who is coming for us than we were after the first move, and it's beginning to wear on us both. "Everett is tracking some unusual activity in the outskirts of the city, but there isn't much surveillance equipment out there, and we're hesitant to send men after your guy died in your entryway."

I nod. After the wedding, both sides are looking a little too lean considering our business interests. We're sitting ducks, and it's not exactly like you can find people that want to do the kind of work we're offering easily. Between us, we employ every criminal in this city, or so we thought. Whoever is after us has substantial firepower behind them, and that's what I'm worried about. If they wanted to, I have no doubt they could take every last one of us out at once. So why haven't they?

"Maybe if we could figure out what their long game is, it would be easier to work out who the fuck they are."

Storm sighs and leans back in his seat. "They're ghosts. They keep hitting us and we don't have so much as a photo of them."

"So what's our next move?"

He stares at me across the desk for a moment before speaking, "I don't fucking know. We're doing everything I can think of, and we're still coming up short."

"We could try another trap," I suggest.

"Because the first one went so well?"

The room falls quiet for long moments and my eyes fall back to the screen where Wynter is perched on the side of Snow's bed. It gives me comfort when she's not alone, even if it's not me there with her.

"I think we should send the girls away," Storm says.

"Absolutely not," I growl.

"Hear me out, Elijah. They're not safe here. Snow was shot. Wynter is pregnant, and the stress isn't good for the baby. Emerson is losing weight every day because she's so worried about Rayne. It's not good for them to be in the city right now."

"No."

Storm sighs. "I know you don't want her far away, but what if this is what's best for her?"

"What's best for her is for her to be here with me, but that's already been taken away from her. Have you seen your sister in the last few days? She isn't coping. She was shot, her chances of having children were halved, and then she was forced to move back to the estate thinking I'm about to leave her. How do you think Snow is going to take the news that you're going to ship her off to another state?"

"Country," he corrects.

"Country?" I shout. "Are you fucking insane? Anything could happen to them in another country."

"I'm not suggesting we send them unprotected, and we have connections overseas that we could lean on. They would keep the girls safe until we're sure the danger has passed."

"How does Everett feel about this? Or Rayne?"

"I haven't broached the subject with them yet."

"I can't imagine they're going to be much more receptive to the idea."

"I just want them to be safe. I know it's an outdated idea that women can't take care of themselves when in fact, the women of my family are more than capable of doing so. But this is a threat we can't see, one who is besting us at every single turn, and the only way I can think to keep them safe is to send them away."

I drop my elbows onto the desk and lean forward. I understand his reasoning. Hell, if it was just Emerson and Wynter going I would be all for the idea, but Snow being on another continent isn't an option. I'm losing my mind with her in a different house, I can't imagine how I would be if she were in another country where I couldn't watch every move she makes. "I can't, Storm. I can't have her that far away." The honest words fall from my mouth before I can stop them. At some point in the last couple of weeks, Storm and I have gone from being mortal enemies to something resembling friends. Perhaps it's because technically we're family now, or maybe it's the mutual trust we're building.

Movement in the cameras catches my attention and when my focus returns to the camera feed, Wynter is helping Snow put shoes on. My brows knit together as I watch her help Snow stand from the bed and pick up a small handbag from the hook by the door.

"Are Wynter and Snow planning on going somewhere today?" I ask, keeping my voice as even as I can manage. One of my conditions of agreeing to move her back to the estate was that I would know anytime she stepped foot outside the front door.

"Do you have cameras in my house?"

"Yes, now answer my question."

"No, not that I'm aware of. Why?"

"Because they're walking out the front door right now." I stand from the desk and look around for where I threw my phone across the room a few hours ago after a particularly frustrating conversation with the guy who took over for David. He's useless, but he's all I've got right now, and the drugs are set to be returned from the Feds tonight. When Storm told me his contact managed to get all our inventory back, I was surprised as hell, but now that idiot is going to actually have something to distribute, I'm a little nervous.

I dial Snow's number, anger burning in my throat as I watch her climb into the black SUV sitting idle at the bottom of the front steps. For long moments I watch her stare at my name on her screen.

"Answer it," I growl.

"Elijah," she breathes.

SIXTY-ONE

SNOW

I've never been much for wallowing. Usually when I feel out of control or my emotions overwhelm me, I find the closest bottle of alcohol and drown my sorrows until I can't feel the pain anymore. It's not my healthiest trait admittedly, but it's always worked for me.

But this time I can't bring myself to move from my bed. I've been here for days, or at least I think I have. The blinds have remained drawn, and my only indication of time passing is when Wynter brings me meals I don't touch.

I thought I'd hit rock bottom in the past, but surely this is it. Surely there isn't anywhere lower than where I am right now.

The door creaks open and my sister sighs from the doorway. I think she's expecting me to snap out of this sooner or later, but if anything, I'm getting deeper into the pit of despair each time she comes in.

Light footsteps grow closer to the bed, and a moment later, the mattress dips beside me. Silence fills the room like she isn't quite sure what to say to me or how to approach me, but eventually she sighs and says, "You have to snap out of this."

I ignore her. She may not remember, but when Everett left her, she didn't get out of bed for two weeks. So I can sympathize with how worried she is right now, but I still have time to wallow before the socially acceptable window closes.

"He's not leaving you, Snow," Wynter says softly, her fingers brushing across my cheek gently. "I spoke to Everett, and he swore black and blue this is only about keeping you safe."

"For now," I murmur.

She sighs. "Have you spoken to him?"

"No."

"Has he called?"

"Yes."

"And why aren't you answering him?"

I pause for a moment, unsure if I want to admit the reason I've allowed so many calls to go to voice mail and haven't been brave enough to check any of the ones he's left. "Because if I don't speak to him, he can't end things. At least if he just has divorce papers delivered, he won't see or hear me break."

Another stretch of silence allows me to burrow farther into my blankets. She doesn't normally stay long, not after the first day. She tried talking to me, about Elijah, about the baby, about work. She even tried to talk about celebrity gossip because that's usually my kryptonite. But at some point, I think she decided it was doing me more harm than good.

"Let's go," she finally says, standing up from the bed and pushing the blankets from me.

"Go where?"

"To see Elijah."

"No way." If I didn't want him to break up with me over the phone, why the hell would I put myself in a position for him to break my heart in front of him?

"Up, now." She tugs the blankets back until they're out of my reach and I'm finally forced to open my eyes. The dim room is too light for me after days on end in the dark, and I quickly slam them shut again. "I mean it, Snow. Get up right this minute, or I will not hesitate to throw a bucket of water on you."

"I was shot," I remind her.

"I've already called Doc to ask if it would hinder your recovery in any way."

"You premeditated throwing water on me?" I ask incredulously.

"Yes. Now do as I say, or I will not hesitate to do it."

I huff and force my stiff body into a sitting position. The only time I've been out of bed since I came back to the estate is to use the restroom, and seeing as I'm not eating, and I'm spending most of my days asleep and not drinking water, even that isn't often. "We can't leave the house, Wynter."

"Of course we can." She looks around the room until she finds what she's looking for and crosses to the far wall to get whatever it is.

"No, we can't. We're on complete lockdown."

"Because that's always stopped you?"

"This is different."

"How is this different?"

"Because I was shot and you're pregnant. And there are multiple men in this house who will murder us if we step foot out of these grounds without their knowledge." When did I become the sensible one? Maybe the baby is making my responsible big sister a little reckless, and I'm not sure I like it. I've always been the wild child, it's my right as the youngest child.

"We're going straight from here to Elijah's house. We won't stop along the way. We'll take one of those ridiculous tank cars Everett designed, and we'll take a weird route to make sure no one is following us. You're not going to believe a word I say until you've spoken to him, and you're not going to believe him over the phone. You two need to hash this out face to face." Wynter returns with a pair of shoes which she immediately kneels in front of me and begins shoving my foot into the white sneakers.

"Should I change?" I ask, looking down at my sweats. I actually got up and showered this morning for the first time since I've been back, so at the very least I don't smell.

"Nope. You're perfect just the way you are."

I stare at her. Is she looking at the same picture of me as I am? Because I'm anything but perfect right now.

"Come on, let's go. Storm went out a little while ago, and

Rayne and Everett are in the gym, so we should be able to sneak out."

I'm all out of excuses and so I force myself to my feet. Wynter wraps a coat around me and before I know it, she's leading me out the front door and helping me into the car.

"Did you get the car out before you came in to talk to me?"

"Yep." She grins, walking around to the other side and climbing in beside me. "I had a feeling this was the only way I was getting you out of this funk."

I roll my eyes and shake my head, but a small smile tugs at the corners of my lips.

My phone vibrates in my hand and I glance down to see Elijah's name on the caller ID. I should answer it to tell him we're on our way over. What if he's out? What if we're putting ourselves in danger when he's not even home?

I draw my bottom lip between my teeth and take a deep breath, pressing the answer button as Wynter turns the car toward the gate. "Elijah?" I whisper, afraid my voice will break under my anxiety.

"What the fuck are you doing?" he snaps.

"What?"

"Tell Wynter to stop that car right this second, or I swear to God you will not like the consequences." The strain in each word makes my stomach tighten. It sounds like he cares, but why would he send me away if that were the case?

"We're on our way to your house," I tell him.

"No, you're not. You're turning that car around and going back into the nice safe house complete with panic rooms."

"Excuse me?"

"You heard me, Snow. I swear to God, if that car leaves those gates, you're going to be in a world of trouble."

My eyes flick to Wynter who shrugs, none of the concerns beating in my chest are visible on her face. I suspect she can hear every word he's said, and she doesn't seem concerned by his anger in the slightest. "No."

"Snow," he growls.

"I'm coming over, Elijah. We need to talk."

"We could have talked any of the three hundred times I've called you in the last few days, but you keep screening my calls."

I pause for a moment, my brow knitting together as something occurs to me. "How did you know I was leaving the estate? And how did you know I've been screening your calls?"

"I've had cameras installed all over the estate for years," he tells me like it's the obvious answer to my question. "Now, can you please turn around and we can talk."

"No, we need to do this in person."

Silence meets me at the other end of the line and continues for so long I pull the phone away from my ear to make sure the call is still connected.

"What do we need to do in person, Snow?" he asks quietly, barely contained anger eating into the edge of his words.

"You're not leaving me. I told you there isn't anywhere on this earth you can hide from me, and I fucking meant it. There is no end for you and me."

My heart jumps into my throat and I meet Wynter's eyes again, an I-told-you-so look on her face. "You didn't send me back to the estate to end things?" I whisper.

"No, I sent you there because you're safer in the iron fortress than you are here. Now please, for the love of God, make Wynter turn that car around and get your asses back within those walls."

I look up at the road and realize we're already a few minutes from the estate. Tall trees surround us on both sides, vibrant green visible even as the sun drops to the horizon ahead of us.

"Turn around," I say softly.

Wynter looks at me for a moment before her eyes flick to the rearview mirror. "Can you put the call on speaker?"

I'm about to ask why when a car in the side mirror catches my attention and I immediately do as she asks.

"Elijah?" Wynter says, her voice even and calm.

"What's going on?"

"There's a car following us."

"Fuck," Elijah roars, but neither of us flinch.

There's a scuffle on the other end of the line and a second later, another voice fills the line. "Where are you?" Storm asks, barely contained anger holding on to each word.

"We're about five minutes from the estate, approximately three miles from the entrance to the highway."

"Can you tell me about the car that's following you?"

"Black, unmarked SUV. Dark tint, so I can't see the driver, but they've been on us since we pulled out of the estate. I didn't think much of it at first, but they're keeping the exact same distance consistently. Every time I speed up, they do the same thing, and when I slow down, so do they."

"They're keeping their distance?"

"I think they're slowly closing the gap but doing it bit by bit, so I don't notice."

"Motherfucker." A loud crash fills the line, and I flinch at Elijah's outburst.

"I don't want you doing anything dangerous, Wyn. You're pregnant, and evasive driving can be risky."

"So is being followed by God knows who," she snaps, the first ding in her perfectly crafted armor showing. Her eyes flick back to the rearview mirror and when the color drains from her cheeks, I chance a look behind me.

"They're getting really close, Storm," I say.

"Tommy is nearby. He's on his way to your location right now. But I need you to both remain calm. It's unlikely they're going to make a—"

His words are cut off when the car jolts forward and Wynter and I both scream. "Not so unlikely," I cry.

"Shit," he mutters.

"Snow, are you wearing your wedding ring?" Elijah asks.

"Of course."

"Wynter, your engagement ring?"

"Yes," she breathes, her eyes flicking between the road and the mirror as the car jolts forward again.

Before he can say anything else, the line goes dead and panic takes hold. Tears gather at the corners of my eyes as I chance another look behind us just in time for the SUV to ram us again.

Wynter lets out a yelp, her hands gripping the steering wheel as tight as she can to keep the car from losing control. "I'm so sorry, Snow. I shouldn't have made you leave the estate. I should have listened to you."

I reach out and brush my fingers down her leg as I try to call Elijah again, but the signal is jammed. That's why they got so close, so they could stop us from calling for help. "It's okay, Wyn. We're going to be okay. It's not your fault. Just focus on breathing and hopefully Tommy will be here soon."

"I did this. This is my fault." Tears drip down her cheeks and there's nothing I can do to bring her comfort. She's past that point now, and all I can do is hold on to her leg to remind her I'm here.

"I need you to listen to me, Wynter. If we are taken, I want you to do everything you can to get away. I need you and my niece or nephew safe."

"Niece," she whispers.

"What?"

"We found out yesterday. Everett was right, we're having a girl."

I squeeze my eyes shut to push the tears down. I can't allow myself to lose my composure, not when Wynter must be so terrified. She has another life to protect, not just her own.

"Congratulations," I whisper.

"I'm not going to leave you, Snow."

"Yes, you are. If you get the chance, you're going to run. I will not allow my niece to become collateral damage in this war."

Before she can respond, the car jolts forward again, a loud crash radiating through the cab. They're getting more and more aggressive because we're coming up on the highway. Once we get on it there's nothing they can do without witnesses, and something tells me an organization like the one coming for us doesn't want any of those.

I lean forward and tug the glove box open, thanking every god that may or may not exist when I find a loaded pistol. "How far from the highway are we?"

"One minute." Wynter glances into the rearview mirror. "Hold on."

Before I can sit back in my seat, the car jolts forward and pain radiates through my temple the moment it hits the dashboard. Black stars dance in my vision as my head falls to the side and Wynter's terror-filled eyes meet mine.

Despite her best efforts, she loses control of the car and the sound of screeching rubber is the last thing I hear before the darkness drags me under. I thought I knew what fear was, but the idea that my sister and niece could be harmed has dread eating at me even as I lose consciousness.

Sixty-Two

Elijah

The moment the line goes dead, Storm and I look at each other, the dread on his face mirroring the emotion raging through my veins. This can't be happening.

"Get them back on the phone," he snaps.

I dial Snow's number again, but it goes straight to voice mail. "They've jammed the signal."

"Fuck!" he roars.

I've already had my freak out, it's only fair I give him a few moments to do the same. I try Snow a few more times, but to no avail. I sigh and scroll down to my cousin. He needs to know what's going on, even if he is going to lose his fucking mind as soon as he hears his woman and child are in danger.

"Elijah," he greets me.

"Why do you sound out of breath?" I ask. It doesn't matter, but it's distracting me from the panic clawing in my chest.

“Rayne and I were working out, what’s up?”

I let out a long breath. “I need you to not freak out until I finish talking.”

Silence greets me on the other end of the line before he finally replies, “Elijah, what the fuck is going on?”

“Wynter decided the only way to get Snow out of her funk was to bring her here—”

“She did what?” he growls.

“There’s more. On their way here, they were followed, and we’ve just lost contact with them.” I could sugarcoat it, but what good would that do us at this point? He needs to know his woman is in danger, and that we have no way to contact them, and there’s no way to break the brunt of that hit.

A roar fills the other end of the line, followed by a series of loud bangs before the line goes dead.

“That went well,” I mutter before returning my focus to Storm who has started pacing up and down the length of the office. The tension in his shoulders and jaw is so tight I’m afraid he might snap something if he doesn’t release it soon, but I don’t see that happening. “I need your phone.” I hold my hand out as he passes me, never faltering in his steps. “We need to know how far out Tommy is,” I say on his next pass, but he doesn’t pause. Instead he continues toward the far wall before turning back again. This time he does pull his phone from his pocket and shoves it at me on his way past.

I quickly unlock the phone and dial the most recent number. “You should really put a passcode on this thing,” I tell him as ringing fills my ear. The moment the call connects, I’m speaking. "Where are you?"

Tommy huffs at the sound of my voice, but I've never known the crazy fuck to hesitate before speaking, which tells me everything I need to know before the words fill the line. "There was an accident. Wynter and Snow are both missing."

I tighten my hold on the phone, the sound of the metal creaking under my hold only makes anger burn brighter. Not only do we not know who the fuck is coming after us, but now they have two of our women.

"The crash site is fresh. They must have got the girls out of the car and taken off in the last few minutes, but there's no way for me to tell which way they've gone."

"Trackers?" I force the word through my clenched jaw.

"Jammed. I've tried tapping into Wynter's engagement ring and it's coming up with nothing."

"They were using a signal jammer to stop them from calling for help. Maybe they haven't turned it off yet."

"That could be it. What do you want me to do?" he asks.

Storm snatches the phone from my hand. "How banged up is the car? Is there blood?"

"The car did exactly what Everett designed it to do and took the brunt of the impact. There was a little blood on the dash on the passenger side, but apart from that I think both girls are okay."

Storm and I let out a collective sigh of relief. "Head back to the estate and keep an eye on the trackers. I want to know the second one of them comes back up."

"You got it, boss."

I drop into my seat and allow my eyes to drift over the cameras I was watching Snow on half an hour ago and the anger grows hotter, burning me from the inside out. I have to get my woman back, but I can't do that if I don't know where she is.

"They'll be okay," Storm murmurs. "They have to be okay."

SIXTY-THREE

SNOW

"Snow," someone whisper shouts from a few feet away, but my eyes remain glued shut. There's something at the edge of my memory that I don't want to remember, and maybe if I can keep my eyes shut and my head buried in the sand, I won't have to deal with whatever it is.

"Snow!" they say louder this time, the voice so familiar it almost pulls me from the abyss of blissful ignorance. "I swear to God, if you don't wake up, I'm going to kill you myself when we get out of this."

Wynter.

The car.

Being followed.

Hitting my head.

Memories crash into me all at once and knock the air from my lungs as panic takes hold. My eyes fly open, and I'm faced with my sister hanging in front of me, her wrists tied and suspended from the beams above. It's only now I realize my own wrists and shoulders are screaming in pain, the rope around my wrists cutting into me until warm droplets of blood run down my arms.

"Oh, thank God," she says, looking around the space.

I follow her eye line and frown in confusion. Where the hell are we?

Burned rubble surrounds us, the remnants of the building scattered around the ground until they're completely unrecognizable. The light is dim, only the moon shining through the stained glass above us illuminates the space.

Wait. Stained glass.

I take another, more frantic, look around us, and my stomach sinks. Oh my god. We're in the church Elijah and I were married in. The one Rayne and Emerson and my parents all said their vows. It's unrecognizable after the events of my wedding day, no longer the church I always knew and loved.

I haven't given much thought to what happened here after Elijah got me out, too wrapped up in feelings of guilt and inadequacy, but seeing it now makes my heart ache painfully in my chest.

"Are you okay?" Wynter asks quietly. "Your head is bleeding and I think you've pulled your stitches."

I follow her gaze down my body to where crimson red seeps through the fabric of my gray sweater. "I think I'm okay. Are you? How's the baby?"

Wynter lets out a breath and winces as it jostles her bleeding wrists. "I'm okay. The impact of the crash was minimal, and they didn't drug me. They just put a bag over my head, so I couldn't see where we were going."

"The baby?" I ask, my eyes falling to her rounding stomach.

"She's fine. She's kicking away in there." She squeezes her eyes shut to stamp down the emotions rising to the surface. Her maternal instincts are kicking in, even if the baby is still months from being born.

"I meant what I said, Wyn. If you get the chance to run, do it. Don't worry about me, just worry about getting the two of you to safety."

"I'm not going to leave you, Snow," she whispers.

"That's exactly what you're going to do. If you get the chance, run. Don't look back. Just get yourself and my niece the hell out of here."

Tears slide down her cheeks despite her best efforts to hold them at bay.

I tear my eyes away from her before her gentle sobs can beckon my own and take another look at the debris around us. The doors and low windows are boarded up, meaning none of them are the escape route we need. There has to be an entry point though, because how else would they have brought us in?

Before I can figure it out myself, the sound of a door opening behind me has a cold sweat gathering at my brow. Being alone in a creepy, derelict church where I married Elijah was one thing, but facing the unknown enemy who has been meticulously destroying our lives is something else entirely.

The sound of heels clicking against charred concrete echoes through the church, and I watch as confusion tugs at Wynter's expression. It's a woman? The person who has been stealing our shipments, and taking out Elijah's dealers, and who orchestrated the attack on my wedding day, is a woman?

"Ladies," she greets as she comes into my line of sight. Holy shit. She's stunning. The woman has long, deep brown hair that curls down her back. Her lithe body is adorned with an expensive-looking red pantsuit, but it's her eyes that draw me to them. There's something almost familiar about this woman, but I can't quite put my finger on exactly what it is. "It's so nice of you to wake up."

"Apologies. It's really quite rude of me to pass out with a head injury. I'll try to remember that in the future." I can't hold back the snark in my tone. What harm is it going to do at this point? And the more attention she gives me, the less she will focus on Wynter.

I'm met with a deep blue glare, but I can't bring myself to regret my words. Whoever this bitch is, she's expecting a pair of spoiled Mafia princesses, and that's not who Wynter and I are. Not anymore at least. Perhaps that's who we were before our parents died, but we've both grown into women they would be proud of and ones who shouldn't be underestimated.

She tears her attention from me and turns it to Wynter, taking steps toward her and giving me a chance to observe her closer. The outfit she's wearing is obscenely expensive, right down to her Louboutin pumps, which means she has plenty of disposable income, especially when she decided to wear it to a decrepit, burned church where she has hostages hanging from rickety beams.

If I were an evil mastermind, I'd be doing it in a more modest outfit, and flat shoes.

"Your sister has always had a smart mouth, hasn't she?" The stranger approaches Wynter before placing her open palm on her growing belly. "The miracle of pregnancy," she murmurs.

I tug at my restraints, hissing through the agony in my wrists until the wood above me creaks from the pressure I'm putting it under.

She turns back to me with annoyance. "You're wasting your time. Even if you manage to get free, the building is surrounded. There's no escape for either of you," she pauses before eyeing Wynter's stomach again. "Or all three of you, I suppose."

"Who are you?" Wynter asks, her voice calm and even. The mask she wears for the world has slid into place, and she looks as composed as she does in the boardroom making million-dollar deals.

Our captor laughs, her head dropping back and her dark hair swaying from side to side. "I thought you were smarter than that, Wynter. I thought if anyone could work it out, it would be you."

"What are you…" She trails off as she stares at the woman closer, the slightest hint of recognition flickering in her eyes.

She huffs out a bored sigh and steps toward the only seat in the building before lowering herself to the clean metal fold-up chair. "I don't really have all day for one of you to work it out, so let me tell you a little story." She crosses one leg over the other and places both hands on her knee, settling in for whatever tale she thinks we give a fuck about. "Once upon a time, there were two crime families who ruled Chicago. The Russo family and the Masters family. As a way to unite the two families and bring unity to the underworld, the Russo's married their baby sister off to the head of the Masters' organization, and the two of them had a son, Everett. But before that, before the Russo's concocted the plan to sell off their sister for the good of their organization, Daniel Masters had a woman on the side that no one knew about. She was young and beautiful, but she wasn't what was best for the family, so he shipped her and their daughter off on the same day he married his new wife."

A small gasp leaves my lips as the pieces fall together. She isn't saying what I think she's saying… is she?

"You're lying," Wynter whispers, the words barely audible despite the deathly quiet surrounding us.

"You're more naive than I thought if you think that." She scoffs but doesn't bother to stand from her seat.

I'm surprised her security team has allowed her in here with no protection, but then again, we're not exactly a threat right now, strung up and powerless.

"In case you couldn't put those pieces together, Snow, my name is Annalise Masters, and I'm Everett's sister."

No one says anything for long moments as her words wash over us, but there's no response I can drag up that does the situation justice. The fact that the man I have considered a brother for most of my life has a long-lost sister none of us knew about, there are no words.

"Why are you doing this?" Wynter asks at last. At least one of us could come up with something to say, and I suppose the longer we can keep her talking, the better chance we have of being rescued.

"Because the Masters' family business should have been handed over to me, not overtaken by a bunch of people who had no ties to the Mafia, and no right inserting themselves into our business."

I stare at her, confusion milling around in my head. "But you would have been, what, thirteen when your father was killed and our family took over. What on earth do you think you would have done with a Mafia empire?"

"That's not really the point though, is it?" Annalise hisses. "The point is that I finally have my revenge, and it couldn't have worked out any more perfectly if I tried. A Russo." She gestures to me. "A Saint James." She points to Wynter. "And a Masters." She smiles fondly as she rubs Wynter's stomach again. Each time she does it, I get more and more agitated by the movement. "It's a shame you all have to die, but that's just the cards you've been dealt."

My eyes clash with Wynter's and despite her best efforts, fear dances behind the ice blue so similar to my own. I should be scared. This woman is clearly unhinged and threatening to kill us as part of some fucked-up revenge plot, but I have to believe Elijah and my brothers will come for us. I have to believe that the reason Elijah asked about our rings is because the sneaky bastards put trackers in them. And I have to believe that Annalise and whoever works for her aren't setting a trap for the rest of our family to knock us out in one fell swoop.

I brush my thumb over the delicate platinum band adorned

with tiny diamonds and pray to any god who will listen that they'll find us in time.

"Where have you been all these years?" Wynter asks.

Annalise shrugs. "Here and there. After Daniel sent us away, he would send money every month to take care of us, but when he died, that money stopped. We bounced around for a while, sometimes sleeping in our car, sometimes on the street. It wasn't much of a life for a young girl, constantly looking over her shoulder, always afraid of being hurt by those stronger than her."

"I'm sorry you had to go through that," Wynter says genuinely. I'm glad she's taking the lead to keep her talking, because there are no words for the level of fucked up this situation is. I thought the whole long-lost sibling thing only happened on those trashy tv shows I like to watch when I'm sick, but I was wrong.

Annalise eyes her for a moment before continuing her story. "It wasn't until I was sixteen that I met Steven. He was older than I was, but he was willing to pay my mother a pretty penny for my hand in marriage, and she took the deal. At the time, he was a small fish, just one of the many players in Los Angeles, but he wasn't looking at the big picture. He only saw the small time, the drugs, the occasional gun, maybe some information. There was so much more money to be made, he just needed to have the vision."

Steven? Why does that name sound so familiar?

"Steven Lounder?" The blood has drained from her cheeks, and if possible, she's paler than she was before.

"So you know of my husband then?" She grins.

Wynter looks to me, her eyes pressing closed for the briefest of moments to gather her composure. "Steven Lounder is a big-time human trafficker. He's the head of the Lounder Cartel on the West Coast."

Understanding washes over me and dread settles low in my belly. It explains everything. The shipments that went missing without a trace. The hits we didn't see coming. The lack of chatter on the street about a new player. There's nothing new about the Lounder Cartel, and their reach rivals even our own.

"The day I convinced him to start dealing in humans was the day our business really took off. There's such a market for pretty girls, so many men with fantasies they can't play out with their wife." She shakes her head, but her smile remains firmly on her lips. "I thought about selling the two of you. Even knocked up, you're worth a pretty penny. But if I were to do that, my idiot brother still has a chance to save you, even if you would be bloody and broken long before he could try."

"What's your endgame here?" I ask, the words falling from my lips before I can swallow them down. "Say you kill Wynter and I. What next? Everett isn't the head of the family, and you're not staking any claim on the Russo family?"

"Smart girl." She smiles. "You know, I really thought you'd be a bit stupid. You have that whole dumb blonde thing going on and the press, boy oh boy, do they have some colorful opinions of you." She blows out a whistle. "You're right. Punishing baby bro is just an added perk to this whole plan. Same as your husband. The Russos ultimately are the reason we were sent away, so they have their own sins to atone for. But although this all started as a revenge plot, it grew into something much larger. It's an opportunity to expand our business to the East Coast and taking over Chicago's underworld will only strengthen that. Angelo Russo had the right idea, but your family stood in his way with your bullshit morals." She rolls her eyes. "Just more reason you never should have had control of the family, and once your brothers are weakened by the loss of the two of you, and Everett is too distracted by his grief to do the job he normally does, it will be easy to take down the rest of the organization, and Elijah. After all, kingdoms always crumble without their queens."

My chest aches at the thought of Everett losing Wynter and the baby, of Storm and Rayne losing both of us, of Elijah losing me. With each minute that passes, the more nervous I become that they're not coming, or that they can't get to us. I can only imagine what's on the outside of this church, and if every other move Annalise has put into place is any indication, she's probably two steps ahead.

I'm surprised they didn't scan us for trackers. That would have been the first thing I would have done, and I'm not an evil mastermind trying to take my revenge. Maybe that's her plan. Lead them all here to rescue us and kill us all while she has the chance.

"Well ladies, it's been lovely speaking with you. I'm sure under different circumstances, we could have been friends." She shrugs. "But I must get going. Places to be, people to see. You know how it is."

The door behind me pushes open and two heavy sets of footsteps fill my ears, followed by the sound of water splashing against the carpet.

Wynter's eyes widen as she watches their movements, horror

creeping into the edges of her mask.

It's not until the scent of petrol fills my nostrils that I realize what's going on, and panic overwhelms me. She's going to burn us alive.

Out of all the ways I've imagined dying, burning to death isn't high on the list of the ways I want to go. In fact, if I had to rank them, it goes right down the bottom with being hunted by a deformed monster from one of those terrible horror movies Wynter and I used to watch when we were teenagers and sleep together for a week because we thought the villain was coming to get us.

The moment metal drags against metal, followed by the sound of a flame igniting behind me fills my ears, bile rises in my throat and fear grips hold of me until I can't breathe through it. The panic roaring through my body is all-consuming as my reality settles over me.

I'm going to die.

And what's worse? I'm going to watch my sister, my best friend, perish right in front of my eyes. I wonder which one of us will succumb to the flames first, who will have to be the last to take a breath and forced to watch the other burn.

The door clicks shut behind me and I'm immediately overcome by a cloud of smoke. Our time is almost up. There's so much I have left to say to my sister, but I can't think about saying goodbye.

You are a Saint James, and a Saint James never gives up, a voice in the back of my mind reminds me.

I tug at the ropes above my head, barely holding in the scream of agony shooting down my arms. Blood drips from the cuts on my wrists, but I don't stop, not even for a moment.

Wynter screams at the top of her lungs. "Help! Someone help us!" The terror in her voice causes a pain in my chest to slice through me, but I can't allow myself to focus on anything I'm feeling. Instead, I lean into the adrenaline, using it to give me the strength I need to not fall apart.

If that bitch thinks she can take out the whole Chicago Mafia in one swoop, she has another thing coming, and I can't wait to see the look in her eye when she realizes she's made the biggest mistake of her life by underestimating us.

Sixty-Four

Elijah

I haven't stopped pacing since we arrived at the estate an hour ago. I can't, because if I do, the reality that my entire world is missing might sink in, and I'll have no control over my own actions if that happens. I'll burn this entire city to the ground if it means getting Snow back.

Every person we trust sits in Storm's office, and despite it being a combination of Russo and Saint James men, it isn't enough to make any impact if we have to go to war to get our women back.

I should have let Storm send Snow to another country, at least she would have been safe there. If I allow myself to dwell on the decisions that brought us to this moment, I'll lose my fucking mind, and right now that could mean the difference between my woman living and dying.

"The trackers?" Storm asks Everett for the tenth time in the last twenty minutes.

Out of all of us, Everett is the calmest. I'm not sure if it's because he knows he's the only one who can find them if we have to lean on technology, or if his fear has numbed him to the point of being placated. "Like I told you the last time you asked, I will tell you the moment I get the sniff of a signal," he mutters, typing something on the laptop in front of him.

Storm glares at his best friend but leans back in his chair without a word. Tension radiates off him, his jaw so tight it ticks under the pressure.

"We can't just sit on our hands and wait for the trackers to turn back on. We should be out on the streets. We should be tearing this city apart," Rayne growls. He's been quiet since we all arrived, silently holding Emerson in his lap. Snow and Wynter being missing it too close to when Angelo took her, he needs to remind himself she's safe, even if his sisters are both in danger.

"Spreading out across the city with limited numbers would only make us easier to pick off," I remind him. We've been over this. If I thought it would make a difference, I would be going door to door and tearing anyone who gets in my way apart. But it wouldn't help. If anything, it would hinder us, and that's a fact Tommy reminded us of when we were suiting up for battle.

I never thought he would be the levelheaded one, but these situations either bring out the best, or the worst in a person.

"I don't fucking care. We're too far away from the city. We should have met at the penthouse," Rayne grumbles.

"There's no guarantee they're in the city," Storm says.

"They could be anywhere," I mumble and barely swallow

down the bile that rises as the words slip from my lips. It's been two hours. Two hours since we lost connection with them. Two hours since their trackers registered. Two hours since the possibility of losing my entire life began to seep in.

"Surely there's something else we could be doing," Rayne mutters.

"There isn't," Storm snaps. "We've looked under every rock, we've leaned on every single contact we all have, and we have no fucking idea who we're up against, let alone where the hell they would take Wynter and Snow. Believe me, if there was *anything* I thought would help us find them, we would be out there doing it right now. But there isn't, so we have to wait for the trackers to—"

"They're back," Everett yells, scooping up the laptop and heading for the door.

"Where are they?" I ask, falling into stride beside him, touching the guns tucked into my waistband. I'm itching for a kill, craving the bloodshed. I need to make someone pay for the pain they've caused my woman.

"The church."

I stop dead in my tracks. "As in the church they attacked on our wedding day?"

Everett doesn't respond, instead he nods without looking back. The man is on a mission to bring his fiancé home, and he's going to do it with or without our help.

I turn back to the group of men standing behind me, including the men who became my brothers the day I married Snow and release a breath. "Let's bring them home."

A few minutes later, we're speeding down the driveway in a convoy. We're taking everyone we trust with us. The businesses and other assets can be guarded by those who may betray us, but we're not willing to risk the lives of Snow and Wynter.

Rayne's in the driver's seat, pushing the large black SUV to its limits as he swerves from the driveway to the road and puts his foot down. Storm is beside him, typing furiously on his phone with his brows furrowed. Everett is next to me in the back seat flicking through camera angles to try to get a picture of what we're going into. If we can avoid going in blind, we have the best chance of bringing them home, but we'll go in regardless. We'll risk everything to bring them home.

"Everett?" Storm turns in his seat just as Rayne pulls onto the highway and pushes the speed to the limit.

There isn't a cop in this city brave enough to pull a Saint James over for speeding, especially considering the amount of money they donate to the department each year.

"There are a few cars around, but nothing seems out of place."

"Are you sure the footage is live? They could have a loop running," Storm says.

"It's not a loop. Not unless their tech guy is smart enough to have all the cameras running on the exact same loop, which I doubt."

"They have been two steps ahead of us in everything else they've done," I remind him, staring out the window as lights pass in a blur.

Everett growls under his breath. "They're not a loop," he

forces out through gritted teeth.

"I'm just saying—"

"Shut up," he snaps, bringing the laptop closer to his face. "There's movement. Someone just arrived. A woman, I think."

"You think?" Rayne asks, not tearing his eyes from the road for even a moment.

"The cameras in the area haven't been updated since the nineties, but by the size of them I feel relatively comfortable assuming it's a she."

"Anyone else with her?" Storm asks.

"Just some bodyguards from what I can tell."

"So the person who has been coming for us, who has been taking shipments and killing dealers, is a woman?" I ask. It sounds bad to ask, but with how ruthless the moves have been, I never would have expected a member of the fairer sex to be the evil mastermind behind it all.

"So it would seem," Everett mumbles under his breath as he flicks through the cameras again, trying to get a visual of what's happening inside the church.

We're too far away. Even with Rayne speeding and swerving through traffic, we're too far from the church, and the longer it takes to get to them, the more chance that something could happen to them.

I've never been afraid of losing anything. When I was a child, I wasn't afraid of losing my cousin and only friend. I was never afraid of losing my father and uncles. And I've never even considered being scared of losing the power that comes with my name. But I'm fucking petrified of losing Snow. Because a life without my Snowflake isn't something I've ever wanted to consider, and I'm not about the start now.

A few minutes pass and I watch Rayne dodge through traffic, never so much as hovering his foot above the brake. The car is dead silent apart from Everett tapping on the keys of his laptop and Storm's fingers on his phone as he coordinates the mission.

We're getting closer. Not close enough, but closer. Traffic is good for this time of night, which has meant we've been able to make better time than I thought we would. We're probably only a few minutes out, but every piece of time I'm away from Snow makes my chest constrict painfully.

"She's leaving," Everett tells us.

"Snow and Wynter?" I ask.

He shakes his head, swapping views to get the best image of our mystery woman. The frame is blurred, but she appears to be well dressed, and she walks with the confidence of someone who has been doing this for a long time. Whoever she is, she isn't new to the scene. She's been doing it for a while.

"Is that smoke?" Storm asks, leaning forward to get a better view of the sky.

I follow his gaze and dread settles over me. It's the church. It has to be.

Everett swears under his breath, confirming what I already know. "We need to follow her."

"No, we need to get my sisters the fuck out of a burning building. Who gives a fuck about her?" Storm hisses.

"We will tomorrow," Everett snaps. "I've checked the streets, they haven't left anyone in the church. There's no one waiting for us."

"Are you sure?" Storm asks.

"I would not be suggesting this if I wasn't one hundred percent sure, Storm. My fiancé and unborn child are in a burning fucking building. If I thought there was any chance this was a trap, I would want every single man who works for us to be here. That's how sure I am."

Storm nods and taps something out on his phone. "I'm sending all the other cars after them. Everett, I know you want to get to Wynter, but I need you to guide them. Rayne, stay in the car, the moment we get Wynter and Snow out, I want to be moving. Elijah and I will go in."

"Do you think you running into a burning building is a good idea?" Rayne raises an eyebrow. "Then you and your succession plan are both in there."

"I don't give a fuck about succession plans right now, Rayne. All I care about is getting our sisters to safety."

The car skids to a stop and I'm sprinting across the street before I'm conscious of my own movements. I reach for the door, some of the panic that has raged through my veins since the moment we realized they were being followed settles, but as my fingers wrap around the handle a large explosion rumbles beneath my feet. I glance over my shoulder and meet Storm's frantic eyes, and don't waste another second before tugging at the doors. My stomach sinks when they don't budge, they're locked.

"Around the back!" Storm shouts, taking off without another word.

I sprint after him, the force of my feet hitting the pavement holds me back from the edge of blinding panic. I've never known fear like this. My everything is in this burning church, and I don't want to live a life where she's not the center of it.

SIXTY-FIVE

SNOW

The smoke is so thick I can barely see Wynter a few feet away. Her coughing is getting deeper with every passing second, and despite my best efforts, my wrists are still bound painfully above my head. Blood drips down my arms in crimson lines and my shoulders ache from the position I'm hanging.

Tears fall against my cheeks in a mixture of terror and rage. The fear makes me want to give up, but the anger, the anger gives me the push I need to fight against the ropes. The need for revenge tugs at the edge of my vision, begging for me to escape and make that bitch pay for what she's done to this family.

"Snow," Wynter cries. "I'm sorry for making you leave the house. You were right. We should have stayed at home."

"This isn't your fault, Wyn. None of this is your fault."

"It is," she chokes. "It's all my fault, and now we're going to die."

"Wynter," I snap. "We are not going to die." But even as the words leave my mouth, the smoke gets the better of me and I bark out a cough.

I've never known my sister to give up. She's the strongest woman I know, I just have to remind her of that. I need to remind her of the queen she was born to be. We were never meant to be the Mafia princesses who did as they were told their whole lives. We were born to lead, and we will live to see our vengeance.

"I just need you to hold on. The fire should spread up the pillars and weaken the beams holding us." I hope. "You are going to get out of this church Wynter, even if it's the last thing I ever do, you and my niece are going to live."

"I won't leave you."

"You will. If you get the chance, I want you out of this building."

"You're my baby sister."

"And you have my niece growing inside you."

I tug at the ropes for what feels like the millionth time. The coarse fibers are so deeply embedded in my skin that I'm worried they'll hit bone soon, but I don't care. The beam above me creaks, I'm almost there, I can feel it. For a moment, relief spreads through my chest, but I don't stop trying to get free, not even for a second.

But all that relief is torn away when a loud explosion sounds from beside us, tearing a scream from my raw throat. The heat of the flames is getting closer, the temperature and smoke almost too much for my body to handle. We can't take much more. The longer we're inhaling the smoke, the harder it is to breathe, and soon the lack of oxygen will drag us both under.

"Snow," Wynter whimpers.

"I'm almost free. The beam is about to give way," I tell her, tugging as hard as I can despite the searing agony.

"Wait! It's going to—"

But before she can finish her sentence the beam above me cracks. I look up just in time to see the moment the rope comes free of where it was tied, and a second later, the entire beam is coming down. It almost happens in slow motion, but I can't move. I'm frozen in place, rooted to the spot as I watch my own demise rush toward me.

Agony slices through my body as I crumple to the ground with the heavy wood laid out over my middle. The pain in my wrists is nothing compared to the weight piled on top of me, digging into my still fresh surgical scar. My eyes fall closed, the combination of pain and the smoke I've inhaled making it impossible to keep them open. My body craves unconsciousness. It craves the peacefulness that awaits me on the other side.

There's so much I want to say to my sister, so many things I should tell her, but there are no more words. All that's left is pain.

SIXTY-SIX

ELIJAH

Storm reaches for the handle of the door and immediately pulls it back, his breath hissing through his teeth. "Fuck."

"Get out of the way," I snap, taking the handle without hesitation. The excruciating pain only serves to keep me focused and the moment the door swings open, smoke billows out into our faces.

I quickly bring my burned hand over my mouth and surge forward. There's no time to waste, we're already far later than we should have been, but we got here as fast as we could. I just hope it's enough.

"Snow!" I yell. "Wynter."

"We're here," Wynter chokes. "Snow's hurt."

My stomach sinks at her words, but I keep moving forward toward her voice. Hurt is still alive. Hurt can be fixed. Dead can't, so all that matters is getting her the fuck out of this place and getting her to someone who can help her.

I find Wynter first, her wrists bound above her head as she sobs quietly between coughs. Her body shakes with a mixture of fear and adrenaline. "We're going to get you out of here," I tell her.

"You have to help Snow," she cries.

"Over here!" Storm shouts and I quickly look over my shoulder. The smoke is so thick I can't see more than a few feet in front of me, but I can just make out the light of his phone.

I hesitate to leave Wynter. She's pregnant and clearly struggling to breathe, we need to get her to safety. But we also need to assess Snow's injuries to see if we need backup to get her out of here. "I'll be right back," I tell her as I take careful steps toward Storm. The smoke only seems to get thicker with each second that passes, and I need to be careful where I tread.

Storm's stocky figure comes into view, crouching down beside a pile of rubble. It's not until I'm almost on top of him that I see Snow, her fragile body crushed beneath what used to be a beam. The moment my eyes lock on her, my stomach sinks and it's almost impossible to drag in a breath through the blinding panic.

I drop to my knees beside him and reach for my woman. Her eyes are closed, her breathing shallow and labored. I've been around enough people in their last moments to know what it looks like and seeing my Snowflake in this position makes me homicidal.

"Get Wynter out," she wheezes the moment my fingers brush her hair from her face.

"No, we need to get you out," Storm argues. "Wynter is okay for a minute."

Snow's eyes pop open and the fire I've become obsessed with all these years flares to life behind them. "I swear to God, if you don't get Wynter out of this building right now, I will personally kill you both." Her words are strong for someone who looks like they're about to pass out from the pain, but then again, she wouldn't be my little spitfire if she weren't threatening us.

I glance over at Storm who does the same. Neither of us wants to leave her because it will take at least the two of us to lift the beam off her and pull her free, but if we do that and something happens to Wynter and the baby, she'll never forgive us.

"Please," Snow whispers. "I need to know she and the baby are safe."

Storm's resolve wavers, and he quickly squeezes her hand. "We'll be right back. Just hold on for us, okay?"

Snow gives us a shaky nod but doesn't respond.

Storm and I both jump into action. We don't have long before the building is going to crumple around us, and more than that, we don't have a lot of time before the flames reach Snow. As soon as we reach Wynter, he lifts her from the ground. I tug my knife from the back of my pants and make quick work of slicing through the thick rope binding her to the beam above her.

She lets out a pained whimper the moment the tension is released, but we don't stop moving even for a second. Storm bundles her up against his chest as we turn toward the door that's almost completely enveloped with flames. I don't allow myself to dwell on the fact that by the time we're back to get Snow out, the flames will have completely overtaken the door, and that's if we can even get back once we've handed Wynter over to Everett.

"You take her. I'm going to stay with Snow," I tell him. I can't leave her. If she's going to perish in this building, I'm going to go down in flames right alongside her. Because I don't want to live in a world where my Snowflake no longer exists. Where her body is little more than a pile of ashen bones in the ground. That's no life.

He doesn't hesitate, quickly moving through the fire while I move carefully back to the pile of wood trapping my woman. There's too much for me to move on my own. I could probably lift it off her, but she's in no position to move without help.

"I'm here, Snowflake," I whisper, taking her hand in mine and squeezing. Despite the rising temperatures, her palm is cold and clammy, and I try not to let myself think of what that could mean.

"Wynter?" she murmurs, her eyes fluttering open for the briefest of moments before falling closed again. She's fading fast, and if we don't get her out of here soon, she's not going to make it.

"Storm's taken her out to Everett and the paramedics," I tell her. "He'll be back in a minute and we'll be able to get you out."

Snow coughs violently, her weak body jolting and causing her to cringe in agony. "Elijah," she whispers. "I don't think I'm going to make it."

"Don't say that," I snap.

She lets out a choked breath. "I'm being realistic. I'm all wet, and I can only assume it's blood. I can barely breathe, and the pain, it's too much. It's all too much," she whimpers.

"I need you to hold on for me, Snow. We're going to get you out of here. I promise I'll make this right."

"Don't make promises you can't keep."

"You're going to live, Snow. We're going to have a beautiful life. You and I are going to rule the fucking world side by side, but I need you to be strong for me. Just for a little longer."

She presses her eyes closed, but tears escape from the corners as she squeezes my hand. "I love you." Her words stop my own breath in my throat. The words I've been waiting a decade to hear. The emotion I never thought I was capable of. Not until I had my Snowflake in my arms, until she became my whole universe.

"I love you too." I lean forward and press my forehead to her clammy one. "Just hold on, Snow."

"I can't."

"You can and you will."

"It hurts," she whimpers.

"I know it does, baby. But as soon as we get you out of here, we'll get you something for the pain, okay? Just hold on, fight for me."

A loud crack draws my attention from Snow for a moment as the beam that held Wynter a few moments ago falls and hits concrete in a loud crash. We don't have long. This whole fucking building is going to come down any minute now, and we need to be out of here before that happens.

Two figures appear in the burning doorway, and I've never been so relieved to see Storm and Rayne, men who I was raised to despise, who I've tried to kill on more than one occasion. They don't hesitate before jumping into action, moving toward us quickly.

"We don't have long," Rayne says, his eyes moving around the patches of fire.

"You lift the other end, I'll lift this one, and Elijah, carefully pull her free," Storm commands. He's moved into work mode like it's the most natural thing to do right now, but work is the furthest thing from my mind right now. I couldn't give a shit about my business, or our assets. The only thing on this earth I care about is Snow and getting her to safety.

"Be careful of her neck, she might have a spinal injury," Rayne says.

I don't bother pointing out that if we don't get her out of this building in the next few minutes, we'll all be dead, so a spinal injury will be the least of her worries.

Another loud crash behind us makes us jump into action, our time is running out rapidly, and while the devil might be ready to meet me, I'm not ready to meet my maker just yet.

"We're getting you out right now, Snowflake. Just hold on for me." I lean forward and press a kiss to her chilled temple. "It's all going to be okay." I'm not sure which one of us I'm trying to convince with those words, but I find no comfort in them.

"You ready?" Storm asks, his hands braced beneath the huge beam, biceps flexing as his muscles prepare themselves to lift it.

I nod once, kneeling on the ash-covered concrete. I won't know the best way to free her until I can see what lies beneath the heavy wood. I suspect it will be easier to pull her out under rather than over, but I won't commit to either until I can assess the situation.

Snow's cries fill my ears as the beam is carefully lifted from her body. I can't tell if it's relief or pain that has broken sobs filling the air, but I don't have time to think about it either. Although every one of my instincts screams at me to comfort my woman, the logical part of my mind seems to be in charge right now.

I carefully pull the remaining rubble off her body and suck in a ragged breath at the amount of blood soaking through her sweater. My sweet Snowflake is stained with crimson, and I will tear the world apart to make whoever did this pay.

SIXTY-SEVEN

SNOW

I thought I was in pain before. In fact, I didn't think it was possible to be in more pain than I already was, but where I expected to feel relief the moment the beam is lifted from my body, all I felt was agony.

The pain that was localized in my torso before now radiates through my entire body, up my arms, down my legs. It's everywhere.

Panic flares in Elijah's eyes as uncontrollable screams tear from my throat, tears soaking my cheeks, but he doesn't pause. He's a man on a mission, and that mission is to get me out of this building before the entire thing collapses.

I squeeze my eyes shut, trying to swallow down the sobs, to be strong at least until we're out of here, but instead I choke on them. It's too much. It's all too much. Mix it with the heat of the flames that grow closer by the second and the overwhelming smoke filling my lungs, I'm not sure how much longer I'll be able to hold on.

Elijah pulls rubble from my body as quickly as he can while still being gentle. I almost tell him there's no point, that no matter what he does, I'm going to be in unimaginable pain, but I can't speak through it. In fact, every breath is a struggle.

"Elijah," Storm grunts.

"I'm working on it," he snaps, lifting a heavy piece of wood from my legs. "I'm almost there, Snow. Just a few more pieces and I'll get you out of here."

As soon as the last pieces of debris are lifted from my body I should feel relief, but there's nothing but agony. I should have told them to leave me. If my injuries are even close to how they feel, I may not make it anyway. I know that's a dim state of mind, but things are looking pretty bleak right now.

Elijah pushes one arm behind my back and the other beneath my knees, lifting me from under the beam my brothers are struggling to hold, and the moment I'm free, they drop it in a heavy thud.

"I've got you," he whispers, quickly standing and striding toward the door that's almost completely engulfed in flames.

I bury my face in his chest, allowing tears to roll down my cheeks and soak through his tactical gear. The heat is too much, the pain is too much, it's all too fucking much. I've never wished for death before, but surely it would be a kinder fate than whatever lay ahead of me.

The flames lick at my bare skin as Elijah carries us through the fire, and if I didn't know better, I would think he's a hero. What else can you call a man who runs into a burning building to save you? Who walks through fire to get you to safety?

But my husband isn't a hero. He's the monster lurking in the shadows. He's the man you cross the street to avoid. And he's the man I trust to hold my heart and body in his hands.

Cool fresh air rushes around us and the moment my lungs fill with something other than smoke is almost as painful as when the beam crashed down on me. The toxic cocktail of smoke and adrenaline rushes from me, and I cough long and hard, jolting every injury I have and causing tears to stream down my cheeks.

Elijah breaks out into a jog. The jostling hurts, but not like breathing does. The very movement that keeps me alive makes me wish for death. The tension in his jaw is tight, but it gives me something other than pain to focus on. The tic of the muscle proves how close to losing his shit he really is, but you'd never know from his hold on me, firm but gentle. He seems to know exactly where it hurts the most, and he's avoiding the areas at all costs. He knows my body as well as I do. Maybe even better.

The moment the cars come into view, Elijah relaxes just enough that I no longer think the muscle in his jaw is going to snap at any second. And when I see Wynter being cradled in Everett's arms on the sidewalk, some of the tension in my own body releases. She's safe. My sister and niece are safe, and that's all that matters right now.

"Snow?" my sister whimpers, her eyes darting over the injuries I haven't brought myself to look at yet. Call it what you will. Blissful ignorance. Plausible Deniability. It doesn't matter what label you put on it, I'm going to ride that train for as long as I can before admitting just how hurt I am.

"Just stay put, Dove," Everett murmurs. "Doc will be finished dressing your wrists in a minute."

"The baby?" I croak. Between the crying, the smoke, and my own screams, my voice is hoarse and barely there.

Everett looks at me over his shoulder, the fear and anger dancing behind the deep blue pools. "She's okay. Doc did a quick handheld ultrasound, and she's rolling around in there happily, her heartbeat is perfect." His hand rubs affectionately over my sister's bump, and relief washes over his tense body, his shoulders visibly relaxing when the words leave his mouth.

I squeeze my eyes shut in relief. I could never have lived with myself if something happened to my niece. Facing my sister and Everett would have been impossible, even if they would never have blamed me.

Another presence tugs my eyes open, and I'm met with Doc's piercing eyes, worry etched into his brow. The man has always had a soft spot for me, even though he hates pretty much everyone else he meets.

"I would rather not take her to hospital," Elijah tells him. "I don't think I can have her out of my sight… ever again. Can you check if you can treat her injuries or if I need to have a team of surgeons meet us at home?"

Doc gives my husband an amused eye roll but nods. "Lay her out on the bed of my truck. There are some blankets already spread out, so it shouldn't be too hard."

Elijah doesn't respond, instead jumping into action and taking long strides toward the deep blue truck. But when we reach it, his grip on me only tightens as a war rages behind his eyes.

"Elijah?" I murmur.

Forest-green eyes meet my own with an intensity that almost makes me look away. His anger and fear are barely contained, and I'm beginning to wonder if the only thing stopping the tether from snapping is his arms around me.

I want to reassure him, to tell him everything is going to be okay and that I'll be just fine. But I don't know if that's true. The more the adrenaline starts to waver, the more pain courses through my body.

"I can't," he whispers, dropping his head to my shoulder. "I don't know how I'm ever going to put you down again."

Before I can respond, Storm appears beside us, his eyes brushing down my blood-stained clothing. "We're all going to the estate." It's not a question and I brace myself for Elijah's anger, but it doesn't come.

"I think we're safest there," he agrees and I whip my head around so fast my neck screams in protest. Did my husband, the man who trained to hate my family, just agree with my brother? Am I dead?

"Why isn't she lying down?" Doc snaps, and if I was capable of smiling right now, I would be from ear to ear. I love how grumpy he is. I love that he puts my scary-ass Mafia boss brother and husband in their place. And I love how Storm and Elijah take it without so much as a blink of an eye.

"I'll be okay," I murmur even if I don't believe the words myself.

He hesitates for another moment before gently lowering me down to the soft linen. My body protests, pain shooting through every inch of me, but I do all I can to keep my face trained. "I'm sorry, Snowflake."

Doc climbs up on the truck bed beside me and carefully pulls the sweater up, the fabric tugging at open wounds and making me hiss out a breath. "I'm sorry, darlin'. I'm being as gentle as I can."

Elijah growls, but Doc just gives me a wink and returns his attention to my injuries. He gives my abdomen a few excruciating prods before picking up my wrist and examining the damage I caused trying to escape.

"I think we should take her to a hospital," he finally says, continuing before Elijah can jump in and interrupt. "I'm positive she has internal bleeding, which means she'll need blood, possibly a lot of it, and it would be safest if she were in a hospital. Additionally, her wrists need to be looked at by a plastic surgeon, and they don't normally make house calls."

Elijah's panicked eyes brush down my broken body and he nods once. If I didn't already know the man was completely obsessed with me, this moment would tell me everything. Despite his better judgment and his own need to have me close, he's putting my health and safety first. "I want the same setup as after the wedding. I don't give a fuck what it costs. Make it happen," he says. "And I want you in there with her. I don't trust anyone else."

Sixty-Eight

Elijah

I never really believed in déjà vu. It wasn't a concept that my family would allow us to believe, and the myths about the feeling were too out there for the likes of the Russo family.

But this is it. I'm pacing up and down the corridor of the hospital wing we've completely taken over. There isn't another patient in this part of the hospital and perhaps I should feel bad about that, but I don't. The only thing I care about is Snow, and everything else on the face of the earth can get fucked as far as I'm concerned.

Not for the first time since she disappeared through the double doors behind the desk, I think about leaving all of this. We could go anywhere, do anything, as long as it's far away from the threat that has almost taken my Snowflake away from me twice in as many weeks. I don't give a fuck about the money or the power, and I couldn't care less about my family's legacy, all that matters is keeping Snow safe.

Of course I'll have a fight on my hands when I tell her she'll no longer live in the same city as her family, but I'd rather she hates me from safety, than love me in the midst of constant danger.

I have no qualms handing my business over to Frost Industries, it would be staying in the family after all, and they could always visit us wherever we end up.

My musings of a life far away from the one we're living now are interrupted when Everett carries Wynter through the double doors behind the counter. She's been getting checked out properly since we arrived, and I have a feeling every time I see her for the foreseeable future, my cousin will be carrying her. I know because that's how it's going to be with Snow as soon as she's out of here. I don't know how I'm ever going to allow her to leave my arms, let alone my sight.

Storm stops his own pacing and takes long strides to where his best friend is settling his sister in his arms. The plastic chairs aren't big enough for Everett in general, but they're certainly not built for a man the size of my cousin, and his woman. "What did the doctor say? Are they sure the baby is okay?"

Wynter tucks her face against Everett's chest and yawns, but there's the slightest smile playing on her lips, just enough to tell me she's amused by her big bad brother fussing over her. "I'm fine, my wrists are pretty torn up, and because it was over existing scar tissue, the healing process may be more painful, but I'll make a full recovery. Baby is perfect."

Everett's hand spreads across the bump protectively, and not for the first time, I find myself craving Snow's body swelling with our baby. I meant when I told her it didn't matter if she gives me legitimate heirs, any child raised by Snow and I will be fit to be handed the keys to the kingdom someday, but the possessive caveman inside me wants nothing more than to claim her in one last way.

"She's bouncing around in there having the time of her life," she says, the affection in her voice clear as she looks up at Everett. The smoke has made her voice more husky than normal, but she doesn't appear to be struggling to speak.

He still looks like he's ready to tear the world apart for daring to touch his woman, but some of the tension has left his shoulders, and his hold on Wynter is gentle but firm.

Storm's phone rings and we all turn to look at him expectantly. We're still waiting to hear from Tommy about whether or not they were able to capture whoever has been making moves against us, whoever just tied my woman up in a church and set the damn thing on fire.

"Yes," Storm says, clicking the phone onto speaker for the rest of us to hear.

"We lost them," Tommy growls. "They disappeared like fucking Houdini. One minute they were ahead of us, and then the next they were gone."

"A convoy of black SUVs doesn't just disappear, Tommy," Storm snaps.

"Well, these ones did. I don't know what to tell you, these guys are pros."

"Find them," he growls, ending the call without another word. The corded muscles in his neck are so tense, they look like they might snap at any second.

"Her," Wynter whispers. "You need to find her."

"What do you mean, her?" Storm asks, barely holding on to his anger as he turns his attention to his sister.

She blows out a shaky breath. "Before she set the church on fire, she told us everything. Who she is. How she got here. What her plan is. She obviously didn't think we were going to make it out alive, and that was the first time she's slipped up since all this started."

"Who is she?" Everett asks.

"Your sister." The words are simple enough, but they send the room into chaos. Storm swears and recommences his pacing. Everett carefully places Wynter down on the seat beside him before walking across the hall and slamming his fist into the wall. And I stand in place, completely fucking speechless. Everett has a sister?

"Everett doesn't have a sister," I point out.

Wynter watches him with concern before turning her attention back to me. "His father had a woman before he married your aunt. He sent them away when the alliance was settled on, and she blames all of us for taking the life she and her mother were owed. In her mind, she should be running both families right now." Her cheeks pale as her eyes dart from each of us before settling on her hands in her lap. "She's married to Steven Lounder."

We turn to her all at once, that can't be right. First of all, Lounder has never dared step foot into our territory. He and my uncles were sworn enemies. And on top of that, the Saint James family have forged themselves into becoming the most powerful criminal organization in the country, and they've always made their stance on human trafficking extremely clear, and that's what the Lounders are known for.

The sound that erupts from Everett's throat is raw and rough, primal anger that's anything but human.

Wynter lets out a shaky breath but makes no move from her seat. "She said that by taking Snow and me out, she was taking someone from each family. A Saint James. A Russo. And a Masters," she chokes on the last word, rubbing her stomach as if reminding herself the baby is okay.

Everett's head whips around and rage fills his eyes. He's past anger. Him and anger aren't even on the same continent right now, but he takes slow, measured steps back to Wynter, dropping to his knees in front of her. He wraps his hand around the back of her head and guides her down until their foreheads rest against one another. He's vibrating with fear and rage, but he's gentle with her. "I will make this right, Wynter. I promise I'll make it right."

"It's not your fault," she whispers. "None of this is any of our faults, and we're going to take this bitch down." Her eyes meet mine and I nod.

I don't need her words to know what she's asking me. She knows if push comes to shove, Everett may not be able to pull the trigger, that even Storm, Rayne, and Tommy will have a moral objection to killing a woman. And normally I would too, but Everett's sister deserves much worse than death for what she did tonight, and I won't hesitate to pull the trigger and send her to meet her maker.

"What's her name?" Everett asks.

"Annalise."

I meet his gaze when it whips toward me. "Why is that name so familiar?" I ask aloud.

"We've met her." Everett pushes to his feet, pressing a quick kiss to Wynter's forehead as he stands.

I try to think back to those days. It was so long ago, and it's a time in my life I would rather forget. My father and uncles changed the day Daniel Masters was killed. They became more cold, more ruthless, and Everett and I bore the brunt of that.

"At your father's funeral!"

He nods, glancing at Wynter to make sure she's still where he left her. "She and her mother came up to us, introduced themselves as friends of my father."

"And Annalise started crying. You wanted to comfort her, but Angelo wouldn't let you." The memory crashes into me all at once. At the time, I couldn't figure out why he was so angry, but it's all starting to make sense.

"I wonder if Angelo kept paying Annalise's mother after Daniel died," Wynter muses.

"I might be able to find out," I say, quickly pulling my phone from my pocket and shooting a text to the accountant my uncle used. I still have him on our payroll despite not trusting him as far as I can kick him, for times just like this. Angelo was into a lot of bullshit, and sometimes I need information about the shit my uncle used to do, just like right now.

Sixty-Nine

Snow

I'm whisked out of the hospital ward the moment I open my eyes after my second surgery in as many weeks. Elijah is right beside me, his large hand enveloping one of mine as I return to consciousness and then all the way to the estate. If I didn't know better, I would think I was in some old heist movie because Rayne is in the driver's seat of the ambulance I'm loaded into, but somehow, it's not the most pressing question I should be asking.

I'm too drowsy to argue about where we're going, too sore and tired to wonder if he's just going to drop me off again. He hasn't said much, just that he doesn't trust anyone in the hospital caring for me, and something about a team of nurses and doctors waiting for me at the estate.

I don't know. The fog of painkillers and sedation is so thick I can barely open my eyes, let alone listen to what's being said to me. I haven't been brave enough to ask anyone about my injuries. What if my ability to have a baby has been taken from me completely? What if I'm unable to give Elijah an heir?

That fear has had its fist around my throat from the moment he told me I'd lost an ovary, but as I consider the possibility that my chance to become a mother altogether may have been taken from me, that fist tightens impossibly.

"Stop thinking so hard, Snowflake. Do you need some more painkillers?" Elijah murmurs, his hand tightening around mine and bringing me a sense of calm.

I shake my head. I'm afraid if I speak, he'll see right through me and see how much pain and turmoil I'm in. And the only way I'm going to be able to stop the merry-go-round of thoughts in my mind will be if they sedate me again.

He shakes his head and lets out a rough chuckle, leaning down until his face is only an inch from mine. "You forget that I've stalked you for ten years, Snow. I know all your tells." His fingers brush the matted hair from my cheek as his eyes move over my face, frowning at the spot where my head throbs. "If you're in pain, you need to take the medication. It's not weakness to admit you need help."

If I was capable of it right now, I would probably laugh, because in what universe has Elijah Russo ever asked for help? But I don't have the energy, and right now nothing seems like it could be funny enough to drag a laugh from my tender throat.

Elijah sighs and presses a kiss to my forehead, his lips lingering there for long moments before he withdraws. "We're almost at the estate."

"Are you going to leave me again?" I ask before I can stop myself.

"Never." He shakes his head. "If I can ever allow you out of my sight again, it will be a miracle, but you'll never spend another night without me beside you." The words do nothing to settle the uncertainty building in my chest.

I squeeze my eyes shut, willing myself to ask about my injuries, but as I open my mouth, the words on the tip of my tongue, the ambulance turns onto gravel, and I'm out of time. In less than a minute, we'll be at the estate, and I'll have lost my nerve to ask by the time we reach our destination.

Five days.

Five days since I arrived back at the estate.

Five days of Elijah monitoring my every movement.

Five days that I haven't been brave enough to ask if my chance of having children has gone from fifty percent to zero.

And each day is longer than the last.

Each one of my family visits during the day, even Storm who has taken to working on his laptop at my bedside.

Despite how much time they spend with me, no one really speaks to me. Not about anything important at least. They ask how I'm feeling. Emerson tells me little anecdotes about the kids from the center, and Tommy has taken to talking to me about Frost Industries' latest venture, an underground fighting ring he'll be managing, but that's about as substantial as conversations have gotten.

Elijah just hovers, constantly watching for signs of discomfort, but it's driving me insane. I need someone to tell me what's going on with Annalise. I need to know if we have any leads and what our plan is moving forward. I need to know how we're going to get our revenge for what she's done to this family.

I've never cared about being out of the loop, I even preferred it at times, but now it's personal. She kidnapped us and set fire to a building with us inside, and I want my revenge. I want to make her pay for what she's done. I don't want to sit on the sidelines and allow everyone else to do all the work and reap all the rewards. But the way they're all tiptoeing around me like they're expecting me to break at any moment, I doubt anyone will even consider allowing me to help.

Elijah, the big bad Mafia king who enjoys ending other people's lives the way normal people enjoy reading a book, pulls the pillow from behind me, fluffs it back up and then carefully sits me forward and places it at the perfect angle. I should be grateful, I know that, but I haven't seen the man I fell in love with, the one who was so obsessed with me that he stalked me for ten years and stole me away from my family, in too long, and I need him back.

"Can you stop fussing?" I snap. "I had surgery, but I'm still able to take care of myself."

His eyes snap to mine, and he opens his mouth to respond, but nothing comes out. To be fair, I've barely said a word since he tried to put me in a hospital bed they'd set up in the living room, and I cried until they finally brought me up to my bedroom. I'm done with hospital beds, and something about seeing that one set up in a space that holds so many happy memories, it set me off.

"Why haven't you told me what the doctors said?" I push the blankets from my lap and swing my legs over the edge of the bed, ignoring the pain that shoots through my abdomen.

"Snow," Elijah growls, placing both hands on my shoulders to stop me from moving any further. "You're going to hurt yourself." He forces himself to sound calm, but he's anything but. I've spent enough time watching him to know the tic in his jaw and the way he tightens his hands into fists over and over again the moment they lift from my shoulders are him barely holding on to his composure, and for some reason, I want to see him break. I want to watch him lose it.

It's like playing with fire and hoping I get burned, the words come before I have a chance to think them through. "Like it matters. Annalise is going to take us all out anyway."

The sound that breaks from Elijah's throat is so far from human it's almost as if there's a wild animal in the room. His eyes flare with anger and I know I've got him exactly where I need him. I just have to push a little bit more and he'll unleash the beast I crave.

"And hey, it will save you having to dump my body in the bottom of Lake Michigan when I can't produce an heir."

I barely get the words out before Elijah has me flat on the bed, his hard body pressing mine into the mattress. His weight settles over me, but somehow, he manages to keep it off my incisions so the only pain that flares to life is the dull ache between my legs. It's been too long since he's taken me. Elijah doesn't do gentle, not when it comes to sex, and I can't imagine he's going to take any chances until a doctor has signed off on it.

"What the fuck are you playing at, Snowflake?" he snaps. His hot breath whispers across my cheek and I barely withhold a groan. "Hmm? Are you trying to bait me? Do you think if you're bratty enough, I'll snap?"

That's exactly what I think will happen, and has already happened to a degree, but I don't respond, instead choosing to look up at him innocently.

"I think that's it." He smirks. "But you have another thing coming, little Snowflake. You can push and push and push, but I'm not going to do anything that will risk your health or safety. Now, if you wanted to know what the doctors said, you should have just asked. And if I thought it was important, I would have told you the moment you woke. You had a lot of internal bleeding, but from what Doc and the doctors said it was very straightforward to fix, and you were out in half the time as when you were shot. There was no damage to any of your reproductive organs and you'll make a full recovery in a few weeks."

I let out the breath I didn't realize I've been holding since I woke up five days ago. The invisible presence telling me that if I can't have children, I'm not woman enough for a man like Elijah, disappears and I can finally fill my lungs with air.

Elijah's lips tug into a faint smile as his fingers brush down my cheek. His eyes track the movement of his hand, committing each dip in my face to memory.

"If I have to tell you every day for the rest of our lives that there will never be a time that I'll consider leaving you, much less ending your life, I'll do it without hesitation. One of these days, you're going to accept that I'm going to love you for every single second we have together, and there's nothing in this universe that will change that. If we can't have kids, we can adopt. If you don't want to adopt, we don't have to have kids at all. Everett is enough of a Russo that his kids could take over the family if something happened, especially now the two families are working together. Get it out of your head that my love and obsession are conditional, because they're not. I will be just as obsessed with you on the day I die as I was the first time I saw you. Just because we're married now doesn't mean I won't still stalk you. I want to know where you are and what you're doing for every second of every minute of every day. I don't care if you're walking to the damn mailbox, I'll need to know about it, because I don't know how to live any other way."

I open my mouth to respond, but before I can, his mouth descends on mine, his tongue frantically seeking entrance the moment our lips touch, and I'm more than happy to oblige.

Elijah groans into my mouth, his hips thrusting into mine of their own accord. I'm not sure he's entirely aware of the motion his body is making, but that doesn't matter to me. I tilt my hips up, ignoring the niggling pain in the hope of some release. If I can just—

Before I can finish my thought, a knock at the door tears Elijah from my body, his eyes flashing with guilt as he calls for whoever it is to come in.

My entire body is still on fire, the need pooling between my legs is so intense I think I might explode if I don't get some relief soon.

Rayne appears in the doorway, his eyes darting around the room once before he says, "We need you in Storm's office, Everett found a lead."

Seventy

Elijah

Dragging my body from the warmth of Snow's is impossible.

Every time I've thought about touching her over the last five days, and hell, even before then, I've stopped myself. What if I hurt her? What if she pulls a stitch? What if she doesn't heal right because of something I do?

It's all the what if's that are killing me. They keep me awake long into the night from where I've been sleeping in the armchair beside her bed. What if we didn't get there in time? What if Annalise stole the only thing on this earth that makes my miserable existence worth living? What if I lost her?

I help Snow sit up, carefully wrapping a robe around her shoulders and tying it above her sutures. I've found I like taking care of her, even if it goes against everything in my nature to do it, it feels right.

"They probably don't want me in there," she murmurs.

"I don't care. I'm not ready to let you out of my sight yet, so you're coming with me whether they like it or not."

Before she can respond, I'm lifting her gently into my arms and strolling out of the room with her cradled against my chest. She leans into my embrace like a sleepy kitten, and something inside me that has been feral and untamed for days settles. Just having her in my arms calms the beast. I was trying to be conscious of her injuries, not wanting to push her or make her uncomfortable, but that was the worst thing I could have done for both of us. The self-doubt has been eating at her for days, and I've been slowly losing my mind with each day that passes.

I stride into Storm's office and sit in one of the leather lounges along the edge of the room, rearranging Snow to make sure she's comfortable.

Storm watches me for long moments, his eyes flicking between his sister and me as if he's not sure what to make of the scene in front of him. He doesn't like either of his sisters being involved in this side of the business, but he lost the fight with Wynter, and if I have anything to say about it, he's going to lose it with Snow as well.

Wynter has her legs tucked underneath her in one of the chairs opposite the desk, her body covered with an oversized sweater that goes to her knees. Everett is beside Storm behind the desk, his eyes darting around the screen with a furrow in his brow, and Rayne is in the seat beside Wynter.

"Is Tommy coming?" Everett asks, not looking up from whatever he's focused on.

"No, he's otherwise engaged," Wynter says cryptically, and I can't help the smirk that tugs at my lips. She and her sister are so similar in so many ways, and over the years, I've witnessed the two of them give their brothers more than a few heart attacks.

"Let's get started." Storm turns to Everett, who finally looks up at the room, his eyes narrowing when he sees Snow curled up in my arms.

I can't help but look down at where her head rests on my chest, her eyes drifting closed with contentment every so often. I could walk away from all of this tomorrow as long as it means she's in my arms. I don't need the death and destruction, or the money and power. All I'm ever going to need is my Snowflake.

"They're trafficking in the city. They started the same day The Legion took down Angelo and the others. Almost like they knew it was happening," Everett tells us.

"We would have known if there were shipments of women coming in through the docks," Storm says.

"They're not coming by boat, that's why it's slipped under the radar. They're coming on goddamn private jets. Just a dozen or so women at a time. They sell them off and then a new group arrives the next day. It's a well-oiled machine and one I imagine Lounder has perfected over the years. I'm not surprised they've managed to fly under the radar for this long."

"How did you pick it up?" I ask, holding Snow a little closer.

"I keep a track of what's going on in the dark web across the country, but with a particular focus on the Midwest, and there were some things that didn't quite add up. The posts are very cryptic, and they read more like an ad for a gun or drugs. They don't use any of the usual terminologies, and that's why it's taken me a while to realize what it is. The only reason I stumbled across it is because of the way they were advertising their… product." He flinches at his own word choice but continues a moment later, "The language was all over the place. In one section the description was very much like your standard gun advertisement, but then in the next line, it was like a description of crack."

"Maybe whoever it is, just sells both and got their wires crossed." Rayne shrugs.

"That's what I thought at first as well. But the more I looked into it, the more it became apparent what was happening. Once I figured that out, I started looking at all the ways to get into Chicago. Boat. Flight. Road. I started with the docks because that was how Angelo always brought the girls in and thought if we had a new player that perhaps they would replicate his model, but there was nothing there.

"The other two options were a little dicey. Chicago has thousands of trucks coming in every single day, so being able to tell if there were women in the back of them would be almost impossible. So I decided to look at air next. There's no way they would bring them in on a commercial flight. There's far too much risk. But the number of private flights that come in per week is substantial considering the number of airports in and around the city."

Wynter looks over her shoulder at us and nibbles on her bottom lip nervously. Even she's not sure Snow should be a party to this conversation, but she's not going anywhere. She's staying right where she is.

"The same jet has been flying in sporadically over the last couple of months. Sometimes twice a week, sometimes more, sometimes less. It's all over the place, but it's the flight manifests that were even more suspicious. Every time they fly in, the plane has been full, or close to, and every time they fly out, there's two, maybe three people on the flight."

"Motherfuckers," Storm growls. The tension in his neck and jaw is so tight I'm almost expecting something to snap under the pressure. He hates this shit. Hell, I'm as close to the devil as you can get, and I hate this shit. "How are they selling them?"

"I haven't got that far yet. But I have got some images from security cameras at the airports they fly into. A different one each time on a random rotation. They're smart, just not smart enough to outmaneuver me."

Wynter turns to us at the same time Snow sits up, her eyes meeting her sister's. "Have any local girls gone missing? Any more than usual?" There's always the odd woman that disappears and you can only assume the worst. I was kept out of that side of our business when Angelo was in charge, but I know for a fact that pimps would sell girls from their stable once they were experienced enough, and fathers would sell their virtuous daughters to put food on the table for the rest of the family. A sacrificial lamb so the rest of the family can survive.

Everett tears his eyes from the screen and watches Wynter, trying to decide how much he should divulge to her. "Yes, there has been a rise in women who have gone missing in the last few months. Quite a steep increase in some weeks, and then as if to avoid unwanted attention, the levels come back to what they were when Angelo was alive."

Storm clears his throat. "What do you know, Wyn?"

"Nothing, it's just…" She pauses and braves another glance over her shoulder, and Snow's body tenses in my arms. There's something they're not telling us, and I get the distinct impression I'm not going to like whatever it is. "When Annalise was telling us about her evil plan, she let slip that she considered selling Snow and I." She flinches at her own words and the tension in the room grows thick in a matter of seconds. "She said that even though I was pregnant, there's a market for that kind of thing. And the only reason she didn't is because she knew you would come and save us eventually, even if we were broken by the time you did," she chokes on the last words, and the sound that tears from Everett's throat is anything but human.

He stands from his seat, shoving it back so hard it crashes to the ground causing Snow to startle in my arms. "I want her dead. I want everyone in that godforsaken organization six feet under. They don't deserve to breathe the same air as my woman, let alone threaten her like that."

Storm rubs his hands down his face and tips his head back against his chair. I've never seen Storm carefree, in fact, I've never seen him anything other than stressed. Even all those years ago when we were trained to be mortal enemies and his family took my only ally, if that's what you could call my cousin, away from me, he had the weight of the world on his shoulders. But this, I've never seen him look so dejected.

"I have a plan," I say. It's more of an idea, but we can flesh it out together, and then we can take Annalise Masters down.

She doesn't deserve to draw another breath after what she's done, and I hope I'm the one to end her miserable life.

I've killed a lot of people, but I have a feeling she's going to be my favorite.

EPILOGUE

SNOW

Warm breaths whisper across my bare thigh, dragging me from my dreamless sleep.

Lips brush against the sensitive flesh, pulling a moan from my throat. It's been so long since Elijah has touched me like this that I think if he keeps it up, I may be able to come just from the gentle touches.

Three long weeks. That's how long it's been since I had Elijah inside me, since he touched me more than a kiss here and there and a few gentle caresses. When we saw Doc yesterday and he cleared me for all activities, I expected for him to fuck me against the door when we walked Doc out, but nope. He helped me dress in a pair of silk pajamas, a routine he seems to enjoy and one I suspect will continue despite my clean bill of health, tucked me in, and held me against him through the night.

I'd be lying if I said I didn't fall asleep full of doubt. Thoughts of Elijah losing interest in me, of not wanting me anymore now I'm scarred from our enemies filled my mind, but a wake-up like this sets me onto the truth. He was just biding his time.

"Good morning, my Snowflake," he murmurs against my thigh as his tongue draws lazy circles into the flesh. The ache of my core is almost impossible to breathe past, and I'm already moments away from begging him to touch me where I need him.

My head rolls to the side and find dark skies through the window. What time is it? "Morning?"

He chuckles. His breath on my hypersensitive skin only makes my desire burn hotter, only makes me need him more. "It's after midnight. I was going to wait, but I couldn't. I needed to taste you, Snow. I can barely breathe without the taste of your cunt on my tongue."

His filthy words drag a moan from my throat. Oh my god. The things this man does to me with his words far surpass anything any other man could do with their entire bodies. Elijah sets me on fire. Every word, every touch, every kiss. My skin heats impossibly, to the point my breaths come in hard and fast, and it's not lost on me that he's barely touched me.

"I can smell you, Snowflake. I can smell how wet you are for me," he murmurs, pressing a firm kiss to the fabric covering my heated core. "Your pussy needs me, doesn't she, baby? I can feel how hot she is for me."

"Yes," I whimper. My heart beats heavily in my chest, a mixture of need and excitement claw at the edge of my restraint. I want to grab Elijah's head and grind my pussy against his face. I want him to make me come so hard I see stars, and then I want him to fuck me in the way that's so uniquely us. Rough. Dirty. Raw.

"I want to tease you, Snowflake. I want to drag this out until the sun rises and sets. I want to make you so crazy with need that you can't fucking breathe without my hands on you. Is that what you want, Snow? Do you want to be so desperate to come that you'll do anything?" His fingers snake into the waistband of the shorts he helped me into a few hours ago, but he doesn't immediately remove them, instead waiting for my answer.

"I need you, Elijah. I need you any way you'll take me." The truth slips from my lips with such ease. I'd like to blame the admission on how desperate I am for my husband, for the man who lived in the shadows of my life, secretly stalking me, biding his time until he could claim me as his own, but it wouldn't be the case. It's not that I haven't had him for weeks, it's that my body is just as obsessed with Elijah as he is me. If the tables were turned and I were the one who spotted him across a crowded room, I could very well have found myself following him, *stalking* him.

We will always find our way to one another, like moths to a flame. We were inevitable from that first day, and Elijah saw that from the very first moment. There isn't a force in the universe that could keep us apart.

"I can't wait though," he tells me. "I can't wait another moment to slide into the heaven between your thighs. You don't know how fucking hard it was to keep my hands to myself while you recovered."

"I do," I whisper. "Because it was just as hard for me."

Elijah growls, impatiently tugging at my shorts and discarding them across the room without ever tearing his eyes off me. He shoves a hand between my legs and groans when his fingers make contact with my wetness. "I need to take you hard and fast, Snow. But I promise I'll kiss it better when I'm done. I'll spend the rest of the day with my face between your thighs, but first, I need to fuck you."

Before I can think to reply, he's hovering above me. He notches his cock at my entrance and I can't help but tilt my hips upward, my body seeking the relief and pleasure he's going to give me.

Without hesitation, he surges forward and a startled scream tears from my lungs. His girth feels like it's tearing me apart as he buries himself inside me to the hilt. I'm impossibly full. Every single part of my body feels like it's being torn apart by him, but equally as if he's putting me back together.

"Fuck," he grinds out. "This pussy is mine." He grasps hold of one of my breasts and squeezes, pulling a groan from my throat and my center to pulse around him. "These tits are mine. Your whole fucking body belongs to me."

I find myself nodding against the pillow despite never commanding my body to do so. He's in control of me right now. He's in control of my body all the time, regardless of whether he's aware of that or not, it's the truth.

"Say it," he roars, rutting into my body with wild abandon. There's no rhythm to his movements, just a man chasing his own pleasure and using my body to take what he needs.

"I'm yours," I sob, tears of pleasure rolling down my cheeks. Each time he slides into me. His cock assaults the spot inside me that threatens to set me off, and I crave the release like I crave my next breath. I won't survive without it, I'm sure that if he took it all away right now, it would be like taking the air from my lungs.

"Fuck yes, you are," he groans long and low, grinding into me with rapture etched into his face. I'll never get enough of this, never enough of him. For as long as we both live, I suspect we will be this desperate for one another. "I want to feel you come for me, Snow. I want your juices to soak my cock, and then I want to fill you so full of my cum, you'll still be leaking tomorrow."

His words are my undoing, and my release catches me by surprise. The rush of pleasure washes over me and Elijah is all I can feel. His body moving against mine, his lips at the shell of my ear whispering dirty promises, his cock dragging every ounce of pleasure from my body like he was born to do so. "That's it, Snow. Give it to me. Give everything to me," he moans in my ear. He's getting closer, his cock pulses inside my pussy as the never-ending ebbs of my orgasm continue to hold me. "Fuck, your tight little cunt is going to drag me over the edge, Snowflake. Do you want my cum?"

I nod against the pillows, words the last thing in my mind. My entire body is hypersensitive and the pleasure borders on pain. But it's the most delicious type, the type I crave.

"Ask me for it, Snow. Ask me to fill you up," he growls, sinking his teeth into the sensitive skin of my throat and causing me to cry out.

"I need your cum," I cry. "Please fill me, please."

The tears are coming hard and fast now. I need him to come because I don't know how much longer my body can handle what he's doing to it.

He lets out a roar I'm sure my entire family can hear, but I don't care. Everything I care about is right here. He ruts into me, his thrusts becoming increasingly less measured, and I relish in the sight of him losing control,

"Fuck!" he growls, and a moment later, he stills, his cock pulsating inside me as heavy ropes of cum fill me.

Before Elijah, I never would have let a man come inside me, never would have risked pregnancy or disease, but with Elijah, it's different. It has been from the moment our eyes locked across his dining room when he took me. I didn't recognize it at the time, but I do now. Our eyes locked, and everything fell into place, I was just too stubborn to see it.

He collapses on top of me for just a second, just long enough that his weight settles me, and then he rolls onto his back and drags me on top of him, never allowing his cock to dislodge. He's craving connection the way I am, and I'm not going to complain despite the dull ache between my thighs from his rough treatment.

We're quiet for long moments, the only sound our rough breaths as we both try to recover from what we just did. Despite my constant insecurities since our wedding, I've had a nagging thought in the back of my mind, words I'm afraid to say because once I put them into the universe, I can't take them back. Words that will change my entire life. Our entire life.

"I want to have a baby," I murmur against his bare chest.

Elijah's head pulls back as one of his palms turns my face

to look at him. The emotions written on his face are mixed. Excitement. Concern. Happiness. Doubt.

"Not because I think you need an heir. I want to have a baby because I love you, and I want to make a little being that is half you and half me." The image fills me with nothing but joy, despite how out of place a newborn will look in their father's tattooed arms. "And if we can't do it naturally, there are so many children who need a loving home, and I won't love them any less because I didn't grow them, as long as we're raising them together, they'll be a little bit of both of us."

Elijah grasps the back of my head and pulls my face to his until our foreheads rest on one another. "There is nothing I want more than to see your belly swell with my baby. But we don't have to put any pressure on it. You're still recovering, and I know I was just rough with you, but I am conscious of that."

"No rush, no pressure," I agree. "But I want us to be on the same page."

Elijah's lips brush across mine, and the kiss is everything. It's like a warm summer's day, and every Christmas rolled into one. It's like everything falling into place after the start of our relationship being such a mess. And I never want it to end.

But when my phone starts buzzing on the bedside table, I groan. I don't want anything to ruin this moment.

"Who the hell is calling at three in the morning?" I mumble, reaching across without moving from Elijah's body.

Storm's name lights up my screen and dread settles in my

belly. "Hey."

"I need you to come down to Empire," he says in a rush. There's something in his tone that doesn't sound quite right, and it has me rolling off Elijah and tugging the sheet around my naked body.

"What's going on?" I ask.

"I just saved a girl from being bought by the Lounder Cartel. She was drugged, and if she wakes up to just me, I'm afraid she'll panic."

My stomach flips, and nausea rolls over me. "I'm on my way."

Thank you for reading Fall of Snow!

I hope you enjoyed Snow and Elijah's story as much as I loved writing it!

This series came to me a few years ago, and has lived rent free in my mind for a long time. Elijah is by far the darkest character to come from my mind so far, and creating him was equally disturbing and fun!

Before the Storm picks up right where Fall of Snow left off.

If you enjoyed Fall of Snow, it would mean the world to me if you left a review on Amazon and Goodreads.

You can follow me on Facebook and Instagram for updates on future releases and sneak peaks.

Keep reading for a look at Before the Storm.

Prologue
Storm

I was born to rule. Born to look out over my kingdom like a king does his lands.

But my life is anything but a fairytale, Chicago is very different to the storybooks definition of a kingdom, and I'm not the king you read to your children about at night.

The city is dirty and gritty. Full of people who will do anything to get ahead in the world. They would sell their own family if it meant they got a leg up.

That's what separates me from them. So many see their loved ones as being a weakness, but recently I've come to know them for what they really are. Allies.

Never in my wildest dreams did I expect I would allow my little sisters to be a part of our organisation. It's not the way the mafia works. Women are to be seen and not heard. They should be protected at all costs. They should never be involved in the darkness.

But times have changed, and although my father would roll over in his grave if he knew about his princesses playing with the big boys, I will never be able to regret the decision to allow it.

I lean my hip into the railing, looking down upon the club I usually spend my nights in. It was the first business I acquired on my own, and the part of the business I feel most at home. I've never found being the boss particularly stressful, but from the moment it was thrust upon me, years before it should have been, it's felt…empty. This place reminds me what it was like before. Before the future of this family rested on my shoulders.

This club is the only place I can allow my walls down, because no one here gives a fuck who I am or what I do, they're here for their own enjoyment, their own selfish needs. It's one of the reasons I conduct so much of my business within these walls, because the oblivious patrons wouldn't know there was something illegal happening if it hit the gun deal hit them in the face.

But I don't have any business on tonight, I'm just here to breathe. This war is taking it out of not only me, but the whole family. Everett is trying to keep Wynter out of it because stress isn't good for the baby, and especially after she and Snow were held hostage in a burning church, he's being extra protective. Elijah doesn't want Snow to know anything because she's such a flight risk. And Rayne is one step away from packing Emerson up and putting her on a plane until all of this is over. They all have one person to worry about, one priority, but I have all of them. Their safety rests solely on my shoulders, and I've failed them too often recently.

My father would roll over in his grave if he knew I allowed my baby sisters to be kidnapped, and then rise from the dead to kill me if he knew that I'm no closer to having a solution than I was three weeks ago. Hell, I'm no closer to having a first step.

The moment the Lounder Cartel became involved, things got a whole lot more complicated, and every step we take, every decision I make, has to be carefully planned so as not to set off a chain reaction of things we can't take back.

We're in a delicate situation, and I will not put my family in an even more precarious situation than the one we find ourselves in now, even if it means we have to bide our time until I can work out how we go about taking out the largest human trafficking operation in North America.

"Sir," Candy says, interrupting my thoughts.

I drag my attention from the club below to the waitress who quickly became my club manager. She's been here since the day I bought the place, and she's the only reason it runs as well as it does. I asked her last year to oversea all our clubs in the hope she would be able to make them run as well as this place, but she turned me down. She's happy where she is, and she doesn't want to take anymore time from her son. "Yes, Candy."

"I thought you would want to know. There's a woman who I think may have been drugged." She looks down at the dance floor before turning toward the far booth and pointing. "See the small girl in the corner booth, she can barely keep her eyes open, and the man her and the other woman met looks like he's ready to eat her for breakfast."

I nod, following her eye line. The booth in question is on the other side of the club, and being the cynic fuck I am I can only assume that they've chosen it for a reason. It's more secluded than any of the other public areas, and they're almost completely hidden from prying eyes. Except for those above.

Four people sit on the black leather bench seat, two women and two men. To the outside would it probably looks like a doubt date, but when you've seen the darker sides of society the way I have, you learn to see the world a little differently.

The two women are closest to the exit of the booth, while the men seem to have been there for a while. Their hungry eyes roam over the smooth planes of the woman closest to them, while the other looks at them with disgust. The men are too old for either woman, but especially the one they are most interested in. She looks barely legal in a tiny black dress that only just covers the tops of her thighs.

The man closest to her brushes his fingers up her bare thigh and irrational anger plows into me. I don't know this woman, and I shouldn't give a fuck what happens to her. After all, that's how we got into all this trouble. Caring about strangers. Trying to stop the trafficking of those who can't protect themselves. But the way they look at her like she's their next meal makes my gut churn and my feet move before I'm even conscious of the decision to intervene.

"I want those men banned. And get me the security footage from the moment each of them arrived. I want to know every move they've made since their stepped foot inside this club," I order over my shoulder, not stopping for long enough to hear Candy's response.

She's used to me now. We've worked together for long enough

that she knows I'm a bossy bastard, and she doesn't seem to mind, I compensate her well enough to deal with it after all.

I take the steps two at a time and push my way across the dance floor. It's not until I'm halfway that I decide I would have been better going around. But I can't tear my eyes off the girl I'm on my way to save for long enough to consider the mistakes I'm making.

I'm vaguely aware of the security guards who are following me, and the people who have stopped dancing to watch whatever is about to unfold in front of them, but I can't bring myself to care about any of that.

She's all I can see. There's something about the barely legal girl that grabs me by the collar and shakes me. The holds my attention when everything else bores me, and the sooner I get her the fuck away from the men who are leering at her like she's their next meal, the better.

Printed in Great Britain
by Amazon

19032194R00317